STAR ANGEL
RETURN TO ANITRA

David G McDaniel

TeamStarAngel.com

Star Angel: Return to Anitra

Published by
Black Helm Entertainment

Cover design by
Ivan Zanchetta

THE STAR ANGEL PENTALOGY IS:

BOOK ONE: AWAKENING
BOOK TWO: RETURN TO ANITRA
BOOK THREE: DAWN OF WAR
BOOK FOUR: RISING
BOOK FIVE: PROPHECY

visit:
TeamStarAngel.com

Jess has been back on Earth only a few months but her hopes for a normal life can't last. She desperately longs for that illusion to be real, wants it more than anything, but "normal" will never again be an option. Too much is at stake, too much has been exposed.

And there are others who want what she hides.

When the hammer falls she's more prepared than she would ever have thought possible, but nothing can prepare her for what comes next. For what waits on Anitra is something beyond anything she could've imagined. An epic reality that will change worlds.

And so, as she heads further down the rabbit hole, no longer able to deny her destiny, she's forced to realize there's only one possible outcome to the terrible convergence of events at which she's arrived.

An outcome that isn't even the end. For, to her growing despair, she realizes life beyond that outcome promises only to become more epic, not less.

Peace, for her, may never come.

Dedicated to my amazing wife. Your belief and support
throughout this journey have meant everything.

This is for you.

"Power is within you. The ranks of the Adeptus have come to understand it. In truth we have learned to wield it. Despite this knowledge we hold no monopoly. Power is within you. It exists within you even now.

"Why you choose to hide it, why you suppress such vast potential can be known.

"True power can be unleashed."

— The priestess Aesha, 5th Kel Dynasty

CHAPTER 1:

NITRO THUNDER

THE VOLUME OF SOUND IN THE AIR was astounding. Jess covered her ears but it didn't really matter. Standing at the fence at the end of the track she braced herself as a pair of Top Fuel dragsters rocketed past, neck and neck, blistering the land with the shockwaves of nearly 20,000 combined horsepower. Her sight warbled as the wheeled darts ripped across her field of vision, so fast her head could barely follow, cone of sonic destruction slamming her with an organ-vibrating assault. Even her eyeballs itched.

The dragsters were past in a blur, through the traps and shut down—tremendous sound gone all at once, chutes popped and twirling madly as they dwindled toward the far end of the track. When they shut off it was as if they released the roar of the crowd, though the thousands watching had been roaring all along, completely inaudible over the thunder of the mighty engines. For those four seconds, when the cars were at full throttle, the rest of the world simply ceased to exist.

Jess cheered along with everyone else. It was a great pass.

"*Yeah!*" Mike enthused. Everyone was keyed up. It was apparently rare for both cars to make it all the way to the end at full power, without one of them at least blowing up or losing traction or shutting down or some other issue that came from being way too high strung. The results of this run were good numbers and the crowd was eating it up.

Throngs had flocked to the bleachers and the fence as the "ground pounders" were announced, every possible viewing space rapidly filled. Mike chose to come all the way forward, working his way through the bodies so they could be as close to the track as possible, down near the traps. Jess smiled at him and his friends as they made excited comments and animated gestures. Levi and Matt were with them, each bursting with enthusiasm at the insane intensity of the Fuel cars. The boys were loving it.

Jess had to admit she was impressed. The physics nerd in her could scarcely believe cars with no more than what were, essentially, V8 piston motors, could accelerate so fast. Each engine made as much power as three freight locomotives, in a car that weighed less than a family sedan, which meant in less than four seconds they went from zero to a good chunk over 300—324.12 was the winner on this one ... it seemed nearly impossible.

Watching them live and in action, however, rapidly disabused you of the unreality of it. It was all very, very real. Standing near the traps, when the cars launched you could actually *see* them move down at the other end *before* the wall of sound hit. From that far away they accelerated so fast they began closing the gap visually before the sound made it to you. You watched the start, heard the cars idling, waiting, the lights went green and ... they exploded off the line, toward you—yet, for that first instant you could still only hear the sound of their idle. The explosive sound of their launch hadn't yet reached the end of the track but they were already well on their way. Silent missiles. Like warp drive or something. Flames shot from the headers in a fire "V", a volcano of death on each side of the car as they twisted under their own monstrous torque, lunging ahead but ... no change in sound. Not at first. Like they were still idling down there, though clearly they were not. Then, when the fierce volume slammed into you ...

Whoa.

On a good run they hit a hundred miles-an-hour in the first half-second, according to Mike. It boggled the mind.

She watched him, standing tall beside her. Having fun with his buddies. They'd caravanned all the way there to Vegas—mentally she pinched herself, still amazed her mom let her go—with three boys no less—nine long hours to witness this spectacle. Mike had been to two NHRA events before and was dying to bring Matt and Levi. His reason, however, for getting everyone to come on this improbable trip was suspect:

This was supposedly her birthday present.

How getting up hours before the crack of dawn and hauling ass through the mountains and desert with three teenage boys just to watch noisy, stinky drag racing was supposed to be a special birthday present ... It was crowded, it was loud, nitro methane and grease fumes everywhere, she was tired ...

But, in a way, it *was* special. Certainly unique.

Way unique.

Coming all the way to Vegas without parents was also a big deal. It was in honor of her recent Sweet Sixteen and there was no good reason for them to let her do this, especially with her boyfriend and two of his rowdy mates, but they had. Mike was nearly eighteen, but even if he was all-the-way eighteen that wouldn't have made him any more grown up and all things considered this was, without a doubt, huge.

The drag racing, according to Mike, was just part of his plans. He had dinner reservations that night. Then they were staying with his aunt and heading back tomorrow. All timed to get home before school on Monday. An exhausting trip, all the way around.

But so far Jess was loving it. As tired as she was she was actually thrilled with Mike's over-the-top gift. It was so much more than anyone had ever done for her and, quite possibly, the most thought anyone had put into a birthday present ever.

"Next one," he announced as another pair of dragsters moved to the starting line far down the track. The rumble of their idling engines drifted on the air, followed by loud roars as they lit up and did huge burnouts. White tire smoke rolled across the starting line, over the crowds, the engines dropping back to a chaotic *Bap! Bap! Bap!*; the unmistakable sound of those over-wound, over-compressed motors weighing heavy over everything as the dragsters backed slowly into position.

Getting ready to annihilate the world.

Jessica's phone buzzed. She dug it out of her pocket and checked the face. It was Mom.

She took the call without thinking.

"Hey Mom!"

"Hi hon—"

The cars launched, sending another round of thunder down the track and completely overwhelming all other sound. Jess flinched and squeezed her free hand to her ear, crushing the phone to her other as the cars reached them in an instant and roared past. One's engine exploded in a ball of flame just shy of where she stood—*BOOOM!*— and that car whirred by—*coasting* through the traps at 200 miles-an-hour—even as the other blasted through victorious.

"My God!" her mom's voice was audible again. "What was that?! Was that the race cars?"

"Aren't they loud?"

"Watch your hearing, honey."

Typical mom.

"I'm fine. Doesn't really hurt your ears, believe it or not. Low frequency. Just kind of rocks your senses."

"Well watch your senses then." Her mom chuckled. Then: "And I mean that. Don't do anything senseless while you're out there. I mean, no nonsense ... "

"I get it, Mom." Jess rolled her eyes. "Mike's been the perfect gentleman."

In the quiet between rounds she could hear her mom clearly, and as she listened she thought she heard ... clicking? Something on the line clicked on and off. Once more, like the connection was going in and out, though her mom's voice remained loud and clear.

Mom was on to other things. "Have you met his aunt yet?"

"We came straight to the track. Nearly missed qualifying."

"Well call me when you get there and tell me what she's like."

"I will."

"I want to talk to her."

Jessica's initial reaction was along the lines of, *God,*

Mom! Give me some space! But Mom *had* given her space. Lots of it. She was all the way in Vegas with no adult chaperone. If all Mom was asking was to talk to Mike's aunt then she more than deserved that. Without any grief from her daughter. Months after "the incident" Mom was only just beginning to lose some of the fear of letting her out of sight, worried she might somehow get amnesia again or disappear. That Mom and Dad let her come to Vegas at all was still, to her, amazing.

"I will," she agreed. "Definitely. I'll call you as soon as we get there." Then: "Love you, Mom."

"Love you too, honey."

And they hung up. Jess put the phone back in her pocket. Mike and the boys were going on animatedly about this or that amazing fact, cool thing or awesomeness about the cars, waiting eagerly for the next run, such looks of expectation on their faces. She smiled.

Boys could be so precious.

She leaned against the fence, closed her eyes and looked up, face to the afternoon sun. It felt so warm, so nice on her skin in the crisp, spring air. She took a moment to soak it up, savoring the sensation, listening to the sounds of the speedway in the background; echoes of tools and cars in the slower classes tuning up, the midway in the distance, simulators and games and everything else that made it sound like a carnival. Noises, smells, a light breeze blowing …

In that moment all was at peace.

Then the next pair of dragsters fired up at the other end, making their authority known. She opened her eyes.

Bracing herself for the fury to come.

* * *

JESS WALKED ALONG behind the boys, feeling very much like a third wheel. Or, in this case, a fourth wheel. They strolled aimlessly through the midway, headed for the nitro pits to see if they could catch what Mike called a "clutch seat". Apparently after the crews installed a new clutch in one of the Top Fuel cars they started it and hit the throttle to apply major torque, thus "seating" the new clutch. In the pits you could stand within feet of the jacked-up cars and, according to Mike, when they hit the throttle and you were that close it felt like standing in the face of an explosion.

She couldn't wait.

Absently she pushed her hair to the side. For the trip Bianca had helped her put in soft curls, giving her long brown hair actual volume and bounce. Mike loved it, or so he said, and it was about the most amazing thing she'd done to her appearance in what seemed like forever.

It was taking some getting used to.

With the hair she wore a flirty sundress, cute sandals, a delicate anklet and necklace and, in the loud, smelly environment of the pits, was starting to feel a little out of place. Too flirty. Most everyone else wore jeans, shorts and T-shirts.

At some point the fried smells of the midway got to them and they all decided they were hungry. Mike curved to one of the concession stands, leading them to the corn dog hut. As they stood in line he let Matt and Levi go ahead, falling back to stand with her.

"Having fun?"

She looked up and smiled and he bent to give her a peck on the lips. He put his arm around her. Mike was the only one among the three boys with a girl on his arm, and he'd been taking every opportunity to hold her hand, or hold her close, or kiss her, not really shoving it in his friend's faces but not hiding the fact either. He had a girlfriend and they didn't.

"I'm getting you your birthday corn dog," he announced.

"Birthday corn dog?"

"I want to start a tradition."

She laughed. Mike had his moments.

"Don't worry," he assured her. "This is just to tide you over. I've got much better things in store." Then, with a sly smile: "The corn dog is just the appetizer."

She had no idea what that meant. Actually, she thought maybe she did, but cringed to think of it in terms of corn dogs. Of course she could be way off. Knowing Mike, which was to say not really knowing what to expect from his mostly juvenile—but sweet— mind, she would just have to wait and see.

He leaned closer. "This will be a birthday to remember."

It seemed he had a real desire for her to have a good time. To be lavished with recognition on this, the celebration of her sixteenth birthday, but she had to wonder if it was truly her happiness he was interested in or his own boyish urges. It seemed a lot of trouble to go to otherwise.

They got their corn dogs and Cokes and continued, eating and drinking as they walked, Mike helping her put mustard on the end for each bite—the way she liked it—juggling napkins and open mustard packets, and bottles and all the things in their hands, laughing and making jokes with the others and generally having a good time. Eventually they found their way to the nitro pits. The crews were busy tearing down engines from the recent passes, getting ready for the next round. It was fascinating to watch and, as Mike promised, you could get right up to the ropes as they worked, hard and fast, almost close enough to touch. They finished their food and kept walking around, looking for one of the fabled clutch-seat events Mike wanted them to witness.

Soon they found a candidate, ready to fire up. Mike hurried them over to stand right by the pit as close as they could. A crowd was gathering. Then ... the crew lit the fuse. The engine whined as it turned, acting at first like it wouldn't start, then it did, struggling briefly at a difficult lope until it caught its stride—sounding like a train wreck in those first seconds—then it settled to a deep, burpy idle. She made a comment to Mike but realized even the sound of the idle, just the idle alone, was giving off such a tremendous bass pulse that talking had become impossible. She tried to imagine what came next. The crew pulled on gas masks and she began to squint as nitro fumes filled the air. They hustled around the car, checking this or that thing, then ...

BRRAP! hit the throttle and she actually jumped. It

was like a body punch. She'd been expecting some sort of shock but was *not* prepared for the ferocity of the engine's hit in that proximity.

BRRAP! again and this time she held. Her eyeballs warbled, her skin tingled, her muscles coiled to flee but she made herself stand in place. Mike stood behind her, holding her around her waist, whooping with the thrill though she couldn't hear him. She couldn't hear anyone or anything. Nothing. It was the engine and only the engine; no other sound existed or could exist in that world. A bomb would not have penetrated the fury of the Top Fuel motor.

BRRAP! and she found herself thoroughly astounded. Then the crew seemed satisfied and shut it off. The engine made a terrific metallic racket as it wound down and ... stopped.

Silent.

The crowd was cheering and whistling.

But the crew was in action, getting everything ready.

"See?!" Mike was pumped. Matt and Levi too.

Jess smiled graciously, suitably awed.

CHAPTER 2:

BIRTHDAY SUSHI

"MMM. MUCH BETTER THAN THE CORN DOG." Jess savored the Dragon Roll, using her chopsticks to gather a little wasabi in preparation for the next bite. "I mean, the corn dog was delicious. Don't get me wrong. Birthday Corn Dog could be a great tradition."

Mike laughed, continuing to stuff his face. She watched him go through three rolls in the time it took her to eat one. Mike was a teenage boy and ate like one, his resting metabolism enough to burn through a huge number of calories with not an ounce of fat on him. Which meant, in order to live, he was constantly eating. Mike was lean, somewhat muscular, somewhat tall with a friendly smile and the kind of sandy-blonde hair you just wanted to rumple. He seemed a little nervous right then, though she had to admit she was nervous too. They were alone in a far-off city—Vegas, no less—on a date like grownups, and the expectations of the moment were driving her a bit crazy. What else did Mike have in mind?

What else do I *have in mind?*

"I got you something," he said, taking a moment between bites. He actually bothered to put down his chopsticks and she could see that, at least partly, whatever he'd brought was contributing to his nerves. Both of them were dressed nice. Mike even wore a dinner jacket, she a cocktail dress, following the weeks-long, mysterious build-up to this "special" trip and, as he rummaged nervously for something in his coat pocket ...

Her mind drew a sudden and ludicrous conclusion:

Is he going to ask me to marry him?!

After all, he brought her all the way to Vegas. What teenager did that? *No*, she admonished herself. That was stupid. He was seventeen, she just turned sixteen. Was

that even legal? Yet her heart raced. She cast her gaze
about the little sushi restaurant, at the other diners sitting
at intimate tables like their own. Candles flickered, mood
lighting, soft red-and-black lacquered wood, romantic
decorations everywhere. It was a couple's spot and she
suddenly began to feel very isolated sitting there with just
Mike.

If he got out of his chair and down on one knee ...

But he didn't. Instead he laid a long jewelry box on the
table. It had a pretty little bow on it. Jewelry, she was
right in that, but not a ring, and at the confirmation of
that her emotions swung from unfounded fear to mild joy—
realizing at once Mike had never bought her anything this
nice. Never dainty pretty stuff. Maybe because she never
really wore stuff like that, the anklet and the necklace of
today being rare exceptions, maybe because he'd always
been too nervous, maybe for a dozen other reasons, but
whatever the reasons up until then the wait was officially
over.

Mike had just given her her first something nice.

"Happy birthday," he said and slid the box to her, then
scratched the back of his neck as she took it and began
undoing the little bow. "It's not much." His nerves were
suddenly terribly cute.

She opened the lid and inside was ... a shiny silver
bracelet, a nice one, set with red stones. She gasped—
actually gasped out loud—and looked up at Mike, hugely
impressed. She took it from the box, holding it across her
fingers and feeling its weight.

"Is this ... real silver?"

He nodded that it was.

Wow. Mike didn't make much, working part-time at a
local auto shop, nor were his parents well off like most of
the parents in their school district. This trip, this dinner,
this bracelet ... these were significant expenses. That
he'd chosen to spend so much on her ... She was at once
flattered and ...

Worried all over again.

Under normal circumstances Mike was giving. About as

much as any boy his age, which meant he usually picked up the tab at fast food joints, tried to win her stuffed animals at the fair—that sort of thing. He was tender. He was also shy, and this trip bordered on extravagant. Even when you considered the fact that he was dying to come see the races and probably would've come without her.

Now this.

"Thank you," she said graciously, continuing to admire the bracelet. "This is so beautiful, Mike. Thank you." It really was. Not a thin, delicate band. It had substance. Perfect width, perfect weight, with an intricate design set with tiny red stones. The little stones were shaped like hearts and, no matter any possible ulterior motive, she was touched by the gesture.

It was wonderful.

She decided to put aside her worries and focus on it. It was truly one of the prettiest things she'd ever been given.

"Try it on."

He watched closely as she chose a wrist and put it on, even helping her a little with the clasp.

"It looks great on you," he said as she turned her arm back and forth for him to see, letting the silver catch the light. It was perfect. Yesterday she'd fixed and painted her nails—bright red, as it turned out—and the fresh color combined with the sparkling red stones of the bracelet did, indeed, look great. She'd wear it as often as she could, she decided. Actually, this being the best gift any boy ever got her, she might never take it off.

After a few moments admiring it she turned to the last of her Dragon Rolls.

"We're getting dessert too." Mike grabbed his own chopsticks. Now that he'd given her the gift he seemed much more relaxed.

"This is all wonderful, Mike." She smiled for him. "Magical. Thank you."

* * *

JESS WATCHED THE CRAZY DIVERSITY of people walking up and down the Vegas strip. Girls dressed way too sexy, guys trying to look way cooler than they were. All of them out to have fun or indulge some craving, each trying to attract the other. The city was full of tourists but many of the visitors were seasoned Vegas-goers, those who knew the venues and knew exactly what they were after. It was a wild combination of lights, sounds and energy.

She sat to the side in Mike's lap, on a bench a step or two away from the moving bodies, watching the action. He held an arm around her and she leaned into him, curved against his shoulder, relishing the strength of his embrace. Sitting in his lap was one of her favorite little pleasures. Mike wasn't a weightlifter, but she was borderline petite and so he was plenty strong enough to hold her. He could even lift her onto his shoulders without bending down. With a little leap from her to help, of course, but still he did it without much effort. She liked that he was strong enough to do that.

"You've got cute toes," he commented, and she realized he'd been staring at her feet as she kicked them idly back and forth. Earlier she'd slipped out of her fancy heels. She followed his gaze, raised her legs and wiggled them. Yesterday she'd painted all her nails the same bright red, and in the Vegas lights the fresh pedi sparkled.

He pushed back her hair, exposing an ear.

"And cute ears," he said and gently kissed it.

This was a record. Two compliments in a row. She smiled, wider as his lips continued to brush her lobe. The kiss triggered a rapturous tingle and she giggled.

It should've been a perfect moment. She was in Vegas, with her boyfriend—once the boy of her dreams. She had more friends now than ever. Her newfound confidence following her ordeal on that other world, an ordeal that seemed an eternity ago, a lifetime, had made things on Earth seem so easy.

So where's my Happily Ever After?

The cutesy dating and going out stuff was okay. Moments like these were sweet. Sitting in Mike's lap, having fun, being together ...

Everyday existence just seemed so boring.

Though she rehashed it constantly her trip to Anitra had become, over the intervening months, almost surreal. Like a dream. She returned. Summer ended. Fall came and went. Winter. Now Spring was upon her and everything seemed so ... average. Definitely *not* Happily Ever After. Only ... It wasn't that life was horrible. Far from it. It was just any action, any challenge, would've been better than the slow death of a mundane existence.

More like Ho Hum Ever After.

Whatever had turned on, whatever triggered during those events, whatever other self rose fighting to the fore, getting her through the trauma, the crisis—whatever impulse drove her then had, in the following months, faded. She was "normal" again, with normal problems, everyday challenges and, at times, it was hard to believe she'd ever been anything else.

Like her time on Anitra never happened.

A quick trip to the barn, however, was all it took to remind her that insane adventure was all too real. The massive suit of Skull Boy armor crammed in the corner, black and ominous, concealed behind burlap sacks and rusty farm equipment, was about the most sobering dose of reality she ever needed.

Her adventure on Anitra was no dream.

For a time, after her return, she'd alternated between a feeling of supreme confidence, at what she'd been through, followed by the feeling of walking around in a nervous daze. Worried someone might actually discover the Skull Boy, the Icon, or come looking for her. Or someone would come dropping through from Anitra, maybe even an army, or someone there on Earth would come knocking, or someone would find her some other way ...

"I'm gonna grab a smoothie." Mike leaned forward. She took her cue and slid off his lap. He stood. "Want anything?"

"I'm fine." She smiled. He smiled back, bent and gave her a kiss, then headed for a little place nearby. She watched him go. Mind drifting.

But nobody came. No one found anything. And the whole situation was killing her. It sucked being the bearer of that secret. How long could she keep it up? She kept imagining a good day would come, when she might say something, or she'd decide once and for all what to do and do it, but truthfully she knew she was just putting off the inevitable. Trying to live her life as if she wasn't sitting on mind-blowing information that could change the world.

What right did she have?

Yet the arguments against it were strong.

If she showed what she was hiding—to anyone—they'd take her away and take the Icon and, not only would she no longer have a way back to Anitra—should she ever decide to go—but Anitra and all of that would be compromised and who knew what would come next. It certainly wouldn't be good. Not for her, not for Anitra, and definitely not for any possible future with ...

Zac.

She looked furtively to see if Mike was still in sight.

Her mind couldn't be any more mixed up.

Zac and Mike and those things were minor compared to the bigger picture, of course, reasonably she knew that, but they were part of it all the same. This vicious cycle had gone round and round her head for months. Was she being a selfish teen brat? Or was she truly being as wise as she felt?

If only she could tell someone.

For any other Earth-bound problem—anything—there would be someone somewhere that had been through it. Someone to confide in or consult. Get them to agree with her that she was doing the right thing or, at least, give her advice. A different point of view. Anyone. For this she had no one. Bianca and Toby, the only two who even had a clue as to what really went on that fateful day—Toby hardly anything—seemed unwilling to talk about it, as if wanting to forget the whole thing. Such that, as the weeks then months scrolled by it kind of became a shunned memory for her as well.

Only, something deeper had been triggered. And though the uncertainty, the fear of what to do overshadowed daily existence, the impulses that trip awakened, the reality of it, had spurred a certain longing that was not to be denied. Fueled by the undeniable fact that, no matter anything else, she could not escape the burning conviction she wasn't finished. That she *belonged* out there. It was a feeling that made no intellectual sense and yet nagged her at all times. An impulse—a *drive*.

Several times on her trips to the barn she'd pulled out the Icon. Carefully, oh so carefully, holding it. Contemplating its power. Contemplating the vast significance of all that went with it, of what it would mean to use it again.

So many consequences.

How it worked, she did not pretend to understand. The Skull Boy armor, though beyond Earth technology, could at least be understood. She got how it functioned, how it did what it did. The Icon, however, was something beyond that. Beyond Earth, beyond Anitra. An instant gateway. With it she could get to another world. A world that, perhaps, was just as troubled as Earth.

Neither planet was in great shape. Earth in particular lacked purpose, with all its gadgets and ways to stay distracted. Earth's problems, much like those of Anitra, were internalized. As if each planet were an insane asylum, full of inmates consumed with playing games or fighting each other, unaware or unwilling to face the fact that there was a whole, vast universe out there.

Unaware the asylum could go up in flames.

The people of Earth *needed* to look to the stars. Of this she was convinced. She'd been convinced of that even before this ordeal, but now more than ever. Of all the times in its history Earth was finally on the cusp. The world was at a place where real progress could actually be made. Never before had the communications and infrastructure existed to unite the whole world so easily in a common cause. To push out, as one, and conquer the next frontier. Now it did. Science was poised. It need only be given the proper priority.

Unfortunately that same technology had the power to suck the entire world into a void of inaction. The same networks that allowed instant collaboration allowed an infinity of distractions. What people's cats were doing, how moody they were feeling at the moment and on and on. All because there was no bigger game. No one had named it. No one agreed to it. And so people burned their time, their valuable time, doing, essentially, nothing.

Long ago, when the MacGreggors fought the MacDonalds, it was all-out war. Their "differences" were insurmountable, no common purpose between them. No unity. Later they got past that and became a whole. Scotland. But then England was the enemy. Soon that, too, changed. And so on up the line. Now the entire world needed to evolve. It was time. Earth needed to become one team. And the new enemy (because there always needed to be an "enemy", another side to the game—total peace, as far as Jess was concerned, with nothing to do but sing and grow beets, was an illusion that only led to more conflict) ... the new enemy would have to be something everyone could get behind. If humanity no longer had itself to be enemies with—and frankly it was time to end that game—a new enemy would be needed. Perhaps an "enemy" like the very real danger of being locked helplessly to a single planet. Or running out of resources. Or wanting new space. Anything to bring the world together. Anything to fight against as one.

Truth was, all it would take would be a decision. A simple, global decision. Wipe the slate clean. Amazing how straightforward it should be, yet how impossible it truly was. If *all* countries banded together, *all* people of Earth, one goal in mind—and the total *intention* of attaining it—their individual, petty problems would, like magic, fall away. A decision. That's all it would take.

Idly she kicked her feet, brushing her soles against the still-hot concrete.

At times she thought of busting out with the Skull Boy armor, of creating her own global wake-up call and give the world a kick-start. But it would never be global. She'd just end up on page ten of the *Enquirer* and the government would sweep it under the rug. What they would then do with the amazing technology she shuddered to think of. Portable fusion generators? One thing was certain: they wouldn't use it to make the world a better place.

Maybe if she wreaked some *real* havoc. That thought, too, had crossed her mind. Earth technology wasn't likely to stop the armor easily. Not before she made a spectacle. *That* would be near impossible to cover up and the whole world would have to address this startling new discovery in a very public way. How long could such a rampage last before it was snuffed? Could the suit take over airwaves, the Internet? Send a message through the public's favorite means of mass consumption? But the end result would be lost lives, including, most likely, her own. And, again, some elaborate cover-up that left things exactly they way they were.

And maybe, just maybe, she was wrong. In all of this. Naïve. Maybe a one-world government, maybe uniting everyone in a single cause *wasn't* ideal. One set of laws for the entire planet? There would be no way to disagree, no way to form your own society or to break off and have your own way. You'd be stuck following along with whatever the "world" decided. There were definite drawbacks to "all for one and one for all", especially when there was nowhere else to go. America was formed, for example, because there was a way for the colonists to make their own world. How could that happen if the entire planet was unified under one flag?

But that was the whole point. Unite in order to find *more* land. *More* planets. *More* places to be different. Soon there would be few options left for that here on Earth.

She sighed. Stared without focus at all the life, the lights, the sounds, the energy all around her, filling the strip with pointless action.

She held a game changer.

The very thing she felt the world needed and she had it. Hiding in a barn. Yet—

Mike walked back with his smoothie, catching her in the middle of a maddening upswing of fresh imponderables and making her wish, for an instant, he would just go away. She watched as he sat beside her, sipping happily. He offered her the large, colorful plastic cup with the giant straw. She reached for it, took a sip and handed it back.

Peanut butter.

All around her people were absorbed with the pleasures of the false utopia they'd created.

Forgetting that utopia had to be won.

Advanced.

Anything left unchanged long enough crumbled.

These were heavy thoughts for a teenager, she knew. She was acutely aware of the fact. People had been predicting the end of the world forever, but she believed the cultures of Earth had finally, after thousands of years, reached critical mass and she worried—rightly—about the future. Especially after all she'd seen. Of all the oblivious people in the world she knew more than any of them. It was a sobering fact: No one knew what she did. None of the thousands of partiers and vacationers right there in her immediate line of sight. None of them. No one on the entire planet, seven billion strong. None knew what she, an unassuming teenage girl, knew. And that was a scary thing. Being the sole possessor of the truth. Or, at least, the Greater truth. In the months following her return, during moments like these, she felt a creeping sort of panicked awareness. Exactly like she was feeling right then. Like one might feel upon waking up in a trap. Feelings that were, in turn, accompanied by a keen sense of responsibility. A sense that she had to do *something*, anything, to get the masses moving in the right direction.

To save her world.

Otherwise the future was grim.

For there was an unforgiving law in nature which drove all things, great and small, from the most basic cell to entire civilizations, forgotten often by those who'd fallen into a false sense of security:

Evolve or Die.

CHAPTER 3:

WHAT HAPPENS IN VEGAS

"Shut up, dude! You're being rude." Mike chatted with Levi on his phone as he walked with Jessica up the sidewalk to his aunt's house. Jess followed a few steps behind, giving Mike space. He'd been talking to his friend for the last ten minutes, since right before they entered the little Las Vegas neighborhood, Levi informing Mike—near as Jess could tell from Mike's side of the conversation—that he and Matt intended to stay out all night and burn Vegas to the ground. They'd sleep in Levi's car if they had to, but they weren't coming home until dawn.

At which point the conversation veered to areas she was trying to ignore. Levi's big plan, apparently, in addition to doing everything in Vegas a teenage boy could dream of doing, was to leave Jess and Mike alone. No doubt Mike and Levi had talked much about this moment, in private, in the weeks leading up to the Big Trip. Now the time was upon them and Jess had to admit Mike looked as nervous as she felt.

"I gotta go, man," he kept trying to end the conversation. Levi made a few more boisterous comments on the other end, things Jess tried harder not to overhear, then Mike finally got in a final "see-ya" and hung up. He turned to Jess as they approached the door to the house. "Those guys can be such jerks."

She attempted a smile. "Hope we don't have to bail them out of jail." Mike laughed, but both of them saw through the joke. It was a weak attempt to cover anxiety. They were home, just the two of them and, according to Mike, his aunt would be leaving. She worked the night shift at one of the high-end casinos, meaning the house would be theirs until morning.

Before Mike could knock the door flew open.

"Mike!" It was Aunt Monica—Mike had already told Jess her name—and she'd evidently been watching for them. She hugged her nephew hard then turned to Jess. "You must be Jessica."

"Hi." She extended a hand but Monica pulled her into a hug. Monica was tiny for a grownup, two or three inches shorter than Jess herself—five feet if she was lucky—and when Jess squeezed her it was almost like hugging a kid. "Nice to meet you," she spoke over Monica's shoulder.

Monica released, smiling. Her hair was jet black and short. She looked to be in her mid-thirties, pretty with angular features, was dressed for work and at the moment seemed hyped up on coffee or something. Or maybe she was just that way all the time. A nervous, flitty person. Like a little hummingbird.

"Come in!" she invited them inside, closing the door. "Did you have fun? How was the birthday dinner?"

Jess looked around the living room, taking note of a few stand-out items. A red leather loveseat. Cubist prints on the wall. "It was wonderful," she said. "Mike went all out." She raised her wrist for Monica to see. "I got this," she flashed the bracelet.

Monica punched Mike. Like, unnecessarily hard, laughing as she did. She was so much smaller than Mike; it was weird she was the grownup and he was the towering child.

"You big romantic," she teased.

"I wanted to get her something nice," Mike defended himself. "This is her Sweet Sixteen. She deserved something to remember."

"Hauling her all the way down here and back over the weekend? That's something to remember all right.

"But I'm sure she appreciates the gesture." She winked at Jessica.

Jess looked to Mike, graciously. "I do. It's very sweet." Then: "Oh. Can you talk to my Mom? She wanted to check with you. You know how moms can be."

"Totally. Put her on."

Jess dug her phone out of her pocket. As she was doing

this Monica stepped over to the front window.

"Check this out," she said. Jess and Mike looked at each other. Mike shrugged and they followed his aunt over to the window so they could peek out the drapes. Monica clearly had something of interest outside she wanted them to see, but was also trying to be discreet. She seemed the type that might harbor a suspicious streak, about many things, so at first Jess didn't think much of her secretive mannerisms, but as she looked through the cracked curtains in the direction Monica was pointing her blood went to ice.

Sitting down the street, in the shadows between lights— Jess had totally missed it on their arrival—was an unmarked car. Like a detective sedan or something. An all-black, late-model with basic hubcaps and tinted glass. The kind of car no one bought or drove as a personal vehicle. The kind of car that was all business.

"It's been sitting there for the last two hours." Monica peeked carefully as Jess studied it, trying to fight off the fear suddenly crashing in. Two heads were inside. If she were a normal teenager she might simply dismiss it. If she were a normal teenager she *would* dismiss it. Call Aunt Monica paranoid and be done with it. What was the big deal? The car was a few houses down and could be there for anything. But she *wasn't* a normal teenager, and her mind turned immediately to the obvious. There was more to her than Monica or Mike could ever, ever in a million years guess. And an unmarked cop car watching the house she'd just arrived at ...

Had someone found out? Were they following her?

Her heart was pounding.

"I think Garth's been dealing drugs," Monica pointed to the house directly across from the car. "I thought maybe they were here for that. But every time I peek I can't shake the feeling they're looking at *me*. Just seems weird." She turned to both of them. "I'd keep an eye on it."

Mike eyed his aunt. "*You* haven't been dealing drugs, have you?" It was a joke but she smacked him all the same.

"Just keep an eye out. I don't want anything happening to you two."

They all stepped away from the window. Monica reached for Jessica's phone, the imagined danger of the car already behind her. Jessica's mind, however, was consumed. She dialed, numb, and handed it to her, trying not to shake, working to calm her racing thoughts. Maybe it *was* the neighbor dealing drugs. *Yeah, that's it.* She looked around the small living room as Monica took the call, barely listening as she heard her Mom answer on the other end. She heard them laugh, heard them having what sounded to be a good conversation.

Who is that?! She couldn't get it out of her mind. Then she grew angry. All at once. Wanted to storm out the door and sprint to the car, jerk open the door, haul both occupants into the street and demand they tell her why they were there.

What do you want?!

At least confirm they were watching Garth, and not sitting there waiting for …

Her.

"Here you go, sweetie." Monica was handing her the phone. Jess dragged herself back to the present.

"Thanks." She took it.

"Your Mom's a nice lady. I told her I'd make sure my nephew was on his best behavior." She turned to Mike. "So be on your best behavior. Got it?"

"Yes, Auntie Monica."

She grinned at him. "You respect her wishes. And for God's sake use protection. You brought protection?"

Jessica's breathing skipped, bringing her fully into the now.

Mike was instantly humiliated. In fact, for a moment he was speechless.

Monica gave Jess a knowing little wink. "Just making sure he thinks with the right head." Jess blinked, stunned.

Mike was turning a deeper shade of red. "Aunt Monica!" he managed.

Well, thought Jessica, *This is just great*. She'd kind of hoped Monica would lay down rules or something. Strict arrangements for the two horny teenagers in her empty house while she was gone. Instead she was more or less giving them her approval to do whatever they wanted. Just be smart about it, were the only implications. You know. Think with the right head.

It was mildly comforting, however, to discover Mike seemed as uncertain as she was. Jess had suspected ulterior motives for his invitation from the beginning but had been willing to come along anyway, unsure of her own feelings and not wanting to shoot him down on such an excessive offer.

"I've got some in my nightstand if you need them," Monica threw them one last curve and began gathering the rest of her things for work, pretending to be oblivious to the ripples in the room. "Just no snooping around." Maybe she *was* oblivious. Maybe she was that dense. Mike and Jess tried not to look at each other.

In a short time—too short a time—Aunt Monica was heading for the door.

"I'll be home around seven," she said. "Maybe we can have breakfast before you two get on the road." Yep. She seemed totally unaware of the dilemma she'd just given them. Jess appreciated the freedom to make her own decisions, but in this particular case would've preferred a little adult supervision.

Mike walked to the door and gave his aunt a reluctant hug. Jess stayed where she was and waved goodnight.

"Have a good shift."

Monica looked up at Mike, about to deliver some other zinger he didn't want to hear. He stopped her with a raised hand:

"Please. Aunt Monica. No more."

She looked between them. "All right you two. Have fun! Call if you need anything." She opened the door and stepped out, pausing at the threshold. "And keep an eye on that car. It creeps me out."

And she was gone.

Jess watched after her, mouth hanging open as Mike

closed the door and stood there.

Great. Some grownup she turned out to be. *Thanks, Aunt Monica.* In a few short minutes she'd managed to leave them alone, for the night, proposing they have sex if they wanted—just be careful—even offering her own condoms, if they needed them, and oh, by the way, there might be stalkers watching the house, so keep an eye out.

Have fun!

Just lovely.

Outside in the driveway the car door slammed and the engine started. Lights came on, backed out of the driveway and headed down the street.

Leaving them alone in a quiet house.

Jess looked around the living room, pretending to study the various knick-knacks and decorations. Willing her embarrassment not to rise. Monica seemed like a party girl and her house reflected that. Nothing frumpy or plain in terms of furniture or décor. In fact, it looked like a bachelor pad. Or a cougar cave.

Making the problem facing them that much more obvious.

"I should've told you she's a little nutty," said Mike. He went to the window, using it as a distraction, a way to mask his own embarrassment, studying the car down the street way longer than he needed to.

"Wonder if they see me looking at them."

Jess checked the time on her phone, trying to convince herself the car was just a fluke. The pressures of the moment were at least making it easier to put from her mind. Eleven-fifteen. They had a long drive tomorrow. She stared at the bright numbers.

Debating how to word her pre-emptive strike.

But Mike spoke first. "You can go to bed if you want. I'll stay up and watch them." He closed the drapes.

It was a sweet offer, unexpected; conceding in one statement that not only was anything they did her choice, but offering at the same time to forgo his own comfort—sleep, in this case—so she could have peace of mind. He would watch over her if she so desired. Be her protector, *and* give up any hope of an evening of intimacy. There was no hint of reservation in his tone. It wasn't a ploy to get her to say "Of course not! You don't have to do that!" She could tell; he genuinely wanted to watch out for her, if it would make her feel better, and was ready to follow through.

She was smitten.

And all at once resisted the urge to give him what he wanted. To give him what *she* wanted, in truth, as she could scarcely deny her own interest in the matter.

Only ... no.

She walked over to him. "That's sweet." She knew her expression spoke volumes, knew he could see in it how much she appreciated the gesture. She put a hand to his cheek. "But you get some rest. We're both exhausted. We've been on the go nearly twenty-four hours and you've got another long day of driving tomorrow."

"Ok," he agreed. "I'll sleep out here. Just in case."

He was working hard to be chivalrous. Mike could be terribly shy at times, and she knew this was challenging him. But in the end she also knew he wanted to do the right thing.

She tip-toed and he followed her lead, bending in for a kiss. It was electric and she very nearly went further, finding it hugely difficult to be smart in that moment. But she shortened the kiss and smiled up at him.

"Let me show you where everything is." He gave her a tour of the small house, then went out and retrieved their small bit of overnight stuff from the car. Changing for dinner had been done in restrooms at the track, and after the busy day Jess was looking forward to cleaning up and putting on her PJs. Mike left her as she brushed her teeth, washed up and slipped them on, then went back out to find him on the couch.

Another difficult moment passed as she saw him sitting there in nothing but his shorts, ready for bed, looking delicious in the light of a single lamp. Bare-chested, hairless, tan skin tight over wiry muscles. She went and kissed him, wished him good night before anything else could happen and made herself go back to the guest room and get in bed. She slipped under the covers and pulled them up to her chin, staring at the ceiling.

Fighting the guilty desire creeping over her.

Should she and Mike just do it? Was it fair to keep holding out? *Did* he bring protection? What would he tell Levi? Doing it just so Mike could save face would be the dumbest reason of all, but she felt his pain. How would he own up to his friends? What would he say? "We just went to bed"? "We made out"? They didn't even do that. Should they? Definitely not, as she was sure that would only make it harder to do the right thing.

But what *was* the right thing?

She lay in the bedroom, alone, wracked by these mental musings that had become such a part of her life. Constant internal evaluations she feared would drive her mad. Indecision. Indecision on everything, it seemed, and now, laying there thinking of Mike and what she ought and ought not to be doing ...

Should she go back out there and do ... other things? Not actual sex, but close enough, no harm in it, no loss of her own integrity but it would be huge for Mike and would definitely make him feel on top of the world. Would that be a bad precedent to set? She had to admit her own intense curiosity in the matter, an overwhelming desire to experience those things firsthand, to be that much wiser, but everything in that direction seemed sure to head her down a slippery slope.

Mike had never pushed the issue, but it was clearly on his mind. They'd been dating for months and plenty of easy opportunities had come and gone, to say nothing of the moments they could've created if they tried. Mike must surely be frustrated. Only, he was too polite, too shy to even bring it up. Each time a moment like this passed she could see the letdown in his eyes, but he never said a word. Sex was what every guy wanted. She didn't blame Mike for that. She wanted it too, only ...

Not with him.

And the voicing of that, even to herself, was like a little

wakeup call. Did that make her a bad girlfriend? Should she just not *have* a boyfriend? As much as she liked Mike, it wasn't fair to keep stringing him along.

So why keep it up?

Did it matter if he was *the* one for her? Her soul mate and future husband, till death do us part? Boys and girls went through many hookups, many "I'll always love you!"s until finding the one they truly would. And some never did. Look at Monica, nearing 40, still playing the field.

So whether or not Mike was "the one", couldn't he, at least, be the one right now? Did it matter if she did it with him? Honestly? Many girls her age had sex. But then, just because it was common did that make it okay?

Like it or not, right or wrong, her role was to please. To keep Mike wanting her. And, lately, she'd begun to worry he might be losing interest. No matter the agenda of feminists or any other equal rights group, men were the takers and girls were the givers. No one could change eons of genetics with an agenda. Girls had it, boys wanted it. And if the boy didn't want it, it wasn't happening. Which meant that, no matter what anyone said, boys and girls would never be equal in that regard. It meant girls would always have it as their job to attract, and boys would have it as their job to perform. Which also meant that, for boys at least, the peer pressure was to do it. To prove their manhood. This was helped, of course, by an overload of testosterone. For girls the peer pressure was different. They were supposed to make the boys want it, to be desirable, to give it away under the right circumstances, but somehow, if you managed not to, that almost made you a bigger person—though most of your friends wouldn't admit it. Giving it away became a selective process, rated by how cool of a guy you could attract.

Was her hesitation even valid? She wasn't hesitating for fear of sex. She *wanted* sex. And if Mike *did* have protection ... What then? What held her back? Was it ... love? To her sex was the ultimate expression of that, the ultimate intimacy. But did loyalty really matter in her case? Would she ever again see ...

Zac.

She moaned at the sudden and clear image of the one who dominated her thoughts—surprised to hear herself make the sound aloud. She'd dreamed about that encounter a hundred times. A thousand. What she'd do, what Zac would be like ...

Since returning she'd tried unsuccessfully not to think about him. Valiantly, each day, to suppress those memories. Zac was an illusion, untouchable, and so wasting time obsessing over him made no sense. It was almost like obsessing over a teen idol, a movie star or any other unattainable fantasy. Which, of course, did not stop girls everywhere from doing it. Still, she should focus on the now. What was before her. Zac himself had told her to live her life.

But she couldn't. Her devotion, like it or not, was to a man she might never see again. And, of course, these self-imposed arguments to forget him were weakened by the fact that, unlikely as it was, she actually *could* end up with Zac. She did, after all, have the Icon. He wasn't totally unattainable.

Part of her thought, maybe, it would be smart to have sex with Mike. Or at least fool around or something. Anything. Use it as an opportunity to gain experience, to be ready for the moment with Zac if it ever *did* come. Driven by that motivation, however, the mere thought of it only made her feel that much more guilty. She couldn't do that to Mike.

Actually, she imagined, *he'd probably be happy to be abused for that purpose.* He was a teenage boy, after all. He'd probably love nothing more than being a sex guinea pig. In fact, she could probably tell him, right in the act, right in the middle—completely matter-of-fact and to the point: "Sorry, Mike. I like you and all, but I'm just practicing so I'll be even better for someone else," and he'd be like "Great! Keep going!"

Ugh! She groaned and rolled over. Annoyed.

Her life had become one big, unhappy problem.

CHAPTER 4:

ROAD TRIP

BOOM! ANOTHER EXPLOSION rocked the metal floor. Jess kept her balance and continued across the room, to an archaic wooden door—a door which seemed entirely out of place against the riveted green-iron surfaces of the small space. Overhead, through an open roof, was a leaden sky, ready to burst, vultures circling. Beside the door was yet another incongruity: a sleek, high-tech access panel, lit with electric lights, some blinking. She braced herself against the wall and studied the scene.

There were no windows. The open ceiling seemed to close off all at once. The sky was simply … gone, replaced with a roof. Diffuse light came from an unknown source. The door before her was covered in complicated runes; alien glyphs that were not any Earth script. A battle of some sort took place outside, rocking the walls with pulsing blasts. Another hit and she caught her footing.

Looking down she saw she was dressed in armor. Skin-tight armor, no gloves. Ribbed and plated yet conforming to her every curve, all except hands and head covered by the hard, satin-black material. In one hand she gripped a long, slightly curving sword of shiny blued steel; like a katana.

But they weren't her hands, were they? Different, somehow. Skin a pale purity, almost that of a child's, though the size and shape of her own. She could feel everything. Could even smell the acrid air, if she thought to take a breath. Tactile feedback was amazing; the wall beneath her palm, the armor against her skin.

This was the most vivid dream she'd ever had.

She looked at the high-tech panel beside the door as the battle outside intensified. As she accepted more elements of the dream its vibrant edge began to fade, dulling that momentary lucidity and bringing with it the usual nonsense one associated with an overactive imagination. Consciously she pressed controls at the computerized panel, caused the door to open and went through, expecting to find something of great value beyond but instead finding a long, featureless tunnel that led to a jungle.

She began running. Why, she no longer knew, but fear rose in her breast and she fled. The jungle extended before her; seemed to grow longer of its own accord. The sword was gone.

Now the dream became entirely nonsensical. A simple nightmare. Faceless, nameless monsters screamed in the trees all around and she ran faster. The jungle closed tighter.

Then a new presence. A powerful figure, demonic, thrashing through the masses of lesser beasts in a rage. Surging after her. She tried to take action and couldn't. Her awareness was too high, however, to suffer the usual panic. Having come from such an initial, clear perspective, the encroaching and unsophisticated dream simply became boring.

Pointless.

She decided to wake up and did.

Looked around the darkened guest room. *Still in Aunt Monica's house.* Moonlight shone through thin drapes, giving everything just enough clarity to be spooky.

She sat up and shook off the last vestiges of the dream.

Never had one seemed so real. A mild shudder shook her and she went with it, added a little to it and finished with a quiet "brrrr".

Since returning from Anitra she'd had many such dreams, odd dreams, several just like this one, flashes of the same settings, fighting battles and running away in the end. As clear as they often were she'd simply chalked them up to some new twist in her mind's eye, following the trauma of the events on Anitra. After all, how else did she expect her psyche to cope?

This dream, however, was different. Creepy how real the images, the sensations. How *she* was not simply a spectator.

How it was *her* in action, but not her.

Dreams were often weird. For her, often very weird. This new and random theme hadn't really bothered her much until now. Now though ...

Now it was starting to seem less like a dream, more like ...

A memory.

She shuddered again and swung her feet out of bed. Rubbed them on the rough rug—vigorously—savoring the tingly scratch against her soles. Checked the clock.

Three-thirty.

After several long minutes she stood and went out to the living room. Mike lay on the couch, sprawled like a true teenage boy, long limbs sticking out or flopped across, blanket scrunched around his chest and half off. Jess went to the living room window, carefully drew back a corner of the curtains and peeped out.

No car.

She looked all the way up and down the street. Quiet. No activity anywhere. No car to be found.

Whoever they were they'd apparently moved on.

Maybe it was nothing after all.

She closed the drapes and headed back to bed—stopping as she walked by Mike.

So cute, lying there.

On impulse she arranged his arms and legs so they were all back on the couch. He mumbled and smacked his lips, pulling in the blanket and clutching it higher. Gently she freed his grip and draped it over his whole body, covering his feet and pulling it up around his chin and over his arms.

There, she thought as she straightened and smoothed the edges. *All tucked in.*

She thought a moment, then bent and kissed him on the forehead, pushing back his hair and looking down on his face in the moonlight.

Deciding she *did* love him.

Mike was a good guy.

STAR ANGEL: RETURN TO ANITRA

But he was definitely not "the one".

* * *

"I know what'll cheer you up." Mike fiddled with Jessica's phone as he drove. They were alone in his little sport import, buzzing down a desolate highway to the drone of the high-strung turbocharged four with the oversized exhaust. Levi and Matt were long gone, having pulled away some time back—after Jess complained a little too loudly that Mike was being juvenile playing their ridiculous game of road tag. That was the way they'd driven down to Vegas and now, after a long weekend and little sleep, her patience for the boys' nonsense had finally reached an end. Sitting there after the fact she kind of regretted being harsh about it, but she had to admit the drive, since insisting Mike slow down, had at least been calm. Seven more hours to go and she was sure, at the end of it, she'd be happier she made a stink. More so than if she'd just sat there the whole time grinding her teeth.

The irony, of course, was that she'd been through more real danger than either Mike, Levi or Matt combined. She'd been shot at, been in a firefight in a suit of powered armor, battled across an enemy battlefield, into and out of an enemy compound, been captured, was in freefall from a thousand feet with no chute, fled cops in a deadly car chase through an alien town—*I've been in—I've driven in—a real, honest-to-God, life-or-death car chase*—found her way, alone, out of the deep, dark woods in the middle of a raging storm, killed an evil Shogun and a dozen other acts of courage far beyond anything Mike and his friends had ever even contemplated. The closest they'd come to what she actually *did* was watching it in movies or playing it in video games.

So, no, she didn't feel so bad insisting Mike take it easy for a while.

"Here we go," he found what he was looking for. He had her phone plugged into the car stereo, selected and cranked up the intro to a song from her list, and as the opening riffs strummed he played a little air guitar, checking for a positive reaction. Jess tried to appear interested but wasn't quick enough. He caught her ambivalence.

"I thought this was your favorite album."

"It is." She tried to come up with a good reason why she was being a poopy pants. Admittedly she'd been an unpleasant companion all morning. "I'm just tired, that's all. Don't take it the wrong way. I appreciate everything you've done." She took the time to put a hand on his leg—the hand with the bracelet. "This has been an amazing weekend." She meant it. "I'll remember it forever." She lifted her arm so he could see the bracelet and jingled it. "I just want to relax." She scooched down in the seat. "We're back in school tomorrow and it's going to be so late when we get home."

Mike shrugged and searched for another song.

"Whoa," he paused. "Purple Rain? You've got Prince?" Jess fought the impulse to just take the phone from him as he eagerly scrolled through this new discovery.

Was that a bad sign? Was her continuing reluctance to share her things yet one more reason she and Mike weren't, in the end, meant to be? Her original vision of crafting him into the perfect boyfriend, visions she'd had since long before meeting Zac, hadn't turned out as planned. As with most such things, perfect dreams did not become perfect reality. More of an imperfect improvement, it seemed. Mike was better than when she asked him out on that first date, to be sure, closer to her absurd fantasies but ...

He was still Mike.

"Ooh," he found one that made him grin. "Here we go. Jess!" he glanced over as he simultaneously drove and thumbed the device. "Look at you! This one's nasty. Nasty girl," he accused and she craned to see what he'd selected. Disappointed to find ... *Darling Nikki.* Terribly amused with himself he put the phone in his lap, turned it up and sat back as the song kicked off, slow grinding, pretending to play the drums with exaggerated movements of his arms as he mouthed along with the lyrics—badly—twisting in the seat and making hip-thrusting motions. She just stared at him, straight-faced with an "are you serious?" glare. But he kept at it, relentless, until ... she cracked. Frustrated she was unable to ignore his immature efforts she turned away, hoping he at least wouldn't see her smiling.

"All right, all right," he said, satisfied he'd won. "Here." He flipped through the phone and selected another album. "Put your seat back," he offered, turned down the volume and settled back a little himself.

She found the lever for the seat and folded it back as far as it would go, lifted her legs and put her feet on the dash, savoring the instant warmth of the spring sun beating through the windshield.

That morning had been interesting enough. Both she and Mike woke early, before Monica returned. They were ready to get going on the long day ahead and, honestly, their bodies were probably still programmed from getting up so early the day before.

What that meant was that when Monica came home Mike's aunt had no idea what the night's sleeping arrangements had been, seeing both teenagers up and about, everything already straightened and put away. Naturally she appeared to assume the worst—or best, from her point of view—and there was no way for Jess to interject with an, "Oh, by the way, we didn't have sex." Which, of course, left Monica with the unfair impression that they *did* have sex—and the equally unfair idea that she'd been right in everything she said the night before.

As the morning wore on and they all went to breakfast and eventually parted company Jess became increasingly anxious that Monica would at least ask, or something, anything that would give her an opening to set the record straight.

She didn't.

And maybe that was part of the reason she was so ready for this weekend to just be over.

CHAPTER 5:

PARANOIA

AMY OPENED THE DOOR as Jess came up the walk. It was dark out. She stepped into the porch light and waved politely to Mike, who sat in his car by the curb; he stuck out an arm and waved back as Jess walked slowly, tired, overnight bag slung across her shoulder. As soon as she reached the porch Amy hurried her inside. Jess got in one last wave as Mike's Nissan ripped off into the night.

"What's the rush?" she pulled away as Amy shut the door.

"How was it?" It was as if Amy knew that should be her first question, but was obviously anxious with other news.

"Fine." Jess began to worry as she noticed more of her sister's edge. Amy took her bag and helped her into the living room.

"What's up?"

Amy wasn't sure where to begin. "There were some guys," she said.

Jess stopped cold.

"In a car."

Now she found the back of a chair and steadied herself.

"They parked out front most of the day. The car was there when I came home, then stayed for, like, hours. I almost went out and asked them what the hell they were doing. I was going to call the cops, but before I did they left.

"I don't know why I'm telling you this." Her sister was still quite disturbed. She'd obviously been fretting over the situation. "I just thought you should know. It really creeped me out."

Jess took a deep, shuddering breath.

Mom and Dad were gone for the weekend. Part of the reason she'd been allowed to go on her short trip. They must've figured she'd be alone with Amy anyway, so what was worse about letting her go stay with an adult in another city?

Aunt Monica, thought Jess. *Yeah. Some adult she turned out to be.* Her pulse thumped harder in her neck.

Amy was shaking her head. "I called everyone I could think of but they were all busy. I didn't want to freak and insist someone come over." Jess could see the awkward desperation in her sister's eyes; the fear at being home alone, mysterious guys outside in a car watching the house, pressed against the fear of looking stupid to her friends by reacting like a child. "I almost left again, but I was afraid they'd follow me. I knew you were gonna be home soon."

"Why didn't you call me?"

"I almost did." Her sister shook her head. "But there was nothing you could do. You were already on your way."

"When did they leave?"

"About an hour ago."

"What did they look like?"

"Cops. Clean cut, in a plain black car. Like undercover cops or something. But I'm pretty sure they weren't cops."

Jessica's heart thundered.

This wasn't happening.

"I snapped a few pictures." Amy grabbed her phone from a nearby counter, brought it over and held the display so Jess could see. She scrolled through a few photos of the car. Taken in the daylight earlier that day, plain black car.

Jess pretended to calmly review the images, stoic on the outside while inside her stomach churned. Could it be the same guys that were outside Monica's house? Sure looked the same, though the details were unclear.

Why would they have driven so far? And ... how did they beat her and Mike? Probably they couldn't have, unless they started last night. Or, unless it was a different car. Different guys.

She fought desperately against the rising terror.

"Do you think we should do anything?" Amy. Jess looked at her. Worked to regain her composure. To match the remarkable outward calm she was presenting. Maybe that was it. Maybe Amy consulted her advice because she thought she was unfazed—failing to see deeper, to recognize the fear knotting her guts.

Jess tried to be the person Amy saw. "Make sure all the doors and windows are locked," she said. "That's all I can think of for now. Get up and go to school in the morning. Hope they don't come back." But even as she said it the mere idea sounded hollow.

"I'm going upstairs to change." She tried hard to convince herself this would turn out to be something stupid. And what else could it be? There was no way that, after months, someone would come knocking now. No one knew what she was hiding. No one knew where she'd been or what she'd done. That trail was long cold.

Amy set off to lock everything, moving around the house nervously. As she checked the front windows she looked like a skittish child, worried Sasquatch or some other monster might be on the other side of the glass, waiting to smash through and grab her.

Jess went upstairs.

And as she climbed the steps everything fell into a sort of fog. Going to her room, throwing down the overnight bag, unpacking it, taking a nervous shower, getting into her sleep shirt, climbing into bed until ... her phone rang.

She jumped; checked the face.

Bianca.

"Hello?" she answered.

"I heard you're back," came her friend's cheery voice on the other end. "How come you didn't call?"

Jess actually began to shake. Nerves she'd been suppressing came raging to the fore. She took a deep breath and held herself still.

"Hey. Sorry. I just ... it was a long trip."

"And?" Bianca didn't seem to notice the strained pause. "Dish, girlfriend."

Jess swallowed. Made herself breathe. She was exhausted, she was overwrought. It took a minute to even process what Bianca was talking about.

"It was fun," she managed.

"Fun? That's all you've got? You went to Vegas! Alone. *With Mike.* Come on! Fun?

"You owe me more than that."

"We had a good time." Jess was starting to wish she hadn't answered the phone.

"And?"

"He got me a bracelet." She looked at the pretty bracelet, wondering if she'd ever get the chance to show it off. Wondering if her life would soon be over. "He took me to dinner." She swallowed down those sudden feelings of doom. Her own voice sounded distant, robotic. "It was nice. We walked around town. Oh, and the races. The drag races were pretty cool, actually." She tried to imagine being a real girl, leading a normal life. She almost cried. "You should go sometime. I know you're not into that sort of thing but it really is amazing. So loud, so fast." She swallowed. "You have to be there. TV doesn't do it justice."

There was a pointed silence on the other end.

"You're kidding, right?"

Jessica's mind swirled.

"Jess! Drag racing? Stop stalling and give me the details." She went straight for the jugular: "Did you guys do it?"

Jess was so consumed with the very real threat before her that the earth-melting significance of *this* conversation had entirely escaped her. "No," she said, failing to realize that, while a simple "No" was enough as far as she was concerned, it would *not* suffice for Bianca.

"*No?!*" Her friend was utterly incredulous. "*No?!* You guys were alone! All night! At least that's what Levi said."

Jess snapped a little from her fog. Did word really travel that fast? The teenage grapevine was truly an amazing thing. Mike didn't seem the type to make up stories, but Levi sure might. And if Levi was already talking ...

Absently she wondered if Levi had pressured Mike into saying something that wasn't true. Guys weren't anywhere near as open as girls about these sorts of things. Mike, sweet as he was, might easily imply something in order to save face.

"We stayed at his aunt's house, yes."

An exasperated pause from Bianca. "And?"

"And what?"

"And?! What did you do when he made his move?"

"Mike's not like that."

"All boys are like that."

"He didn't push."

"Did you? If he's shy then *you've* got to be the one." Bianca's frustration was clear. "I thought we went over that." Jess was like a project, and this project had just come back with a big red F.

"It will happen when it happens."

"Jessica! God! You're so naïve."

"I'm not naïve."

"You didn't do *anything* for him?"

"No."

"Come on. You guys were in Vegas." Her friend seemed to be shaking her head on the other end of the line. Jess could almost see her disappointment. "You're lucky he didn't sneak out and just hire a hooker."

"Bianca! You are so weird sometimes."

Her friend pressed on. "He's a boy."

"We're in love." But even as she said it she felt a twinge of guilt. Knowing it wasn't true love.

"Love schmuv. You've got to work it, Jess! If you don't he'll find someone who will. He's a guy!" Bianca, of course, was only repeating arguments Jess had already had with herself. "They play with it, like, every day. Their main purpose in life is to use it. They don't have any common sense when it comes to that. You've got to do *something* with it or he'll find someone who will."

Jess did *not* want to be having this conversation right now. Probably ever.

"It's like it's out of their control," Bianca was unrelenting. "Do you know how many times each day they think about sex?"

"I don't know. Like, a million? Look. I'm exhausted. Can't you just lecture me tomorrow or something?"

"You know I'm only doing it because I care."

"That's what you keep saying."

"That's not fair."

"Sorry." It was true. Bianca, misguided though she was, had Jessica's best interests at heart.

"You're strong, Jessica. You're an absolute bad-ass. When it comes to boys, though … It's like you've got a blind spot." B really was trying. And Jess really did want to get off the phone. "Teenage boys aren't men," her friend continued. "They're high maintenance. It takes a lot of energy to keep them around. Even men are high maintenance but boys are double bad. Triple."

This caused Jessica to drift. Maybe she didn't care whether she kept Mike around or not. Maybe she *did* want a man.

And she knew exactly who.

She groaned, louder than she meant and was immediately worried Bianca would misinterpret the noise.

But her friend either didn't notice or finally realized Jess wasn't paying much attention. "You're tired," she said. "Get some sleep. We'll sort this out tomorrow."

Jess didn't want to sort it out. But she was polite, said goodbye and hung up. Wondering if she should tell Bianca *exactly* how much there was to sort out.

Boys were the least of her troubles.

Nervous, she put down the phone, got up and went to the study across the hall, at the front of the house and, from the shadows, peeked out the window at the front yard and curb. Nothing. Warm, inviting streetlights designed to look like old gas lamps lining the streets of the affluent neighborhood. Nothing else in sight. No stalkers. No secret agents.

She turned and walked from the darkened room, back across the hall—

Right into Amy.

Amy screamed; covered her mouth. Both girls caught their composure.

"I just checked outside," Jess hurried to squash her own reaction. "Nothing. The car's gone."

"Good," said Amy, eyes still a little wide with fear. "I'm

going to bed."

"Night."

"See you in the morning."

And Amy was gone. Moments later Jess was back in her own bed, turning off the lights and pulling up the covers. She lay there, listening to the silence of the house.

Wishing she could just be one of the ignorant masses.

CHAPTER 6:

VISITORS

"Higher!" barked Master Lenny.

Jess nodded in response to his command, set herself and kicked again—higher, as instructed.

Whack! her foot impacted the vinyl of the heavy bag and made a solid dent.

"Good!" Lenny smacked her shoulder. "Ten more minutes," he instructed in his thick Brooklyn accent, "then switch to the left." He walked off to check a pair of students grappling on the mats nearby.

Jess delivered another walloping kick to the bag, returned to a strong stance, set herself and delivered another.

Whack!

Lenny began "encouraging" the students on the mats. As he did Jess took a moment to cast another nervous glance out the big front windows of the MMA gym. Cars moved back and forth in the street, people walking by on the sidewalk outside.

No sign of anything suspicious.

She returned her attention to the bag.

Whack!

That morning she'd been beyond nervous on her way to school, riding with Mike, obsessively checking the mirrors for sign of anyone that might be following. The car from the day before hadn't returned. At least, it wasn't waiting in the morning and she hadn't seen it all day at school. School was patrolled and pretty secure, but she nevertheless found herself staring out every window and across every parking lot, looking for signs; nerves amped all day, playing with the idea that some official with a badge might show up and demand her presence in the office.

Who the hell were they?!

Were they government? Why were they following her?

And so blatantly? Was it even her? Was it just some amazing coincidence?

That seemed totally impossible.

After what seemed the longest school day ever, watching all the other young faces laughing or shouting or talking or otherwise caught up in their very small, *very* dramatic worlds—knowing nothing of what *real* issues were like, having no idea what incredible things *she* was going through ...

Nothing happened.

After school Mike brought her here, to Lenny's gym, then ran off to work on Levi's injectors. Since that time she'd been unable to stop glancing furtively out the gym windows.

Whack!

She checked her form in the long mirror covering one wall.

Whack!

After returning to Earth—it still felt bizarre to even think those words—after returning to Earth she started going back to MMA class, attending more often even than when she was a busybody kid, improving steadily. She'd been working hard and was now more in shape than she'd ever been. She kicked again, watching herself in the mirrors, exhaling forcefully through her mouth as her foot impacted the vinyl.

Whack!

She returned to her stance and bounced on the balls of her feet. Her reflection, geared up for fighting, looked different than the usual Jessica. Black-and-red fighting shorts, red compression shirt, MMA gloves, black mouthpiece where her teeth should be, hair braided tight into twin ponytail whips that swung at the sides of her head, sweat beading above an intense stare.

She looked like one bad-ass bitch.

That was until Master Lenny walked up, dwarfing her.

"Good. Now watch this." He moved her aside and stepped back, demonstrating a few kicks at half-speed, leg well up the bag. Lenny was a one-time heavyweight champ, with high belts in several fighting disciplines, stood about six-three or four and probably weighed close to three hundred pounds, most of that still muscle. Years of no competition combined with age—age caught everyone eventually—had provided him a layer of softness which no doubt added a few of those pounds, but beneath it he was still hard as a rock.

Staring at herself standing next to him in the mirrors she imagined this was what she'd look like standing next to Zac. Though Zac was even taller than Lenny and definitely leaner. Shredded; not an ounce of fat on him.

Forcibly she turned her mind from the tingle rising in her belly.

Zac and I would make an interesting couple, she thought. Not because she was tiny. She wasn't. A little shy of average, maybe, but not tiny. It was just that Zac would dwarf any girl.

And he could kick this bag into a cloud of stuffing. She looked at the heavy sack as Lenny kicked it harder. Wondering just what a kick from Zac would do to it. Vaporize it, no doubt.

"Try that," Lenny brought her back to the present, moved her shoulders and positioned her stance. "A little more like that. Now try."

She did. *Whack!* delivered a solid blow, way high, foot coming well above her own head—high enough even to kick Lenny's. In the mirror her form looked great.

"Yes!" he enthused.

He left her to check on another student.

She continued kicking.

The exertion felt good. It was helping to burn the adrenaline running through her system. Wailing on the heavy bag was intensely gratifying and she was glad Master Lenny chose strikes for her this afternoon. She turned up the heat.

Whack!

Checked her form. Set herself.

Whack!

Checked the clock and switched to the left foot.

Whack!

Not high enough. She pivoted and ...

Whack!

Good. That one was better.

She glanced around the room. Saw the other students practicing. Flashed her eyes across the windows, returned her attention to the heavy bag ...

And froze.

The car was there.

Desperately she steadied herself and controlled her breathing. She angled her vision in the mirrors so she could see the street outside without having to turn.

It was no illusion. There it was. Sitting at the curb on the other side of the street. Two guys inside, looking back and forth between the front of the gym as they talked to each other. Her heart began that steady pounding with which she was becoming so familiar. Even over the exertion she could feel it. Hammering in her chest.

It was unlikely they could see inside, bright as the afternoon sun must be against the glare of the windows. They likely only saw their own reflections. They weren't using any special equipment that she noticed, no polarizing lenses or anything of the sort.

But surely they must know she was in there.

And with that she was forced to accept the fact that she *was* being followed. This was not wild coincidence. And it occurred to her in that same instant that these guys were either amateurs, inept pros, or were such ultimate experts they just plain didn't care—because they pretty much sucked at stealth. Even Aunt Monica had spotted them with ease. There they sat like a couple of dweebs, blatantly casing the joint in their stupid black sedan and "Hey! I'm a G-man!" suits. Only, it was hard to really think of them as dweebs. They were grown men and had, somehow, figured out how to track her, from Vegas to home to the gym. She shuddered to think what else of hers they might have access to. Phone calls? Emails? Social sites?

"Come on," Lenny startled her from behind and she suppressed a scream. Her physical reaction, however, was less controlled. She jumped severely.

"Whoa," he put a hand on her shoulder and her head drooped, mortified by her lack of composure.

"You okay?" He was genuinely concerned.

"Sorry," she said, slurring around her mouthpiece. She took it out and spoke more clearly: "I was just thinking of something.

"I'm sorry, Master Lenny."

But he could tell this was no simple case of daydreaming.

"You sure?"

She met his gaze. "Yeah."

He studied her eyes, not convinced.

"Need to take a break?"

"Probably best if I keep going." There was more truth to that than he could possibly realize. He paused, then decided to let her have her way.

"Fine. But get some water."

She went to the fountain. Drank a few sips, peeking furtively out the windows. Lenny continued circulating but kept his eye on her as she went back to the bag, gaze locked on the black sedan outside. She put her mouthpiece in and resumed drilling.

The next hour rolled by, her body on automatic. Lenny checked on her a few more times. She kept kicking then switched to punching, coming out of her trance only when she looked out the window for what seemed like the hundredth time and ... found the car was gone. Had anyone been left behind? Frantically she scanned the handful of people in view on the sidewalk—were they coming inside?!—but found no one that looked like a secret agent or a G-man.

At length Master Lenny called them in for the closing pep talk then dismissed them with bows to him, the class leaders and each other. When all was done Jess wandered in a daze among the other students, gathering her gym bag and taking off her gloves.

Lenny found her.

"Sure everything's okay?"

"Yeah."

She felt like a dead man walking.

"If you need someone to talk to, let me know."

For an instant she almost took him up on his offer. In fact, Master Lenny was such a friendly guy … his tough-guy accent combined with the reality that he was, in fact, an actual tough guy, gave her the fleeting thought of asking him to help her go find these guys and kick their heads in. Fear had risen slightly to rage, and she really just wanted to confront them and get it over with. Who were they? What did they want? She wanted to scream at them.

But that was all fantasy. "Thanks, Master Lenny. I will."

"Listen," he was on to other things, "I've been watching and you're getting good. How would you feel about a competition? There's a grappling tournament coming up."

All she could do was look at him, expression blank.

"You up for it?"

She knew she was supposed to respond. She nodded. "Maybe." She must look like a zombie. Competition was the furthest thing from her mind right then, but Master Lenny was zeroed in.

"I've seen some of these other girls," he assured her. "You'd kill in your division." At that he grinned. "You could bring the school another trophy."

The school already had dozens of trophies but Lenny was always on the quest for more. More recognition. More prestige. His back wall looked like it belonged to a bowling league. It was kind of the running joke.

But Jess couldn't think about that right then. All she could think about was how fast things were spiraling out of control. She might not even be alive by the time any tournament happened.

No. She reined in those dangerous thoughts. Too fatalistic. There had to be a way to figure this out.

"What do you think?" Lenny.

"Good," she agreed. "Sounds good." Then, remembering the real question: "I'll ask my parents. See what they say."

Lenny smiled, excited by the prospect of her grappling for the school. "Great. Let me know."

She returned his smile and headed reluctantly for the

door.

He called after her: "And let me know if you want to talk." She nodded that she would. Off the mats she found her flip-flops and stepped into them, pulled on a fleece hoodie, pulled the hood over her head until it cast her face in shadow, opened the door and stepped outside into the chilly spring afternoon. There were people on the sidewalk. She drew some comfort from standing by the building with them crossing back and forth between her and the street. No one was going to pull up, rush through those other bodies and grab her.

She hoped.

Shaking a little, from both the cool air and the fear, she called Mike. He was already on his way. She went in her gym bag and pulled out the bracelet, glinting silver in the sunlight, red stones shining, put it on and put her hands in her pockets, counting the minutes, relieved when he finally pulled to the curb and bripped the throttle. In no time they were surging toward home.

The whole way back he talked about what they'd done to Levi's car and how he was heading back after he dropped her off to finish the project. Being alone right then terrified her but she told herself she wasn't going to make a bigger deal of it. Like Amy, she didn't want to freak in front of her friends, Mike included. Her parents weren't due back for another day which meant that, if Amy was out, she'd be home alone. But she was determined not to be put off her game by these assholes, whoever they were.

As they pulled into her neighborhood, Mike chatting away—oblivious to her sullen mood—she realized her emotions were definitely rising more toward anger. Fear still gave a sharp edge to everything yet, right then, she was starting to get pissed. These guys were messing not only with her peace of mind, they were messing with her life.

Again she checked the mirrors, heart rising into her throat as Mike rounded the last curving corner and ... no sign of the spy car as her beautiful two-story house came into view. They weren't waiting. Maybe they'd just go away, she thought, but by then she knew that wasn't happening. And so she began to resolve to go right up to them, with witnesses, the next time they showed their faces. Which, she had to admit, would probably be soon.

At the house she kissed Mike goodbye and he ripped off, chirping the tires as he upshifted through the neighborhood and out of sight, then ... all was quiet. She shouldered her gym bag higher and pulled out her keys, glancing up and down the street as she headed for the front door.

As she reached the steps a black car pulled around the far corner. She froze ...

Then recognized it as Bianca's little Fiat. Gloss black with shiny black wheels, red, pinstriped tires, tinted windows; like a California girl, which Bianca fancied herself. Jess leaned her head back and squinted to the sky.

Wanting this nightmare to be over.

She waited as Bianca pulled in, sunglasses on and looking cool, music pouring from the open sunroof. Oblivious to the danger Jess was in. She shut off the car and got out.

"What up, G?" She laughed at her own silly greeting. Jess tried to smile. It failed utterly. Bianca, who was the only person who even had an inkling of what Jess had really been through, always seemed to be on the lookout for signs of that past trauma. Anything out of the ordinary to indicate there might be something on her mind—beyond the usual slew of micro-dramas on the mind of the average teenage girl. And, in that moment, her friend saw it.

Something bad was up.

She dropped the goofy smile and came around the car, taking off the sunglasses. Jess looked past her, at the neighborhood and streets beyond.

"Let's go inside," she said unsteadily. Bianca followed her gaze down the street, seeing nothing, still straining to find what held her friend's attention as Jess took her inside and shut the door.

"What's going on?"

Jess motioned her further in, stopping in the foyer.

"I'm being followed," she said, peeking furtively out the window. Ready to jump out of her skin.

"By who?"

"I don't know."

"Does it have anything to do with ... that stuff?"

"I don't know." Then: "Come on." Jess led her up the stairs to her room. She shook her head as she entered and threw her gym bag on the bed; took a moment to take a deep breath and try to center herself.

She looked at Bianca. "I don't know what's—"

A knock at the door downstairs. Both girls jumped.

Jess rushed passed Bianca, out of the room and across the hall to the front study, checking out the window. *There was no one outside just a second ago!* Her mind raced. Maybe it was a salesman or something ...

Never would she have been so happy to open the door to a salesman.

If only.

Bianca joined her and together they peeked out to the front yard below. And there, down on the walk at the front door ...

Three guys in suits. Looking just like the G-men in the car. Parked at the curb were two black sedans.

Jessica's knees buckled. She actually had to grab the wall to catch herself from falling. Slowly she slid to the floor beneath the window and squatted in horror. Bianca, now very alarmed, squatted with her.

"Is that who's following you?" she hissed. Jess, who'd been seeing these guys off and on over the last few days, mind crafting all sorts of terrible scenarios, tried desperately to be calm. Nervously she peeked back out the window, noting the men wore small earpieces. She strained to see anything else about them that might give her a clue.

And as she did so noticed ... guns. They had guns, in shoulder holsters. Two of them anyway, inadvertently exposing shiny black pistols as they pushed back jackets and put hands on their hips. Idly they looked over the house and yard.

Then one looked up and she recoiled from the window.

Did he see me?!

She jerked her head to Bianca. Stared into her face—

knowing her wide-eyed panic would likely freak her friend even more but unable in that moment to control it. She could hear her own heart thumping in her chest and was sure Bianca must hear it too.

Desperately she tried to remind herself what she'd been through back on Anitra, what amazing dangers she'd already overcome. How strong she'd been, how capable. How fearless.

Unable to feel anything in that moment but absolute terror.

CHAPTER 7:

DECISION TIME

IF SHE FLED, just got up and bolted out the back door and didn't look back ... that was the same as an admission of guilt. Guilt of what didn't matter. They'd catch her and no one was likely to help. People weren't going to take the side of a frantic teenage girl being chased by a bunch of official-looking dudes in suits with guns. The guys in suits—she had to assume they had badges too—would just claim she was a nut-job and haul her off screaming, while any witnesses simply stood by and watched.

Poor, sad, crazy girl. What a shame.

Now that the moment was upon her she realized there was no way to execute her earlier plan. Gathering a mob and confronting these guys and finding out just who the hell they were wasn't going to happen. Not now.

Could they be there for something else? Was she blowing it out of proportion? Could their intentions be benign? Should she just go down and answer the door?

That was the obvious, most expected thing she should be doing, but at the thought of it she nearly laughed—and would've if she hadn't been so far gone. These guys were *not* there to ask a few questions. They'd tracked her across two states and certainly well before that. These weren't regular cops. If they just wanted to ask her a few questions they would've already done so. She had to assume the worst. If she went to them now, whether peacefully or otherwise, she'd disappear and probably never be seen again. They'd get the Icon and get the armor and all her fears would come true.

Freedom did not lie with those men outside.

If only Mom and Dad were here! Anyone. Not just her, all alone. She looked at Bianca, everything flashing before her eyes. Should she call? Her parents? They wouldn't be home till tomorrow, but even if they *were* back ... would it matter? Bitter tears stung her eyes as she almost laughed again. This was not a Mom and Dad problem. Dad wasn't going to just open the door and tell all the men in suits to go away. This was far bigger than any of that. Maybe, in a sad way, it was better her parents *weren't* there. Or Amy. That way they didn't get sucked into the wake of her destruction—

"What do we do?" Bianca's voice startled her. She'd been sitting there staring at her and Jess couldn't form a coherent thought. As her friend's face moved, though, it snapped her from her trance.

"I don't know," she looked around the room.

"Should you just go answer?" Bianca rose up to peek out the window again but Jess pulled her back.

"No."

"Why not? You can't hide up here. Jess, they'll find you."

The truth of that was more than she could bear.

Desperate, she rose to a crouch and hurried back across the hall to her room. Bianca jerked at her sudden movement and shadowed her, growing more alarmed by the second.

As they entered Jess waved her to the side. "Stay here," she instructed. Best if her friend just stayed in one spot. Bianca obeyed without question, leaning against the wall and sliding slowly to the floor. Getting a sense of just how serious this was. Jess searched her room, deciding action— any action—was the only way out of this. Eventually the guys downstairs would break in. Right now they were waiting, but they had to know she was in the house. And there was no way she was going to turn herself in. Not now, not here. She had no idea what to do but it did not involve handing herself over to whatever authority these guys were.

And there was still the chance they weren't authorities at all.

What if they were some sort of international group?

It was all happening too fast. Her mind was absolutely whirling with indecision.

She realized she was pacing. Caught a glimpse of herself in her dresser mirror. Hair pulled tight in the braided pony whips from MMA class, still wearing the pullover hoodie and board shorts.

Time to move.

She kicked off her flip-flops, went to her closet and dug out a pair of canvas high-tops—her favorite Chuck Taylors—black, white laces, well worn; her flattest pair of shoes with the best grip. Considerations of the best shoes for what she was about to do, her conclusions as to why she needed them and the pure mechanics of that evaluation made her swoon, so absent were they of any emotion, so final. Quickly she sat on the floor and pulled on the Chucks in a rush, taking no time to think any further about it.

"What are you doing?" Bianca asked from across the room, scrunched up on the floor against the wall, knees hugged to her chest. Her voice had a tremor in it. It was clear by now that Jess intended something rash.

She didn't answer; finished lacing the shoes, tight, and went to the window overlooking the back yard ...

Three of the guys were back there now, walking toward the playhouse. Was it the same ones from out front?

No. Two were different.

Their numbers were growing.

Fearful she raced back across the hall to the study, staying low, telling Bianca once more to "Stay here" and hoping her friend would just do as instructed.

Entering the study she went and peeked out the window ... finding a new vehicle parked at the curb. A black SUV, plus several more guys in suits. One of them looked up at the window, saw her—this time she was certain—and ...

Hardly reacted.

And as she crouched to the floor it all clicked. They were definitely out to get her. There was no doubt now. They were no longer knocking downstairs, no longer "requesting" to see her. They were surrounding the house. With guns. Knowing full well she was up there, hiding, taking their time about getting to her.

This was definitely it.

She took a deep, shuddering breath, crouched and hurried back across to her room. As she entered Bianca watched her, wide-eyed, following her every move, practically pasted to the wall. Her friend's normally radiant face had grown completely pale.

"They stopped knocking," she said. "Are they still down there?"

Jess went back to her bedroom window and peeked into the back yard.

The guys had passed the playhouse. They were now heading down the hill toward the barn. The old red structure was clearly their destination.

Shit!

Who are you?! She wanted to thrash them. All of them; shake them until they gave up their secrets. Were they the local police? Why in the hell would Boise have a detective branch like this? Were they FBI? That seemed more probable. Only, they weren't acting like FBI. If they knew she was up there the FBI wouldn't keep her waiting. They'd barge in all official like, or use a megaphone or something. *This is the FBI! We've got the house surrounded!*

Which meant they must be some other organization. Probably with all kinds of latitude to accomplish their mission.

She peeked again. Saw they were definitely headed for the barn. And decided, with terrifying clarity, what must be done.

They could *not* be allowed to find the suit of powered armor.

The Icon is in there.

Her only way out.

It was all happening too fast. *I need time to think!* But there wasn't any. No longer time to consider rational options—if any even existed. They were here. Now. She had no contingencies, had never made plans for a scenario like this, had no idea how to react and it was down to this. She couldn't talk her way through this or confront them or let them continue. They were heading right for what she'd been hiding from the world, and she had to either get away or stop them—both of which must involve the armor and the Icon. In short, she had to move.

Now.

Whatever it took.

She turned to Bianca. "Stay here," she said again. Then, thinking a moment, knowing her friend deserved more, went closer to kneel beside her. She put a hand on her shoulder.

"No matter what. Okay? Just ... stay here."

The "no matter what", the chilling certainty working its way into Jessica's demeanor ... these things made Bianca start to tremble.

"You're not part of this," she told her friend. "You stay right here and nothing will happen to you. Okay?" Of course, the implications of that were that something was going to happen to Jess, and that just made Bianca shake harder. Jess desperately wanted to believe her friend would be spared. Desperately wanted to just wake from this horrible nightmare.

But she knew, part of her knew—that part that had been through so much already, so much more than any person ever had been—let alone any girl her age ... that part of her knew this nightmare was only just beginning. Waking would not come sweetly.

Desperately Bianca searched her face. "Jess. What's going on?" she whispered, voice cracking. Tears welled in her eyes. Jess knew her friend sensed, at last, the full scope of what was about to transpire. Bianca knew this was about to be their last moment together. For what could possibly be a very long time.

Jess was going away.

And as the realization of that hit home Jess began to shake too.

"I never told you," she said, taking a deeper breath, "but I brought something back."

Bianca just stared at her, eyes glistening.

"Something they want. I'm sure that's what this is all about. Somehow, some way, they've zeroed in on me."

Bianca whispered: "Why don't you just give it to them?"

"I can't."

"Why not?"

Jess had no words.

And Bianca cried. Jess wanted to cry too, to just sit there on the floor with her friend and break down, hold her and bawl and wait for someone to come save them. But no one was coming. There was no savior on the way. It was time, no matter how much she dreaded it, to rise. To become the Jess that survived. The Jess that, when called to action, became something beyond the simple teenage girl she appeared. She didn't want it, wanted no part of it, but the fears that had been building over the last days, the denials—those things were over. Her choices were stark. Hide and die or ... confront this and, possibly, live. There were no other options.

"You're my best friend," she felt herself switching to that other plane; more and more ready each instant, impatient to face up to and annihilate the threat before her; rising higher even as her friend broke further down. "Don't worry."

"But you haven't done anything wrong," Bianca sobbed. Then: "Have you?"

"I haven't. But if they find what I've been hiding ... I can't explain. Not now. It's too late. Too late for all that. I have to run, I have to get out of here and that's all I know."

Bianca wept openly now, sobs wracking her body, tears streaming down her cheeks as she shook her head in disbelief. It was everything, Jess realized, the magnitude of what was happening, beyond anything Bianca had ever experienced, and it was hitting her like a truck. Jess knew how powerful this cocktail of emotions was. She'd been there. And she'd wept too.

"Stay here," she said one last time, kissed her friend on the forehead, rose and ran back down the hall to her parents' room.

She tried to frame the situation in crystal clarity. If those men were allowed to reach the barn it was over. They'd find the armor and that the jig would be up. More importantly, the Icon would be gone. Her only way back. The gateway between worlds. Why hadn't she ever hidden it separately? The armor *and* the Icon were right there, in the same place, hidden under a bunch of hay.

Stupid!

In a rush she entered the master bedroom, heading straight for her objective. As she threw open the closet in haste and fumbled to reach the small dresser inside she ran mentally through a laundry list of over-analyzed objections. What right did she have, really, to decide if the Icon was revealed? This God-complex had plagued her since returning; whether or not to tell the authorities, whether to reveal the technology for the evaluation and benefit of all. Should she just let those guys find it?

No!

Again, as always, she came to the same conclusion— though she had no more to base it on than childish fears and gut instinct—that revealing either the armor or, especially, the Icon, would do more harm than good. And so she'd kept them both to herself. Waiting for some perfect moment, some perfect opportunity that might never come. And now here were a group of guys she *knew* would be the *last* people she'd choose to reveal it to and they were about to force her hand. How they'd tracked her after all this time … Why they hadn't come sooner …

None of that mattered. Not now. The brief flash of sanity, the months of peace and quiet and normalcy as Jessica Paquin, regular teenager, were over.

As if she could ever have gone back to that life.

She hunted in the dresser where she knew the key to be. Dad kept it in a little box with other stuff, there in the top drawer. She pushed aside underwear, a small cigar humidor, a spare set of keys, earplugs, cufflinks, tie pins, camera, watches. *Dad keeps a lot in his underwear drawer.* Then she found it. The little black box, inside …

The key to the gun box.

She took it out, reached for the top shelf and pulled down the heavy case. She took it over and set it on the bed. Inside it had room for several pistols. Dad was a small-time collector and had taken her shooting many times. With two daughters and no sons Jess, girl number two, had become a sort of stand-in for his subconscious desire to pass on stuff to a boy. Amy was left to her girly devices leaving Jess, in turn, to bear the brunt of those fatherly impulses.

Right then she was glad for it.

She rushed to the window and took another look out in the front yard. Not much change. The men in suits were still milling about, checking things. Surely the neighbors would be looking out their windows. The police might even have been called. The G-men didn't seem to care.

Should she just call 9-1-1? Likely as not these guys controlled all that. All that would do is waste time and, most likely, just bring even more people to try and chase her down. She could imagine the 911 operator getting instructions to keep her on the phone, assuring her to stay calm even as they quietly expanded their ring of force.

I'm the only one that can save myself.

Whether that was true or not, whether she'd just seen too many movies, she believed in it strongly enough to act. There was no one to call who could dig her out of this.

She was on her own.

She hurried back to the gun case and opened it. Of the selections available she chose the most powerful: a gleaming Ruger Super Redhawk, short-barrel, combat grip and sights. It would make the loudest bang. Leaving everything open she went back to the closet, got out the ammo box, threw it on the bed and opened it, grabbing a handful of 454 Casull rounds—the most powerful pistol bullet made. *With rifle round pressures, designed for big-game hunting,* she recited the facts as taught by her father. *Great for predator defense. Big predators, like lions, tigers or bears.*

Oh my! The old line played in her head. She shook it clear. Tried to clear her mind of *all* thoughts as she loaded the big chrome revolver and snapped the cylinder shut. She debated pocketing extra rounds but decided against it. Those in the pistol would be enough to make her point and, hopefully, slow any pursuers.

And at the thought of that, as if a fog had been lifted, she realized, quite suddenly, she was holding a loaded gun. A big, heavy, loaded gun, in her own house, preparing to use it on other people. Not shoot them, just scare them, but the fact of going against another person with a loaded gun at all ...

She began to shake. All at once, and she dropped the gun to the bed and stepped back. Breathing came in gasps.

This was too much. Suddenly it was unreal. What she was about to do ... this "plan", if executed, would be permanent in a way that could never be undone. This was Earth, not some other world. Whatever happened here would change her life forever. Those were men out there. She was in high school. She had homework due tomorrow. Mike was supposed to call in an hour. *I've got a boyfriend!* She'd planned to lay in her room later and try and read a book. Try to put all this out of her mind. Maybe make homemade brownies for when Amy came home. Fresh brownies were about the best thing you could ever want to eat. She and Mom made them from scratch sometimes and, all at once, as if waking to a dream, she imagined the smell of their wonderful aroma filling the house ...

All that was about to be gone.

Where will Nana send my Christmas card?

And the world came crashing in.

She stood there, shaking harder. Staring at the shiny gun on the bed, unable to move. The crux of her entire life squeezed her so tightly in that moment she couldn't breathe.

Just as she was about to lose it completely, just as she was about to fall to her knees ...

Bianca came into the room.

"Jess ..." she froze as she saw the scene before her. Guns and ammo on the bed, Jess in a state of deadlock with herself. *"What the hell are you doing?!"* Her whispered scream echoed Jessica's own deadly thoughts, eyes like saucers as she stared at the open cases, guns and bullets. Dried tears streaked Bianca's cheeks but shock quickly supplanted her fear. Her friend's reaction was enough, however, to yank Jess back from the brink. To kick her back into action. She focused, went to the bed and took the gun in hand once more. Used both hands and steadied her grip.

"*Jessica! No!*"

I'm on my own.

She stared into the eyes of her quivering friend, big shiny gun in her outstretched hands, steeling her resolve.

"*You've got a gun!*" Bianca sputtered, waving a hand in its direction. "*You're holding a gun!*"

"I know."

And as it became clear Jess was committed to whatever insanity she had in mind, as it became clear there would be no reasoning with her and this was truly the end, Bianca, mentally, collapsed.

"Oh my God," she turned this way and that, nowhere to go, "oh my God oh my God," trapped, at last, dropping to the floor and curling into a ball. She hugged her knees to her chest and pinched her eyes shut, muttering between sobs.

"I love you, Bianca," Jess said quietly, not knowing whether her friend heard or not. "I wish it didn't have to be this way."

But there was nothing more to be done. She was about to leave again.

About to leave everything behind.

"I have to go."

And, with one last look, she went around her and walked out into the hall.

Even as downstairs the men began banging on the door.

CHAPTER 8:

SHOOTOUT AT THE RANCH

Move! JESS COAXED HERSELF FORWARD. *Move!* Down the stairs, tight against the banister, hugging the corner at the bottom as she curved right by the front door where the men outside banged—sounding as if they'd knock it in at any moment. She saw their forms through the stained glass, muted in the sunlight, and prayed they couldn't see her. It was dark in the foyer so they probably couldn't, but the sensation of being right there, with a gun in her hand—*I'm holding a gun!*—nothing but a door between them and her ...

She hurried across the living room, spine crawling with fear.

Out the far windows she could see two more guys in the back yard, the other three that were heading to the barn now down in the field, closing on its dilapidated red form.

They'd nearly reached it.

Driven by their proximity she crouched low and hurried to the kitchen, hiding behind the couch on the way, then the kitchen island with its shiny brass sink and marble top and, finally, the microwave stand near the back door—fighting hard—so hard—with the recognition that these familiar things, these things that had always been associated with calm, with family, with peace, were now being used as cover in a deadly game. Fighting to ignore, in truth, the fact that these things were about to be lost forever.

She took deep, forceful breaths, making herself breathe, staving off the debilitating panic. Consciously she honed her edge. This was the point of no return. At that moment she could, in theory, put down the gun and go answer the front door.

Bang! Bang! Bang! It reverberated through the house.

She eyed the back porch; the kitchen and the screened

area through which she would have to run. Peering around the corner she estimated the distance to the barn. There were two guys in the back yard, three more out in the field she'd have to beat. *Then I have to get into the armor and go live before they stop me.*

Would the armor even work? Though she remembered how to run it she had no knowledge of its function. How did the fusion reactor operate? Had it remained "hot" all this time? Would it have shut itself off and need to be restarted? Gone to sleep or hibernated or otherwise need time to get going? Would she get in and ... nothing?

And where would she go? Assuming it *did* fire up—and this was starting to seem like a dangerous assumption— what then? Obviously flee these guys. That was the only reason she was down there in the kitchen holding a gun in the first place. Any reveal of the Skull Boy had to be on her terms and these guys were all of a sudden right there, in her face, swarming her, and it wasn't going down like this. Now that her hand had been forced, whatever she did with the Skull Boy her first goal was to keep it away from *these* guys.

But ... what then? Where *would* she take it? To a military base? Reveal it in broad view of everyone? She trusted the military. People in the military were patriotic, with a love of country and a desire to protect and serve.

Soldiers, however, worked for people. Soldiers would have no say in what was done with it, even if she could get the Skull Boy to them. Nor would they be able to protect her if a bunch of agents with high-power badges showed up and told them to turn it over.

Going to the military would not solve her problem.

Silently she cursed her failure to give this more thought before now. It was the same thing she'd neglected to figure out after all this time, and suddenly she had to, all at once, and there weren't any more answers now than there ever had been.

Of course there was the one.

The one option that had been there all along. And as she realized she now had no choice, no more excuses; as that option took hold, the *only* option, washing over her; as she realized, subconsciously, that option was the real thing driving her ... the sense of possibility it brought, the sense of excitement, made her feel suddenly lighter. It was a giddy feeling, like a nervous glee, and she knew at once she was for real losing it. In that moment, however, she didn't care. She went with it. It gave her hope amid the hopelessness and, though extreme—her life *was* extreme, the intervening peace just an illusion—in that moment, with absolute clarity, she realized where her future lay.

Where it always had.

With Zac.

There were no more "carefully" thought-out reasons not to go back. In her heart she'd known this day would come. Dreamt of it, of the day conditions would be right and all would be as it should be. Only, like most people and their dreams she'd managed to procrastinate. To make excuses, putting it further and further into the future, waiting for some perfectly opportune time that might one day come, where things were just so and everything was just right and only then would she act.

Except, that perfect day would *never* come.

And so here it was. Imperfect timing, fraught with difficulties, uncertainties, terrible circumstances, people and things to leave behind and a long shot to boot.

And she was doing it. She was returning to Zac.

And for the moment she let that soaring feeling rush through her, riding the fleeting wave of insane euphoria.

The banging at the door behind her stopped. She rose a little, peering over the microwave and down into the field. The three guys had spread out, the old red barn getting closer with each step. The two guys in the backyard had now also started toward it, toward the grassy hill down to the field, following their partners.

Her last thought, oddly, as she crept forward and opened the kitchen door, was a desperate wish that Bianca would be spared.

Quietly she snuck onto the back porch, over to the screen door, gun in hand, finger on the trigger. *Put your finger on the trigger only when you're ready to shoot.* Her dad, a former Marine, had trained her. *Don't point at anything you don't intend to kill.* She didn't want to shoot anyone. She certainly didn't intend to kill anyone. But if she had to use the gun to scare them down or buy time, she would.

Sorry, Dad.

Under the circumstances, he would understand.

She put her hand on the screen door, in danger of lapsing once more into a state of emotional shock. Too much was about to be lost. She had to stay on that other plane, stay in action if this was going to work. The decision had been made.

Follow through.

With a deep breath she flung open the door.

Bolted upright and through it; hit the soft grass outside at a full sprint and laid on the speed. Wind rushed in her ears, afternoon sun and fresh, open air washing through her senses. Pleasant memories, happier times. She lengthened her stride, whipped around the other side of the playhouse and down into the open field; arms pumping, the giant revolver heavy in one hand. She caught a glimpse of the two guys in the yard as she passed but raced on, flinching in expectation of the shots she prayed would not come.

They yelled. Both of them, and she couldn't resist a glance over her shoulder.

They'd picked up the chase.

The three guys down in the field were further away but reacted to the yells. In an instant they were running too, converging on her. She huffed, in her own world of speed and intention, closing on the barn, closing on her objective, realizing she'd never make it without being cut off.

The three in the field drew parallel, still dozens of yards away. These were grown men, maybe faster than her, maybe not, but the physics of this foot race were not on her side. They had an angle on her and began heading toward her from the side, arms and legs pumping fast in their suits, far enough ahead to intercept her before she could reach her target. *Shit!* She flew. Running so hard she nearly tripped, heels smacking her ass with each adrenaline-charged kick, tall grass whipping at her shins.

Realizing there was no choice ...

She raised the gun, as best she could in the furious sprint, showed it to them, pointed it at them—knowing full well where that would lead but seeing no more options. If she didn't make the barn ahead of them it was all over.

Reflexively they ducked and slowed, as hoped, yelling as she kept hauling ass. She lowered the gun.

Maybe she wouldn't have to use it.

Pow! a shot split the air and she hunched but kept going, too desperate to stop and take cover.

This was it.

Pow! another. She zagged left, then right, tall field grass ripping at her feet, conspiring against her. The barn was still too far away. *Pow!* and that time she heard the bullet rip the air by her head with a shrieking whiz and her skin jumped. She tucked and rolled. Her mind was racing—like Jason Bourne or something—tactics coming at her faster than she could think. On instinct she leaped to a new position, staying low in the tall grass even as a bullet *thunked* the ground where she'd just been, a plume of dirt whipping into the breeze.

They're trying to hit me!

Gripping the big revolver with two hands she rolled again, stopped and crouched just below the grass; raised it, aimed in their general direction, over their heads and up in the air, braced herself for the expected shock and squeezed the trigger.

BOOM! the Redhawk rocked in her grip, thundering. She'd never shot it without ear protection; the roar dwarfed the pops of their nine-millimeters, echoing back sharply from hard surfaces in the distance. She debated another shot but held, wanting to conserve her limited rounds. A quick peak revealed they'd dropped to the ground, taking cover from the bark of the cannon.

And she was up and sprinting again. Checking back; throwing her head over her shoulder to see where they were.

The closest two were back up and crouching, barrels

on her. She extended the revolver behind with one hand, before they could shoot, held on tight and … *BOOM!* sent another thundering shot in their direction—nearly losing the gun as it wrenched in her single-handed grip. The muzzle flash was brilliant in the afternoon sun and the three agents dropped back to cover.

Pow! Pow! Pow! Pow! the ones further back unloaded. Bullets whizzed all around and she went low again, the red of the barn in the corner of her eye, then dove back into the grass, rolling over and over on her side, hearing the bullets hit nearby, catching glimpses of dirt flying as she whirled beneath the grass-line, rolling toward the barn as fast as she could. It was a crazy tactic but it got her the remaining distance and on the last roll she looked up, dizzy, and there it was.

Faded red, rotting wood; above her a window. Sanctuary. *Freedom.*

She spun back toward the house, rose and steadied her aim over the heads of both groups and emptied the cylinder. Thunder. Pure, hammering thunder, rocking the neighborhood and the hills beyond. As the last of the giant rounds echoed across the land, booming, coupling and magnifying upon themselves, she wondered absently what the neighbors must be thinking.

Gun empty she clambered through the window, hit a pile of hay inside and rolled to her feet. She tossed the gun to the side.

Her life on Earth was now officially over. She was a fugitive. Back on Anitra, when it happened there, she could at least console herself with the notion that it really didn't matter. She didn't belong there. But now she'd created the same situation there on Earth, her home. And now; now she was going *back* to Anitra. A fugitive on both worlds.

If it weren't for the pure adrenaline of the moment she knew she'd be having a nervous breakdown right then.

She ran to the heap of burlap and hay in the far corner and began yanking it off. The guys outside would be all over the barn any second. Fear of the big revolver and a scared teenage girl wielding it might give them pause, might keep them from rushing in, guns blazing, but not for much longer. She had to move like she had no time. Likely as not they had no idea what was waiting inside. It was killing her to know how they knew to look there at all. What *did* they expect to find? Why hadn't they come when she wasn't home? Whatever led them there, whatever drove their actions, she was certain they had no idea she was hiding *this*. And she pulled off the last sack, exposing the menacing skull helmet of the towering Skull Boy armor.

During the intervening months, since returning, she'd carefully removed the cover now and again to peek at it, always nervous it would be found, always wondering if it gave off signals that would be detected by this or that form of scanning. But, until today, those concerns had never borne out. The massive suit of Skull Boy powered armor might well have been just another piece of farm equipment, tucked away rusting in the old barn. No one ever went there, no one ever stumbled on her carefully hidden secret.

Exposed now, in full view, it was almost like seeing it for the first time. Scarred from battle, black, standing about nine or so feet tall. Like a giant man, helmet cap menacing, molded in the shape of an inhuman skull with a fearsome grimace.

Her plan was to put it on, activate the Icon and pop out of existence before they stormed the barn. They'd hear the pop, get up the courage to charge in and ... the barn would be empty.

And she would be falling through the air over Osaka. Back on Anitra. Falling over the very city where she was a wanted criminal. Home of the enemy. And her, alone, falling smack into the middle of it.

She opened the front satchel box and checked the real treasure, nestled inside:

The Icon.

Chrome and unassuming, it was the key to her escape. It would shift her from one danger to another, but on the other end there was hope. On the other end she could find

Zac, and there she could find her freedom. She shuddered again.

With a simple twist it would send her.

She stripped off the hoodie and paused, catching sight of the shiny silver bracelet Mike gave her in Vegas. Forgotten in the heat of the moment but still on her wrist, red stones glinting in the soft, dappled sunlight, streaming through cracks in the wood ceiling. Bitter reminder of what she was about to do. As recently as she got the bracelet, just days ago, it was from a time that now seemed so far away. Sadness welled, squeezing her with its deadly grip but, holding to the surge of new purpose, she kept her focus and forced her thoughts back to the task at hand. She found the bulky operator jumpsuit, dug it out and pulled it on, fumbling with the straps in her rush.

The moment of truth was upon her.

A glance out the high barn window showed no sign of pursuit. Maybe they thought they had her trapped. Maybe they were surrounding the barn, confident they had her where they wanted her. If that were true she couldn't ask for better luck. Their confidence was giving her the time she needed. She would either be gone, leaving a mystery in her wake, or her fantastic escape would end there. Things at that moment had become about as black and white as anything could be.

The armor was dusty but wiped away clean, its advanced metal skin as shiny beneath the dust as the day she put it in the corner. Would it start? No sign of rust or any sort of decay. No sign of anything, really. It just stood there, completely inert, totally silent. Like a statue.

She shook off her hesitation and climbed up, popped the helmet cap like she remembered, slipped in and punched her legs and arms into their proper slots, lined up the suit, found the activation node, flipped it ...

And the armor came alive.

It works!

Just like that.

She trembled with relief—actually trembled—and for an instant the suit magnified her shaking to a spastic reaction that knocked a heavy plow crashing into another piece of equipment and very nearly took down a ceiling beam. Forcibly she calmed herself. *That was loud.* She stood still. Inhaling, through her nose, exhaling with a steady hiss. *Calm.* Listening to the fading echo of the metallic clangs.

The guys outside had to have heard it.

No matter. The suit was operational and she was about to be on her way. She pulled down the helmet cap and the inner dome came alive, old memories flooding back. Cool oxygen rushed in and she relished it. Took a moment to clear her head. Amazing! *Like I just turned it off an hour ago.* She spoke to the suit, instructing it to bring up telemetry data on her surroundings. It hummed to life. Walls became transparent. Outside the barn the five guys were indeed forming a wide circle, surrounding it as she guessed. More agents were on their way from the front yard and she adjusted her scans, bringing various wavelengths into play, scanning through the surrounding houses and out to the street. More vehicles were pulling up out front. Her yard was turning into a battlefield.

Time to go.

Quickly she checked the suit's metrics, finding all systems in order and functional. It was incredible; as if it had never been turned off. Like an instant boot or something, all your programs where you left them.

She stood straighter and stepped clear of the last bits of hay, feeling entirely invincible. Now that she was in the armor, now that it was working and all those fears were laid to rest, now she could not be stopped. The Skull Boy was like an extension of self and there was nothing these guys could bring to bear that would even scratch it, much less hurt her. Besides, she wasn't sticking around.

Phase One was behind. Now the only unknowns lay ahead.

What had happened on Anitra? Were the Venatres and Dominion still at war?

How will I get out of Osaka?

Carefully she took out the Icon and held it in the giant

metal hands. The device was small in the Skull Boy's grip, but it packed enough power to send her and the suit clear across space, or time, or through dimensions—or wherever—to Anitra.

To Zac.

Her entire body tingled. Her heart raced.

She scanned the house one last time, thrilled to be returning to the one man who, no matter how she'd tried to move on, consumed her heart and mind, and yet filled with an infinite sadness she could *not* take time to experience. She had to keep all those emotions at bay, like she'd been doing since she made this irreversible decision minutes ago; could not dwell on the dire finality of the moment. And yet it hit her like a ton of bricks as she stared longingly at the outlines of everything inside her home. Each wall, each piece of furniture, each cherished memory, brought to life by the suit's scanners in monochrome relief. All her stuff, all her things, her life, her existence ...

All right there.

She rode the waves of loss, managing to maintain the strength that had gotten her this far. There would be time for grief later. Zac would hold her while she bawled her eyes out, about everything she'd left behind.

She drew in a deep breath of the fresh oxygen. The guys at the front of the house hadn't broken in. Instead they'd been drawn away by the gunfire out back. That meant Bianca was, so far, safe. Jess scanned the top floor, looking for her friend, hoping she would get out of this without being subjected to anything horrible. Bianca knew so little, after all, yet ...

Where is she? Jess had left her curled in a ball on the floor of her parents' room. Had she moved?

She scanned more closely, finding her parents' room empty. *Did she go to my room?*

But her room was empty too. The upstairs bathrooms, Amy's room, the halls, even the closets ...

Then there she was.

Coming down the stairs.

Shit.

Bianca was coming down the stairs, stepping timidly, heading into the living room ...

Outline of a hard metal pistol in her hand.

CHAPTER 9:

COMPLICATIONS

No! BIANCA HAD one of Dad's guns. *What the hell is she doing?!* Jess froze. Already her heart raced in anticipation of what was to come, already she'd steeled herself to leave all this all behind, now ...

Now Bianca was coming down the stairs carrying a gun.

Her friend's outline glowed on the scanners as she moved inside the dull x-ray of the house, toward the back door, skin radiating the heat of her fear. But Jess couldn't take her eyes from the cold metal shape of the gun.

Bianca raised it, hand shaking.

No!

Slowly she came out the back door.

Shouting.

"Stop shooting!"

Jess increased the audio pick-ups as her friend stepped across the porch, out the screen door and into the grass, gun up and trembling, eyes squinted tight.

"Stop shooting at her!" she yelled. Enraged, spittle flying as she screamed at the agents in the back yard, pointing the gun. They turned their attention to this new threat, guns up and on her. It was like Bianca had gone from one extreme to the other; from terror to absolute rage, shouting in fury. *"Stop shooting!"*

Jess unstuck herself. Put the Icon back in the front satchel.

Damn!

"Stop shooting at her right now!" Bianca screamed. Jess wasn't even sure B saw what she was looking at, waving the gun left and right, over the heads of the agents in range.

"External comm," she remembered that command and the suit blurped that it was on and ready.

Time to make a scene.

Jess took a step forward, adjusted to the suit's movement, took a longer stride, followed by another that powered effortlessly through the barn wall—*Crack!* wood panels and beams splintering into the field, a cloud of debris shooting outward with the Skull Boy right behind—and she was outside, into the sun.

Everything laid out before her.

She kept stepping, crunching the shattered wall underfoot and on into the tall grass, the agents surrounding the barn scattering in alarm as she lurched past, stunned by the sudden appearance of the giant black machine, and she was beyond them and accelerating, covering the rest of the distance to the back yard in three leaping bounds.

She stopped just at the edge, not far from the playhouse and swings. For a moment she stood there, shifting her weight, letting her towering presence impinge. Open-mouthed stares on every face reminded her just how shocking this must be. The sudden, dramatic appearance of the Skull Boy had frozen time. No one moved. A few looked like they wanted to. Most looked like they wanted to flee.

She gathered her composure and fixed her gaze on her friend.

"Bianca!" Her voice boomed, amplified through the suit's PA. "Go back in the house!" The throb of the speaker reverberated through the suit. Bianca stared in mute horror at the massive Skull Boy calling her name. Surely her friend must realize it was her. Surely she must now realize this was the thing Jess ran from the house to get.

"Bianca! It's me!" She wondered if using her friend's name was a good idea. *Why don't you listen!?* "Go back in the house!"

But the shock was too much. Before Bianca could act the agents did. Jess watched in horror as the two closest got their wits, scooped her up and hustled her away. They had the gun out of her hand and were dragging her back into the house before she showed the first signs of resistance. Jess continued to watch, helpless, unsure what to do, unable to act fast enough as they dragged her inside. She watched on scans as they hauled her through the living room. Bianca started kicking furiously but by then it was too late. They had her.

Jessica's heart sank.

On impulse, barely taking time to consider the consequences of doing so, she pulled the long plasma cannon from her back. Every agent in sight dropped to the ground. She really didn't want to use it but maybe the threat would be enough to scare them. Scans had already confirmed there was nothing bigger among them than a shotgun, making them, essentially, harmless. She eyed them, angling the massive rifle back and forth over their heads. The gun itself was bigger than a man. Surely they'd come there expecting *something* unusual. Could they ever have imagined this?

"Let her go!" she boomed. Struggling to come to grips with the fact that Bianca was suddenly involved. *Why?!* Jess just wanted to hide. To run away and wish this all to be over.

"Bring her back!" she yelled. "Now!"

But the two agents who'd grabbed Bianca were already through the house and out the front door, dragging her friend toward the street. Jess could see them clearly on scan, a fact they probably didn't realize. She watched them head toward one of the SUVs. There were several more parked in the street along with the sedans; a small army of FBI-style agents. This was definitely not a routine police action. Maybe not even an ordinary government action.

These guys had balls.

Only they've got no idea, she thought grimly, assessing the comparative firepower of the Skull Boy armor versus a bunch of guys with guns, *they brought matches to a bonfire.*

"Let her go or I start lighting shit up!" She meant it, and the thunder in her amplified voice reflected it. For an instant she thought to make an offer she knew she wouldn't keep; tell them she'd turn herself in if they let her friend go, some nonsense like that. But they'd never honor such an offer. Never truly let Bianca go. And she herself would be doomed.

Out front the guys continued toward the street, Bianca fighting all the way. They bundled her into the SUV and slammed the door. Then, suddenly, out of her peripheral vision, amid the surreal setting unfolding before her, Jess noticed two boys a few houses down, peering over a fence. Joseph and Hicham, she recognized them; guys who went to her school. It was Hicham's house. Sometimes they hung out, but not much. So utterly normal, they seemed, trying to see what the commotion was. Drawn out by the gunfire, no doubt. And the yelling. Trying to make sense of this giant metal robot with cannon in hand, speaking at absurd volume. She wondered if they recognized her voice.

Well, boys, she tried to smile at her own humor, *Jess won't be in school tomorrow. Tell Miss Farrington she won't be getting my report. Oh, and by the way, hold onto your hats. You're about to get a show.*

"I warned you," she told the agents. Many of them scrunched further as she shouldered the plasma cannon, but no one tried to stop her, no one yelled "Wait! Let's talk!", and so she sighted one of the empty SUVs at the curb out front, far enough from any people that it should be safe, drew a bead and ...

Fired.

WHOOOOOOM!!!!! the star-bright lance of plasma cast impossible shadows in the afternoon sun, coupled with a staggering concussion as the beam cooked the air. Jess felt it through the armor and every agent threw hands over head and ears, hugging the ground as the SUV went up in a fantastic plume of superheated light. *Way* more than expected, chunks ejecting up and out on trajectories away from the impact, atomized streamers of metal that shot straight and high like a giant sparkler.

Slowly Jess lowered the gun.

She'd forgotten just how powerful the Astake cannon was. The SUV Bianca was in was untouched, thankfully, though a few vehicles closer to the target were ablaze. *Zac lived through one of those*, she marveled in absolute awe.

Pieces from the blast fell like rain. She looked at the agents, on the ground all around her, every one of them cowering.

She now had their full, 250% undivided attention. A gorilla in glasses and a bowtie could've walked up and started reciting Shakespeare, in perfect Victorian English, and not a single eyeball would've blinked from the Skull Boy standing in the yard with the glowing plasma cannon. Joseph and Hicham were gone. Behind the fence or back in his house or fleeing in horror down the street, they were no more. No one in sight moved. Jessica's mind raced. For a fleeting instant she noticed Bianca's Fiat in the drive, blocked in by all the official vehicles, thoughts of happier times flitting across her mind. Bianca had only had her license since Christmas but they'd done so much in that little car since then. Windows down, listening to music as they cruised town. Ski trips to the mountains. Trips to the mall. Things Jess would never, ever do again.

Her private nightmare had come home.

One of the agents stood slowly. As he did the SUV out front holding Bianca came alive. The engine went hot and Jess watched as the agents inside hurried to put it in gear and then lunged away, squealing into the street, racing off into the neighborhood.

"We've got your friend," said the standing agent, drawing her attention to him—so nervous he shook visibly. His knees were actually wobbling, gun on the ground, voice cracking. He was obviously being ordered to stand and stare her down. "Give us the device or we'll kill her."

Device? The word sent a chill down her spine. But the words that fell out of her mouth were in response to the other part of his threat: "Kill her?" She leveled the giant plasma cannon right at his chest and she was sure, from the man's expression, he'd just pissed his pants. "I'll kill *you.* I'll kill all of you unless you bring her back. You're not calling the shots here. *I* am.

"Turn that car around."

The man quivered and nearly collapsed. But his statement shook her, distracting from her rage. *Device?* Could they be talking about the Icon? *Must be.*

Had to be.

She spoke directly to the suit's computer. "Computer. That vehicle that just left, can you track it?"

"Stand by."

Standard scans had already lost the SUV through the density of the neighborhood. Jess didn't think that, even using the jump jets, she could catch it. The guy driving was hauling ass. Her only hope now was to find it when it stopped. She wished she'd run around front and tried to do something before it left instead of standing there making idle threats.

But that was then. This was now. Regret solved nothing.

The computer beeped. "I have unit IDs and can triangulate. Units in vehicle have mapped IDs and are traceable through the local infrastructure."

Jessica wondered just what else the suit might be capable of.

"Good," she told it, "track it." Then; "External comm," and the PA blurped to life. "Well?" she challenged the quivering man before her. "Is she on her way back?" Then, when he didn't immediately respond: "I'd be curious to see if there's even any of you left after a shot from this." She bounced the cannon once in her grip, listening to the sheer power of her own amplified voice as it boomed across the neighborhood. She could tell from the man's wince every time she spoke the volume was painful. She gave him a long moment to ponder; everyone laying on the ground was looking up, the man about to faint; the ball of slag that was the SUV out by the curb crackled and popped, white-hot as it burned. It was the only sound, it seemed, cutting the oppressive hush.

Jess had had enough.

"Call your little friends in the Escalade," she said with false patience, "and tell them to get back here." The man just stared at her. Helpless, it seemed. *Now,* she said. Clearly he had no idea what to do next. Jess shifted a little in the armor, that action alone causing him to fall to his knees. She shook her head inside the helmet, suddenly disgusted. She could see this would go nowhere.

"Let me make it easy for you," she went on. "Here's

what you do. Pick up your little phone, call them and have them bring the girl back here. Simple. Do it now."

The man didn't move. She'd never threaten him enough to make that call. Nor, even if he did, could she expect the guys in the SUV to listen. To suddenly change their minds and, oh, what were we thinking, bring Bianca back and let's just put this whole thing behind us. Sorry about everything, really. Hope you can forgive us.

She would have to go rescue her friend.

There was no other way.

"Computer."

"Yes."

She relished the private conversation inside the helmet. "Can you flatten the area? Like an electronic pulse or something? Shut off their communications?"

A moment's consideration, then: "I can burn the transistors in their devices at this range. The devices are not hardened."

Jess thought only a second. "Burn them."

And the Skull Boy complied. There was no delay. No "are you sure"—nothing human about it. The suit simply did as it was told, a short buzz thrumming through the armor. The men stayed as they were, not realizing anything had happened. Then, slowly, a few began checking earpieces. Most conspicuously the one in front of her. He reached, hand jerking with fear, tapping his ear. Nothing. Everything was quiet. Confusion began to spread across their faces.

"Done," the computer reported.

Jess took one long step toward the kneeling agent, knocked him tumbling with a casual sweep of her arm before he could get out of the way and strode on toward the street. It took a moment but bullets began popping, first a few then more, zinging off the armor, hits barely registering. Those agents in her way hurried aside and she crunched through the lush green grass of her yard and stepped all the way to the front yard and into the clear.

"If you're in a car or near it, get out," she boomed, the suit projecting her warning like a rock concert. She raised the cannon. "Five," she began, "four," and continued a countdown to zero, watching as a handful of agents fled the scene. Honestly she didn't care if any of them got burned, but nevertheless waited to finish her count before opening up.

And, with a small amount of misplaced delight, methodically hammered each car and SUV in sight with a blast from the cannon. One after the other, sending them up one by one in vaporized starbursts of liquid metal—a string of giant firecrackers, white-hot trails of debris firing into the air in all directions, creating a concentrated war zone right there in front of her house. Explosions coupled upon explosions, rocking the neighborhood. She was certain the whole thing could be seen—heard—for miles. A quick check confirmed every agent had fled far, far a field. Many were still running.

She felt hugely empowered in that moment.

"Computer," she queried as she watched the sun-hot remains of one of the cars melting into the asphalt. "Show me where the vehicle is now."

"I have discovered an existing asset that may be of use," the computer reported. "I can overlay tracking."

The screen before her lit up with a transparent, aerial map of the city—probably something pulled from the Internet—a blinking icon marking the SUV that carried Bianca moving along the street graphics at breakneck speed.

Clever computer. She'd never had the chance to call on it as much as she was now. On Anitra the battles had been too intense, the demands too strained to need the computer like she needed it in that moment. She was finding it nearly miraculous.

And as she noticed the trademark logo on the overlaid screen, small in the corner but standing out like a beacon, she couldn't help but grin.

Google Maps.

Pulled from the web, pressed into service by the suit's computer and combined with real-time GPS data to give her the info she needed. *Very clever.*

Then she laughed aloud as, whether the computer had any awareness of the significance of it or not, the Google-enabled map began throwing up little bubbles of "useful" information next to the SUV as it tore through town: local restaurants it passed, hot spots, places of interest. A theater with movie times; a menu, more info following.

She shook her head in bemused wonder.

How far to the nearest Applebees? she thought.

How cute.

CHAPTER 10:

BATTLE IN BOISE

JESS THREW THE PLASMA CANNON over her shoulder and locked it to the unit's back. Eyes on the houses ahead, she crouched and ... leapt. Up and out, calling on the jump jets, remembering how it all worked but forgetting in that instant just how alarming it all was. *Whoa!* The jets hit her in the back and suddenly she was surging high—a hundred feet before she caught her breath. Vertigo gripped her in that sickening instant, the soaring leap hitting its peak, the whole thing a slap in the face.

This was for real.

Beneath her sprawled her neighborhood; streets, cars, many of them pulled to the side of the road—likely in reaction to the fiery drama burning in the sky back near her house. A pair of kids on bikes spotted her from far below, mouths agape as their heads rotated skyward to follow her unlikely passage. And ... a house, right at the end of her arc. Falling up to greet her. *Shit.* A measure of composure returned as she cursed her own failure to think this through. Frantic, she called up the jets once more, a brief pulse to kick the Skull Boy over the roof, pulled her legs to her chest just in time and ... cleared it. She hit the jets on the other side for the landing and *whumped* into the back yard like a long jumper, kicking out a huge gouge of sod in front of her.

Gonna have to do a little yard work, she thought as she carried the momentum into a run and another leap, *but at least you won't have to buy a new roof.*

The jets hit; kicked her over the trees and she was on to her next impact.

* * *

IN THE BACK SEAT OF THE SUV BIANCA had finally stopped struggling. It was useless anyway. She bounced between the two burly guys as the car jerked back and forth, hands tied in front with a plastic band. Both men gripped her as the Escalade drifted and rolled around corners, tires howling, the driver spinning the wheel with white-knuckled intensity. Swerving, braking, accelerating, drawing involuntary gasps from her and—to her mild surprise—a few squeaks from the guys who held her.

A car pulled across their path and she screamed. It freaked; braked; the driver of the SUV skidded, wrenched the wheel left then hard right, drifted around the car— snap-snap—fishtailed back onto their previous path and hit the gas. Bianca looked between the faces of the two men holding her.

They were scared out of their minds.

"She'll find me," she announced, mustering courage she didn't feel. "You saw that thing? Scared? You should be. I know what it can do." Jess had told her so very few details, actually, of what happened those many months ago, and what she *did* tell her was mostly so fantastic it was impossible to believe. But rage was helping overcome some of the fear and Bianca gave it free rein, wanting these guys to burn. She in fact knew nothing of whatever that big, black robot thing was but was all too ready to act like she did. "You saw what it did to that car? That's what she's going to do to your faces!" Absurd, but she let the anger flow.

"She's tracking you right now," she kept on. "You can't stop her. I don't know where you're taking me but it doesn't matter. She'll pick us up on radar and—"

"Can you reach anyone?" the driver talked over her.

"Hold on," the guy to her left took out his phone and tried making a call—as he'd been doing off and on since racing away from Jessica's house. Now, as then, he seemed to get nothing.

"Nothing," he confirmed.

The driver was growing more agitated by the minute. "Shit! What the hell is going on back there?!"

"She killed them," Bianca informed him, a little too full of herself but not caring. These guys deserved whatever they got. "Your friends are gone."

"Try HQ," the driver zigged then zagged, hooked the SUV down a smaller street, swung right onto another empty road and slowed the frantic pace. A little.

"You sure?" The guy on the left wasn't.

"Just do it!"

The man hurriedly tried another number.

"Getting a ring," he said, then: "Hello? Yes. We have a package. No, not *the* package. *A* package. A girl. From the site. Right. Okay." And he hung up. "They'll contact us," he said to the driver. "They said don't use our phones."

"Can they raise the units at the house?"

"Didn't say."

"Shit!" The driver smacked the wheel.

Bianca grinned. "You know. I'm happy, believe it or not. You guys can't be legal, what you're doing. Whichever ones of you she doesn't kill are going to jail."

"Gag her," the driver ended up sounding more exasperated than pissed. "Somebody," he turned down another road, eyes straight ahead. "Please."

* * *

JESS RAN DOWN THE SHOULDER of the 84 at about forty miles an hour, passing jammed-up after-work traffic. Heads inside vehicles jerked to watch as she loped past with long strides, a giant black interloper that no doubt left a few gap-jawed accidents in her wake. She had no time to look.

The SUV carrying Bianca was putting distance on her. It was difficult to tell where it was headed; the driver seemed to be executing random moves, off the main roads, back onto the main roads; avoiding a hunter he only imagined was there but couldn't see. At the moment the vehicle icon was closing on an area of old buildings on the outskirts of town. Many of those were abandoned or at least empty, if Jess recalled. *Maybe they'll try to hide.*

Though the suit did all the work she still had to exert

the effort of a normal run. The machine simply multiplied that effort a hundred-fold, hydraulic rams surging along with quiet power in response to her movements. Thanks to youth and recent, dedicated conditioning she wasn't winded yet, but there was still a ways to go and by the time she reached Bianca she would be tired, she was sure. Adrenaline ebbed and flowed, as it always did at times like this—for a surreal instant it struck her that, at her age, she'd even *had* "times like this", but she had—and she knew it would flow again. When the moment came she'd get the surge she needed. Absently she thought of Master Lenny and all the cardio he always made her do and how Master Lenny, like everything else, was soon to be gone forever.

All at once the sounds in the helmet began to weigh on her. Her heavy breathing, echoing in there, the subtle whine of the suit mechanics as it ran, the solid impact of each armored footfall.

She needed to get out of her own head.

"Computer?"

With a little work she was able to hit her online account, make a selection and begin streaming music, in stereo, complete with fade and balance. Like a mini-concert hall right there inside the helmet. The music came out a little tinny on the suit speakers, but it did the trick and soon she found her groove. Kind of like being out for a jog with her earbuds in.

Thankfully it took her away.

She raised the volume. Rhythmic bass covered the last of the outside sounds, she got a second wind, cut right, off the highway, scanned the path ahead and made a beeline for her friend.

* * *

"WHAT DO WE KNOW?" the driver stormed into the abandoned warehouse ahead of the other two men, who dragged Bianca between them, gagged. "What the hell is going on?"

Inside was what looked to be a hastily prepared field

base, more guys in suits and ties sitting at folding tables with laptops and a few big screens, coordinating whatever they were up to. Bianca's eyes darted around the room, teeth clenching the gag that wrapped her head, plastic band pinching her wrists. Defiantly she dragged her feet as the two burly guys jerked her along.

"We're trying to fix this," came the preoccupied answer.

The driver continued striding briskly, over to the nearest set of tables and up to a man who appeared to be in charge. The two carrying Bianca stopped short.

"This is a fiasco." The driver was turning up the volume of his frustration in an effort to divert attention from his own shortcomings. His boss, however, wasn't impressed. He wasn't about to be distracted from the man's failure.

"What happened out there?" he demanded. "Where's the device?" At that Bianca noticed, quite to her surprise, a shiny chrome device on one of the tables, incongruous where it sat between two laptops near several of the "agents". Was it ... the same like the one Zac and Jess used last summer? In the playhouse? Looked like it. The thing that started this whole mess, and now these guys had it.

When did they get hold of it?

Other questions formed and raced through her over-taxed mind. Many questions.

"We think she has it," said the driver. "I can't reach anyone back at the house."

"She flattened the whole area." The boss stood straight, clearly unhappy with the way things were going. His field unit had evidently failed miserably. "Unit Five called from a land line in the house just before you arrived. They found nothing. The girl destroyed every car they had, fried their electronics then took off after you. After *her*." He pointed to Bianca. "What in God's name were you thinking taking a hostage?"

Between the two men holding her Bianca smirked, stretching the fabric of the gag. The driver tried not to notice her shit-eating grin but, for some reason, couldn't take his eyes from her. The whole thing had him steamed.

This situation must be going terribly wrong from his point of view.

"And you threatened to *kill* her?" the boss accused and Bianca's smile faded. "Who gave that order? Who told him to say that? Did you not see that thing her friend was in? You're going to lay a threat like that on a teenage girl, obviously at the end of her rope—who happens to be in control of a machine we have *no* intel on? A weapon that just vaporized an entire frickin car in one shot? What the hell were you thinking?" He gathered back some of his composure. "Well guess what? She found you. Tracked you here, near as we can tell. That's right. She's headed right for us." The boss turned away, disgusted.

The driver looked pale. Despite the fact that it seemed they had nothing but bad intentions for her, Bianca giggled. Couldn't help it, really, though she felt no mirth. The sound was muffled through the gag but the room fell quiet and everyone looked at her.

The driver regained a little composure and waved her away.

"Get her out of here."

* * *

JESSICA'S SPRINT ACROSS THE CITY in the powered armor felt like some kind of freaky, mechanical parkour. Running and leaping, heading straight for the area where the SUV had finally stopped, through yards, parking garages, over walls, across intersections, bounding over cars and commuters, even short buildings, jump jets roaring as needed, timing her landings, clearing it all, trying to leave behind as little impact as possible. So far property damage was, remarkably, minimal. Damage to the psyches of those who witnessed her passage ...

That she could do little about.

"Any more communications?" she queried the computer, breathing heavy from the steady exertion. *Turn the Lights Out* by Hadouken! was on, the lyrics cracking the whip: *Go! Go! Go! Go!*

"Unable to correlate any current signals."

The phones the agents were using back at the house were fried. So far the computer had been unable to make any new connections related to the agents' activity. Once or twice the phones in the SUV had been used but no trace to the recipients on the other end. Now the SUV was stopped, a few miles ahead, parked, just across this next section of town, having been stationary now for about five minutes. Jess hurried to reach it before it moved again.

Across the city, here and there, came the sound of sirens, filtered through the suit's audio, police cars crisscrossing her path but never close enough to interfere, trying to predict her passage, unable to zero in. Whether they were on the side of the agents or not mattered little. If they *were* on their side it wasn't out of any understanding of what was really going on, of that she was sure. If they weren't, well ... she had no time to stop and deal with police. Too many variables lay in that direction.

And so she pressed on.

She scanned ahead, trying to scope her path and make decisions before obstacles were reached, rushing along just on the edge of control in the thick of the metro area; not wanting to waste a second yet not wanting to hurt anyone either. A tall, block-spanning building lay directly ahead. *Have to go through it,* she decided. She leapt a car that screeched to a halt in front of her, landed in the street, ran up the sidewalk past a dozen gaping pedestrians—one even dropped his coffee without taking his eyes from the Skull Boy, empty hand still in place holding the cup that was no longer there, just like in a movie scene—ducked, hit the big revolving door out front and sent it shattering into the wide hall inside, glass and metal framework bouncing far ahead of her thundering strides.

Okay, she thought, checking for her next exit point, *that was probably expensive.*

"Any other threats?" she huffed. No people in the hall.

"Unable to determine."

So far the suit was having a hard time making sense of the million different things in the city. As awesome as the computer was turning out to be, the density of signals in the metro area had finally proven too much. Cars, buildings, people—input everywhere. Jess looked up as she ran. The helmet just cleared the ceiling of the hallway; it was a sort of business mall, suites of offices connected by an internal walkway. Next up was a crossway ending at an office door and, at the last second, rather than go left or right, all the way to the exit at either end, she chose to go *through* the office directly ahead. One heat signature inside. On scans she could see a window on the other side, her way out, just a few dozen feet away, so she stopped outside the door and, as carefully as she could, pushed it open. There was no way to turn the knob, not with the suit's massive hands, so she decided instead to put a hand on it carefully and push it in, shattering the bolt and the knob but leaving the hinges intact as it swung inward.

That will cost a lot less to replace, she thought, crouching and turning to the side to squeeze through without doing more damage. The suit scraped badly. A man sat at a desk inside, the only one in the office. She waved meekly to him as she tromped through and out to the back window. She half expected him to scream or dart out the door behind her or faint or something but he just sat there, wide-eyed and unmoving, a lot like the guy with the coffee cup. At the window she stepped through, *use the money you save on the door*, she thought as the glass shattered, put her feet on the sidewalk outside and picked up the pace.

"New targets," the suit notified her when she was outside and running. "Two, airborne."

Airborne? She looked up, still deep within the canyons of the city. Slices of sky were visible but she saw nothing. Then the suit overlaid profiles in her line of sight, moving along above the rooftops, racing toward her general location.

Helicopters.

She killed the music.

"Weaponized," the suit added. "Projectile weapons, missiles. Threat level high."

Great. Not police choppers. Not frail little civilian craft painted with a police badge, a spotlight and a rifle or two.

These were gunships. She identified their scanner profiles. Military-spec. *Apaches.* Not good. Then she caught a glimpse of them on visual as they passed across a clean patch of sky, moving on a sweeping arc around the area she traversed. Blacked out and unmarked. And it struck her, once again, just how far outside the bounds of convention these "agents" were operating. Those helicopters were all business; full-on gunships which meant they were, potentially, about to call down an air strike right there in the middle of a major city.

"Targets have identified our location," the computer threw up info on the Apaches. They were now banking sharply, angling right for her, snouts coming online and rotors pitched, accelerating to speed. They'd spotted her. Jess ran faster and bounded out of the shadows of the last low-lying buildings, onto an open stretch of single-story offices and garages. The sky was a clear, deep blue, sun heading for the horizon, the helicopters bearing down on her like dark birds of prey. Her spine tingled, muscles spasming as she made herself keep running toward them. Faster. Warnings sounded as the gunships locked on.

Here was something that could hurt her.

And all at once she was directly in the crosshairs of an aerial attack. She'd seen videos of what that looked like, death from above from the view of the attackers, raining Holy Hell on ground targets that had little or no defense. Now she was about to experience it firsthand.

From the wrong end.

"Recommend evasive positioning," the computer seemed to make a bid for reason as she kept running straight ahead. She *should* be looking for a place to hide.

What the computer didn't realize, of course, was that she'd already leapt beyond the immediate. Though it might not seem it she was acting, not reacting. The Apaches were on the hunt and, deceptively, so was she. Right then she was in an area that was, near as she could tell, free and clear of collateral targets. It was an empty street, mostly empty buildings.

Perfect place for a showdown.

Closing the gap the lead gunship opened up. Jess saw the orange muzzle flash of its chain gun even as the computer reported the weapon going live. An instant before that, however, she was lunging to the side—*knowing* the gun was about to start firing, sensing it—breaking stride and turning her forward charge directly into the grill of a parked car. A Volvo, ironically. *Safest car in the world*, she thought, keeping her momentum hot. She hit, grabbed under the front bumper with both hands and, using a combination of the Skull Boy's forward speed, surge with its legs and a full snatching effort with her arms, flipped the car up and backwards, nose over tail, somersaulting directly into the helicopter's line of fire. *Well*, she thought as she watched the shiny red Volvo hurtle end over end into the stream of bullets*, keep me safe.*

It did. Flipping directly through the hail of armor-piercing rounds, shielding her, metal flying as the car was fragged by the heavy-caliber stream. The bulk of it continued its flip, hit the ground on the other side of the street and slid in a shower of sparks. But Jess was still in motion, leaping onto her chest and hitting the jump jets, launching the suit across the street like a rocket-powered sled, trailing her own shower of sparks as the Skull Boy skidded across the asphalt—crashing through the wall of a small office building as the helicopters continued their strafing run down the street behind her. Hundreds of bullets kicked up chunks of the road in their high-speed flyby.

Might as well forget about property damage, she thought as she jumped to her feet inside the office. The whole front wall of the building was gone, nothing but a smashed hole leading back out to the street. The helicopters had been flying a little too fast, perhaps thinking they had her, and were now pulling back, braking hard for a return run. She wasted no time hurrying through the hole in the front wall and back into the street, took a wide stance and calculated the position of both; made a check of her conscience, decided on the greatest good—these guys were trying to kill her, after all—yanked the plasma cannon from her back, shouldered it and ...

WHHOOOOOM! burned one chopper from the sky. Much like the cars back at the house the beam went through it, vaporizing most of the armored fuselage and sending the rest flying away in chunks of white-hot metal. Blades went cartwheeling—an effect she had *not* planned for—and she cringed as they launched off in opposite directions like giant spears, hoping they didn't kill anyone.

The other Apache lost control in the wake of the explosion; she saw it wobble and go into a dive. Whether from the startled reaction of the pilot or the shockwave she couldn't be sure, but it nearly went down on its own. It was over an occupied building. Lots of heat signatures. She took no shot.

It recovered, continued its arc and was suddenly hooked around facing her. *Shit!*

A flash and a missile launch and a Hellfire was on its way, streaking toward her.

Fast.

Reflexively she leapt up and over, hitting the jump-jets—clearing the area just as the missile hit the street where she'd been. *BOOOM!* the blast impacted behind her, hard, kicking her forward, altering her trajectory and causing her to land wobbly atop a building on the next block over. A quick turn to the right and she saw the Apache pivoting to track her. Another missile rushed from it, trailing smoke impossibly fast. She barely made it off the roof before it hit, tucking into a shoulder-roll in the street below as the building went up in a thundering fireball. As she rolled to her feet and sprinted off to the next section of cover, on the run, she couldn't believe they'd just shot two missiles right into a city block.

These were definitely *not* the good guys.

Desperately she scanned her new location; oriented herself, looking for the best place to lead them.

"Is that all of them?" she fairly yelled, panting but full of the expected adrenaline surge. She was "on", in a way that could scarcely be described.

"No more targets identified."

On scans she could see Bianca was being held less than

a mile away. *Nearly there.* One chopper down, one to go.

She only hoped there were no more coming.

She darted down an alley and called up a rear-facing overlay, watching the Apache maneuver aggressively as it tried to lock her in its cross-hairs, appearing and disappearing in her line of sight as she used the buildings of that block to elude. The chopper went high, gaining enough altitude to look down on her. Making her little more than a mouse in a maze.

She realized her brief tactic was at an end.

But the chopper may have done itself in. It was so high now she could blast it to pieces without fear of striking anything on the ground. As she realized this she jumped, in advance of yet another missile, using the jets to land atop a four-story building as the Hellfire incinerated the alley below—right where she'd just been. *Shit!* The impact actually shook the building beneath her. In fact, sensors warned the structure had been compromised and would probably go down. She should get off. Now.

She whirled atop the roof, shouldered the gun, aimed up, locked the chopper high overhead and ...

WHHHOOOOM! vaporized it. Then, as the larger pieces fell away, *WHHOOOOM!* shot the biggest and, *WHHHOOOM!* the next, picking them off until the sky was filled with sparkling, drifting fireballs. Like the end of a massive firework, falling to earth.

Harmless.

Then the building was shaking and ... crumbling to the blast side, into the alley. She leapt away, to the far street, hitting with a crunch and turning to watch in disbelief as the whole four-story structure collapsed in on itself like a demolition, a cloud of dust billowing into the air.

It finished its fall. Nervously she took in her surroundings. The street was a busy one, cars stopped in mid-commute, drivers staring slack-jawed in all directions. Into the sky, at the dwindling fireballs that had been a helicopter just moments ago, smoke from the missile attack and, no doubt, the eye-popping flashes of the blistering plasma blasts. Staring in disbelief at the building that had just collapsed, a haze of dust and debris still roiling into the air.

Staring at her.

Towering, nine-foot-tall robot girl. Menacing black skull face, glowing cannon in hand, standing right in the middle of the storm. Orchestrator of destruction.

A nightmare come to life.

She turned and ran.

CHAPTER 11:

RETURN TO ANITRA

BIANCA WATCHED AS THE AGENTS in the room grew increasingly agitated, becoming short with each other—clearly not prepared for this contingency. She'd heard the distant blasts across the city and tried to overhear any word of Jessica's progress, but all she could conclude was that the suit of armor was hunting them and that, somehow, other elements had failed.

Good enough news for her. Jess would find her, of that she was now certain. Fear, however, continued to wash over her in waves and, though she was confident in her rescue, she had no confidence whatsoever in her life after that.

* * *

THE WAREHOUSE WAS JUST AROUND THE CORNER. Jess slowed the Skull Boy to a walk; steadied her breathing as best she could, still shaking from the encounter with the helicopters, stopped behind a building corner and waited. She peered at the warehouse a few hundred feet away, watching the agents inside on the suit's scanners and trying to decide what to do next.

Shock, as a tactic, was probably out of the question. The agents were now fully prepared for what she was capable of. Nor could she hope to sneak in. Somehow, some way, she had to get in there, find Bianca and get her out. Bianca, who was not wearing a suit of armor. Bianca, who could be killed by a single stray bullet.

Staying behind cover she scrolled through a multitude of scans, mapping the scenario as best she could. The SUV along with a few other vehicles were parked outside the warehouse. Inside were about a dozen bodies, working at computers or other electronics. The suit's computer now had their frequencies marked, though they weren't communicating at the moment beyond the warehouse. Focused audio amplification wasn't enough to hear what they were saying at that range. The building was empty otherwise, situated in a section of others like it that were also abandoned or for sale. All sirens in the city converged on the wake of destruction behind her, sweeping in to make sense of the two helicopter explosions and multiple other chaotic events. No other activity within a mile.

Where are you? Desperately she analyzed the heat blobs, searching for Bianca. One looked like it was probably her. Sitting alone to the side, not moving, smaller than the rest.

What next? And, of course, the *real* question: What after that? Take Bianca with her? To Anitra? That wouldn't work. She had to get her friend to the authorities before she herself used the Icon to return. Which meant more running, more exposure for them both.

And what authorities? The cops were all she could think of. All she could get to, really. There was still the very real likelihood these agents were so powerful Bianca would not be safe no matter which "authorities" she took her to. After all, look what they'd just authorized right there in broad daylight. They clearly answered to no one, short of the head of the CIA or something. Or even higher.

And what of my family? The thought of that sent a wave of sadness rushing through her and she was wracked by a sudden sob. Those emotions, held at bay, broke through and she fought to contain the unexpected torrent of despair. *Will I ever see them again?* Quickly she reined in that line of thinking before it cascaded into a fit of grief she could not control. She needed to maintain Strong Jessica. The one that survived. This whole thing would fall apart otherwise.

But ... they needed to know. Needed to be warned. And this could be her last chance. The last moment of calm before she was gone again, her family left behind, lost and confused in her wake.

She couldn't bear the thought of telling Mom or Dad. Amy, too, wrenched her heart to think of, but someone had to know. Amy, by default, was it.

"Computer," she sniffed, making the call before she could talk herself out of it, "call this number on the local network." And she gave it Amy's. A moment later the phone dialed, ringing in the helmet like it was right there with her. Her heart pounded in anticipation and, for a few terrified rings, she hoped Amy wouldn't answer. That she could just leave a message. Deep down, though, she knew she had to talk to her sister. A message wasn't enough. They had to connect, if only this one last time.

"Hello?" Amy answered and Jess started crying. Right away, before she could say a word.

"It's me," she choked through the sudden tears, trying too late to compose herself.

"Jessica?" Amy sounded confused, but Jess could tell she knew it was her. "What number is this?" Then, scared: "Why are you crying?"

"I'm okay." *Don't worry about me, Amy. I'll be okay.* "I can't talk long." Her voice pitched up and down as she sniffled. *Be strong!* she commanded herself, clenching her teeth tightly. "Some crazy shit has gone down," she said more steadily, "but I'm okay. Understand? I'm not hurt, but you need to call the police."

"Jess you're scaring me." Amy's voice was on the rise. "What's going on? Why are you crying?"

"You may see it on the news." Still she wondered if these guys had the ability to sweep all this under the rug. So much had been witnessed. *Exploding helicopters over the city!* But part of her worried even that wouldn't be enough.

"Jess where are you?!" Amy now sounded completely desperate.

"I'm fine." Jessica's voice was stabilizing, but she could feel powerful emotions teetering at the edge of control. "Listen. Call the police. Get somewhere populated. Call Mom, call Dad. Have them do the same thing." She paused long enough to choke back a burst of bawling tears. "It's the guys in the car," she explained, shaking. "They're after me. I never told you what really happened last summer but I have to get away. I have to go."

"Go where? Jessica?! Go where?!"

"Away. Where they can't follow."

"You are really freaking me out. Please tell me this is a joke. Please, Jessica. I'll laugh, I swear I'll laugh. Tell me I'm being pranked." Her sister's voice echoed large in the confines of the helmet. "Tell me you're joking!"

"It's no joke, Amy." And she could no longer contain it. She spluttered and started weeping. She heard Amy start crying with her. Together in spirit, a vast gulf between them that might never again be crossed.

Jess tried valiantly to calm herself. "It's no joke," she said, but it was a lost cause. "I'm so sorry." She wept like a baby. "I'm so sorry, Amy." Wanted so badly to hold her, to hug her sister and, at least, share that last moment. To feel her embrace before she was gone forever. Of a sudden she was acutely aware of the cold, impersonal armor, unable even to wipe away her tears.

"Don't be sorry, Jessica," Amy cried around her in stereo. "Just come home! We'll figure it out. Don't run away! Please! I can't lose you again."

"I can't lose you either. I love you." Her words slurred. "I love you so much." Her vision blurred, nose running. She just wanted to curl up on her bed and rub her eyes. She wanted so badly to rub her eyes.

"Come home," Amy pleaded. *"Come home Jessica!"*

Slowly Jess pulled herself together. Slowly, forcing aside the debilitating emotions; grateful that, at least for that moment, she'd let them run their course. "I can't," she sniffed. There was no way back. Only forward. "You have to leave. Go somewhere safe. Get around people. Call Mom. This is serious. If I go now I may be able to return." She didn't see how. "If I don't … they'll capture me and it will all be over."

Rather than plead further, however, Amy just kept crying.

"I love you, Amy. Tell Mom and Dad. Tell them I love them and I'll be home as soon as I can. You'll see. You'll see what this is all about and then you'll understand."

Still no more response from her sister. Just uncontrolled

sobbing. It was all too much.

"Goodbye, Amy," Jess steadied her voice, made it the strongest it had been for the entire conversation. "I love you."

And ended the call. For a long moment she simply stood there, watching the warehouse. A frightened girl, packed into the middle of a ton of high-tech mechanized armor. Invincible on the outside, slowly collapsing within. Her mind was a million miles away. Gone. Buzzing with disbelief. But she knew better. Deep down strength remained. Incredible resilience. There was only so far she could fall. Only so deep her despair might plunge before yielding to this inner core. Like a neutron star, eventually the collapse would end, leaving power in its wake. And so she waited, breathing, letting the tears fall until, at last, they dried and she began to see clearly once more. She breathed deeply, still shaky but better, a rasping echo in the helmet. Then, deliberately, turned her thoughts to the next actions that would set her free.

And as she studied the scene before her, blinking away the last of the blurry images, new heat signatures began appearing at the periphery. Outside in the alleyways.

First two, then another. Then more, moving slowly; cautiously, closing on the same target she had in her sights.

The warehouse.

"Computer," she queried. "Who are those guys?"

"No info," came the answer. "They are armed."

Jess watched them, growing ever more alert. What were guys with guns doing creeping up on a warehouse filled with other guys with guns? Was it a SWAT team? Would the cops help her after all? Could they save Bianca? But if the guys creeping up on the warehouse were the police, then who was inside? Or, if the guys inside were the police, then who were the guys outside? A hundred possible scenarios. There was a chance this new group might protect her, but that idea seemed so unlikely she realized she could *not* afford to entertain any such hope. Crippling indecision would be the result, of the sort that could cost her and Bianca both their lives.

She bristled in anticipation of this new threat.

"Are they communicating with the guys inside?" The guys on the outside sneaking toward the warehouse were equipped like commandos, now that she had more data from the suit; like the Army or something but not quite. The guys on the inside were in suits and ties and appeared not to know anything about them.

The computer evaluated the developing scene. "No," it concluded. "Units are observing communications silence. Appear to be using hand signals only."

By then Jess had very nearly forgotten her meltdown. The sudden discovery of a new group preparing for an assault on the group inside yanked her mind quickly back to action. There was about to be a shoot-out and Bianca was about to be in the middle of it. She had to move fast if she was going to rescue her friend.

"That's my target," she continued communicating with the computer, "right there." She looked at the red/orange blob that was Bianca, knowing the computer was tracking her eyes and where she was looking. It highlighted her friend.

"Understood."

Whether the computer actually "understood" or not was debatable, but so far it had proven uncanny in its resourcefulness.

"Once the shit hits the fan," she told it, needing someone else to talk to right then, someone to share this deadly moment with—anyone, even if it was only a machine, "if you have any advice, let me know. Okay?"

A brief pause then, just as she was about to clarify what shit hitting the fan meant, the computer said: "Understood."

Jess didn't want to kill anyone. *Else*, she reminded herself, recalling the fireballs that consumed the helicopters. Had there been any collateral? *So much destruction ...*

Not killing anyone was dreaming. People had already died. Someone else would die. If not from her directly then from all the shooting that would follow. There was obviously about to be a firefight, whether she made a move or not. She had to stay focused. Her only objective was to rescue her friend.

There were going to be casualties.

"I'm going straight in," she said, stepped into view of the warehouse and …

Started running.

"Understood."

She picked up the pace, identifying targets on either side as the commandos continued closing methodically on the building. The agents inside sat idle, unaware of what was coming for them.

Yeah, she thought, trying to maintain her own internal dialog, *commandos are the least of your worries. You're about to get a visit from something a whole lot worse.*

She blitzed up the alley at an accelerating sprint, across an open parking lot and into view of the nearest commandos, angling for a section of warehouse wall. The commandos crouched behind cover, attention on the building ahead and, as the sound of her heavy boot strikes reached them, they looked back in her direction. She could only imagine the reactions inside their masked helmets. Here was a giant, nine-foot-tall suit of black armor with a skull for a head appearing out of nowhere in a full-on, assholes-and-elbows sprint, gravel spitting from its boots as it kicked heavily off the pavement straight toward them, hydraulics whining.

Surely their eyes must be popping behind their goggles.

Sorry to crash the party, fellas, she imagined telling them as she charged past. *I'll try not to eat all the chips.*

And she threw a shoulder low and, *BAM!!* punched through the warehouse wall, directly past where Bianca sat. *Oh yeah!* Bricks and mortar flew, scattering before her in a cloud of destruction. That impact alone could've killed someone, she realized, and steeled herself for the chaos to come.

"External comm!" she ordered. *Blurp.* "Bianca!" the PA blasted the large open space.

Bap! Bap! Bap! Bullets. They were flying—and not from the agents.

From the guys outside.

What—?! The commandos had hardly been fazed by her rushing assault. In fact they were using her attack to further their own. Opening fire through the gaping hole she'd just created.

Bap! Bap! Bap!

Son-of-a-bitch!

"Bianca!" she whirled, taking stock of the scene. Behind her, through the hole, masked commandos began leaping in in pairs. Bravely or stupidly didn't matter. Here they came. Across the way more had burst in the front door, capitalizing on the sudden pandemonium.

She couldn't believe it.

Agents snapped from their momentary shock and began returning fire, the drifting dust from her entry casting a thin cloud of obscurity across the scene.

"She's there," came the computer voice, surprising Jessica. Bianca's blob was highlighted to the right.

The expected firefight was erupting, hot lead crisscrossing the room as bodies fell or dove for cover, voices yelling above the din. The fact that the commandos had chosen to take advantage of the shock of her entry to press the assault still held her frozen in place. Her arrival should've paralyzed them, all of them, at least for a few moments. It should've changed their game plan. They should be diving for cover, looking to see what had happened, not charging into the fray, heedless of the intentions of the lethal Skull Boy. Their careless disregard for her presence, for the clear threat she presented, was suddenly disconcerting.

Then she heard her friend scream; choked but piercingly high above the pulse of gunfire. It unstuck her. She leapt to the side, cleared the melee and landed directly between Bianca and the action. The two groups of men were, fortunately for the moment, bent on fighting each other.

"Bianca," she said through the PA. Practically blaring, but there was no time for subtlety. Bianca looked up from the floor where she lay, hands tied, gag in her mouth, disheveled and looking weary. She mumbled around the gag. Bianca knew it was her, she had to by now, but the expression on her face was still a mixture of terrified relief.

Such a conflict of emotions, and in that moment Jessica's heart went out to her.

You should've stayed upstairs!

"It's me," she said. She extended her hands and lifted Bianca carefully to her feet. Her friend seemed tiny from the vantage of the armor. *So frail.* Bianca stared up at her, gag pinching the edges of her mouth in a mute smile, wide-eyed as Jess checked the bindings at her wrists. Zip-ties. Hard plastic. The armored hands of the suit were suddenly clumsy; unable to pull the ties free without hurting her. At least she could remove the gag. She fumbled with it at the back of Bianca's head, eliciting a cry of pain as she pulled too hard, then had it free.

"Jessica!"

"I'm going to get us out of this," she assured her, continuing to shield her with her giant body. Desperately she cast about, searching the area for anything to remove the zip-ties. There was nothing. "Let me know if this hurts," she told her finally and, carefully—as gently as she could—pinched the plastic band on either side between thumb and forefinger, pressed the suit's fingers together, twisted slowly and … popped it in half. Bianca winced but was okay.

She rubbed at the red marks on her wrists.

"Stay behind me." Jess turned to the gun battle, a blitzkrieg of shots that had, thankfully, moved further away. Gun smoke filled the air, adding to the dust being stirred up by the flurry of action, the rapid-fire crack of shots and ricochets, pistols and short bursts from semi-auto assault rifles, men moving between positions of cover around the room.

Then something caught her eye.

Across the way; a thing entirely out of place amid the bedlam, standing apart from the madness in full force around it. On one of the tables. Shiny, chrome, glinting in the late afternoon sun streaming through the windows, far across the melee, tethered by some sort of cable to one of the laptops.

Another Icon.

For a desperate instant she looked down and checked the Skull Boy's front satchel. Had the Icon fallen out?! Had they taken it somehow after all?!

How?!

No. Hers was still there. Which meant ...

This was another one.

Another Icon!

Sitting in plain view, on one of the tables.

She felt herself wobble. Stuck out a foot; widened her stance and stabilized. Mind racing to build new possibilities. Did that Icon go to Anitra?! Did they know anything about hers?!

They must.

Give us the device. Their demand echoed in her mind.

Then movement. From the corner of her eye. A man, holding a gun aimed right at Bianca. *No!!* Bianca was behind her, safe from the larger gun battle but right in this guy's line of sight. And there was no time to act.

She'd failed.

A blur of action. Her own arm snapped straight, right in front of Bianca's head as the gun fired, *POW!!* the muzzle flashed and kicked in the man's grip but ... the Skull Boy's armored hand was directly in its path.

CLANG! the round sparked off the palm.

"He will try again," the computer advised. Jess realized the computer had just moved her arm, thus blocking the shot and saving her friend.

Without further hesitation she lunged for the attacker, covered the distance in a single stride and hooked an uppercut into his mid-section with every bit as much rage as she would've if hitting him with her bare hands. *Bastard!* Only, these weren't her hands. A fact which registered only as she completed the swing.

People will die today.

Her movement was so fast the man's expression barely had a chance to change as she connected, folding him in two with a loud *whack*, body wrapping around her fist in a mushy mass that went flying. Momentum sent the broken form arcing away from the impact, limbs twisting unnaturally, mouth spewing blood until it flopped with a crack and a thud to the concrete floor.

Behind her she heard Bianca retch.

Jess nearly did too.

Then a voice: "Are you injured?" For a moment she couldn't place it. Turned to the side, looking.

Injured?

The computer.

She shook off the gruesome image. "No." Her arm ached, yes, having been jerked so quickly by the computer's automatic reaction to deflect the bullet, but it was a pain she could live with. Bianca was alive.

"I'm fine," she said.

Then: "Thank you."

"In my estimation the shit was hitting the fan," the computer informed her. "I had no time to give advice."

"Thank you," she said again. "That was perfect." She turned to Bianca. Her friend was doubled over but still on her feet, heaving up nothing, looking like she might collapse at any moment. Jess understood how she felt. She called up the PA.

"Take some deep breaths," she said, amplified voice loud. Slowly her friend did. "There isn't much time," she added and, carefully, reached and lifted Bianca into the crook of one arm.

There really *was* no time she thought desperately as she searched everywhere, not wanting to be surprised by any more attackers. Bianca was hugely vulnerable, and behind them the battle was only heating up.

But ... the other Icon.

It was too much to ignore.

"Hold on," she told her friend, held her close with her other hand and ... jumped. The surge jolted a scream from her but Jess made sure the leap wasn't too abrupt. Her target was a ledge one floor up, filled with boxes and stacked with unused crap—far enough from any agent or commando, well away from the hail of bullets. Jess landed and set Bianca down.

"Stay behind cover," she said, turned before her friend

could protest and jumped right back into the fray. The agents were in a fight for their lives, hugely outgunned by the commandos who, Jess was now convinced, were there for one thing only:

The other Icon.

Whether they knew she also had one she couldn't be sure. At that point it really didn't matter. The agents clearly knew. She'd given up on trying to imagine who was who, who was up to what, which was working for which or any other explanation. Every man in there was an enemy as far as she was concerned, every man there was dangerous, and none of them should be in possession of *either* device.

She ran across the open floor between the warring sides, bodies sprawled here and there, hurrying with the impunity of a kid charging between two sides of a snowball fight. She cringed reflexively as bullets struck, crouched a little as she ran but, ultimately, was in no danger. Sparks flew, hits zinged off the armor, information scrolled and she made a bee-line for the table. At the last, too late, a handful of the closest agents saw what she was up to and reacted. Funny no one had thought to tuck the Icon away; though the nearest commandos were still far enough from it and the agents had the table surrounded.

Not for her though. She kicked the men away easily as they tried in vain to stop her. Their efforts to tackle had no more effect than their bullets. One, two, three on each leg, grabbing futilely. She peeled them off like children. Less than children, stripping them off and flinging them away, yelling, beating them to the Icon before any could snatch it. Without hesitation she knocked the last man free, grabbed the Icon—deciding to take the connected laptop as well— and threw both into the front satchel with her own. At the last instant she had a thought and scratched the end of the new Icon with an armored finger, before she tossed it in— hoping to mark it as distinct from the other—did so, then turned and ran as fast as she could back across to Bianca.

She had the Icons, she had Bianca, and she was leaving.

Marines, we are leaving! she imagined that famous line from *Aliens*. The yelling intensified, became more focused. Directed at her now. As the shock of what she'd just done registered the remaining agents shifted to a panicked frenzy, nearly ignoring the deadly assault of the commandos. A fact that didn't seem to matter, she realized, as the commandos, too, had turned their attention to her. Confirming immediately everyone's objective. The massive suit of armor had now, quite suddenly, swept right through the midst of everyone's focus, stealing away that which they all sought.

In one swift stroke she'd made herself the immediate target of everyone in the room.

And it crystallized for her: Even though one of these groups *had* to be allied somehow with American interests, both would kill her without hesitation to prevent her escape. Which meant not only was she not safe, neither was Bianca.

Things had gone too far.

Neither of them could go back.

You should've stayed upstairs.

"Bianca!" she yelled as she ran, PA voice booming in the warehouse above the din—heart sinking with the realization of what had to be done. "Stay down!"

With her next step she pushed off, leaped up and out at a run, a little too far away but eager to get back to her friend, arms and legs windmilling to keep her balance as she arced through the air with tremendous forward momentum. At the ledge she pulled up her feet and hit with a skid, crashing into several boxes. Bianca screamed off to the side, well protected but terrified nonetheless. Bullets whizzed. More bullets; striking the armor in a shower of sparks and whistling ricochets. Down on the floor both groups had nearly forgotten each other, moving with haste toward the ledge—almost as a team, though they surely were not—barely sticking to cover, unleashing a deadly rain of lead. Bursts cracked in rapid-fire volleys; pistols; rifles; muzzle flashes popping in strobe-light staccato from every corner.

There was no way Bianca would survive this.

Quickly, frantically, Jess scanned the rest of the

building from her elevated perch. Behind them was a thick wall which led down to another section of floor— more commandos laying in wait. Outside the building still more had moved in, making it clear which way this battle would've gone had it been allowed to last. The agents were severely outnumbered.

None of that mattered. All that mattered was that Jess was completely surrounded. There was no way to break through the warehouse walls while holding Bianca, shield her absolutely from the fury of the gunfire coming from all directions and run. Her friend's unarmored body was far too vulnerable for any of that.

Jess agonized over the dead-end at which she'd arrived. The time was now and ... she had no answers. Bianca had somehow fallen into the same mess as her.

"Bianca," she said, pushing aside a few boxes and stepping over to kneel beside her. "You're in too deep now," she said as quietly as she could, armored skull just a few feet from Bianca's trembling face. Tears streaked her friend's cheeks. "I can save you," Jess tried to sound reassuring. "I can save us. But it won't be pleasant. There is no other way.

"Do you understand?"

Bianca shook her head slowly. She didn't understand any of this.

Wasting no time Jess reached down to the armored satchel and checked the two Icons inside, pulled the one without the scratch and held it in one hand. With the other hand she reached for Bianca. Held up her palm— as invitingly as she could, imagining how terrifying the gesture must actually be. Especially considering what she had in mind.

Bianca nervously eyed the Icon in her other hand. She knew what it did. She'd seen Jess disappear once.

She was terrified.

"Come," Jess tried to calm her with her voice alone; it projected so harshly from the PA no matter how softly she spoke. But this was it. Bullets were striking close, shattering wood, cardboard exploding in a steady, bursting cloud of brown and white paper.

They had to go.

Slowly Bianca rolled toward her, flinching with every near miss. No choice. Jess took her back into her arm and snugged her close. Bianca hooked her arms across the metal shoulders as best she could and Jess could see her friend up close, just a few inches from her on the internal video screen, face pressed against the outside of the helmet. As if right there, though a layer of high-tech armor separated them. Tears flowed freely down Bianca's cheeks.

Jess felt her sadness acutely.

Yet, a corner of her mind held hope. Far from the end of their lives, this was merely a change. A monumental one, no doubt, but there was hope. They could make their own future.

They would be alive.

And, quite out of place for the moment, she felt again that surge of exhilaration. That giddy tingle of excitement.

She was going to see Zac.

"Hold on," she told Bianca. "I'll save you."

And she gripped the Icon and ...

Twisted.

CHAPTER 12:

REALITY CHECK

Pow! THE PRESSURE WAVE CLAPPED THE AIR, sending a pulse through the powered armor. Jess felt the tingle of vertigo, felt the vibration of the suit's gyros as it corrected for orientation, bringing its legs down toward center of gravity. More than anything in that first jolt she felt Bianca; the vague tactile feedback of her friend's small mass, heard her scream, felt her body jerk and begin to writhe. In that first instant Bianca's survival was most in jeopardy. And not just from the fall. If Jess—herself working to control a frantic, panicked reaction—forgot herself, even for an instant, if she jerked and clutched Bianca even a little too tight or a little too loosely ... she could drop her or snap her spine.

But that first instant passed, Bianca safe and very much alive at the end of it. In the midst of the ensuing madness— careful to maintain her grip on the Icon with as much care—Jess cast her gaze far and wide, taking in as much as she could as they plummeted from the sky. It was early morning; she could tell by the direction of the light. Dawn had not yet broken; the sun was still below the horizon, casting its red glare up into the clouds. No battle took place. Not like last time. Calm prevailed below. Osaka was the same burgeoning military/industrial complex she remembered, stretching in all directions below her like a walled Manhattan—the two tallest spires at the center dominating the rest—but it was a quiet, almost peaceful morning they materialized into.

Bianca scrabbled in her grip, screaming as the streets rushed up to greet them. *Quite an entrance*, she thought. First the sonic pop of their arrival, followed by Bianca's screaming ... they'd no doubt drawn a few skyward stares. Lucky—*real lucky*—they'd arrived at such an odd hour, before many were awake and after most had gone to bed. Few things moved in the streets below. Whether that mattered or not had yet to be discovered. If anyone *was* looking up at that moment she imagined what they were seeing. A glinting, black Skull Boy falling from the sky, screaming like a girl.

She pulled Bianca closer. Hit the jets once to slow their fall. Unlike Zac she had a way to brake their descent. With a little skill she might actually make it a soft landing. She hit the jets again, the thunderous roar adding yet one more noisy herald to their arrival. Quickly, with as much finesse as she could muster—like playing *Lunar Lander* or something; little, controlled bursts of thrust—she angled them past rooftops into a canyon between buildings, down to the street below. They skimmed one wall, scraped along it as they headed for the street ...

Whump! she bent her knees deep, squatted all the way and soaked up the remaining momentum. Immediately she checked her friend. Bianca had stopped moving. An instant of alarm then she confirmed her friend was breathing. Passed out. From the fear, from the rush of air, the impact, the sheer adrenaline overload—from everything, probably. Jess put the Icon carefully in the front satchel, checked the contents—all good—snugged Bianca closer, gently supporting her head like holding a sleeping baby, and made a sweep of the street. More good fortune: the buildings around them were empty. No people as far as she could detect. And as she looked closer she noticed signs of obvious disuse. She and Bianca had ended up in a section of Osaka not unlike the one they just left in Boise. One that, for the moment, was abandoned.

She began moving. No one out walking. She wondered who in the city had seen her fall. Surely someone did.

Gotta get off the street. She searched the nearby buildings. The dark, empty lobby of a tall one looked inviting. Deep scans revealed no hidden threats. Not even a bum asleep in the hall. Absently she wondered if the Dominion had bums. She went to the building, found an open window and stepped through. The glass was out and wasn't boarded up, lending strength to the idea that there might not be any vagrants or homeless in the city. That or they were too scared of some law to enter abandoned buildings. At any rate, the thing was wide open and easy to get into.

She continued to safeguard Bianca's body as she passed inside, chipping edges with the suit's wide shoulders but not disturbing her friend. Bianca didn't stir as she strode the interior halls, making her way eventually to a large lobby and a place with more room to move. Carefully she laid Bianca on the dusty cushions of a long bench, feeling like King Kong setting down Fay Wray or something. Gently she straightened her friend's neck and legs, laid her arms by her side and turned to survey the space. Nothing inside or out. For a minute she played with the suit's scanners, checking things, then tried with no enhancements, seeing everything as if with unaided eyes. The entrance, here in this room, was a single door, probably locked, with a pair of double doors immediately to the side, chained closed. Streetlights outside shone through high windows, illuminating everything in deep shadows.

Looks like an old theater lobby, she decided as she moved around slowly, nervous in the momentary peace. The parallels between Anitra and Earth were uncanny, just as she remembered, reminding her of the depth of mystery surrounding both.

I'm back.

Other than the Emperor Kagami, who formed the Dominion over a hundred and fifty years before, no one on Anitra had been to Earth and no one on Earth had been to Anitra. She and Zac were the only ones. Yet, both worlds were full of humans and, thanks to Kagami, both spoke English and had many things in common. To the common Dominion man Kagami came from divine origins and would return to rule them one day. Falsehood tied together by one, simple device. The Icon. And now she possessed it. The very device that had shaped so much of this world's history.

And now there's the other.

Curious, she looked down into the front satchel box, comparing the two. There had been no time to look closely until now. She examined them both. Except for the scratch she'd put on the one they were identical. Leading her to believe these devices must've been common at one time. There must've been a time in the distant past when Icons were used for regular travel. Where did the other one go? Did it also go between Earth and Anitra?

Or somewhere else?

Bianca screamed. Jess jerked toward her, slamming the satchel shut.

"*Where am I?!*" Bianca was frantic, on her feet looking this way and that. Utterly disoriented. Jess could see she was about to bolt.

Then she noticed the looming Skull Boy and did.

"Nooo!" she fled into the dark, absolutely terrified. As if waking *into* a nightmare rather than from one. Which was, more or less, what had happened.

Seeing this coming Jess was already taking a long stride to intercept her. Before Bianca got far she had her by an arm and was gently pulling her back, thrashing, desperate to escape.

Jess decided not to use the PA. Instead she popped the helmet. The skull hinged back, startling Bianca and revealing Jessica's human head beneath. Smells washed over her, sounds, the naked-eye view of the musty old theater. It was a rush of sensations but she ignored it and looked down on her friend; as calmly, as reassuringly as she could.

"Bianca," she said, adjusting to the sound of her own voice outside the helmet. "Bianca. It's me."

Bianca looked up, pure horror distorting her face. She saw Jessica, looked into her eyes. It wasn't registering.

"This is the place," Jess tried to sound soothing. "The one I told you about. The other world."

Bianca stopped thrashing. Fitfully she cast about, looking up, sharply side to side, back along the dark hallway down which she'd just tried to flee, around the dimly lit lobby.

Back at Jessica.

Jess caught the dark reflection of them both across the lobby in a polished marble wall. The giant Skull Boy, holding Bianca who looked like a toddler with a man holding her hand. Jessica's own head was tiny atop the massive shoulders. She knew the dried tracks of her earlier tears must still mark her face, which meant she probably didn't look a whole lot more composed than Bianca. She just hoped her friend could see the sincerity in her eyes.

"Come," she said. "Sit."

Slowly Bianca did, face full of dread, breathing short but starting to get a grip. Jess guided her back to the bench and she sat, numb. Jess stood straight and waited, watching her friend from her perch nine feet in the air.

Bianca looked up, head tilted dramatically back to look Jessica in the eyes, looming so high above her.

Said her name quietly: "Jessica."

Jess nodded.

Bianca slumped a little. Resigning herself to the truth of it. "It's real," she said.

Jess took a nervous look around the room.

"Very."

* * *

"DOWN HERE," the guard sergeant called to his three men sweeping the street behind him. They picked up the pace, shifting from a meandering, lazy scrutiny of the surrounding area to a more purposeful walk. Their lack of interest was to be expected, of course; all of them had been winding down from an overnight shift, ready to go home when they got the report of a disturbance in this section of town. No one liked getting a call in that gray area between watches, especially a call as vague and potentially involved as this one. Dispatch had little info. Just that several people heard a series of loud noises in the sky, followed by some sort of exaggerated commotion in the street. As was usually the case with such things, now that he and his men had arrived all was quiet. No sign of anything.

Except for a little evidence.

"Take a look at that," he pointed up as his nearest officer drew close. Overhead, midway up the face of a nine-floor building, was a long, fresh gouge, starting at about the seventh floor and extending in a ragged arc down to the third. Like something heavy had been dragged along it. Particles of stone and brick dust powdered the street below.

His officer looked up at the gouge. Then, considering what might've caused it: "Meteor?"

There was nothing in the street.

"Where is it?" asked the sergeant, looking pointedly at the ground in the area.

"Maybe someone carried it off," one of the others suggested. "Kids or something."

The last officer reached them. The sun was rising, the city waking with it.

"Kids are all in bed. Even the naughty ones."

"I say we call it and go home," one of them suggested.

The sergeant looked up at the gouge. "Something made that," he pointed. "We patrolled this section earlier and it wasn't there. We can't just call it quits."

"The report was of something falling out of the sky. That looks like it was made by something falling out of the sky. Whatever it was made that."

"So where is "it" then?"

"Maybe it *was* kids," the man said. "You know how they get."

The sergeant looked at him like he was crazy. "Do you not see that?" He waited while the guy looked up. "And this?" he pointed down at the fragments of building on the ground underfoot. "Whatever made that was big. Kids did not carry it off."

"Maybe it broke into smaller pieces."

The sergeant stared levelly at him.

"Look, I don't know," the other was tired.

"I understand we're all ready to go," said the sergeant, "but at a minimum there's property damage to report. We can't—"

"It went that way," an old man's voice interrupted from

across the street. All four of the guardsmen looked, to a third-floor window on the neighboring building. An old man leaned at the sill, barely visible in the dim illumination of the street lamps. A cup of fresh tea was in his hand, steaming in the chill morning air.

The sergeant called across: "What did?"

"Armor," said the old man. "Didn't look Dominion, that's for sure. Skull Boy, if I had to say. Carrying a girl."

The sergeant looked to his officers, then back at the old man.

"Heard the noise," the old man explained. "Came to the window. Saw a black suit of powered armor, carrying a girl. Headed that way." He pointed down the street. "Think they went in the old theater."

The sergeant studied the old man carefully, though his face could barely be made out from that far away. Was he senile? Hallucinating? Playing some twisted old-man joke for his own amusement? Let's send the guard off chasing ghosts and watch and laugh. Only ...

"Come on," he motioned for his team. "Let's check it out."

CHAPTER 13:

NEWS

"THAT THING CONNECTS OVER YOUR HOUSE," Bianca said quietly. She'd been slumping on the bench, posture one of someone who was thoroughly lost. Which, of course, she was. Her comment broke what had been a long period of silence. "Doesn't it."

Jess stood tall in the armor, helmet retracted.

"Look, I know what you're thinking," she said. "We can't go back. Not yet. We need to wait."

"But it does, right?"

Hesitation. "Yes."

Bianca seemed to weigh a decision. At length she spoke.

"Do it," she said, voice full of false patience. "Take me back." Desperation was in her expression, thinly veiled by an obvious effort to sound calm. "I promise I won't say a word. If they ask me anything I'll play dumb. I'll pretend like I—"

"Bianca. Those guys will hurt you."

"They won't. Just leave me and you come back here. You were trying to come here anyway, right? I mean, what were you planning?"

"I didn't have a plan."

"So just take me back. Drop me and come back."

"They're swarming my neighborhood. That won't work." Then: "I can't leave you with them."

"I'll be fine."

"They were going to kill you!"

"Kill me?" She latched onto that; spotting an objection she was sure she could reject. "They weren't going to kill me! It was all a bluff. They were just saying that." She leaned forward, imploring: "They won't kill me, Jessica. I know. I was with them. They may be assholes but they won't kill me. Just take me."

"Look at all they did already. And now there's commandos involved. It's too dangerous, B. We don't know *who's* at my house right now." The thought of that sent her spinning. She kept talking: "One of those groups has nothing but bad intentions, probably both, and I can't risk *either* of us getting caught in the middle."

But Bianca latched onto this train of thought. Trying to be rational, trying to act as if she was giving this very careful consideration, anxiety clear in her eyes.

"It's okay," she said. "I promise it will be okay."

It reminded Jess how hard she worked to convince Satori of the same thing, back when she was stuck here the first time. How she fought the red-headed commander to let her do something equally insane, to go to the Crucible and retrieve the Icon so she could go home. No different, in a way, than what Bianca was doing now. In the end Satori caved. Should she? And for a sudden, frightening instant she panicked. A sharp wave of madness during which she struggled to resist the irrational impulse to give in. To just do it; grab Bianca and get the hell out of there, go back home and figure out the rest. Go before it was too late. Before something happened and she lost the way. She was in the heart of the enemy stronghold, Osaka, capital of the Dominion, and cops and armies and Astake and Kazerai and Shoguns and all others against her would be coming and the chase would be on, and there was no guarantee she could find Zac—he could be anywhere—and what the hell was she waiting for anyway, and if they were caught *both* Icons would be gone and she'd never get home and her life would be over ...

Icy sweat chilled her spine as she fought the paralyzing fear. Her heart thumped in her chest.

She wanted to take Bianca back. Maybe it even made sense. Bianca might be able to claim ignorance, might be able to endure a million hard questions, thorough interrogations—might even be released back into a normal life. *Big "might"*. Jess, however, never would. Never could. And as she reminded herself of that sobering fact the brief, silly thoughts evaporated.

She looked around the room.

This was the end of the line for her. Which meant, if she was to survive, she had to stay on task. For her, the end had to become the beginning. Right or wrong she'd done what she'd done and now they were both committed, and now, while she had a moment to think, she needed to decide what came next.

"Just do it, Jess." Bianca's desperation took on an edge of pleading. Jess could see the same panic building in her friend and wondered if Bianca, like her, would be able to control it. "Please?" Bianca kept her voice level; deliberately quiet. "Please take me back." Tried to make a joke: "I actually *want* to go to school tomorrow." Tried to laugh and couldn't. "Can you believe that? Me. My assignment's not even done."

Jess looked down at her from a lofty height, Skull Boy in form, girl and best friend in countenance, unsure how to handle the breakdown she saw coming.

"You'll go to school again," she said, with as much sincerity as she could manage. As much hope. "I promise. Just not tomorrow."

"Take me back." Bianca's voice dropped to a whisper. "Please."

Deep down Jess tried to make herself believe what she was doing was the right thing.

"Please, Jessica," Bianca's voice cracked. "Please take me home." She started to cry softly, quiet tears of despair. "Please take me home." All at once she looked like a child. Hopeless, lost. Jessica's heart ached for her. So vulnerable, out of place in that dark theater, on that alien world; wearing regular Earth clothes. Fashionable, teenage dress.

So far from ready for this.

Why didn't you just stay upstairs?

Jess couldn't stop thinking how much that little failure to listen had ruined.

"Jess I can't do this," Bianca put her face in her hands and began to sob. And in that moment, as if on cue, a shaft of morning light broke through the high windows with the rising sun, casting her in soft illumination. Dust motes swirled about her head in the gentle beam, a halo of quiet suffering.   Beautiful, child-like Bianca, head in hands, the muffled sound of her quiet sobs, illuminated in yellow sunlight; angelic light, a spotlight on her tragedy.

It was bitterly poetic.

Jess looked to the day outside. The city was becoming noisy; the activity of a waking populace preparing to go about their lives. Soon she would have to move.

Bianca looked up, tear-stained face beautiful in the yellow morning light. Jess turned her attention to her.

"I was hoping you were just crazy," her friend said. "I was hoping everything you told me was just your imagination.   That somehow this was just your mind's way of coping. Of shutting out the pain. I never thought that thing really went anywhere." She meant the Icon, of course. "It didn't matter what really happened, all that mattered was that you were okay. Maybe you got raped, maybe you got beaten ... I didn't know, it didn't matter. See? All that mattered was that you were back and you were okay." Her voice hitched. "You were okay, Jess. That was all that mattered." Jessica's whole relationship with Bianca suddenly felt shaky. *Raped?* What did her friend think really happened? How had she pretended to believe her? All those months.

You never believed me?

After a short spell Bianca continued. "I listened to everything you said. When you came back. Everything you told me. I pretended to go along. You seemed fine. I thought maybe it would all be forgotten. Now this." She looked around the room, shaking her head as if finally realizing it wasn't going away. "I told myself I just blacked out when you disappeared last summer. After a while I started to believe it. Everything else, everything you said just seemed so ... impossible." She looked up, plaintive. "Even Toby thought maybe what we'd witnessed was all our imagination. That the shiny thing just knocked us out, like a tazer or something, and the guy kidnapped you—"

"Zac saved me," Jess bristled—more than was necessary,

perhaps, but the mere idea Bianca could think Zac would harm her ...

She calmed herself, not wanting to argue with her friend. Not now. Hastily she looked around the room, concerned they'd been there too long already. "There was a war going on last time I was here," she put all that nonsense from her mind and moved on to what mattered. "This city was the capital of the bad guys. I have to imagine it still is." She turned back.

"We've got to keep going."

"You should've just left me!" Bianca rose from her despair. "Why didn't you just leave me?! Why did you bring me?"

"*I told you to stay in the room!*" She cowed and Jess regretted the force of her outburst. She softened her tone, though anger still edged her voice: "You would've died in that warehouse." Would she have? Who knew. "What I did may not have been the best decision but it saved your life. Now we're stuck with it. Now we have to make it work."

Bianca sank into hopelessness. She kept her chin up, but the realization that she was stuck in a nightmare was sending her spiraling out of control. Jess watched her eyes fill with fresh tears. She pitied her, in a way, but didn't know what else to say. She had nothing in that moment, and the loss for comforting words was killing her.

"Jess?"

Bianca was starting to shake.

Her friend whispered: "I'm really scared."

Jessica's lip trembled. Consciously she held it still. Her voice, however, was not so steady.

"Me too."

And for a crushing, horrible moment she wanted, more than anything, to hug her, to join her on the bench and hug her and just fall into her arms and be there for each other, to take that moment and share their pain, but her friend was as far away from a hug as her sister, her mother, her dad and Nana and anyone else and it was the most terrible feeling.

* * *

OUT IN THE WASTELANDS, on a scorched plain of fused sand that reflected the rising sun like glass, a team of Dominion scientists worked the irradiated ground, instruments pinging and buzzing, telling them the same thing they had been for months: there was nothing out here. Nothing but death. The protective suits they wore were good only for short forays into the Black Lands, former site of the Crucible, but the suits kept them alive in that waste, where nothing at all could live.

"Can you believe another day of this?" One of them asked. There was no reason for an answer. None of them could believe it, though each day they asked the same question.

The team leader gave an audible harumph.

The search for the Holy Relic, the Icon, had been consuming the Dominion in the most absurd ways. The team leader shook his head. The search had started here, at the site of the Crucible's destruction, the last known location of the Icon, and continued in earnest around the globe, agents tasked with looking far and wide to discover if the Relic had been stolen by the Venatres. Maybe they took it after all. But the alternative, the idea that, if it *had* been here at the sight of the Crucible, it might have survived the nuclear blast that atomized everything around it for miles, that it might still be buried beneath the ground somehow … that idea was, in his humble opinion, the most absurd.

Holy technology or not, nothing survived that explosion.

"Next they'll have us start digging," one of them added unhopefully.

The team leader nearly responded. Nearly pointed out how ridiculous that was, how it would take an army of construction equipment months to dig up the dozens of square miles of glass, layer by layer, searching for a device the size of a shoe, but he stopped short. Of course that was *exactly* the sort of thing the Council might order. Their new head, the cleric Fezna, was obsessed. And Yamoto, the new Shogun, did nothing to keep him in check. Yamoto had become little more than a mouthpiece.

The leader cast his gaze back across the shiny ground, to the large wheeled vehicle they'd driven to that spot. Thorough scans were difficult and required this sort of manual scrutiny as they swept the terrain, layer by layer, looking for sign.

Then a beep.

"Whoa," one of his guys reacted to the instrument as it went off scale. Within an instant the rest of their instruments began pinging, indicating something beneath them that was generating a none-too-subtle reading.

"What is it?" the leader crowded closer with the rest. Everyone's instruments were now picking something up.

"Not far down," came the answer. "At a depth we've scanned before."

"How's that possible?" They'd been meticulous in all prior passes across the area.

The lead tech shook his head.

"Curious." A few of them made further checks. "A live source. Emanating energy."

Something new.

"Wavelength? Quantity?"

"Hold on."

The rest started to murmur as the specialists zeroed in, working with sudden, keen interest. After being so long engaged upon so futile a quest this unexpected bit of action had them all instantly excited. It was clear this wasn't the Icon—not as they knew to look for it—but the fact that *something* was down there giving off energy was, scientifically, stunning.

"It's a harmonic," one said. "A vibration." More checks, then: "Rising."

Suddenly the team leader began to grow worried. What the hell could this be? And why now? If it had been inert all this time ... By now everyone was studying every reading coming in, trying to make sense of whatever was beneath them.

"... I'm refining it. The energy signature is painting a

form. It's a pocket of fused glass. Different structure than the silicate surroundings. More of ... a crystal.

"Like a giant gem."

A giant gem. Now the leader's thinking went in another direction. A gem of that size would be a treasure.

"Why is it radiating energy?" he asked the greater question. "And why now?"

"Unknown."

One of the others grinned humorlessly. "Looks like I was right.

"Now we *are* going to have to start digging."

* * *

GENERAL LYTO YAMOTO—*SHOGUN* YAMOTO, he reminded himself, as he often had to do, frustrated with how he'd failed to come to terms with that transition—exited the elevator to the lavish Shogunnate chambers. His suite of rooms covered the entire uppermost floor of the Tower of Light, filled with the colors and fabrics of royalty and there, awaiting him as always, was the High Cleric, Fezna. With Fezna stood numerous aides, lesser clerics, officers of the Dominion's senior ranks, and the new General over the Dominion forces—the man who took Yamoto's place in that capacity when he "ascended"—his old adjutant, Damas.

Several "Good morning, Lord"s greeted him as he found his way to the throne and sat stiffly, smoothing fancy robes. Having stood so often before that very seat he'd come to realize, now that he occupied it, just how much he despised it. An over-opulent symbol of power. He'd never despised the Shogun he served. The now-dead Ashikagi had been a military man like himself. Together they shared many like-minded views on affairs of State, most specifically their distaste for the ranks of the self-appointed Elite, the Clerics and the High Council in particular. But for Yamoto to suddenly be wearing the golden silks, to be sitting in the golden chair ...

It was difficult not to be acutely aware of the frivolous trappings—and the unnecessary layer of command they represented. He wondered how Ashikagi felt during his tenure.

"Begin," he said, voice as stiff as his robes. Upon reflection he realized it had been Fezna's insistence that brought him to this. Once Fezna himself secured his position as head of the new High Council, following the loss of the entirety of the old Council in nuclear fire at the destruction of the Crucible, he'd come to Yamoto. Offering advice and, at the time, seemingly in need of an ally. Now it mattered little what Yamoto thought. It was too late for more careful evaluation of those decisions. Following events at the Crucible Yamoto, himself in need of an ally, had been too quick to maintain the old ways, too quick to lapse, to relinquish those things to Fezna and the lesser clerics, who then wasted little time installing themselves in the necessary positions of power. Almost as an afterthought they elevated him to Shogun, despite his misgivings, assuring him of his worthiness, demanding his service; that the vaunted connection between the religious codes of the Dominion and their Emperor and the might of their conquering military be maintained.

Yamoto was sure he made a fine puppet.

Damas came to him and stood at a respectful position, as he did every morning, hands behind his back.

"Lord," he addressed him, himself long since adjusted to the transition. In some ways Yamoto was jealous of Damas. His old adjutant had risen in rank, gaining power within the same structure, ultimately reporting to the same man he always had.

Yamoto.

Yamoto, however, had shifted altogether, reporting now to buffoons. Now, at least in name, he served the dead God Emperor and, though the military was his to command, he was no longer a part of it. Divine posturing was what it amounted to, and it did not suit him any more than it had Ashikagi.

Damas kicked off the morning report. "CQ at Monterey intercepted an encrypted communiqué last night," he delivered what sounded to be an intriguing bit of news.

Damas had a way of giving an edge to the otherwise tedious routine that had become the meat of these morning briefings. "Originating from border operatives along the Vasek," he went on. "We believe they were attempting to set relay electronics along the coast. The communiqué was a notification of these.

"Forces were dispatched at once to the intended location. A sweep has begun and more information should be available later today."

Yamoto nodded. Dominion forces on the Venatres coastline had been holding ground. Those forces were sent across the Vasek Ocean in the wake of the incident at the Crucible, in such quantity that they easily overwhelmed the unprepared Venatres. Since that time the Dominion had maintained a center of operations at the old Venatres city of Monterey, controlling a major slice of Venatres coastline and a big chunk of their land. The Venatres had so far been unable to take any of it back, making it a huge thorn in their side; one that had been festering and, in the end, like a lethal poison, would spell their demise; the first in a series of assaults that went beyond mere retribution. The Dominion, finally, had its focus on the taking of the entire world. An old ambition, certainly, but one which now commanded the absolute and total concentration of their every resource. Perhaps the only real goal on which Yamoto and the clerics saw eye to eye. Consequently he worked to make it the center of the Council's every interaction.

"Their efforts grow desperate," Fezna spoke from across the room. Until then he'd appeared casually engaged with one of the other clerics, not listening—an affected distance by which Yamoto was no longer fooled. Yamoto may have been unused to the subtleties of politics between Council and Shogun but he could read men. And he knew Fezna was, beneath his humble façade, a greedy, self-important ass, much too convinced of his understanding of things.

If only Yamoto had seen that sooner.

Fezna came closer, deigning to involve himself in the conversation.

"They realize," he said as he approached, "too late,

that we, and only we, are the custodians of the Emperor's legacy." At this he stopped across from Damas, before the throne, flowery silk robes a contrast to the pressed military uniform of the other. Yamoto regretted deeply his inclusion in that group of robed men. Almost reverently Fezna looked back across the room, as if inviting the rest to join him in gazing out the panoramic windows at the other tower, Vivitak, home of the Emperor himself, sparkling in the early dawn light.

Neither Yamoto nor Damas bothered.

"Don't underestimate them," cautioned Yamoto. "The Venatres are powerful. They have brilliant scientists. You know the reports as well as I. They were looking for something when they invaded Osaka. The Icon was more than just a simple treasure. They saw more in it. That move, otherwise, was far too risky.

"We need to be wary of whatever drives them," Yamoto noted. "Conquest is the only solution."

"Curious you should mention the Icon," Fezna brought his attention back to the throne. "I just received news." He seemed suddenly proud of himself. Immensely more than usual. "We've found it."

Yamoto straightened. Damas, too, without thought; neither man able to conceal his surprise.

"The Icon?" Yamoto spoke. "How?"

Fezna smiled. "The team. In the Wastelands."

Impossible. Yamoto had gone along with Fezna's wishes months ago, sending a scientific team to scour the blasted lands where the Crucible once stood, ridiculous as the idea was. It seemed harmless enough: Agree to waste the time and effort of a handful of scientists and technicians, maintain a bit of harmony.

He never expected it to yield anything.

"They found it?"

Now Fezna retreated a little. "It has not yet been extracted, but we have it. An object, beneath the ground. Giving off its signature energy." Yamoto knew a stunned look had crept across his face yet could not wipe it away.

"But they say it's there?"

Fezna nodded. "The team is beginning to dig even now."

Yamoto sat back, still unconvinced but trying to think with the possibility. What if the Icon *did* survive?

For starters, if it did, he would make it his mission to study it, Holy Relic or not. Anything that could endure a blast like that and remain whole—in any form—was a scientific marvel and he would *not* allow it to simply be put back on a shelf and revered. Would not allow it to be stuck in a sealed case high in the Emperor's chambers to collect dust with all the other baubles. Yamoto was done putting religion before science.

The Icon must be understood.

Silently he began preparing himself for a battle of wills.

CHAPTER 14:

NO REST FOR THE WEARY

THE DULL BLUE EXCAVATION MACHINE rolled toward the survey team across the thoroughly glassed plain. Various pieces of equipment had been stationed on-site, in the event the unthinkable happened and they actually found something, and today, much to the team leader's unexpected yet growing sense of excitement, they finally needed it.

He was mildly surprised at how dramatically moods had changed. Perpetual boredom, if not outright resentment, had been the order of the day for so long it was hard to believe he and his group were actually experiencing such a high level of anticipation. What was this mystery object buried beneath the shining sand? All were eager to find out.

So far all they knew for sure was that they'd found a large concentration of fused silicate, showing on instruments as being roughly the size of a car, compacted into the shape of, more or less—and quite curiously—an egg. Did it encase the Icon? Was that even possible? Word was that was the interpretation of the Council. The clerics had, of course, taken that vague information and turned it into a huge discovery. The team leader wasn't so sure. Actually, he was pretty damn sure. The Icon was not fused into a silicate egg. But let the robed freaks think what they wanted. They always did anyway.

The more curious thing was that they hadn't discovered this before. How it was now, quite suddenly, emanating a definite and unique energy signature where it hadn't before ... that was the biggest mystery.

One he looked forward to solving.

He shook one leg, trying to make an annoying pinch go away. Week after week in the sealed suits had not made the bulky gear any easier to wear. Each new day as they suited up they steeled themselves for the inevitable string of annoyances; dripping sweat, muffled voices, fogged lenses, painful little pinches, chafing ...

He had to admit at least part of his excitement stemmed from the fact that, after this, he'd get to go home and, at last, wear regular pants again.

The machine rumbled and hissed to a stop at the designated spot. His team moved into action, hooking up instruments, entering settings, bringing hydraulics to life and slowly raising the drill ram.

Beginning, at length, the tedious process of boring into the hard ground to extract the crystal egg.

* * *

JESS LISTENED TO THE TILE FLOOR CRACK ever-so-slightly beneath the weight of the powered armor; a hundred tiny shatterings with each step as she paced the deathly-quiet theater lobby. She stopped and looked down, helmet still retracted from earlier, studying her "footprints" with unaided eyes. Sunburst spider webs of thin cracks marked each heavy footfall on the tiles. Absently she looked out the grimy windows at the steadily rising sun. The urgency of the situation gnawed at her, compelling her to move, to take action, to keep things going. Waiting was solving nothing. She told herself she was giving Bianca a chance to calm down. Most of her hesitation, however, came from indecision.

Whether they tried to fake it as citizens of Osaka and just walk out of there, whether she charged into the streets in the Skull Boy armor, guns blazing, whether they snuck out on foot ... there was no reasonable way to continue. Every plan had a hundred opportunities for failure. There was a false calm to their current surroundings, an illusion of peace, of time they didn't have, but none of that was real. Any moment someone could walk in; a cleaning guy, a realtor, anyone. It was like being boxed in, and the more she thought of it the tighter the box became. They couldn't go back, they couldn't stay there.

They were stuck.

In that moment she had no idea why she ran. None. There were reasons, she was sure, but right then she was simply drawing blanks. She should've just given the agents the Icon and the Skull Boy and let happen what happened. Now she was right back at the center of a huge mess and could never return.

She glanced at her friend. Sitting on the bench across the lobby, quivering even after all this time, trying to hold it together even as she made little, involuntary whimpering noises. Bianca looked so weak sitting there all alone.

Maybe I should *just take her back*, thought Jess. Drop her off behind the house and let the assholes take her. Lock her up; whatever. Probably they *wouldn't* kill her, which meant at least her friend would be alive.

Though things were calmer than they had been when she and Zac first fell into Osaka, though she stood in a quiet room with a deceptively calm moment to think, the road ahead was no less treacherous. They were in the middle of a hostile city, surrounded by people ready to either capture, fight or kill them. If they *did* manage to escape Osaka she had no idea where to go after that. Where would they run? Her, carrying Bianca across the wide open plains, to the distant woods, hoping she made it to a Venatres outpost?

Absently she thought of Darvon and the Conclave, the ones that had saved her before. Had Darvon made it home safe? Did he go with the Venatres? What of his family and the rest of the Conclave? Could they be any help this time around?

How would she find them without being seen?

Had they been disbanded? Rooted out after the chaos of her escape?

Maybe she and Bianca could sneak out and walk around the city asking questions.

Nervously she checked the Icons in the front satchel. Now she had two; one which was considered a Holy Relic, the other which would no doubt create an even huger sensation were it discovered. Plus the laptop, whatever it contained. And she could only imagine the sensation *she* would create if they found *her*. After what she'd done. She had to be at the top of the Dominion's Most Wanted list. Probably on posters and everything. "Jessica. Murderer of the Shogun." Girl who helped bring down the Crucible.

And what about her family back on Earth? Would they be safe? Would the agents go after them? What of the commandos? Now that the damage had been done, now that Bianca had effectively ruined any chance of slipping away quietly, now that *that* was ruined, now that the cat was out of the bag—*boy was it!*—should she just go back and wreak bloody havoc? Back to Earth, fight everyone who stood in her way until her world snapped out of its waking coma and was forced to make a turn in a new direction? Even if that meant fighting to the death in a blaze of glory? These were thoughts she'd already had before. She could probably last against the Earth forces; long enough to raise quite a ruckus.

And what about Zac? Her mind was racing but she couldn't stop it. It was all the same paralyzing indecisions, only now she was on Anitra instead of Earth. Was Zac here? In the city? When she left he'd been with the Venatres. Had he gone back to the Dominion? Why would he? But if he had, and he was in Osaka, might he find her? More than that, now that she was back on Anitra, how would she find *him?*

Could things have changed dramatically? Could the Venatres now be in control of Osaka? Was she hiding unnecessarily?

What if the Dominion were now friendly?

Was that even possible?

God!

She was going mad just standing there.

When she came the first time Zac got her out in spite of all obstacles. She looked across the room at her friend. Could she do the same with Bianca? For a surreal moment it struck her just how far beyond Bianca she truly was. How much more she'd been through and, as a result, how much more capable. Back home, in their normal lives, Bianca was the wise one. The one Jess looked to for advice.

Now the tables were turned. Now Jess was the wise one. The warrior with the skills, experience and composure to get them through.

Bianca needed *her* to survive.

Despite that realization, she agonized over how badly she did *not* want to be the warrior. Did not want to be carrying the full burden of their predicament. How badly she wanted it all to just go away, back to Bianca being the one with the answers. How badly she wanted to be listening to her friend right then—a desire she thought she'd never actually feel. To be on the phone with her, getting advice on what to wear to the party.

She could hear them talking.

Do you think I should wear the plain skirt? How 'bout the plaid?

Sure.

The black and red?

No, no. Wear the green one. It goes with your eyes.

Thanks, B. What about guns? I know they're not a popular accessory, but should I carry the revolver? You know, just in case a bunch of G-men show up and crash the dance.

Sure, Jess. Definitely. Take the chrome one. And wear your silver earrings. They'll go good with it.

Jess snorted. A short, curt noise with no mirth in it and Bianca looked at her from across the room.

Just as the door to the lobby burst open.

Four guys; rushing in, dressed like police. For the briefest of instants Jess was in awe of the fact that she didn't flinch—even as Bianca shrieked, recoiling in terror. Followed by another, equally brief instant in which she marveled at how quickly she snatched the plasma cannon from her back, trained it on the wall above the men—who were still assessing the scene—and ...

Fired.

WHOOOM! a short burst that bored a hole straight through to the sky outside, sending chunks of wall collapsing down on them. The Skull Boy helmet was retracted and the sound of the blast in that proximity, unshielded, crushed her skull. She staggered in the wake of it, fighting the brilliant spots that danced across her vision, a deafening throb pounding her ears from the massive concussion in the enclosed space.

Blinking away the spots she saw all four men had been knocked to the ground. They were, for the moment, immobile.

A quick check confirmed Bianca was too. On the floor; whether unconscious or frozen in fear she couldn't tell.

She triggered the helmet. *Zzzzp,* it slid closed and the dome came alive.

"Computer," she checked telemetry, catching her breath at how decisively she'd reacted. In a bizarre way she felt energized now that she'd been forced to action. No more time to think.

Time to act.

"Wide perimeter," she told the computer. "Anyone else?"

"No threats," came the report, even as she made a visual sweep of human forms within range. People were up and about outside, morning commuters and the like, though not too many in that section of town and none on that side of the theater. Many, however, would've heard the massive blast of the plasma cannon.

One of the policemen began to stir, bringing up his pistol. Jess stepped to him, locked the plasma cannon to her back in the same action, reached with one hand and grabbed him up. Barely thinking—on that other plane again—she clinched a handful of uniform at his neck and hurled him sliding down the long hall. His gun flew in one direction, body flailing in the other. As he skidded away into the shadows she turned to the other three who were also scrambling to get their bearings—fearful of the Skull Boy suddenly looming over them. She bent and knocked away the sidearms of two, grabbed both men before they could flee and hurled them, one-two, after the other, down the hall.

Pow! the fourth got off a shot that clanged her armor. She turned and smacked his gun away, eliciting a sharp cry as she probably broke his arm, grabbed him carelessly by the uniform at his chest and slung him screaming and flailing after the others. Without pause she took a step back and pulled the plasma cannon, leveled it at the ceiling over the entry to the hall she'd just thrown them down and ...

WHOOOM! brought down the arch in a tremendous ball of flame—worrying for a moment it might be too much. Bianca was perilously near the explosion. The shockwave alone would probably injure her, to say nothing of the heat and flames. Too late to rethink it, though, and she watched as the whole front of the hall piled down on itself in a cloud of dust and debris, sealing it off and sealing the guys inside. Making a spur-of-the-moment prison.

"External comm," she slung the cannon. *Blurp.* "Bianca!" She went to her crumpled form. As it turned out her friend had been far enough away not to be hit. Still, she was curled up in shock, a layer of mortar dust settling over her from the destruction.

"Bianca." She crouched beside her. "Bianca. We've got to get out of here." Impatiently she looked to the collapsed hallway entrance. No doubt the guys would be on their feet soon, calling for help or circling around. More police were certainly on their way.

"Bianca." But her friend wasn't moving. This must be what it meant to be shell-shocked. Gently, trying not to hurt her, she lifted her into one arm and stood. Then, sensing the need to take a moment, to do everything she could to calm her before she had a heart attack or something, retracted the helmet.

Zzzzp. The smells of the lobby, tinged now with the acrid edge of electric, burnt air, returned. She held Bianca close, looking at her over the rim of the helmet, face to face; listened to her shallow breathing. Her eyes were about as wide as they could get.

"Bianca," she said quietly. "It's me. Jessica."

A glimmer of awareness passed behind her dull stare. Just a glimmer, but Jess zeroed in on it, searching Bianca's eyes with her own, looking deep until she found her friend.

"I'm no different than you," she said, ever conscious of how quickly they needed to move. "I went through this once and survived. You can too."

Bianca took a deep, shuddering breath.

"If there's one thing I've learned," Jess tried to appear both calm and confident, "it's that no one really fails. No one ever fails. They just quit." She made sure she had Bianca's full attention.

"Don't quit," she told her. "Okay?"

Bianca just kept looking at her. "Okay?" Staring like she was from Mars or something.

"Don't quit and we'll make it through this." Jess noticed, however, that her friend's shock, very subtly, seemed to be easing, replaced by what appeared to be a rising fear. *Good*, she thought. Fear was better than shock. Fear, at least, could take action.

Slowly Bianca nodded. Jess nodded with her.

And thought of something.

CHAPTER 15:

A PHONE CALL

OF COURSE! The thoughts had been there, circling, vague ideas, just not the final conclusion.

Now she had it.

If it works.

But it had to.

"I'm going to get us somewhere safe," she spared a moment to reassure Bianca and, with an encouraging look into her friend's eyes, re-sealed the helmet.

"Computer," she said as the interior came alive. "Can you access the local phone system?" Everything depended on this. A simple question, a critical response. Her breathing nearly stopped in anticipation of the answer, and as she waited, nerves twitching, she felt her heart pounding all the way in her ears.

"Yes," came the answer.

She closed her eyes, breathing again.

"Good." She steadied herself. "Dial this number." And she recited the number Darvon gave her, what seemed an eternity ago, back when she was in the Daimyo's penthouse, the one Darvon told her to call when she was ready to meet and, once more, she fought debilitating nerves as the computer dialed. Would it be active? Was it some kind of temporary number, long since abandoned?

It has to work.

45809. Somehow, some way, she remembered it. Like her first home phone number. Somehow it got stuck, one of those unintended circuits that got locked in your brain. Not on purpose, and she'd never really thought of it before, but whether from the stress of the situation or something else the numbers rolled through her mind right then and she was suddenly getting a vivid recall of dialing them those many months ago. The sound of the computer trying to make the connection seemed to fill the helmet, ringing, ringing, and as she listened with simultaneous dread and desperate anticipation she recalled that night months ago; could see her reflection in the windows of the penthouse, beautiful city lights beyond, standing there looking at herself, phone in hand, pushing numbers ...

"Hello?" A male voice.

"Darvon?!" it came out so enthusiastic she nearly overwhelmed the speaker. She was sure it startled the person on the other end.

But it wasn't Darvon.

"Who is this?" came the answer.

Her heart sank. "Is Darvon there?"

Another pause. A repeat of the same question:

"Who is this?"

Should she just hang up? Panicked, she looked at Bianca, face on the other side of the thick helmet armor, overlaid with data projected onto the interior screen. Objects of interest were moving closer outside. The guys down the hall were moving, not doing anything yet; indistinct heat blobs, three of them on their feet, one still on the ground. Was someone tracing this call? Would they use it to home in on her? A slew of Earth movies where they'd done just that began to impinge, compelling her to hang up and just start running.

"Who's calling for Darvon?" the voice repeated, growing more suspicious ...

It sounded like they recognized the name.

Hope swelled. "Is Darvon there?"

"I asked who's calling." The voice was terse, but she was convinced that, whomever this was, they knew Darvon.

"Tell him it's Jessica." It wasn't like any more harm could be done. She was already so screwed.

Another pause. "... Jessica?"

"Yes."

Hesitation. Then: "This is Chom."

"Chom?!" she spiked the audio again; remembered him at once, putting the sound of the voice with the face. Familiarity that had been hovering at the edge of awareness came crashing in. *Chom!* The Conclave leader that talked to her in the penthouse. Right before she and Darvon left on their quest.

Chom!

"I can't believe it," she said needlessly.

But he was already speaking to someone in the background. "It *is* her." The background voice said in response, ecstatic: "She came back!"

Chom was back to the phone. "Darvon isn't here," he said—even as other voices in the background took up the news, a minor cacophony rejoicing at her return.

It worked! The number still worked! But as she overheard them chattering in the background she accelerated the moment, remembering their level of fanaticism. "I'm in trouble," she said. How could she have forgotten? To them she was an angel, or something like it, and if she let them they'd probably marvel at her return indefinitely.

She had no time for awestruck swooning.

"They're closing in," she said. With rising apprehension she watched the scanners as threatening objects moved toward the abandoned building. Down the sealed hall all four policemen were on their feet and congregating. Looking for a way out.

"Where are you?" asked Chom.

"I don't know. Computer?"

It chimed in obediently, adding its voice to the conversation. "Yes?"

"Computer, can you tell them where we are?"

For a moment it seemed to consider the best way to transmit that information, then engaged a short conversation with Chom. Jess was impressed with the way it answered the Conclave man's questions, giving him verbal directions until, at last, he knew exactly where she was.

"Jessica," he spoke to her, "leave that building and head around the back. There's an alley there. Go down to the next alley then go right.

"Call us when you're there. We should hang up now."

Jess nodded. "Got it."

A voice on the other end blurted, "We're so glad you're—" but the computer was already hanging up the call. Just then there was a roar outside, coming from the sky, and she realized there must be an airship on the move. News that a Venatres Skull Boy was loose in the heart of the city must surely have escalated the Dominion's concern. *Quite a bit, I'd bet.*

"External comm." *Blurp.* "Bianca," she whispered as quietly as she could, still loud, "we're going to run. Hang on."

Her friend leaned in and clung to whatever she could grab. Jess snugged her closer with one arm and headed to the chained double doors off to the side of the entry.

Metrics were in-band and scans showed armed units at range down the street. There was no good way out, but if she moved fast she might get around the corner before anyone took action. Quick, unexpected movements might get her past their methodical positioning.

She held Bianca with both arms, shielding her, and ... kicked open the double-doors. *CLANG!* they banged outward with a suppressed scream from Bianca, bent metal and snapped chains flying, one door hitting a parked car across the street as it flew much farther than expected.

Jess was right behind, charging out and hooking left around the corner, holding her friend tight—catching glimpse of a small squad down the street to the right, stunned for the moment as expected. She sprinted around the theater building and into the deep canyon between the tall structures, putting distance on her would-be attackers. Anxiously she looked up, to the slices of sky connecting the rooftops overhead.

"Computer. Can you track the airship?" The roar seemed to have gotten closer. She ran to the next alley on the right. In response to her query an icon for the airship illuminated on the scanning image, oriented downrange. It was moving toward the area. Sirens sounded in the distance.

She checked Bianca. Face plastered against the outside of the helmet, grimacing, eyes squinted shut; holding on for dear life as the Skull Boy ran. Jess hooked right.

Down the next alley, a busy street visible at the far end, vehicles crisscrossing at regular intervals. Like any alley on Earth this one had things in it; trash cans and so forth, back doors to various homes or businesses. Cops would probably be on that main road up ahead.

"Computer. Call the same number," she instructed. The computer established a new connection and Chom answered.

"Jessica?"

"I'm in the second alley."

"Good."

"Hurry," she huffed. "I'm nearing the end." She widened her scan, trying to pick out what she could in the increasingly congested surroundings.

Chom talked faster. "Cross the main street ahead. Into the same alley on the other side. At the first cross alley go left. Three doors down on the right is a red door. That's the closest we can get. Go to it. Get to the red door." Then, thinking: "But don't leave the armor there! Leave it far enough away."

Jess realized how difficult that was going to be. *Perfect.*

Chom finished with: "Good luck."

"Thanks," she said, unable to conceal the sarcasm in her voice. Chom had already hung up.

Must be nice being the guy who sat around dreaming up dangerous things for others to do. She wondered if Chom had ever been caught in the middle of something like this. *Cross the street?* That should be fun. *And don't leave the suit anywhere near the door.* That meant they'd have to go on foot.

Maybe she should just leave the suit now.

The idea of leaving its security was frightening. She'd known that moment would come but wasn't ready. However, the Skull Boy was about the hugest beacon possible. Whether she got closer to the red door or not, at some point, in the next few seconds, she'd have to get out.

Might as well do it now.

A large generator was up ahead on the left, big enough

to hide the suit behind. She veered over and stepped into its shadow. Bianca looked up, panting and terrified but conscious. Inside the helmet Jess stared at her.

There was the laptop and the two Icons that had to be carried. Bianca was *not* dressed like anyone in Osaka. She herself still wore the clothes from MMA class; board shorts and red compression shirt. Most definitely not like any other fashion statement on that world. Especially the Dominion who wore nothing but plain black. If she and Bianca went on foot they would, the two of them, dressed like space aliens and carrying two shiny Icons and a laptop, have to make their way through morning traffic, elude any followers, find a red door and sneak into it without being seen.

Or, charge across in the suit, create an even bigger scene, ditch it somewhere further away on the other side and do the same thing.

She took a deep breath. Retracted the helmet and the sounds of the city came flooding in. Bianca jerked in alarm as the helmet slid back. She looked directly into Jessica's face, trembling. The airship's mighty pulse had risen to lay heavy over all other noise, somewhere in the near distance and closing.

That and the sirens made for a harsh, audible reminder of the extreme jeopardy they were in.

"We walk from here." Jess told her. An old *Indiana Jones* line, if she remembered correctly—which she wasn't entirely certain she did. Her mind was bouncing between every possibility of what they were about to do; every way they could be caught or killed.

There were many.

"Here," she leaned and sat Bianca on the ground, before the terror became overwhelming. *Just keep moving*, she told herself. "Stand back," she instructed. "Over there," and she pointed to a recess behind the generator. Realizing in the same motion that it would be the last time she pointed with the massive Skull Boy arm. Bianca stepped deeper into the shadows, eyes wide and getting wider. Quickly Jess popped the locks and started getting out. Then it hit her: the suit was loaded with everything she'd done, everything she'd said.

Darvon's number. Scans of Earth.

Shit!

"Computer?" Could it hear her without the helmet being shut? The roar of the airship approached. It seemed as if it would appear in the narrow slice of sky overhead any instant. Sirens grew louder. Far down the alley a group of armed men would no doubt run around the corner into view any second.

The noose was tightening.

"Computer?!" she leaned her head back into the open helmet.

"Yes," came the tinny response.

"Can you purge yourself? All data?" Overhead the sound of the airship crescendoed. Her skin crawled in deadly anticipation.

"Yes."

"Do it," she said hastily. "Erase everything."

"A full purge will render the suit inoperative," it informed her. "All control centers will need to be reset." The matter-of-fact—and very human—way in which it said it was a bit chilling, considering the act would amount to suicide.

"Yes. Do that. All data." Even as she confirmed what had to be done, however, she felt a fleeting sense of camaraderie with the machine she'd been through so much with. The Skull Boy armor she'd worn to rescue Willet, bring down the Crucible; the very armor that returned her home safely, sat in the barn unused for months then, when called upon, had been so key in helping her escape, save Bianca and get them both here. In many ways it was a hero. And as she fought away a tinge of sadness—no time for that now—she added, impulsively: "Thanks. For everything."

"You're welcome," it said and the sadness bit. Then: "Purging all systems." Pause. "Goodbye."

"Goodbye," she said. After a moment there was no indication of change so she queried: "Computer?"

Nothing.

"Computer?'

It was dead.

Hurriedly she finished climbing out and dropped to the ground, stripped off the operator suit and left it in a pile at the Skull Boy's feet—the incongruity of Mike's bracelet catching her eye as it had back in the barn. Should she just get rid of it? Would they be able to tell it wasn't from Anitra? Everything else there, the suit, the armor, was. Best to leave it on, though it hung as a painful reminder of all she'd left behind. She knew well the importance of forgetting that attachment. Mike, wonderful, friendly Mike, was simply her last boyfriend. He was not her soul mate after all. And the confirmation of that, in that moment— oddly—brought a sense of relief.

She knew exactly who was.

The changing roar of the airship snapped her into focus.

Turning back to the suit she popped the front satchel and drew out the two Icons and the laptop. "Bianca," she motioned for her, extending the computer, "take this." Hesitantly Bianca stepped over and took it.

Now Jess looked for something to do with the Icons. She needed her hands free, and all she was wearing were the board shorts and compression shirt. She decided to stuff them up the shirt. It seemed the best solution and the Icons did, in fact, snug into the tight elastic, firmly if clownishly large, and it felt like they would stay. They were much lighter than their size made them appear. Of course there was the chance of either one twisting, but she was far too amped right then to be slowed by such concerns. The Icons would stay and they wouldn't activate and this solution would work.

Carefully she adjusted them. Though it left her hands free, the Icons were the size of small dumbbells and looked ridiculous. Of course, how they looked really didn't matter, did it? She and Bianca already looked painfully ridiculous. Jess with her Chuck's, black and red board shorts and tight red shirt—now bulging with Icons—bare legs and arms, hair pulled up in twin ponytail whips; Bianca a colorful teenager in the latest fashion.

She took Bianca by the arm, pulling her to the edge of

the generator to look down toward the street. Traffic had slowed, which made her think the police must be blocking it off.

"Jessica." Bianca was plaintive. "Why can't we just keep using that thing?" She glanced at the Skull Boy, standing inert against the wall. "We'll never make it."

"People are waiting on us." Jess eyed a door across the alley. "Let's go," she tugged her across, checking left and right, expecting to see policemen burst around the corner at either end, wondering at the wisdom of going through an unknown door but unable to think of any other course of action at the moment.

"Come on," she urged, pulling Bianca faster, "hurry." Together they reached the door and Jess tried the knob.

Locked.

She looked back down the alley, trying not to become frantic; yanked Bianca along toward the main street ahead, toward the next side door. Tried the knob and ...

It opened.

Roughly she snatched Bianca through, checked the alley to make sure no one witnessed their passage and closed it behind them.

Bianca stumbled on into the room. "Stop jerking me!"

Jess checked all around the space, senses on high alert. "Keep your voice down," she warned. "I know you realize this is for real, but come on. Really *get* that this is real. Really get it. You've got to start thinking like a soldier if we're going to get out of this. You can't keep running around like some useless High Schooler."

"I *am* a High Schooler!" Bianca hissed. She clutched at the laptop, hugging it close.

Jess exhaled, sorry for her outburst. Determined to make her point. "You're not," she said, deciding not to apologize. "Not any more. So grow up and snap out of it."

Bianca just gaped at her.

"This way," she led them toward the front of the building, to another door, staying behind cover as much as possible. There were lights on in the room and it was filled with boxes. Like a storage room or something. Maybe there was a storefront on the other side that let out onto the street.

At the door she stopped and listened. No voices. No distinct noises. Slowly, with Bianca huddled close behind, she cracked it open.

Beyond the door was a store, as suspected. A bookstore of some sort, shelves filled with them. Windows at the front showed a street. *So far so good.* The street looked to be empty of cars. Sirens continued in the distance.

Now she heard quiet voices and looked across to see people at the window staring out, each of them dressed in plain black Dominion garb. *Great.* There was no way she and Bianca were going to just waltz through there and out the front door. Give a friendly little wave as they passed, *Oh! Hi. We were reading in the shelves. Didn't you see us come in earlier? Hey, what's all the commotion? What's going on outside?*

"What now?" Bianca whispered, too loudly, and Jess cringed. One of the guys at the window turned. Then the others.

Looking right at them.

CHAPTER 16:

THE RED DOOR

"HI," JESS STOOD, going with the first thing that came to mind. Maybe waltzing through was *exactly* what they were going to do. No way back now. She opened the door and stepped confidently into the store, like there was nothing at all odd about it, Bianca pressed tightly behind. The people standing at the window stared at them in open shock. Jess smiled sheepishly.

Too late for anything else.

"We saw the police and ran in here," she said, acutely aware of the Icons, huge beneath the form-fitting shirt. Unable to catch herself she glanced down at the ball-shaped lumps. As if she and Bianca weren't suspicious enough, the Icons made her look like some kind of circus-freak. *Come see the quadruple-breasted woman!* Absurdly round, hard ends stretching the fabric of the compression shirt. Wonderfully symmetric and inhuman, a perfect four-pack of ball boobies.

All the girls will be getting them.

Bianca cowered behind her, clutching the laptop, hardly looking better. Earth clothes so flashy in that setting.

This is bad. Jess swallowed. *Really bad.* But they were stuck. *Keep moving.*

"We thought there might be some danger," she blazed on, stepping boldly into the store with as much confidence as she could maintain. *Man does this sound weak.*

"Yeah," Bianca's voice startled her from behind, "sorry."

Jess glanced over her shoulder, then back to the people at the window. So far they weren't moving. She could see their minds were going a mile a minute, though, trying to make sense of these two non-threatening yet oh-so-bizarre girls who just suddenly appeared from the store room.

"What's going on?" Jess pretended to care, continuing

further toward the front, steadily toward the windows, toward the people and, toward her real objective, the front door. Bianca continued to crowd behind her, too close, stepping on her heels, but at that point her friend's obvious nerves mattered little. At that point it was more a matter of making no sudden moves. If they just kept pressing on, nice and easy, the people might remain frozen long enough ...

"Who are you?" one of them broke the stupor.

"We're from up the road," Bianca said. "Uptown."

Jess looked over her shoulder and locked eyes with her friend. *Uptown?* But Bianca made a little *Go with it!* face and Jess tried to fall back into character.

"Yeah," she turned to the people, making sure to maintain a methodical pace toward the door. "Uptown."

The man spoke again, something about who they were or what they were up to, but Jess just kept walking. Slow, steady. Nearly there.

"That's right," she answered, nodding and smiling.

"You aren't supposed to be here," the man was saying and, at last, he was moving. Toward the counter, back toward the storage room. The others remained standing by the window, staring. Jess ignored them; ignored the man, ignored the people—ignored them all, turning her full attention to the street outside. They were close enough now. Traffic was indeed being held at either end, by police cars, green lights flashing. She saw one now. The old steam-powered roadsters she remembered.

"I'm calling the police," the owner informed them from the rear of the store.

"Don't think that matters now," Jess muttered to herself, then to Bianca: "Ready?"

Bianca was pale. Her brief effort to get through this charade had faded and now, faced with what waited outside, flashing lights and all, she quaked with fear. Jess could see her friend was, in fact, not ready at all.

But they were going.

"Follow me," she said as the man in the back spoke loudly, on the phone, ratting them out. "It's not far," she added, even as she reached a hand and pushed on the door. "We'll make it."

If we don't get shot, she thought grimly.

Not giving Bianca more time to think—not giving herself that opportunity either—she took a deep breath and, with a firm: "Now!" shoved the door all the way open and ... bolted into the street.

Her strides were instantly long and fast, wind whipping at her ears as she hit a full sprint, pressing the Icons tight to her chest with one hand as they bounced and threatened to fly free. After a few steps she checked to ensure Bianca followed. Her friend was there, running faster than she'd ever seen her move, clutching the laptop just as hard, head tucked and eyes squinted as if someone was about to start throwing things.

Which they were.

POW! the sound of the first pistol echoed from the buildings, followed by more and the whipping *zip!* of invisible bullets slicing the air. Jess cringed, that feeling of imminent impact—not knowing when, or if, a strike would come.

Behind her Bianca screamed. A quick check, however, confirmed she still ran. No hits. Following. Running as fast as she could.

POW! POW!

Miraculously each shot missed.

"In here!" Jess yelled as she made it across the street to the alley and flew in, hauling ass, shielded for the moment by the surrounding buildings. Bianca was right behind.

Bap! Bap! Bap! chunks of stone fragmented from the corner of the closest, the deadly bullets barely a step behind. Jess kept on the speed. Up ahead she could see the next alley, the one down which they would turn. The one, according to Chom, with the red door. No movement at the far end. She threw a quick look over her shoulder, knowing the cops would be rushing in behind them any second, hot on their tail. She and Bianca had to make the cut before they did. Before anyone saw.

"Come on!" she yelled, breath heavy and running harder;

desperate to make the next alley.

Even as two cops came around the corner right in front of her.

* * *

"AMAZING," one of the team members said aloud, giving voice to the slack-jawed stares of everyone present. The extraction arm of the blue excavator was slowly withdrawing from the ground, the upper edges of a scintillating crystal shape emerging with it.

"Watch as it clears the sides," the team leader instructed, motioning. The rough rim of the bore hole looked as if it might scratch the crystal's surface, though in truth he had no idea if that mattered. As yet they had no way to know the value of this bizarre, energy-emitting formation. Was it just a massive gemstone? *God* was it massive! If that was all it was (*all!*) then a few scratches would hardly detract from its worth. Not even a little. If this were a true gemstone its value would be worth more than the planet. Priceless.

He suspected, however, that the value of this thing would prove far more than that of a precious stone. There was more to it than that. There had to be. The energy signatures they were getting kept fluctuating, changing and, now, as they brought it slowly to the surface, were pegging off the scale. He fully expected to see the thing start glowing.

Could it actually contain the Holy Relic? Preserved, somehow? That was what the clerics were reading into it. *It's the Icon!* they screeched. He could sense the salivating enthusiasm coming down the lines, eager to see what his team found.

"There," he directed as the crystal cleared the hole. "Hold it there." And the machine stopped, crystal hovering in mid-air at the end of the machine's firm yet delicate grasp. Grime clung to its surface, and as the rays of the morning sun struck it from behind it *did* seem to glow, magnifying and radiating those rays into a myriad of sparkling prisms that floated ghost-like in the air. The team leader squinted, holding up a hand to shield his eyes from the sudden brilliance.

And noticed something.

An object inside. Like a kernel or something. Or a seed. *Inside* the crystal.

For a fleeting instant he thought maybe it *could* be the Icon. But how?!

"What *is* that?" someone asked. The team leader glanced at the man, then back at the crystal dangling in the crane's grip, waiting for further instruction. Others were now stepping closer, squinting into the shiny, shifting depths of the magnificently formed egg.

The guys with instruments had turned to them with a vengeance, checking readings, adjusting, scanning ... trying to get a read on whatever was fused into the core. There were no seams, no way anything could've ended up in there save being formed within the crystal itself.

Now that it was out and in plain view the team leader was beginning to suspect the crystalline object was new. That it had formed in the heat and pressure that cooked the land and everything for miles when the Crucible's nuclear furnace detonated. Perhaps whatever was at the center was what got cooked, like a smaller crystal or a piece of metal or something, sand fusing around it in the blast like ice forming around a rock.

But what could possibly withstand that kind of force? Whatever it was it was giving off some kind of force. Instruments pinged and buzzed, men murmured or made increasingly perplexed comments ...

Then the crystal *popped*. A thunderous, sharp sound, like a tiny snap magnified a thousand-fold, and the entire team leapt backward in surprise. Everyone recovered quickly, no more sounds forthcoming. Checks confirmed nothing had broken, nothing had shattered, yet ...

A crack could now be seen snaking through the interior lattice. One that hadn't been there before, working outward from whatever was at the center, wending its way slowly.

POP! it went again and, again, everyone jumped. The

crack inched visibly closer to the surface. Like a lightning bolt in slow motion. Branching. Crawling toward them.

Then they heard it. A deep, resonant groaning, the grinding of some terrible force deep within the crystal itself. A vast internal stress, barely within their range of hearing but unmistakable.

Whatever was in there was pushing out.

* * *

THE COPS WERE RIGHT THERE. Jess was racing head-on, coming from the opposite direction, running at them at full speed as they rounded the corner. Two cops, and for an instant they recoiled in surprise, startled by the suddenness of the encounter.

Not her.

Rather than pull up she ran faster. Even as her blood went to ice she attacked; two more huge steps and she covered the intervening space with a surge, barely registering her own insane action as she actually ran *faster —what are you doing?!*—hit the closest at full speed and collided with him, snatched his gun and, in the same move, threw an elbow into his jaw. *Whack!* With the full weight of her charge behind it the blow knocked him back, even as she wrenched the pistol from his grip.

Just like that she had his gun and he was falling.

Not missing a beat, moving like a machine with no thought or hesitation, she turned the alien yet quite familiar gun (a gun was a gun, after all) on his partner—who was so far failing to react to the fact that she was *attacking*—and ...

Shot him; point-blank, right in the leg. He screamed and grabbed for the wound, dropping his own gun as he went down. Bianca screamed too, a distant sound that reminded Jess her friend was still there, but even as the second cop was in the midst of his agonized collapse she was turning back to the other, that man still reeling from the elbow strike and ...

Pow! the sound of the shot ricocheted down the alley as he, too, rolled with a scream and a shot to the leg. Bianca screamed again, even as Jess turned her attention up and in all directions, gun in both hands at arm's length, quick-scanning their surroundings.

Nothing in sight. No more targets.

Certainly not for long.

She rushed to the other cop's dropped pistol and kicked it to Bianca.

"Pick it up!" she commanded as it skidded across the pavement to her feet. Only then did she notice Bianca was rigid in shock, standing there hugging the laptop, screams fresh on her lips. And why not? In a matter of seconds Jess had disabled and disarmed two men, two *cops*—both much larger than her—taken their guns, *shot* them, and was now demanding Bianca join her. *Come on! Grab a gun!* Bianca managed only to look at the pistol at her feet.

Some of Jessica's awareness returned. She checked the Icons. Still there. She understood how Bianca felt. But there was no time to process emotion. That would come later.

If they lived.

"*Take it!*" she yelled and went to the alley end, the one the cops had just run from, the one they needed to go down, desperate to get out of there, hoping it was clear.

Still no other cops in sight.

They had to move *now*.

"*Come on!*" she blasted Bianca. The men on the ground were writhing in pain but either could make a call or shout for help. Both would see the alley they ran down. Neither would see which door they went in. Should she kill them? The logic of that option teased her, reason fighting to overpower emotion, nearly winning the battle in her current, heightened state. It would be quite logical to put a round through each man's skull. Would even be smart.

With great difficulty she forced the thought away.

"*Come on!*" she yelled, adrenaline surging through her like lightning. Without waiting she sprinted down the alley, gun tight in her grip. Halfway to the red door—she saw it ahead—she looked back and saw her friend running, laptop under one arm, gun in the other hand—she'd actually picked up the pistol—a look of frightened determination on her face. It was an interesting transformation, but Jess scarcely had time to appreciate it.

At the red door she skidded to a stop and grabbed the knob.

Locked.

She banged furiously. The injured cops started yelling behind her, calling out around the corner, out of sight as they shouted agonized pleas for their comrades. Bianca reached her and stood close, panting hard. Somewhere overhead the airship had drawn closer and was circling. As yet it had not appeared.

There was no way that could last.

"Open up!" Jess yelled, desperate, banging on the red metal surface until her hand stung. If anyone spotted them entering she was sure it was over. It was probably over anyway. The end felt perilously near.

"Open up!"

Bianca bounced up and down behind her, utterly freaked.

Then the door opened from inside.

* * *

THE GUARD COMMANDER moved closer to the suit of Venatres powered armor, standing against the alley wall behind the large generator. Skull Boys, the suits were called, and he'd never seen one this close. He'd heard stories of how they were no match for the Dominion's own Astake powered armor. He had to admit, however, right then, with one of the giant black suits directly in front of him, he didn't care how much better the Dominion armor was. This one looked plenty dangerous when you were standing next to it.

Gunfire up the street had brought his squad to high alert. Radio traffic reported not one but *two* girls making a break for it, one of them fitting the description reported earlier. It appeared that, in addition to there being a girl outside the armor, there was a girl *inside* the armor as well. Or had been. He looked at the Skull Boy now. Empty.

Listening to the radio exchange he continued his survey of the abandoned unit, noticing the Dominion plasma cannon locked to its back. Not Venatres. *Curious.* He looked closer, only half paying attention to the communication continuing to pour in as the conflict across the street heated up. Gunfire could be heard popping off. He was far less concerned with the ability of his men on the scene to capture two young intruders than he was with the mystery unfolding before him.

How did this combination of things come to be? A Venatres machine of war, carrying a Dominion weapon, in the possession of a colorfully dressed teenage girl who, in turn, had been carrying another teenage girl.

Inside the city walls.

Nothing made sense.

He couldn't wait to interrogate them. In a way he hoped they didn't get killed in the action unfolding.

Somehow that frantic noise seeped through this gathering fog of incredulity, drawing his attention back to the radio exchange. He thought to issue instructions not to kill them, which sounded like what might happen if the furious shooting continued, until he heard the startling discourse indicating ...

The girls were getting away.

That, somehow, two of his men had been shot.

What ...?

And the girls had ...

Escaped.

* * *

"This way," a middle-aged man in the plain black civilian garb of a citizen of Osaka hurried Jessica and Bianca inside. Right before closing the door Jess glanced down the alley in both directions and saw nothing. No one at either end. They hadn't been spotted going in which meant, unless one of the cops came around the corner in that absolute last instant as the door slammed, they'd made it. No one knew which door they entered.

"This way," the man repeated and Jess noticed he wasn't alone. It took a moment for her eyes to adjust, but as they hurried along and the lighting began to change she saw another man in the lead, one who looked like he was probably the heavy. Capable looking and athletic. Not that two guys, even if one of them was big and strong, were going to save them from a bunch of cops if it came to that, but she appreciated the effort.

She put her attention on their surroundings.

What the Conclave did well, it seemed, was hide. And these two, presumably Conclave men, led them on a twisting journey through a maze of rooms and hallways until she was sure no one could ever follow. Even *if* they managed to discover they'd gone in the red door.

Without a trace. She glanced back at Bianca who walked directly behind. The man who'd opened the door for them fell back and brought up the rear. Bianca looked almost normal in the shifting shadows, the face Jess knew so well, beautiful Indian features passing in and out of the variety of lighting. In her eyes, though, was burned that persistent look of terror.

At length they entered a room with one door in and no other, and Jess was reminded of the room Darvon brought her to when rescuing her outside the city. This one was different but she suspected that, like the other, it held a secret exit. Sure enough the big guy went to a bookshelf and, like an old-school spy movie, rolled it to the side to reveal a stairway leading down.

Moments later they were at the bottom and entering a large room with several more people in it, all dressed in the drab Osaka clothing, and an older woman was coming up to Jessica. Jess recognized her from her visit before, the kind-faced woman who brought her food and drink and took care of her when confronted with the Conclave for the first time.

"We've been watching for your return," she enthused, reaching out a friendly hand to Jessica's cheek. A look of reverent awe was upon her, as seemed to be the case with most of the others. "This is a sign!" she said. "There is still work for you here." The rest nodded agreement.

Jess smiled patiently.

"Graced," someone added.

"Victory is at hand," said another.

Then began an exchange among them over what she'd done, how she'd brought an end to the Crucible, the Shogun, the High Council and the Witch. In their effusive commentary she realized an awful lot of embellishing had been done, whether by Darvon or simply through the distortion of multiple retellings, but it seemed they had her pegged as the sole force responsible for all of that. *She* was the one that killed the bad guys, *she* was the one that destroyed the Crucible. There was no way to correct that misconception now, nor did she have the energy to even try, so she just let it all slide. It was true enough, she supposed.

They went on about how the Dominion was crumbling, in its death throes—again, thanks to her. How the end of tyranny was at hand, how her return marked the next phase of their efforts for freedom, how her actions had— and would—usher in a new age. As more crowded in, coming as word of her arrival spread, a gathering of people surrounding her, heaping praise and gratitude, she grew increasingly uncomfortable, hugging the Icons to her chest beneath the shirt, police gun still in hand, eyeing the gun Bianca held and the laptop she clutched.

Bianca offered no refuge, stunned as she was by everything and everyone around her. Overwhelmed was more like it. Nor was Bianca a target to which Jess could deflect any attention. All eyes were locked to her, and though Bianca was another Earth girl who must seem just as strange and possibly even angelic, it was almost as if she didn't exist.

Jessica was the center of their universe.

Finally the old lady took charge and led the two girls to a side room, away from the crowd, shutting the door and sealing off the awed conversation that continued outside. Jess was thankful for her intervention, too tired, too amped with everything that had happened over the last hours to do anything but stand before their waves of admiration in stunned silence. In the quiet of the windowless room she went to the center and stood.

"Wait here," the old lady smiled graciously. "Others will come." And she left.

Voices continued on the other side of the door, enthusiastic discussions, not loud enough to penetrate the thick wood with any clarity yet a constant buzz nonetheless. Otherwise the room they were in was calm. A sort of momentary sanctuary.

What now?

The furious adrenaline rush leading to that moment was ebbing and, though there remained a million unanswered questions, Jess was reluctant to jump to the next round of agonizing speculation and internal debates about what to do. Her life had become far, far too complicated, even for her normally analytical mind. Should she ask right away for Zac? Was she really about to start a brand new existence on a whole different world?

It felt suddenly unreal to be standing there at all.

Exhaustion was setting in. Not only was it getting late in the day for her (though the day was just getting started there in Osaka), the non-stop intensity of the last hours was abating. After all, you could only run scared for so long, she'd learned, until the body began to shut down.

She decided not to sit, afraid she might nod off. Bianca had already found her way to a couch and lowered herself to the edge, leaning forward with the laptop and the gun in her grasp. All at once she seemed to realize she was holding the pistol, held it out like a dirty tissue and set it on a nearby table. She clutched the laptop with both arms and Jess wondered if she was even aware she still held it.

Jessica's own cargo was getting annoying. The Icons, stuffed against her chest inside the skintight shirt. She decided to pull them out and set them on the same table, along with her own gun. She listened to their solid metal thunks as she set them down, then stood straight and stared at the four items. Two guns, inert, potentially deadly if used. Beside them two ancient alien artifacts, also inert.

Not much bigger than the guns, simple metal devices on the surface; so far beyond the guns in technology it was hard to imagine any similarities between them at all.

The guns could kill. The Icons were potential world-changers.

She held Bianca's gaze.

"Sorry I snapped," she said, partly to apologize, partly to engage her friend. Bianca stared back, eyes empty, then looked away, numb; straight ahead, to the far wall. Through the far wall. To infinity.

"This is happening," she said quietly, more to herself.

Jess felt her pain. She took a deep, steadying breath and let her gaze drift around the room, seeing details but registering none of it. At some point her stare came to rest back on the table, the Icons and the guns.

"Thanks," she said. "For trying to save me. At the house." She didn't want to remind Bianca too vividly of the actions that, in truth, were responsible for her even being there, but the intention behind her friend's amazing deed weighed on her. She wanted to thank her for the tremendous act of friendship. "I know I told you to stay in the room. And you should have. But when I saw you coming down the stairs, with a gun, ready to defend me. To fight for me ...

"What you did was beyond anything anyone else would've done. So thank you. For trying to save me."

"I couldn't let them shoot you." Bianca's voice was distant, though not as fearful as Jess would've imagined. She could see Bianca was calming.

It was a good sign.

At length her friend asked: "Who are these people?"

Jess sighed. "I met them last time I was here. They call themselves the Conclave."

"What did you do?" Bianca's question was couched in awe. Out in the other room she'd looked catatonic. Apparently she was listening closer than Jess thought. Apparently she'd heard everything about which the group marveled.

Jess shrugged, unsure what to say.

Bianca continued to study her. "They think you're their savior." Then, as if making a connection: "You're not normal, Jess. And I don't mean that in a bad way."

Great. Now her friend was making her feel uncomfortable. What she'd done, even till now, was driven by events beyond her control. *She* hadn't planned to come to Anitra the first time. *She* hadn't planned to do all the things she'd done while here. She had to do those things to get home. Everything else along the way just sort of happened. Same thing with escaping from the warehouse and everything that got them to the relative safety of this room.

Wouldn't someone else have done the same?

But even as she thought that she was forced to consider the possibility they might not. Maybe others would simply have failed. Maybe others would've just curled up and died. Jess definitely wanted to. More than once.

Bianca was shaking her head slowly.

"What you did to those cops ..." She couldn't finish, consumed with the recollection of what just happened.

Then she looked away. "It was scary. Like a whole different you. I mean, you got us through everything. All of it. From the warehouse, through the streets, past those cops to here ... each time the shit was going down ..." Her head continued shaking, ever so slightly, side to side. Bianca simply couldn't believe it. "You're a beast."

Jess inhaled. Forced to consider it.

Maybe I am *different.*

Then a knock at the door. She turned even as a man let himself in, followed by two others.

It was Chom, with Grisha and ... Perra? Jess tried to remember their names.

"Hello again," Chom smiled in greeting and closed the door. "You remember Grisha and Perra?" His introductions confirmed her recall.

"Hi," she said. Then, extending a hand toward the couch: "This is my friend, Bianca."

Chom and the others nodded to her. Bianca gave a small wave.

Then Chom's gaze drifted to the table and the guns, and

...

The Icons.

An expression crossed his face that Jess could not read, but which seemed like ... greed.

She began to grow nervous.

CHAPTER 17:

FUGITIVE

THE TEAM LEADER STEPPED back several paces. Everyone was reacting to the sounds within the crystal, moving away even as they continued, almost out of professional habit, to monitor readings. Instruments were now well off the scale. Indications from the crystal grew increasingly ominous as it popped and pinged with rising frequency, sound overlaying sound, each a sharp warning of the force contained within. Something titanic was about to burst forth, pressure stemming directly from whatever was in the center, and it was looking less and less each moment like a good idea to be standing near it.

For the team leader that primal fear came to a head all at once, unleashing a frantic impulse. "Drop it!" he ordered, wide-eyed and in action, waving to the operator—whose focus, like everyone else, was consumed with the slowly splintering crystal. "Drop it!" he shouted. "Everyone! On the excavator!" He began rushing around, snapping them out of their sluggish stupor. "Get out of here!"

The operator got the sense of urgency and unlatched the egg. *Whoomp!* It thudded to the ground, crunching into the glass sand even as it continued making obscenely powerful, deep-frequency pulses that foretold a catastrophic ending.

They had to get out of there.

"Let's go!" His team was moving, finally, following his direction, everyone sensing it now, hopping on the outside of the big blue excavator, grabbing onto whatever they could and holding on and, as the last man climbed aboard, the team leader yelled at the operator to drive. Fast. To get them out of there. The excavator lurched away, wheeling around and accelerating. The steam turbine rumbled with torque as it pulled harder than it probably ever had, racing away as fast as it possibly could.

Everyone held on, the team leader checking to make sure they all made it, that no one was left behind. The crystal had suddenly become a ticking time-bomb. There was no way to be sure what would happen, but it was long past time for being safe rather than sorry. The crystal might simply crack and fall apart. It might stop cracking and just sit there. All he knew was that, based on the amount of force registering at the center, there was a very good chance it would explode in a deadly hail of shards.

"Stop here!" he yelled, struggling forward to get the attention of the driver. "Stop here!" he yelled again and the guy saw him this time. Heard him.

"Why?" the man leaned out the window and yelled back, barely audible over the roar of the turbine. He was now as frantic to get away as the rest of them, reluctant to stop moving.

"Do it!" the leader yelled. "We're far enough! We've got to get behind something!" Right then, if the thing blew, the flying pieces might impale them.

The driver backed off the throttle and braked, turning the excavator to the side to form a barrier and brought it to a lurching stop.

"Everyone behind!" the leader yelled as he jumped to the far side of the machine. Anxiously he waved everyone over.

They got the idea. Scurrying awkwardly in their hazmat suits, the last man made it around the edge even as ...

The crystal exploded.

* * *

CAREFULLY JESS INCHED CLOSER to the table, not wanting to alert the three men to her concern yet suddenly fearful of the distance between them and the Icons. The shiny alien devices were the ticket to everything and, though she trusted the members of the Conclave, or thought she did, she didn't want to find out too late Chom was some sort of Dominion plant, a spy, or otherwise operating on greedy self-interest and after the Icon himself.

There were too many who would stop at nothing to get their hands on it. Let alone *two* of the priceless devices.

Chom looked away from them, away from the table and the Icons, to her, and as he did his expression relaxed and she realized it wasn't greed. More a reaction of disbelief. Or ... something like alarm.

Two Icons?! he seemed to be thinking.

"I see you have another," his attention fell back to the table, unable to look away though he was trying. It was as if he wanted to pretend they weren't affecting him as strongly as they were. "Darvon told us you escaped with the Holy Relic," he said. "Was there ... another? Back on Earth?"

Jess nodded. "I found that one right before I came here."

With an effort Chom pulled his eyes back to her and this time was able to hold her gaze.

"Forgive my surprise," he said. "It's just, you understand the significance of that single, small device. Now to see two ..." And he smiled. A genuine smile, filled with tired, resigned humor, and he seemed to relax a little more.

"Well," he said. "It looks like the adventure begins again."

She tried to smile with him. To share a little levity.

It wasn't easy.

"Is Darvon okay?" she skipped ahead. Chom's mention of Darvon reminded her how little she knew of current events. So much must've happened since she left.

"Yes. He slid back into life here, in Osaka. He filled us in on your heroic, some would say angelic," Chom gave a wry grin; he knew how she felt about her angelic status, "deeds."

Jess had already gotten a taste of what flourishes Darvon must've added to the story as he spread it among the Conclave. She'd just had to listen to them going on, back in that other room. On top of that the mythology must surely have grown on its own. By now, from what little she'd heard so far, they apparently thought she single-handedly brought down the Crucible; that she flexed her holy might and brought an end to the Shogun's rule and all else that came out of those events.

Chom, at least, seemed to have a more realistic impression of things.

"Now that you're here," he said, "the first thing we have to do is get you out. I'm sorry, but you won't be safe. Not in Osaka. From our sources we know the police are connecting the dots. It won't be long before they realize who you are and, from that, deduce how you got here. The Dominion seeks the Holy Relic, convinced it somehow survived the inferno of the blast."

"They don't know I left with it?"

Chom shook his head. "You they assumed dead with the rest. If they learn you're back then they'll know you escaped with it and, logically, used it to return. And, of course, that it must be with you, here, in the city.

"Even we won't be able to hide you."

"What about Zac?" She asked it, the biggest thing on her mind, bad timing and heedless of anything else that mattered right then but this mattered most and she had to know. "Is he here? In Osaka?" The three men looked at her with curious expressions.

Chom, of course, was the one to answer. "The Kazerai?" He shrugged. "We haven't heard much. He went with the Venatres."

Yes! Jess breathed an inward sigh of relief.

Zac stayed with the good guys.

Chom went on: "The Venatres used the opportunity of the ensuing chaos following events at the Crucible to withdraw, back across the ocean. Their fleet returned. Our operatives are in contact with Venatres agents and we're told the Kazerai, Zac, has been helping them." Chom paused, then continued with what Jess was sure he believed to be illuminating information: "Yamoto has been named the new Shogun. Fezna, a former cleric, is head of the new High Council. Fezna has Yamoto's ear. Together they've waged war, bent on taking over the entirety of Anitra. They have invaded Venatres land.

"At the moment they control the offensive."

Suddenly there was a commotion in the other room.

Chom and the two others turned to the door; Jess stiffened. The door opened and …

It was Darvon, behind him a sea of expectant faces, all looking eagerly for another glimpse of the Angel.

"Darvon!" she ran to him. He grabbed her up in an embrace, even as he enthused right beside her ear: "*Jessica!*"

Darvon! The same, short, pudgy Darvon she remembered, lifting her from her feet and spinning her around. He squeezed himself full of her and she squeezed him back, looking over his shoulder at all the smiling faces behind him, grinning at them both.

Darvon!

He sat her down and she looked up into his face—not far up, as they nearly saw eye-to-eye—Darvon absolutely beaming. Her own face ached with how wide her smile stretched, so happy was she to see him. She almost couldn't believe just how happy she was right then. All day she'd been panicked, afraid, running or in tears and now … she was smiling so hard it actually hurt. *Probably showing every tooth in my head.*

"I knew you'd come back!" His jovial cheeks were red and so relieved. She laughed and nearly cried but decided not to let herself go. There were too many strong emotions washing over her in that moment; letting go could turn into a festival of bawling.

She sniffed. Then, remembering Bianca, stepped back and looked to her. "This is my best friend, Bianca."

"Hello," Darvon went to her. Bianca stood from her seat and shook his extended hand, still confused by everything but rising from her earlier grief, fear and outright terror. Looking at her now Jess figured she was doing better, for the moment at least, much of the earlier trauma eased behind a wall of simple exhaustion.

Behind them in the other room the people of the Conclave continued to crowd around, trying to see. Chom restored a bit of order, politely shooed them back and closed the door. Darvon rocked eagerly on his heels, from his heels to the balls of his feet, smiling and smiling some more. Like a kid, so excited he couldn't stand it.

"I was just telling them we have to move," Chom informed him. "It won't be long before the police step up their search. Jessica's little sprint through the city created quite a scene."

To this Darvon grinned even wider, if that was possible, imagining the trouble Jess had caused, knowing what she was capable of, and she grinned happily with him; two adventurers, sharing something only they, together, understood.

She *did* have a way of making a scene.

"We've got to figure out how to get them out of the city." Chom was already planning what to do next. Darvon, on the other hand, was having different thoughts.

"She has to meet my family," he said.

For a moment Chom looked confused. "What?"

"My family. They want to meet her."

Jess stared at Darvon, equally bewildered.

Darvon's purity, however, that he could even think of something so seemingly unimportant at a time like this, touched her. Made her see the moment a little differently. And that, perhaps, was what it boiled down to. Meeting Darvon's family *was* important. In his simple way of looking at things it was *very* important. She was there. Now. And while she was, before she went away again, before she ran off to the next adventure, in his mind she had to—

"She saved my life," he explained. "Now may be their only chance to meet her."

Part of Darvon's disregard for the urgency of matters at hand, Jess realized, came from the fact that he truly believed she was near immortal. No harm would come to any of them as long as she was around. Everything would be okay, in his mind, simply because she was who she was.

Chom shook his head. "Darvon, that isn't going to be—"

"You have to make some connections," he insisted. "Right? I mean, she's not running out the door this second. Can't she go with me in the meantime?" He turned to Jessica. "It isn't far."

She couldn't help feeling the intensity of his love. How he

cared for her. Darvon was no idiot. He knew the pressing nature of the situation. Despite that, he believed with all his heart in what he was asking.

It was hard not to be affected.

She looked to Chom. "Is there time?" Then back to Darvon. "I mean, I *would* like to meet your family."

How Darvon could keep smiling wider, how he could keep getting more excited escaped her. He was such a friendly man. You just wanted to hug him. She very nearly did. Very nearly just randomly stepped over and grabbed him again in an embrace.

But in the midst of this Chom saw he would lose the fight.

"Fine," he agreed. "But don't make a spectacle of it." He stopped at that, making this point most strenuously: "There's too much anticipation spreading. This is bound to leak if we don't contain it. Do I have your word?"

Darvon stood straighter. "My word."

Chom went across the room and rummaged for a large sack. He brought it back and handed it to Jessica. "Put the Icons in here for now. I'll meet you at Darvon's." He looked at Darvon with another stern expression and took a moment to give the look to her as well. "When I come for you you need to be ready to go. Immediately, as soon as I arrive."

Both of them nodded and Darvon eagerly took Jessica's hand.

Thrilled.

CHAPTER 18:

A TYRANT IS BORN

THE CRYSTAL SHARDED VIOLENTLY. Giant chunks, sailing into the air in all directions, smaller pieces pinging off the excavator—at least one impact large enough to rock it, lifting the wheels on one side briefly off the ground. It was a tense moment, filled with yells and cringing fear, waiting as the large machine teetered above them, off balance, before slamming roughly back to all wheels.

For what seemed an eternity after that pieces of crystal both large and small continued crashing to ground, larger ones falling from height, throwing up plumes of glassed sand. There was no fire from the explosion, no heat, just a massive release of energy as the crystal egg gave from within, popping ears with a tremendous wave of overpressure that shot out in all directions. As the last chunks rained down all was quiet on the breezy plain.

The team leader hazarded a glance skyward, looking from beneath arms clasped tightly about his head. The rest of the science team were crouched around him against the excavator, holding their heads similarly, trying to make as small a target as possible.

He checked them. Everyone seemed unharmed. No injuries. Suits looked intact. That was the next biggest concern, as radiation exposure in that desolate wasteland would kill in short order.

Slowly he stood and the rest followed. He inched toward the rear of the excavator to get a glimpse of the site of the explosion. Was there anything left? Gleaming shards of crystal peppered the ground in a radius all around, almost as if the glass field had been salted with diamonds.

After the excitement of earlier, would this just end up some amazing mineral find? Mere gems to add to the Dominion coffers? Was the misshapen form at the center of the thing part of the crystal itself? Something with the built-up pressure that, once released from the ground, blew the whole thing apart?

But, he told himself, even if this were just a large gem, forged by the heat and fire of the Crucible's destruction, there were still things of scientific interest to be discovered. How did it form? What could be gained by it?

There would be much to learn.

And as he peered further around the back of the excavator, toward the site of the extraction, jaw falling open and eyes going wide, some distant corner of his mind began to scream.

* * *

THE PAIN! KANG HUNCHED. On his feet, doubled over in agony.

Aaaargh!

The rush!

He bellowed again. *"AAAARGH!"* This time he heard it. Other sounds came to him.

A breeze.

Sights now.

Light. Sunshine?

He squinted.

It was bright.

So bright!

Coalescing until ...

Shiny, glassy land, as far as he could see.

Like standing on a mirror, one that spanned the horizon.

But there was something else. Something breaking the uniformity. Something ... blue, off to his left.

A machine.

Still hunching, he turned his head and focused on it, squinting harder as it took form, markings and other things he recognized, frustrated at length when he was unable to dredge those memories from the depths of consciousness. Unable to make a connection. The familiarity of the thing teased him, flitting just at the edge of awareness. Sitting alone on the mirrored plain.

With an agonized effort he straightened. Stood tall. Taller. All the way, bellowing as he came fully erect, muscles stretching—tearing, it felt more like—bones cracking, yet he forced them even so. Extending his arms to either side, tilting back his head, face to the brilliant sun. He roared and the sound of his roar echoed heavy across the empty ground.

After a moment he turned his head back to the blue machine. Lowered his arms slowly.

It was ... a machine for digging. At that he noticed a hole nearby. Then, focusing further, crystalline objects of all shapes and sizes ranged around him, twinkling in the bright sun, incongruous with the flat landscape. More variety.

Judging by the sun's position it was either late morning or early afternoon. He could tell that much, and something else told him that, whatever his past, he'd been there before. Knew this world and its things. This was not Heaven, or the Great Beyond. This was not the Valorous Beginning, of which all great warriors dreamed.

And as he thought of that one word raced through his mind, burned and stuck. Like a flaming image imprinted in space:

Kazerai!

He was. Had been. Hand of God. A warrior, greatest of all warriors, and this was *not* the end. He had *not* passed on. He had remained, somehow.

Fueling yet another recall.

The last battle, fire and blackness, an instant among instants, fleeting, barely enough to register before ...

Darkness. Nothingness, in truth, as this awakening brought with it no sense of the passage of time. That blistering, agonizing, instant, then ...

Now.

Even in the Crucible, when being forged into a Kazerai— he remembered that time, vividly of a sudden, relishing these gathering thoughts, the memories that made him who he was—even when in the Forge, he'd known things.

Yes.

But not now.

How long have I been dead?

How long have I been ... alive?

Slowly he took a step.

Feeling returned. Pain.

Vigor.

Yes!

The breeze blew audibly past his ears.

He looked down, noticing his skin was a yellowed version of what had been. As of disease. Images of himself, of his former self, danced across his mind's eye, and what he saw was nothing like what he recalled. Yellowed, scaly; more like hide than skin.

Was this merely a dream? Or had he been ... reborn? If so, what had he become?

He turned to the blue machine, and as he did so his shadow cast across the ground before him.

In witness of it he let loose a titanic bellow.

A man in shape, two arms and two legs yet ... disfigured. Horribly. Thick limbs, muscular. More than that his head ...

Looked like the shadow of a demon.

He reached for it. Repulsed with what he felt.

He yelled again into the distance, inhumanly loud, clenching his fists in rage. Whipped his head furiously, trying to shake loose those infernal shapes.

They remained.

"What am I?!" It was a voice he recognized, his own, but with a rasp he could not clear. He tried. Coughed. Coughed again. It did not change. Would not. Like gravel.

Evil.

"*What am I?!*" Desperation gripped him. More recalls flooded back, more memories, more images and he began to get a terrible sense this was not a dream.

Something was very wrong.

"What am I?!" Nothing answered. No one was there. He stared at the machine sitting in the distance. No one inside. There was a smell, though, on the air. More distinct than he ever remembered any smell. And sounds. *Yes.* Faint—

so faint—the sound of breathing. Beating hearts.

There were men on the other side.

Hiding, sweating with fear.

With a roar he leapt into the air, clearing the distance in a single bound, over the machine and far across to the other side. He hit with a tremendous impact and crouched, smiling with the liberating sensation of the exertion. It took nothing to leap that far.

He stood and turned, as far away now on this side as he had been a moment ago on the other.

Yes.

There were men there. He saw them now. Quivering. Amazingly he could smell the suits they wore, their sweat, their fear as it was processed through ventilators and out over the wide, open plain.

With more restraint he took another leaping stride and was standing in front of them, a spray of glassed sand ricocheting from the machine as he slid to a stop. They squinted in terror, cowering before him.

He snorted, a reaction to the shimmering cloud—beyond his control, like a sneeze—and he paused at the sound of it. It was the sound of a beast, clearing its nose. He shook his horned head and snorted again. Studied the pale, sweating faces staring at him from behind shielded masks.

Dominion ...

He recognized the markings on their suits, on the great blue machine. Memories were returning.

"Citizens of the Dominion," he mused, listening to the rumble of his voice; a rumbling edge of power.

I am Kang!

Then he caught the edge of his reflection in a long section of metallic plating. Behind the driver's cab, a sheet of polished steel covering an access panel of some sort. Slowly he stepped before it, stunned at the visual manifestation of his disfigured shadow. He raised an arm, watching the image move with him.

No.

He raised the other arm. The reflection was a perfect mirror of his movement.

Of course it was him.

Of course.

His skull looked as if it had been hit with a blast beyond reckoning. Blown into two, crooked, misshapen extensions at either side, like a pair of terrible, hideous horns, bending away and out, one longer, the other curving almost forward. No hair to be seen. Skin a jaundiced yellow. And his face ...

His face. That was his.

It's me.

Locked into the middle of a demon's skull, sneering, eyes red, teeth jagged and nearly fangs yet ...

Me.

He started to laugh. A broken chuckle, somewhere deep within his chest, building to maniacal fervor. Laughter reserved for the damned. He watched himself, threw back his head and let it go, turning up the volume. It became a tremendous sound, echoing across the land into the distance; grim thunder that bounced back a haunted spirit. Before, as a Kazerai, he'd been proud, vain, in love with his handsome physique. Now he admired this monstrous body, kept looking at it in the reflective plating; yellowed and scaled, a man in form yet so much more. Hugely muscled limbs, clawed hands that were yet human; short, horned protrusions at his shoulders and, if he turned, along his spine.

Magnificent!

Only after some time did he notice the men were running. Had been, stumbling away as fast as they could in their little environmental suits. Hardly moving, it seemed.

He turned back to the large blue machine. Considered it. Once his strength had been legendary.

He reached and grabbed under the frame with one hand, set his stance and ...

Flipped it to its side.

He laughed again. As with the leap it went over *easy.* Flopping and creaking as tons of machinery twisted under the sudden, unusual movement, load stresses moving in entirely different directions than were ever part of its design.

He watched the blue, metallic mass settle, then went to the front. Grabbed a solid section of frame and ... flipped again, harder this time, sending it *into* the air, end over end, cartwheeling, hitting the ground several of its own lengths away. Loose pieces flew from it, braces and other parts reverberating with booming metallic clangs as it broke apart on landing ... *WHUMP!* in a fantastic plume of shining sand launching skyward.

Like a toy.

"*Yes!*" he bellowed into the distance.

Never had he been *that* strong.

As the cloud of glass rained down, cleared and drifted, he saw several of the men had fallen from the shock of the impact but were getting to their feet. It was a panicked escape, no sense or reason to it. A dozen of them, running in every direction, every man for himself, no possible destination in sight on the gleaming wasteland.

He needed answers.

With a single leap he reached one, hitting right by him in a landing that sent the man tumbling. Kang stepped and grabbed him, turned him to face him and lifted him high, holding the suited man at arm's length.

"Is the Dominion still in power?" he growled. The man writhed futilely in his grip, kicking.

Kang was patient. "I see you wear their insignia."

The man realized he could never escape. "Yes," he fairly whimpered. Kang could smell his sweat, his soiled suit as he shook, but at least the man was not too terrified to speak.

"Where is the Shogun? Ashikagi?"

There was a distinct tremor in the man's voice. "Ashikagi is dead!"

"Dead?"

Interesting.

"Yamoto is the new Shogun!" the man offered, perhaps growing a bit braver.

Yes, thought Kang, *be brave.*

He looked around. "This is where the Crucible stood?"

"Yes!"

And Ashikagi was dead. Yamoto the new Shogun. That must mean whomever was at the Crucible when it detonated—which was assuredly what had happened—was also killed. The Council. All of them.

Had Horus made it? The unpleasant image of that final encounter came to him, bitter-sweet in his moment of triumph.

What else had changed?

"Which way to Osaka?"

To this the man simply pointed a badly trembling hand. Kang followed his finger, over the horizon.

And grinned. This rebirth, whatever had happened to him, was truly momentous.

Casually he cocked his arm and hurled the man away, body fluids and shreds of environmental suit pinwheeling around the rubbery form as it arced into the distance—result of the massive acceleration. It was so sudden the man didn't even have a chance to scream. He was dead as soon as Kang made the toss.

Detached, almost serene, he watched the messy form until it hit the ground far, far away, curious with his own decision. It happened rather suddenly but, upon consideration, was the right thing to do.

Methodically he killed the rest. *Fascinating*, he thought as he worked his way through them, *how easy it is to bring a fragile life to an end.*

As he tossed the last, limp form aside, realizing by then the truth of what had happened—that he had, some impossible way, survived the fusion blast of the Crucible's detonation—he wondered if he himself could ever die.

* * *

SHOGUN YAMOTO KNELT FOR TEA, a delicacy brought by the Emperor Kagami more than a hundred years ago when first establishing the Shogunnate and the Dominion itself. The Emperor said tea came from Heaven. Whatever its actual source, Yamoto had to admit it was delicious. Special blends were grown there in Osaka for the royal ranks, using seeds from that original gift.

The thing Yamoto could do without, as with all the frills of station he found so annoying, was the ceremony that went with it. Make the tea, drink the tea. That was all that was needed, as far as he was concerned.

That, however, was not the way it was done.

Ceremony, too, came from the Emperor. Geishas, meant to mimic the angels in Heaven—from where the Emperor supposedly came—were trained in the Ceremony and administered the tea daily with tedious efficiency.

Yamoto watched, growing sleepy and impatient all at once, as he did most days, as the one nearest poured a cup with methodical precision. He adjusted the scratchy Shogun robes, themselves made of gifts from the Emperor, silk from special worms bred for that purpose alone. As with every day he used the quiet time to dream of a future where this nonsense did not exist.

"There was a disturbance today," Fezna spoke as the geisha finished her pour and rose to move to the next person. Fezna was at the ceremony, as were Damas and several clerics. Aides stood around the room, geishas executed the ceremony and Yamoto waited impatiently to drink his damn tea.

"Yes?" He stared at the steaming cup of brown liquid. Fezna had a habit of smiling no matter what news he delivered—while simultaneously making all news seem a bit troubling. He looked no different now. Yamoto could only imagine what little bit of information he was about to share. Probably nothing.

How he loathed the clerics.

"A Skull Boy," said Fezna. Yamoto looked up.

"Here, in the city," Fezna added, smiling that unreadable little smile. As if his mission were to cast shadows of alarm.

"A Skull Boy?" Yamoto noticed Damas was also surprised, though the clerics seemed unmoved. "Here in the city?"

Fezna nodded. "More info is coming. I just heard of it myself, before we arrived. City police are seeing to the investigation. I'm sure they have the matter well in hand."

At that moment a messenger came brusquely into the room, not waiting to be admitted. Two of the aides reacted too late, rushing to stop him, but the man was a soldier and pushed them aside. He stepped directly to Yamoto's end of the table.

"Sir," he stood respectfully before Yamoto and Damas, effectively ignoring Fezna and the others. Urgency was clear in his manner. "Something is wrong."

CHAPTER 19:

PROPHECY

"SHE'S SO CUTE!" Jess bounced Darvon's baby girl on her knee. Ereena was her name, just a year old, and she had the most adorable giggle. Mother had put blue bows in her hair, which matched her brilliant blue eyes, she wore a diaper just like a baby on Earth and was, in every way possible, human and, again, it struck Jess that they were on a completely different world. She held Ereena's face up to hers and touched her nose with her own, whispering a quiet little encouragement. And again Ereena let loose one of those magical little laughs.

Darvon had a family of girls. Ereena plus her two older sisters; one eight, one fourteen. Those were their Anitran reckoning of years, which didn't seem far from Earth's. Darvon's 14-year-old looked to be Jessica's age, more or less. They were all pudgy like their dad. Mom, in contrast, was short and skinny. All of them, however, had cherubic smiles that seemed incapable of a frown, filled with a jolly sort of built-in happiness that was difficult not to be affected by. Though so many terrible things had happened it felt safe in that room, the living room of their little apartment, sitting among them.

"She really likes you," said Darvon. Thrilled to have Ereena meet the Angel, to see his little girl showered with such divine attention.

"She's wonderful," said Jess. Then, directly to Ereena: "You're wonderful!" To which Ereena wriggled in delight.

The living room was a central room with no windows, Darvon's apartment not far from where she and Bianca had been brought after entering the red door. Darvon had apparently been headed to work when he got word of her return. A quick call to say he was sick and he was on his way at once. Now they were back at his place, waiting on

Chom.

To that end Jessica's head was still spinning. Trying to get a grip on what might come next, wrestling with an infinity of possibilities—the one, the only thing she knew for sure that she and Bianca needed to get out of Dominion lands.

In the meantime they had the Darvon's to distract them.

"Do you have a last name?" she asked. It was an odd, random question, but no one seemed to care.

"Hestron," Darvon's oldest daughter answered. "It's Anitran. Not one of the Emperor's names."

"The Emperor brought many things with him," Darvon explained. "Names among them."

"Do *you* have a last name?" It was the 8-year-old. Jess could see that, while the girls were in slight awe of her from everything their father must surely have told them, they studied her with barely concealed scrutiny. As if trying to determine how she was an angel after all or, the other possibility, if she was just a regular girl like them. Jess welcomed their effort. She wanted them to see her for what she truly was. No wings. No halo. No special powers.

"Paquin," she said. "I've got an older sister too. You're lucky. Older sisters are awesome."

The two chubby girls looked at each other and smiled.

"More tea?" The mother.

Jess nodded. "Sure."

Mom went to the kitchen as Jess continued playing gently with Ereena. Off to the right Bianca sat in a recliner, slightly removed from the group. The conversation so far hardly concerned her, everyone enthralled with Jessica, and as the rigors of the day set in Jess could see her friend was about to be out like a light. She knew she herself should rest too, not knowing when she'd get another chance, but there was no way Darvon and his family were going to leave her alone, even for a second.

Mom returned with a fresh cup of tea. Jess shifted Ereena to one side and took the little white teacup. She blew on it, then noticed Ereena's fascination with what she was doing. She held it lower so she could see. "Tea," she informed her, then blew on it and showed her the ripple across the clear brown surface. She blew again gently so she could see the effects of her breath. "Mmmm," Jess closed her eyes in rapture, sniffing the steam. Ereena watched all this with huge interest, then smiled at Jessica's yum face. With all ten little fingers she reached and touched her lips, the contact bringing instant joy. Ereena smacked her hands together, giggling with pure excitement. Jess laughed and so did everyone else.

"What a great mother you'll make," Mom said as they shared in Ereena's amusement. Bianca roused a little at the commotion, but as the merriment faded so did she, and as the room quieted once more she was gone, head lolled to the side in a deep sleep.

Darvon watched Ereena, who in turn studied Jessica as she began taking careful sips of the hot tea.

"She can't get enough of you," he said.

At that Jess noticed the mother admiring her intensely. Too intensely for the moment, it seemed, then, unexpectedly, Mom's lip trembled, ever so slightly, and she said with absolute sincerity: "Thank you." And all at once her eyes were glistening in the soft light. "So much."

Jess lowered the tea.

"For saving our Darvon," Mom cried a little then stopped. Still smiling that rosy-red smile, tears trickling onto her cheeks. "For getting him back to us." The sudden emotional shift choked Jessica up, before she even knew what was happening, before she saw it coming, and she looked at Darvon who was also tearing and ... the daughters' eyes, likewise, had turned red.

Jess did not want to cry. Not there. Not then. She felt like she'd cried enough for an entire lifetime. She wanted to be done with crying. But she couldn't hold it back. Not at first. She was tired, exhausted, emotionally spent and ... the sadness came, welling up, and in seconds she and the Hestrons were sitting there looking at each other, silent tears rolling down everyone's cheeks. It felt instantly silly, and Jess got herself in check, but it was too late to hide the mark of her emotion.

"*He* saved *me*," she said to all of them. "Didn't he tell you?"

Mom and daughters looked to Dad.

"I called for help," Darvon admitted. "But only after I ran. Jessica was the hero. She saved us all."

They all looked at Jessica as if, indeed, she were the angel she truly wasn't.

The 8-year-old shook her head. "The car chase," she said. "The police. The fight in the streets. Escape from the city."

"The attack on the Crucible," the older girl chimed in. "Death of the Shogun. The Council. Everything. We owe you." Now that they were remembering the fantastic nature of her actions—as related by their father—their regard was tilting back in favor of angelic status. Awe returned. In Jessica's lap Ereena considered her sisters, much too gravely for a baby; looked up at Jessica, pointed a finger at her face and goo-gooed something very profound. As if admonishing the angel, that she should consider herself more carefully.

You are *powerful*, she seemed to say.

Somehow even Ereena had the image.

Jess wanted desperately to take the focus from herself. She got the idea to speak to Ereena directly, to acknowledge her for whatever she'd just said. "Thank you," she lowered her face to look right into Ereena's upturned eyes. "Thank you for saying so."

Ereena smiled. Then, helping to reduce the weight of the moment, Bianca snored. A snort, followed by a long drag of air and a shift of her head. Drool sparkled at the corner of her mouth.

Lovely, thought Jess.

Mom smiled and wiped away her brief tear fall and looked more closely at Ereena. "Either she just said something incredibly meaningful," she stood and came over, "or she's trying to tell us she needs a new diaper." She reached and took Ereena from Jessica.

"Or both," offered the older daughter.

Mom peeked inside the diaper leg. "Yes," she finished

her inspection, "I think both." She gathered Ereena all the way into her arms. "Looks like a little pee," she announced and turned to the 8-year-old. "Help me change her?"

"Sure." The younger girl rose and went with Mother to another room, leaving Jess alone with Darvon and his oldest daughter.

And the drooling Bianca.

"You seem so normal," the older girl commented when Mom and her sisters were gone. Jess regarded her, round face pretty in a chubby sort of way. Essa was her name, though her pet name was Egg. So far Darvon had called her that exclusively.

"I am normal," Jess insisted. "So many things could've happened differently. If I wasn't there when Zac fell none of this would've happened. He probably would've come back once he figured out how to use the Icon and that would've been the end of the story. My story, anyway."

"But it wasn't," Darvon pointed out, as if that were proof enough. "You were there for a reason." He was emphatic. "You're *here* for a reason."

Egg added: "The Prophecy says a lot about these events."

Jess looked at her. She seemed smart. Like one of those honors-type kids who got perfect grades and was wise for her age, not easily fooled by the wiles of the world. How could she buy into any of this?

Darvon smiled. "I know you think we're simple—"

"I don't," Jess corrected. But Darvon held up a hand as if it were completely okay if she did.

"The Prophecy is old," he said. "The Conclave has just been the most recent to revive it. It was lost long ago, in the anarchy following the Darkness, after the Great Wars. As I mentioned before, when you were last here, the Prophecy was foretold by a powerful priestess. Aesha was her name. During the Great Wars. We know of her and the Prophecy as, despite the ruin and catastrophe of that time, her legacy was preserved. When all else fell to ruin, after the Wars, the Prophecy was passed forward. It may have been altered, we don't know, but the message is clear: an Angel will come, bring down evil and herald a Golden

Age."

Bianca snored. Jess glanced between Egg and Darvon, curious at this greater explanation.

"So that's all it predicts?"

Darvon looked at his daughter then back at her. As if to say, *It's okay. She may be the Angel, but she doesn't actually know anything about why she's here.* Perhaps that was part of the mystique. Perhaps her resistance to these things, perhaps her genuine ignorance only re-enforced their convictions that she was in fact the One on whom they waited.

It was frustrating.

"When the Emperor came Anitra was in bad shape," said Darvon. "Ripe for dramatic change. In the wake of the horrors of the Darkness our world had begun a new religion that, we believe, was slowly becoming a ray of hope, but it was yet unformed, unstable. It became Kagami's greatest competition. Once he began his path of conquest, eliminating all challenges became one of his earliest objectives. And the Prophecy and what it promised was his biggest threat. Unfortunately the majority of the world saw more hope in what *he* promised. After all, he was a living, breathing deity incarnate. All the Prophecy had to offer was the words of a long-dead priestess. Kagami was real. He brought real hope from another place, from Heaven, so he claimed, and the rate at which he gained followers was unstoppable. Soon he had swept away the old, the Prophecy and all things connected to it.

"As is the case with such things, however, you can never completely remove the truth. Believers remained. There were those who preserved the knowledge and brought it forward."

Jess regarded them both. "You guys."

"Eventually, yes. The Conclave brought back the Prophecy and stands ready as its guardian. Ready to assist the angel when she comes." At this he smiled. Jess shook her head.

"So you think Kagami is from Heaven," she said. "Yet you also think he was evil."

Darvon's expression confirmed this was so.

"Kagami was cast out," he explained. "He presented himself as a god. Most believed that. Most followed him, and the Dominion was formed. *They* believed he was divine. Others believed he was just a man, from some fantastic yet explicable origin. That, mostly, is how the world has been divided.

"There are those, however, who believe the truth is more sinister. As I mentioned before, they—we—believe Kagami was a demon, cast from Heaven. The same demon the Prophecy foretells would come, at the head of a powerful army, bringing much suffering and sorrow before the dawn of our victory. The angel would herald that moment. Aesha saw that clearly."

Aesha. At the second mention of this name Jess rolled it around her head. *Aesha.* Priestess. The one who created the prophecy that, inadvertently, thanks to a bizarre set of circumstances, had set her up as an angel. At least in the eyes of the Conclave.

"And this, Aesha," it felt strangely liberating to say it, "was a priestess in your ancient world?"

"We know little of her, in fact. Only that she was central to events of that day, and that she set in motion a future that, according to her prophecy, would lead to this day."

Jess was reminded of the various prophecies of Earth. Both religious and non-religious. It seemed there was no shortage of predictions for future doom and, in some cases, salvation. Some prophecies had criteria in order to be saved, others gave no options whatsoever. In those cases fate was fate. This prophecy hardly seemed different from any of those except, somehow, she'd ended up right at the crux. *She* was the one that would bring salvation. To an entire world.

Ugh.

Darvon regarded her. "So you see why we believe. You've come and done everything we've waited for, everything the Prophecy predicts. You're from the same place the Emperor came from. The priestess, Aesha, long ago, saw the future. *You're* the angel she foretold. *You're* who she saw. Now, in one short visit, you've turned the tide of this world. Now you've returned and you see how we believe there are great things for you yet to accomplish ..." he trailed off, reflecting. "This is a wonderful time." He looked directly at her, full of that deep, trusting admiration that made her so uncomfortable.

She looked to Egg, hoping to find her a little less enthralled.

No luck.

Both of them held her, at least for that moment, in infinite regard. The snoring Bianca was the only thing giving the scene any perspective.

"I don't know how many times I can say this," she tried to reason with them, "but I'm not the person this priestess predicted would come. I'm not an angel, that's for sure. What makes you think she could see the future? How could she have known any of this? How could anyone? I'm just Jessica. I got caught up in all this stuff but I'm not driving it. If anything it's coincidence."

Darvon just looked at her and she realized she was heading down the wrong path. No matter the contradictions, no matter the impossibilities, she had no right poking holes in anyone's beliefs. She herself had never been religious, though she made it a point not to attack anything anyone else held sacred. Anything was possible, or so she told herself, and though this whole Prophecy thing was about as far from likely as you could get, she had to allow for the possibility that it could, somehow, be true.

If nothing else, she couldn't undermine Darvon. Any of them. He was too sweet and so were they. They'd helped her and were helping her and would help her again. And they weren't, at the end of it all, sitting around telling her what to do. They weren't saying, "Go do this, go do that," or, "the Prophecy says you're supposed to blah blah blah." No, they simply believed she would do whatever it was she was going to do, and the result would be peace and prosperity.

No pressure.

"I guess it doesn't matter," she said. "But try and see

my point of view. I'm from another world, a lot like this one—a *lot* like this one—and if that's where Kagami came from then he's a normal person like me. Not something beyond you. Not a demon. I'm not saying the Prophecy can't be true. I'm just saying it may not be as mysterious as it seems."

"It's not mysterious," said Darvon. "Aesha had power. Real power. She said the one who came would be like her, and likewise would have power unrealized.

"Look at all you've done."

Jess wanted to argue but couldn't. How could she deny it? Even though she herself knew what she'd accomplished had nothing to with extraordinary power or angelic forces.

She just … did stuff.

Darvon seemed to know exactly what she was thinking. "I'm not necessarily talking about mystical power," he said. "Things we can't understand. Wings and halos and all that. Kagami was powerful. Do I think he was a true demon? But look at all he did. He formed the Dominion, a legacy that lives on even to this day. That's power. Could he fly? Could he shoot lightning from his fingers? Probably not. All that matters are results. And he achieved vast, terrible results. Already you've undone great chunks of that. You've achieved results, Jessica, and the Dominion is crumbling." He smiled at her; one of those friendly, *I'm so sorry but you're wrong*, smiles. *Tsk tsk* that she couldn't see who she really was. Said: "You can't deny that."

To her increasing agitation she allowed herself to be baited. "Then why didn't this Aesha just set things right? If she had power? When the world fell into chaos the first time? If she had real power why didn't she use it?"

Of course Darvon had an answer. "There was too much evil," he said. "Too much decay within the ranks of her own forces. She tried. Everything she did … She tried. All was brought down from within, even as the Great Wars swept her civilization away." Darvon became more insistent: "Even the most powerful need support. Aesha couldn't do it alone. Nor can you.

"This is why we stand ready."

Egg sat straighter. "I know it sounds crazy," she said, and it looked, at last, as if she saw that it did. "We don't know, obviously, if any of this is real. We can't. But we do have evidence. Scientific evidence, of the Great Wars and all that went before, and we can see that some of the things the Prophecy makes reference to did happen. What we believe is that this priestess, Aesha, discovered some great knowledge, something that struck fear into the leaders of her day, that they forbade this knowledge, the people cried out and, as a result, the Great Wars began.

"The Conclave believes the Wars had to do with this forbidden knowledge. An ancient secret and Aesha's effort to make it known. Her effort to bring enlightenment to everyone. Freedom. That was her purpose." Egg shifted a little in her seat; made herself more comfortable. "It scared those in power. The idea of an enlightened populace threatened their control.

"Ultimately it got Aesha killed."

Eve, thought Jessica. It was the Eve story. Yet another crossover concept. In Earth lore Eve was portrayed as wicked, but in truth it was her threat to a greater power that brought about her ruin. Her effort to spread knowledge. *History is written by the victors*. Aesha, as Eve, was crushed by the wrath of something greater. Eve was painted as the bringer of ruin when in fact she strove to bring enlightenment. A dangerous proposition when dealing with a vengeful god or a would-be enslaver. Information, truth; these things were poison to one who wanted unquestioning devotion.

And for a moment Jess wondered if Aesha, too, was simply the mythology of some religious text. Not a real person at all but, rather, a metaphor for the perils of disobedience.

Egg went on. "The Prophecy foretells of this future angel possessing similar knowledge," she said, "the power to prevail. To use it to elevate the world to a Golden Age."

Jess shook her head imperceptibly. She held no special knowledge, that was for sure.

A knock at the door shattered the conversation. Darvon rose and went to the other room. Jess and Egg looked at each other as he answered, out of sight, greeting people. Bianca roused at the changing noises, coming a little awake as Darvon returned, followed by Chom and another man Jess hadn't yet seen.

"This is the Daimyo," Chom introduced him. Egg stood and Jess did as well. Jess extended a hand out of habit and the man took it and shook. Though she knew he was of considerable rank among them, he nevertheless looked on her with the same awed fascination as everyone else.

Chom spoke to her. "We need to get you both something to wear."

Egg took that as her cue and rushed off. Bianca was fully awake now, sitting in the chair looking at the people standing around the room, starting to freak again as reality interrupted her fitful slumber.

"Come," Jess reached a hand for her, making a pre-emptive strike at staving off the terror. Bianca looked at her like she was an alien, then got a grip, took her hand and stood.

"This is the Daimyo," Jess introduced him. Bianca pulled herself together and shook his hand. It was what she knew she was supposed to do, but Jess could see the confusion on her face.

"They've ramped up their activity in the city," Chom kept things moving. "Military and even Astake are involved. The whole Skull Boy thing combined with everything else has them on high alert. We can't use our normal channels."

The Daimyo spoke. "We have deals in place for such situations." He looked at Chom, then back at Jessica. "We've found a way to get you out of the city, to Venatres lands."

And Jess thought immediately of Zac.

CHAPTER 20:

AN EVIL WIND

STORM WINDS PELTED KANG with rain as he strode the rolling hills, headed in the direction of the city. Recalls flashed through his mind, images like strobes, in sync with the crack of lightning, replaying from his final moments as a Kazerai. *Horus!* Their epic battle on the fields outside the Crucible. Sounds of the warning klaxons. The imminent destruction. The agony—no, the fury—at losing that battle, at being handled by Horus at every turn, at being unable to defeat him. Vivid now, these memories, where before there had been only darkness. In the hours following his "awakening" many things had returned to him.

Foremost among them his failure.

He walked now, done for the moment with leaping. Not because he was tired. He doubted he would ever tire. No, he walked because these memories had gradually consumed him and he found the steady pace less distracting. He knew he was brooding. Could nearly imagine the rain hissing from his seething hide.

He chose to let the hate run its course.

To let the memories inspire him.

Horus himself must surely be dead. At the last Horus had jammed him deep into the ground, presumably to contain him while he made his own getaway. That was the last thing Kang remembered. Whether Horus escaped or not ...

Angrily he lashed out at a tree. It was off the path he traveled but he lunged for it, swinging two punches and bringing it down. The first punch was enough, as it turned out, cleaving the mighty trunk in a splintering snap, the second already on the way and simply making the destruction that much more thorough.

He reveled in this new power. He *was* stronger than

before. Much stronger. A wicked grin stole across his face. At the moment he made for Osaka, but for what purpose? To turn himself in? Subject himself to the grip of the Dominion once more? Become its faithful servant and tool?

Truthfully, he had not yet thought it through.

As he continued on in the pouring deluge, leaving behind the felled tree, a distant sound reached him. He looked up. It was a continuation of the random thunder but ...

Was not thunder.

Steady. Powerful. Still far away but clear to his greatly attuned hearing.

Something approached.

* * *

AKIDO, GREAT KAZERAI, stood on the bridge of his airship as it cut the driving rain. The craft moved ahead steadily, not too quickly, high enough to scan wide sections of the hilly terrain yet low enough to spot a man-sized target.

A monster is more like it, he thought, hands behind his back, surveying the lands ahead with supreme confidence. The wide bridge monitor afforded a spectacular view as they flew. He glanced occasionally at his crew as they, too, scanned for any sign of their objective. So far nothing, and though he devoted his full attention to the effort Akido could not stop replaying the images from the brief video in his mind, the ones relayed by the scientific crew at the site of the Crucible before they were slaughtered. Video of the yellow, horned beast, a living demon, destroying one of their machines then turning its wrath on them.

A monster indeed. Whatever the science team found out there was unlike anything ever seen or recorded.

Akido had been dispatched to capture it, if possible, destroy it if not. The thing was last seen heading toward Osaka, and though the city was a long way off they had to assume that was its eventual objective.

It could never be allowed to reach it.

"There," one of the crew pointed.

"I see it," Akido had just spotted the small form below, striding along a section of open ground between hills. It was the thing from the video, and as the crew zeroed in on it he studied it more closely. It looked up and, though he knew it was impossible, he felt as if it found his gaze and locked eyes with him. Somehow, right through the monitor. An involuntary shudder shook him and he immediately admonished himself for the reaction.

No beast could stand against a Kazerai.

Still, it was ...

Hideous. An abomination from God knew where. He tried to imagine how it had come to be.

No matter its origin, he thought as he prepared himself to confront it, deciding all at once how this would play out. *I'll simply kill it and tell them there was no other way.*

Capture would not be part of his efforts.

This thing does not deserve to live.

* * *

KANG WATCHED THE TREMENDOUS MACHINE move across the sky. He stared into it though he saw no windows, knowing there were yet men inside. It was an airship, one such as the ones he recalled flying during his life as a warrior for the Dominion, and as he stared at the markings on its side memories took form and he recognized the sunburst emblem of the Kazerai.

Excellent.

Could he leap to it? Pound his way in, wrest control and fly it away? It was massive, far larger than the excavator and far more powerful. He wondered if even his vast strength would be enough to bring it down. There was no need for further debate, however, as the ship began heading for a landing.

He was its target.

Of course they've come for me. After all, he'd killed their little science team, hadn't he? And even if he hadn't, he himself must be quite a curiosity. Survivor of the nuclear blast, reborn; once great Kazerai, once under their control now ... what? Enemy? His existence must surely be challenging their response. Did they even know it was him? Their faithful servant, Kang? Like as not they didn't. Not yet. But no matter. Decisions crystallized. Any lingering doubt ... falling away. He had a mind for another option. Had a mind, with this new power, to see exactly what heights he could reach. It seemed he had nothing to lose, everything to gain. And here, on this rain-soaked field, would be the first test of his transformation. The first step on his road to Godhood.

Slowly the airship descended. As it drew near, the power of its mass impinging on him, he made himself move closer. Closer still, testing his might—until he was standing directly in the face of its fury, seeing what he could withstand. Wind, then rain, then finally wet earth whipped him with incredible force as the airship settled to ground, engines thundering white-hot with a blast that destroyed the ground beneath. He was so close that, he was sure, anything living would have been killed. Trees, people—nothing could withstand that force. Nothing, even, could've withstood the mere energy of its sound. His skull should've been crushed, sensitive ears destroyed.

For him, however, it was but a gentle breeze. He found himself laughing in the face of it, unable to hold back the mania. Soon the colossal machine was on the ground, settling it's bulk and ...

It shut down. The sudden silence was nearly as overwhelming as the prior ferocity and his laughter boomed in its absence. He was still laughing, in fact, when a door on its side opened. He reined it in, as out stepped ...

A Kazerai.

Kang recognized the clothing. Recognized the stature, the bearing, the cocky confidence. Remembered how he himself had once stood the exact same way, a sneer on his once-human face.

His laughter faded further.

"I am Akido," the man announced, as if it mattered. He paused a moment, then jumped easily to the ground and stood several paces away. "Do you speak, monster?"

Akido. Images gained form and Kang recognized his brother, even as he debated his first move, eager to test his might against this formidable foe. He knew well how powerful a Kazerai was. Akido, one of the Five that were part of his past brotherhood, along with the despised Horus. He had no particular hate of Akido, now that he knew him, and in fact had gotten along with him, barely, working together at least in battle. But Akido and any other surviving Kazerai would only stand in his way.

Therefore Akido must die.

Kang smiled. Akido did not recognize him.

"Do you not know me, friend?"

And suddenly Akido did. Saw Kang's face pasted on the monstrous skull and quailed. Briefly, only briefly, but Kang could see his foe recoil within himself. He grinned wider.

"Yes," he confirmed. "It's me."

The resulting stare-down stretched. Akido, alone, no one further emerging from the ship, standing in the mud, rain falling steadily from the heavy, gray skies, mind working to understand the monstrous vision before him, working not to react further or show fear. Kang grinning the whole time. Though a glimmer of concern haunted him, for as yet he had no true measure of his new power. In the past a fight between he and Akido would've been legendary. As had been the fight with Horus. The thought of that sent a wave of anger rippling through him. But now how would he fare? How much greater had he become?

Time to find out.

"You must be wondering where my intentions lie," he eased his grin, staring deep into Akido's eyes. Akido did not speak. "I think you deserve the truth. I could attempt to do this otherwise. I could rely on your faith, in my past, perhaps, use some clever trick to gain control. Claim helplessness, pain, dementia.

"But this is my new beginning, and I intend to command by force." At this he mused a little, imagining the glory of it. "Yes. And I believe fear will be part of my reign." Then, raspy voice clear through the storm: "Whatever happens, however, I do not intend to begin my rule with a trick.

"So, my dear Akido, here it is: I intend to kill you, take your ship, return to Osaka and assume my rightful place as Emperor. This isn't personal, you see. The simple fact is I have no room for competition." At this Kang gave him a fanged smile. "And," he added, taking a more aggressive stance; preparing for combat, "in order to do that I must fully explore just how powerful I've become."

By then Akido had come to grips, at least, with the fact that the fight was at hand. And, fearful or not, afraid of what Kang had become or not, the unshakable confidence he had as a Kazerai, the knowledge through both training and experience that he was nigh-on unstoppable surged and he was ready. He set himself, leaning forward.

Kang moved first. In that instant between instants, as Akido made to do the same, Kang beat the Kazerai to the punch.

BOOM! the impact rang loudly through the wet air, across the soggy land, Akido driven into the side of the airship with epic force; as much as Kang could muster—so much so that the airship actually *moved.* Slid in the muck about half a pace, landing struts digging grooves. The impact actually formed a dent in the massively thick armor.

Impossible!

Kang rebounded, hit the ground on his feet and dug in, watching as Akido's body held briefly against the side of the ship—stuck to the depression in the armor—then slid away and flopped to the sloppy ground. It was his eyes, however, that held Kang's keen interest. Akido's eyes were glazed! Stunned! And when he hit the ground, in that first instant, he did not move.

He was unconscious.

Dead!?

Could it be?! Kang reveled in the possibility of it. *That fast!* He stood there in rapture, chest heaving, himself barely affected by the force of his own attack, fists curled at his sides, staring with immense satisfaction at the fallen Akido.

Then the downed Kazerai stirred and pushed himself to

his knees. And for a moment Kang's glee collapsed into fear, and he wondered in that terrified instant if a Kazerai could be killed. Could this battle go on forever?! One had never been killed by an outside force. Even he, in the wake of a nuclear blast, had not died, but had instead grown *stronger.*

Could Akido die?

Kang lunged at him, before he had a chance to gain his feet. Before his own fear could take hold. Akido let out a pained grunt as Kang slammed into him once more, tumbling across the ground beneath the airship and out the other side in a spray of rain and mud. Real thunder punctuated the attack, shaking the ground with a low rumble and adding, in Kang's mind, a sense of drama. He laughed a short laugh, right on the heels of the fear of a moment before, and he wondered if he had, in addition to the other, more obvious changes, become insane.

Akido struck him, alert now, and Kang let him, wanting to know just how far he might go. The punch was painful. Enough to make him decide that experiment needed no further testing. The Kazerai were powerful and they could hurt him.

But not defeat him.

He blocked and redirected two more punches, keeping Akido near, then grabbed his fist with the third and hurled him skidding away. His own center of gravity seemed much better than when he was a Kazerai. Like he could plant himself with more authority. And as he watched Akido tumble and flail across the watery ground he noted he himself hardly moved from the effort.

Akido arrested his motion and stood, a hundred or so paces away. Now he was fully recovered from Kang's initial attack and looked to be deciding how to proceed. Kang pushed off in a horizontal leap right at him and Akido met him with one of his own.

WHACK! they hit in an explosion of skin and rain, locked in a deadly embrace, flying away from the impact as one twisting, writhing form, each trying to gain purchase on the other.

Kang won the effort before they hit the ground.

WHUMP! they hit and rolled, Akido working desperately to free himself from what had become a rear choke. Kang, at his back, had one forearm locked around his neck, the other across his head. He looked up as they rolled to a stop, fending off Akido's efforts with relative ease. The Kazerai were strong—he was remembering just how strong—but he had clearly become much stronger. Sinking in the choke he looked across the field through the driving rain, seeing the airship and how far they'd moved from it in just a few quick actions. He squeezed tighter, knowing the Kazerai did not necessarily need oxygen to live, as their bodies had become so radically changed from the Crucible. Attempting to choke Akido would be pointless.

But that was not his objective.

With a grunt, one that followed into a deep, bellowing roar, he locked his grip on Akido's neck and squeezed. With every bit of power he could bring to bear, losing himself in a cloud of red, filled with a primal rage, knowing nothing beyond the effort of the clutch. Nothing beyond his absolute determination to destroy his opponent.

RRRRRRAAAAR!

Then a snap. Sooner, perhaps, than expected. A titanic snap, beyond that of any bone or anything human, echoing sharply across the distance. The sound of a neck breaking that was stronger than steel. Stronger than anything, that neck, able to withstand any force and yet ...

It broke.

And Akido went limp in Kang's grip.

For a moment he stayed that way, then Kang eased his efforts. Laying on his back, looking up, vision clearing, feeling the drops of rain hit his eyeballs in a steady rhythm as he cooled, splattering away; beginning to feel Akido atop him.

Dead.

"*Yes!*" With an exultation he hurled the body away and stood.

He'd killed a Kazerai!

And with a rising sense of victory he turned and looked

at the airship.   Symbol of Dominion power; mighty, indomitable, sitting across the rain-soaked field.

Waiting.

CHAPTER 21:

THE WAY OUT

THE EXTRACTION WAS URGENT, made more harrowing by the obvious tension in their handlers, the two men tasked by the Conclave to get them out of the city.

"This way," Aber directed, the muscular "heavy" from earlier who met Bianca and Jessica at the red door and led them to safety. He had returned to lead them to their next destination and they'd been following him for some time, along with another man, named Tenko, a swarthy, quietly efficient guy who was supposed to have the connections to get them safely away from Osaka and on across the ocean to the land of the Venatres.

Jess hitched her backpack tighter. In it was the laptop and the two Icons and, again—as had been true since they left the hidden rooms of the Conclave and forged into the bustle of the city—she felt the weight of their burden. Far beyond mere pounds or kilograms.

She carried the treasure of two worlds.

Behind her Bianca stayed close. That they could be out there, just the four of them, in the heart of the enemy capital, rubbing elbows with the oblivious masses, a simple backpack all that stood between the priceless artifacts and the rest of the world, made her feel naked beyond belief.

Both she and Bianca wore the plain black clothes of the Dominion, uniform shirts and slacks from the closet of Darvon's oldest daughter, Egg, having left their own clothes behind. In that they blended with the other pedestrians on the streets, though the look of dread on their faces must surely give them away. Jess felt like she was positively beaming fear; like a lighthouse or something, even as she tried her best to hide it. Bianca wasn't hiding it well at all. Her friend looked absolutely terrified, jumping at everyday things. Jess had long since stopped trying to calm her, worrying that, as soon as the pace relented and they had time to sit, Bianca would finally lose it.

As she hitched up the backpack for the hundredth time she saw her bare wrist and thought of the bracelet Mike gave her. Before leaving she gave it to Egg. The girl had been so wide-eyed at the gift Jess though she might actually faint. During their short stay with Darvon's family she noticed Egg eyeing the shiny silver band set with its sparkling red stones, as if imagining it to be some sort of supernatural talisman. At least that was the wonder she displayed when Jess handed it to her. Jewelry, any sort of affectations, really, didn't seem common there in Osaka, so whether the bracelet bore divine connection or not it was still quite a significant gift. Egg was beyond thrilled. Jess knew she would take care of it.

Letting it go panged her, of course, but there was no more use for it. In fact getting rid of it was necessary so as not to draw attention for the next leg of their journey. The bracelet was all she had left of Mike but, sadly, Mike, like most of the things she cared for back on Earth, had become simply another part of her past. Her future, her survival, lay along a different path. One that did not include him.

They turned as Aber led them briskly down stairs to a subway train that was arriving, queued up with other passengers making the afternoon commute and got on. As everyone grabbed a handhold Jess swayed a little, steadying herself. She was exhausted and on terrified alert all at the same time.

The train pulled away.

Nervously she scanned the other faces aboard, trying not to make eye contact. Bianca looked straight ahead, across the car—through it, really, a thousand-yard stare—zoned out, freaked out, the train only strengthening her self-imposed cocoon.

Surely someone will stop us. Two teenage girls, the precise description of the Dominion search, pale, frazzled, obviously not relaxed, being hustled along between a meathead and a wary-looking businessman. One girl wearing a suspiciously lumpy backpack. *Aren't many people wearing backpacks*, she noticed. Unlike Earth, where every city around the globe was full of them. The Dominion was *looking* for two teenage girls. And there they were. *We might as well be wearing signs!*

The train clacked along.

Earlier Chom introduced Tenko at Darvon's place. For a while after that things became all business, the men briefing them on what was to occur, who would do what, where they would go and so forth. Getting them dressed, packing the Icons and prepping shifted things back to the urgency of action. It was only near the end of their preparations, as they finally made to leave, that the gathering sadness in the Hestron family poured out. Darvon was the first to cry, followed by his wife and two daughters. When Ereena saw her sisters crying she fussed as well, getting a sense, it seemed, that Jessica was about to be gone. Her sad little face nearly made Jess cry but she stayed strong, reassuring each of them as best she could—Ereena with kisses and a big smile—leaving them with a sort of sad joy on their faces. Tearful smiles, they were, but the tears were, in truth, tears of hope. She was an angel, after all, come to usher in their salvation, and everything would be just fine. Reluctant to fully embrace the role they had mapped out for her, she nevertheless used it in that moment of parting to comfort them. She *was* an angel, and she would do as they claimed.

It worked. They believed.

Then she was off and moving through the city, as naturally as possible, following their two unlikely guides; Bianca a zombie, Jess shouldering the lumpy backpack. It was a secure, military-like affair with sturdy straps, but still managed to feel slippery against her back. Like it would come off, or get blown away, or snatched, or something would fall out. Far too much was at stake for her to ignore it, even for a second.

As it turned out it was believed, by enough members of the Conclave, at least, that the Icons were part of the Prophecy and therefore part of Jessica's destiny. She hadn't had to fight them for the devices. None were eager to send them with her like this, in the open and in such peril, but all knew it must be done. After all, she was to save them in the end, wasn't she? How could she do it without the fabled Icons? There was confidence among the group that the Venatres handlers waiting at their final destination would know exactly what to do. The Venatres had been after the original Icon in the first place, using Zac as a pawn to get it, and though the Conclave wasn't privy to what the Venatres wanted with the Icon they supported the Venatres in their efforts to undermine the Dominion. They knew the Venatres could help lift the oppression of the Emperor's ancient rule, believing Jessica and the Icon—now Icons—were key. Proof of that had already been achieved: With the help of the Venatres Jess and the Icon brought down the Crucible and severed the head of the Dominion. The Conclave believed that, with Venatres help once more, she might complete the Prophecy and bring about the much-anticipated Golden Age.

And so the Daimyo ordered the Icons be sent with the angel. And that was that.

So Jess had them—and the Earth computer—bundled in the most inconspicuous way possible, which wasn't very inconspicuous at all, in a large, military-grade rucksack, and she was on her way, off to the safety of the Venatres, off to fulfill her supposed destiny. In their minds she was off to fulfill the Prophecy.

In her mind she was off to find Zac.

She watched out the windows as the walls of the tunnel flashed by. The steady motion combined with the thrum of the car's mechanics made it hard not to drift. She held tighter. It was already hours past her bedtime on a day that had been filled with non-stop near-death intensity. Hopefully they'd get a chance to rest aboard whatever transport they were taking. Chom wasn't clear on how they would travel and Tenko wasn't much more forthcoming, so she hadn't pressed, but they knew it was to be by sea. Somehow she imagined it would not be first class. Or even coach. They were being smuggled, so wherever they ended up wasn't likely to be comfortable.

But at that point she didn't care. She could almost fall asleep right there, standing on the train. Except, of course, for all the jacked up emotions washing through her. Beneath the feeling of exhaustion, overlaying her uniquely stimulating fear, was the giddy excitement that she was on her way across the ocean, to Venatres lands, where Zac now lived. Tickling at the edges of *that*, to her dismay, were yet other, difficult considerations, all of them so in conflict with each other that, truthfully, she wasn't sure if she would ever sleep again.

What if Zac has re-married? What if he had a girlfriend? Did Kazerai even have girlfriends? Though he wasn't really a Kazerai anymore, was he? Apparently he'd defected to the other side, which made him a sort of free agent. Which would mean he was able to do whatever any normal man did, no matter what a Kazerai did, and normal men dated and had girlfriends.

I'm his girlfriend, she thought and winced at the idea. That wasn't official. That was just her own personal fantasy. It had been months since they kissed, since they said goodbye, not knowing when—or if—they would see each other again. And at that time he'd told her explicitly to go live her life. Had he lived his?

Was he spoken for?

The thought of that very real possibility was crushing. Made worse by the exhaustion sitting so heavily on her. *We might never be together.*

Forcibly she turned her mind to other things.

Tenko stood across from her. A Conclave man with one foot in the seedy underworld of Osaka vice. Hard to believe, really, that such a rigidly governed society had an underworld at all. Yet they did, apparently, and she knew most every society of Earth did as well. China had one. The old Soviet Union had one. North Korea had one. Everyone had one. Most of the time such things were just too far removed from the average person. Strictly need to know. You wanted drugs, you could get them if you knew where to go. They were always there. Stolen goods? Same thing. Slaves? No problem. And in Osaka, Tenko knew where to go. He could get Jess and Bianca on the right lines and out of town. Of course that meant putting them into the hands of increasingly shady people, further and further removed from the protection of the Conclave. But Tenko, or so he claimed, had it figured out.

Jess studied him in the quiet moments as they traveled. An average-looking man, mid-forties, with a suspicious gaze, always looking without looking. Seeing everything without staring, aware of what could be waiting around every corner.

She hoped they could trust him.

Several stops later, people getting off and on between— none of them, thankfully, giving the odd group more than a cursory glance—Aber led them from the train, onto a platform and back above ground, to the street and into the daylight.

As they emerged Bianca's voice startled Jessica from behind.

"Where are we?" She'd crowded up close as Aber paused to check their surroundings.

"I don't know," Jess answered honestly. Of course she didn't know, but Bianca was scared and, in her mind, Jess had this well in hand, having been here before. Truth was she was just as concerned about where they'd arrived. Now that she looked around she saw they were in a run-down district, everything projecting an air of decay, which only seemed to heighten the sense of danger.

"Stay close," Aber finished his survey, including Tenko in his warning. He started across the street.

The giant wall was close, looming before them over everything, only a few blocks away. It towered above the two- and three-floor buildings in the area. Most of them looked empty, in obvious disrepair, some even showing signs of vandalism—something Jess hadn't yet seen in Osaka. People were out and about, though not many, lacking the purpose evident elsewhere. Some milled about, others walked but seemed to have no real destination in mind.

Up ahead were a few lighted building fronts. Dusk

approached and it struck Jess that they'd arrived that morning before the sun rose, making it a full Anitran day that had passed. Add to that the fact that they'd begun their adventure back in Boise in mid-afternoon and she estimated it must be, like, 5 am for their bodies with hardly any rest.

I am so tired.

A quick check of Bianca confirmed she was baked as well. Both of them stumbled along, following Aber robotically.

At the end of the block he turned toward one of the lighted buildings. It looked active, unlike many of the others around it, and in fact appeared to be the destination of more than a few people in the area. Aber took the group to the building's front door and followed two men in coats who were arriving, heading inside.

Standing in the pitch-dark foyer Jess panicked for an instant, losing sight of the bodies she knew were around her—worrying there might be others she couldn't see. She gripped both straps of the backpack firmly and jumped as an equally fearful Bianca pressed against her.

Music issued from somewhere deeper within; rhythmic, thumping, almost like a dance club or something. As her eyes adjusted she saw the two men in coats who had entered ahead of them pass through another set of doors, past a doorman. The room beyond was the source of the music, large and better-lit, colored lights strung around the ceiling, and as she caught a glimpse it looked as if it were mostly dark-clothed men inside watching a show. The door closed and the momentary light was gone, but by then she could see Aber and the doorman ahead of him, Tenko and Bianca to the side. Aber spoke to the doorman, who looked around his considerable bulk to study the two girls.

A few moments of conversation and they were passing into the large room beyond, the eyes of the doorman following them all the way until the door was shut.

As they passed within Jess shuddered at the sense of perverted interest she felt beneath the doorman's gaze.

The large room beyond was indeed like a dance club,

though no one other than the performers were dancing. Almost like a strip club. At the center were two lighted stages, men sitting on all sides watching. Powerful, greedy men, some captivated by the dancers, others all but ignoring the girls on stage as they talked among themselves. Waitresses delivered drinks, more men stood around the walls at the fringes, but all that receded behind the realization for Jessica that the girls dancing on the stages were, in fact, *girls*, not women. Several years younger, even, than her.

They weren't naked, and it didn't look like actual stripping was part of the act—though there was no way to be sure—but they were done up in makeup and wearing provocative clothes and moved around the stage suggestively, two girls on each. Four girls who had probably just hit puberty, bending and grinding and fueling the fantasies of this roomful of decadent men.

Movement caught Jessica's attention. A figure walked up to Aber and Tenko, eyes firmly on she and Bianca. He looked like an owner, or at least not one of the patrons. All business. Jess listened as best she could over the thumping music, catching his words and the response of their chaperones.

"Sedra," the man introduced himself, continuing to look Jessica and Bianca up and down. "These the girls?"

Aber nodded that they were. Aber either didn't notice the way the guy was looking at them or didn't care.

"A little old," Sedra wrinkled his nose, then grinned wolfishly. "Pretty, though. I can fit them in."

Jess swallowed, wishing Zac was there. Wishing she'd run off to find him first, knowing that was impossible yet wishing it all the same. She wished he was there to pound in all their faces and whisk her away to safety.

But Tenko spoke. "These are going out," he cut short the man's regard. Tenko was firm, not gruff, making sure there was no mistaking Sedra knew exactly what was required and wasn't to be questioned. Sedra's greed faded.

"You're paying?" he asked, acting a little surprised.

"That's the deal."

Sedra raised his hands. "Hey, news gets twisted. I

thought you were here to sell." Whether he really thought that or not, whether he was just taking a stab at what he saw as an opportunity, didn't matter. He had his eye on them and, to judge by his avarice, saw profit.

Jessica looked at Bianca, whose barely-controlled terror was on the rise. Ready to bolt at any instant. More or less the same way she'd looked at every step since leaving Darvon's house, but now intensifying to the point Jess thought she might actually do it. Thankfully there was nowhere to run. *She's so pretty*, she thought. Even harried and strung out as she was her exotic beauty shone through. The greedy guy must really have his eye on her. Bianca would certainly make a great addition to his stable.

Jess tried to get a grip. Once Tenko paid and handed them over, who was to guard them then? They had to go on alone in order for this to work. That meant passing through the hands of others. But others such as these?

Suddenly she wanted out. There had to be a better way.

But Tenko was moving on. "Half your usual rate now," he said to this Sedra character. "Then, once we have proof of delivery, we'll pay you another double."

The man's eyebrows raised and he looked back and forth between the girls and Tenko, nodding his head in cautious optimism. "Double, eh? That also wasn't in the news. I'm not arguing, mind you."

"Double is the deal," said Tenko. "And." He paused after this, letting Sedra know this was the sort of "and" that needed to be listened to. Carefully. "And," he repeated, "if you do *not* deliver them. Safely," he made sure to add. "Whether your fault or not. If we do *not* get confirmation to our satisfaction of their safety, we will kill everyone involved in this transfer, including you. We will kill your family, all of them.

"Do you understand?"

Jess stared at Tenko in disbelief. *Whoa.* She had no idea the Conclave were that serious. Killing Sedra certainly wasn't a horrible thing to imagine, in a way she wanted to do it right then, but the fact that her protectors were ready to kill *anybody* was a bit of a shock. The Conclave seemed too peaceful for that. So far their whole stance had been about freedom, not killing people.

But it set her mind at ease. With that kind of send-off it was unlikely she and Bianca would come to any harm. Not if Sedra could help it.

And as she thought of this she realized her delivery was so important to the Conclave they were willing to do whatever it took. They had no way to deliver her themselves, either openly or covertly, so they had to make use of these underground channels. A risky proposition and, knowing that, they were prepared to take every measure to ensure it worked. In this case they would pay double for success, and they would kill him if he failed. And as the understanding of *that* washed over her Jess continued, slowly, to calm. It might be a hairy journey ahead, but if these people knew what was good for them they would do everything in their power to make it happen. They would have to.

When Sedra didn't answer right away Tenko filled the stunned silence. "Is that clear?"

Reluctantly Sedra nodded that it was. "You need these two across the sea that badly, I'll make it happen."

"Please pass it along." Tenko's threat was made that much more menacing by the matter-of-fact way he said it. "As the actions of everyone after this will directly affect whether you live or die."

Jessica was impressed. There was no force behind Tenko's words, no grabbing of Sedra's collar, no "you better or else!" It was simply the cold, hard truth. If Sedra did not deliver, he would die. Simple as that. No emotion, no regret. That was the penalty and that would be the result and Sedra could count on it. Apparently Sedra believed it, as he'd begun to sweat and his tune was shifting even as they stood there. The music played, the girls on stage danced and Jess could see Mister Sedra was fast becoming their friend. Maybe he knew Tenko. Maybe Tenko had a reputation. Whatever, it was clear Sedra believed him fully. The seedy club owner would do everything in his power to make sure he got his double-plus-half fee and did not, as the alternative, end up dead.

"Come with me," he turned and led the group to his office.

The club was in the port district, as they soon discovered, wharfs and docks at the edge of a wide river that flowed right by the city out to the ocean. Tenko took them aside and gave them their last instructions, telling them how they would be met on the other side, what would come next and every other bit of info he could impart, then Sedra took his initial payment, took charge and moved them through bustling loading areas that were much like Earth, large metal ships waiting for cargo, arriving or heading to sea. Machines and men moved about, cranes lifting and lowering, horns sounding, the smell of the salt water, of fish, heavy on the air.

Storm clouds gathered on the horizon.

Jess made sure to keep Bianca close, though she hardly had to give it much attention as both of them practically clung to each other, nerves totally fried by that point. Sedra handed them off to another who, in turn, passed them aboard to an officer on a fairly decrepit looking cargo ship who then took them below decks.

As night fell and the ship's horns sounded they were in a dingy compartment, sitting on the floor, holding each other, tears dried on their faces as the groaning vessel surged steadily against the waves, rising and falling, making pace.

Steaming out to sea.

CHAPTER 22:

ARRIVAL

YAMOTO STOOD AT THE EDGE of the terrace looking out into the night, high above the lights of the city on the roof of the Tower of Light. Highest point a person could reach in the city of Osaka, though the Emperor's great tower, Vivitak, soared higher. That holy pinnacle, however, was off limits. Even to Yamoto, Shogun of the entire Dominion.

A gentle breeze blew in the passing of the rain.

Vivitak, he thought bitterly, never having outwardly expressed discontent at the enforced legacy of a dead man, simply following along like all the rest, keeping his resentment obediently to himself. Vivitak, built for the sole purpose of housing the Emperor's body, looming in Yamoto's vision as he looked past it. Both towers, Vivitak and the Tower of Light, standing tall within the inner walls of the Imperial Compound, a walled fortress within the fortified walls of Osaka itself. Symbols of the mighty Dominion.

But Vivitak was not the focus of his attention. Dread, not distaste, consumed him, fixing his concentration firmly west, toward the lands where the Crucible once stood. Storm clouds hung in that direction, far out on the horizon; invisible in the pitch of night, illuminated now and again in stark detail as threads of lightning raced within their dark masses. Following each strike the blackness fell once more and thunder rolled; low, distant; remnant of the titanic force.

Video had come earlier of the beast. Of the fight outside the airship, out on those same, rain-soaked fields. Yamoto refused to believe the Kazerai Akido had actually been killed yet, by all indications, he had. An impossibility come to life. *What is that thing?!* Some sort of monster, spawned from the radiation of the Crucible. Perhaps from some other source. Sketchy data from the science team offered little to go on. Some images, a few readings ... that was it. Then Akido. Great Kazerai, sent to intercept the creature which, even then, continued to hold Osaka in its line of approach. Akido, unable to contain or destroy it, the thing more powerful than the Kazerai, somehow, and the thought of that caused Yamoto to shudder in the cool breeze.

By now the search for clues as to how a rogue Skull Boy came to be in the midst of Osaka had taken a back seat to this greater threat. After a short time, during which Yamoto's advisors and generals did their best to come to grips with what happened out there on the plains, tempers rising—fear, rising—the clerics frozen at the thought of some apocalyptic end, Yamoto's adjutant, Damas, took charge and dispatched airships to search for Akido's own. The last they knew it had been boarded by the beast and took off, immediately after the epic fight, and began moving low over the ground, disappearing from any means of tracking it. The beast was probably flying it, or had commanded the crew to do so, and all communications ended. Finding the rogue airship from the air at night, even with a dozen airships, was unlikely, but they hunted it nonetheless. If that thing truly meant to return to the city ...

It must be stopped.

At first Yamoto debated ordering his remaining two Kazerai to assist with the search, but decided against that. After what happened to Akido he wanted them close, just in case the beast slipped through.

Another flash of lightning, a delay, then the clap and roll of thunder.

Each rumble brought him more alert, straining his overwrought senses into the void, looking for sign of the hijacked Kazerai craft. Though each time he saw the lightning first, though each time he knew the thunder would follow, he could not stop the lurch in his heart when each rumbling sound hit.

What kind of beast was it? What could it possibly be? Had the explosion of the great forge truly created it?

They knew so little scientifically of the process by which the Kazerai were made.   The original effort had been an accident, an experiment that bore results in entirely unexpected ways.   That process had then become part of their most closely guarded secrets though, in truth, they had little real understanding of it.   A religious mystery, of a sort, one they subsequently used to great effect in the control of their populace.

Had something else gone awry?   Was that thing out there Maza? The last Astake to enter the Crucible? Maza's conversion process had only just begun when the whole thing went up.   Could someone close to the reactor have been affected?   Was it a bug or an animal or something that got transformed, mutated in the blast?

There was no reasonable explanation.   All they knew was that something had been spawned out there and it was on its way here, to Osaka, for God knew what purpose.

Thunder rumbled.   Yamoto jumped and admonished himself. *It's just thunder.*

Only this time ...

His blood went to ice.

This time there was no lightning.

The thunder continued. Steady. His heart rose further into his throat and he saw it: the glowing exhaust of an airship, distant, curving fast toward the city across the open plain, rumble of its approach deep and ominous— reverberating against the hard surfaces of the city's skyscrapers as it closed.   Fresh lightning arced in the distance, herald to its approach, flash-lighting the landscape and illuminating the far-off form of the airship in stark contrast, jagged shadows wrapping its dark, irregular shape for a shuddering instant.

It was Aikido's.

Yamoto swallowed. In that same flash he saw another airship, beyond it, coming in from on high, racing in at the rogue from a different direction; one of the hunters, which had at last spotted the enemy.

On the attack.

* * *

ASTAKE COMMANDER RAGNEL pushed back in his command chair, feeling the tug of the harness as his pilot banked hard and over, angling the mighty airship down toward its prey and accelerating.

"Coming on-line, sir."

"Steady. Target the spine."

They'd spotted Akido's craft moments before and turned their methodical sweep into a charging rush.

"She's making speed."

"It's too close. Bring it down."

"Yes, sir."

Somehow it felt wrong to mercilessly pursue and attack one of their own but this was, technically, no longer one of their own. The crew had been compromised and, aboard with them—whether they lived or not—was a beast that must be stopped, by all means. It could not be allowed to make its objective.

"Locked."

Ragnel checked and confirmed at his own console. It was their only chance.

"Fire."

And missiles were away. Recessed blister turrets popped and released; two missiles piercing the night, headed with haste toward the target—which was now making changes to its flight. As if sensing the attack, it changed pace suddenly and angled down, toward the city.

But the missiles were locked and found their way home.

BOOOM! BOOOM! twin fireballs, white-hot energy erupting against the spine of the intruder. The concussion of their impact slammed it wildly to the side and harder down, into an immediate and deadly spin, shedding chunks of its outer framework as it went, out of control and tumbling.

An instant too late. Ragnel watched in furious dismay as the blazing mass managed to gain enough final control to clear the outer wall of the city, raking across the top edge in a shower of flame before slamming down inside.

"Damn," he cursed aloud. Then: "Circle it. Call the others."

He surveyed the damaged structures below as the pilot hove them around, collateral fires bursting through the impact zone. Against the overall breadth of the city the destruction was small, yet that isolated inferno burned bright in Ragnel's eyes, mark of his failure. A few seconds sooner and they would've brought it down harmlessly on the empty plain outside the walls.

"The others are on their way. Ten minutes."

He continued staring. Now that the intruder was grounded, now that the damage was done, the all-consuming question became: was the monster destroyed? Looking at the hulk of the airship down there, laying crookedly across the buildings it had squashed, upended and tilted radically to the side it was mostly ... whole. Which meant the thing inside could still be ...

Alive. Even as Ragnel thought this a door blew open on the airship's side, knocked away by some colossal force within. And there, behind it, moving into the opening and standing at the flaming threshold, was the beast. Looking out over the wreckage and, in turn, looking completely unscathed. Horned head, scaly yellow skin, wearing what looked to be Akido's pants. A mockery.

A monster.

Standing like the devil incarnate amid the flames, the fires of Hell having no affect on it. Then it looked up at him, or seemed to, gazing at the airship circling high above.

It grinned.

"Target it," Ragnel ordered, urgent, motioning with his hands as if to direct the flight of the airship himself. The pilot throttled them out, accelerating hard in a sweeping arc and banking around, bringing weapons to bear on the wreckage below. Ragnel gripped the chair as they came to, determined to finish the destruction in that section of the city, if it meant killing that thing. But ... when they came online again it was gone.

Leapt away. In the city, somewhere. Gone from sight.

Ragnel's frustration was tempered by his doubt. What

foolishness had that been? The thing was far too quick to be hit by anything the lumbering airship could bring to bear. And even if they *could* hit it, would it die? His skin crawled. This was a nightmare come to life. A cancer, loose in the city; one that might kill them all before they could cut it away.

"Scanners," he ordered, numb but knowing they had to continue. "Find it. Track it."

"Yes, sir."

CHAPTER 23:

NIGHT OF THE BEAST

LINDIN TOOK A SIP OF TEA; looked again at the screen of information on the desk before him. Displayed was a field brief from agents tasked with liaising between his Venatres Intelligence Command and the small group of Dominion revolutionaries across the sea known as the Conclave. The Conclave who, while admittedly useless in terms of a real, active rebellion, had proven useful in other ways, most notably when fencing the contacts and information needed to execute Lindin's grand plan to steal the Holy Relic: The Icon, closely guarded treasure of the Dominion. That plan nearly succeeded those many months ago, when Horus—Zac, he reminded himself—stole the thing right out of its tightly guarded spot at the heart of the Dominion's Imperial Compound, almost getting it into Lindin's hands.

But somehow the initial promise of that operation went terribly wrong. Rather than bring it directly to Lindin and company Zac used it to flee and, unexpectedly, returned, bringing a girl with him. A girl that, frustratingly, ended up a force more powerful than they could ever have expected and, at the end of it all, vanished with the Icon. Thus ending any hope to which Lindin held. Success, elusive—*so elusive!*—so close yet, ultimately, the gambit failed. The Icon was gone, lost forever.

Until now.

As if the forces of cosmic fate were teasing him, laughing at their favorite plaything—the gullible Lindin—now ... the Icon was back. *Two* Icons. The one once held by the Dominion plus another, an Icon from "Earth".

Brought back by the same girl that took the original. *Jessica.*

In the wake of that news Lindin fought a cascade of powerful emotions. Working to remain calm even as he waited for the arrangement of passage and the arrival of those treasures, leaving to fate the intervening moments over which he had little control. By report the girl, Jessica, was, even now, on her way to him. Aboard some nondescript freighter out to sea. And so his excitement was, again, inflamed, barely contained, along with the fear that all might be lost.

It was a difficult time.

Jessica. He remembered her vividly. A face he would never forget. Not because she was too young to be in the middle of all this, so alien and yet so human—the first visitor to Anitra since the Emperor himself. Not because she was memorably ... compelling, though she was; a timid teenage girl, unassuming, trapped by circumstance yet quickly, through her own determination, becoming the center of everything. Nor did he remember her so well because she'd caused so much trouble—though surely she had.

No, he could not forget her simply because of the first time he looked into her eyes. Such depth to that stare, a disarming intensity that, at first, seemed little more than the fear of being so far from her known elements (he assumed) but, only later realized was, in fact, something greater. As if *she* was the one calling the shots. One step ahead of everything—and everyone. It was this image, this memory of his first look into her face, expression filled with something he could not quite grasp, that made the deepest, most lasting impression.

Lindin had been in intelligence for some time. Rarely— *never*—had he seen one such as this girl.

Jessica.

Following the loss of the Icon and the stunning victory at the Crucible he'd discovered the details of her final escapade. At the time he'd been a little surprised to learn it was Satori that fell victim to her guile. He'd thought more of the capable field commander. It was Satori that let her go. Satori let her use the Icon to return to her world, probably never to return. Ruining, in one simple, idiotic move, everything on which the future of the Venatres hinged.

At the time Satori, of course, had no idea what was at stake.

Rather than punish her—for there was no way reasonably to do so—Lindin had, instead, brought her in as an agent. Enlightened her. Satori was battle-tested, in the extreme, with a proven record for getting things done. In fact she'd turned out to make a great intelligence agent. Lindin had a gut feeling he needed to keep an eye on her anyway.

But there had been little additional light she could shed on those final hours. Jessica left with the Icon, returning to Earth, and no one at the time knew the importance of the device beyond that. Only Lindin and a handful of elite operatives had any idea of the *real* significance of the Icon; of what they'd lost. At the time Satori let it go she thought simply, reasonably, she was doing everyone a favor. Disposing of the Icon and giving Jessica a deserved exit from this world where she did not belong. They'd given their hero a ticket home. Who could punish that?

And so Lindin and his group were left empty, no hope of completing their objective.

Until now.

"They should arrive in a few days." One of his inner circle sat across the desk from him, quietly reviewing the same brief. Trying, as was Lindin, to see his way through the minefield of ways this whole thing could fall apart. Their eagerness to get their hands on the Icon was unmistakable. But there were too many points of failure yet to come. Already it was little more than pure luck that they suddenly had another opportunity at all, and as close as it was, as well as things were going, to simply have to wait a little longer as they were ...

"Has the free trader redirected?" Lindin asked.

"Yes," came the answer. "So far our ... guidance, is being followed. They should arrive at Port Sanvers, north of Midbay as instructed."

"The tac team is on standby?"

The man nodded. Lindin took another sip of tea and looked back at his screen. Reviewing the same lines he'd read a dozen times.

It was too good to be true.

The Conclave saw Jessica as some sort of prophet. An other-worldly force—heavenly—an angel that was to herald a Golden Age, according to their legends. A simple girl who would sweep away tyranny and despair. What that meant for Lindin and his group was that the Conclave entrusted Jessica—and the Icons—to the Venatres as part of divine fate. Lindin was more than happy to go along with their prophetic notions. Truth was, he and the Venatres *could* bring an end to the Dominion and their oppressive rule. If only they got what they needed.

A knock at the door brought him from his thoughts. Lindin's associate turned. Neither expected a caller at that hour.

Lindin shut off the screen. "Enter," he called. The door opened and one of his junior aides entered.

"Sorry for the interruption, sirs. We just got an update from the Osaka branch."

Lindin motioned him in and the man shut the door, including both seniors in his delivery.

"Channels are a bit choked at the moment, but we have word of a major disturbance. Our spies just got hold of new information. The supposed thing the Dominion found in the wastelands, the anomaly, may be on its way to Osaka." The man swallowed. "Apparently it killed one of their Kazerai."

Unconsciously Lindin leaned forward in his chair.

"Killed a Kazerai?"

The man nodded.

Lindin couldn't believe it. "Do we know yet what 'it' is?" He could see the aide was uncomfortable with the information. As if he either couldn't believe it or felt silly relaying it. Or both.

"Some sort of horned monster, sir." He shook his head. "We don't yet have many details. There is apparently a video we haven't gotten our hands on, taken by a scientific team. They sent a recording before it killed them."

Lindin leaned back. "A horned monster?"

"That's the way it's being described. There's a lot of confusion on comm channels right now, probably as a result. Whatever it is it's got the full attention of the Dominion. Word is it killed a Kazerai and they believe it to be on the way to Osaka."

Lindin looked across to his associate. Back to the aide. "Anything else?"

"So far that's all we have."

Lindin shook his head. Tried to imagine it. "Killed a Kazerai," he mused. If that were true …

"That's the report, sir."

He cleared his thoughts. "Ok. Keep us informed."

"Yes, sir." And the aide left. The click of the closing door marked the end of that interlude, leaving the two men alone again with their thoughts.

"A monster, eh?" the other wondered aloud. "Can't wait to see what that's all about. Probably another one of their freak accidents."

Lindin shook his head. They were both tired. He flicked back on his screen, bringing up the field brief. He agreed. Sounded like another of the Dominion's misguided experiments gone wrong. For such a technologically advanced culture the ranks of the Dominion were steeped in truly mystic practices. He only hoped that, if this *was* one of their mistakes, it ended up wreaking a little havoc back on them. They certainly deserved what they got.

He took a sip of tea.

"Guess we'll find out."

* * *

UP AHEAD LAY THE WALLS OF the Imperial Compound. Kang recognized it; remembered the place he so frequently haunted as a Kazerai, subject of the Emperor, servant of the Shogun and the Council of useless clerics. He stared at the twin spires of Vivitak and the Tower of Light, rising into the night. Lit, full of power. Staunchly set against him. Surely they must realize by now.

I come to conquer.

The towers had been visible for his entire, brief journey across the city. Beacons to his destination, fortified walls within the fortified walls of the city itself.

Useless.

He'd been moving through the city much too fast for organized resistance. No forces had been able to predict his movement or position themselves to stop him. Not that they would've been able to stop him anyway. Still, he was glad he'd managed to avoid the distraction.

The attacking airship had been joined by others, circling above, watching, catching sight of him now and again, unable or unwilling to rain down destruction and kill so many innocents in the bargain. Part of Kang despised that weakness but part of him, the better part, perhaps—the part he must call upon if he was to rise as leader of these people—knew it was the smarter thing for them to do.

He paused from his perch atop one of the business district skyscrapers, shouldered up along the outer walls of the Imperial Compound. A building of forty floors or so, with an angled roof and various objects atop it. He stood at the edge, having leapt there from another, gazing over the walls of the Compound, down to the Imperial court within. Gardens and walking paths wound throughout, visible in great detail with his acute vision; decorative buildings and palace-like constructions surrounding the two massive towers. All of it so delicate. So frivolous.

All of it waiting.

In the shadows down there he saw figures preparing, setting themselves against all possible angles of attack.

He leapt. Forty floors to the street below, the thunder of the circling airships loud in his ears, hoping the remaining Kazerai would be part of his welcoming party. If there were any. It was possible, he imagined, that Akido was it. Maybe the rest were gone. No more could've been made without the Crucible, so if the others had been retired then Akido was it. A disappointing thought, in a way.

He wanted to ensure his defeat of Akido had been no fluke.

At the compound wall he leapt easily to the top, fully

expecting a hail of bullets or missiles or plasma blasts or whatever to come streaking his way.

What *did* hit him took him entirely by surprise.

The agony! He ground his teeth as a blast struck him like a wall, bathed suddenly in a purple light that filled his vision. It locked his jaw so tight he was unable even to scream; a monumental groan escaped his clenched teeth but that was it. Muscles spasmed, tensing him atop the wall until he teetered, off balance, powerless to take control. At the last instant he found the will, somehow, to force himself backward, not forward, so he fell outside the Compound, away from the field of the beams.

He screamed as he fell, now that he could, hit the street and blacked out.

But only for an instant. His eyes flicked open and he was on his feet, shaking off the pain even as his mind filled with primal rage.

The priests! How had he forgotten?! Those masked, faceless, golden-robed priest warriors, wielders of the Raza energy, only force able to contain a Kazerai. Overhead the airships circled, preparing for an attack, perhaps thinking he was vulnerable though he'd snapped to and was fully awake.

But he was no longer a simple Kazerai, was he?

And maybe that was it. Maybe the shock of the Raza energy had just taken him off guard. From his higher perch he'd seen the golden-robed demons moving inside the compound, seen their shiny chrome staffs in hand but somehow, in his arrogance, failed to make the connection. What struck him now, however, as he stood outside the wall, chest heaving, fists clenching, was that he'd withstood the sudden shock and recovered. Even felt as if he could overcome it.

Yes! His ascension had elevated him in all ways. Even the Raza was no match for him now!

With that thought he leapt again toward the top of the wall, waiting no longer for reason, for evaluation, giving no opportunity for further attack, pulled his legs and continued over, landing on the other side inside the compound—facing directly half-a-dozen of the robed priest warriors, staffs leveled squarely at him.

"You will die!" he shouted. The beams came even as the words left his mouth, violet and brilliant in the night, gripping him as if a tangible thing, seizing his entire body. He rode the convulsions and retched; tasted bile and ... began to laugh. It was the laugh of the damned, but he could feel strength mounting. Slowly he lowered his head, locked his gaze and ... took a step. Toward them.

Then another.

Yes!

Shaking from the resistance, from the rage; moving forward nonetheless. He could not see their eyes behind the masks but could nearly smell their fear, even through the acrid tang of the Raza beams. They dared not lower the staffs to run, yet holding them on him was not, as was now becoming painfully clear, going to save them. All they were doing was prolonging their own end and, as the realization of that came over them, Kang laughed louder; moved faster. Step after step, closing, gaining tolerance with each, building power.

As he neared them, all other observers in the compound held motionless in a state of shock at what they witnessed, he saw two new forms move out of the edge of his vision. Sparing an instant of focus to identify these brave souls he confirmed they were Kazerai. Two, and he recognized his old brethren. He smiled at them—for them, so they could witness the grim madness in his fanged maw—then turned back to the matter at hand.

The priests.

The Kazerai would not dare attack while he was enveloped in the grip of the Raza. For now they watched. Horrified, perhaps, knowing they were next.

He reached the first of the golden-robed wretches and seized that man in his grip. As he did one beam dropped, then the others, the priests terrified enough at last to flee, a disorganized retreat and Kang surged in the freedom, snatching them one by one in a flurry of death blows that left shredded, gore-stained piles of golden robes and bright red flesh scattering the grounds. The finale happened in an instant.

The Kazerai remained a cautious distance away, if there were such thing, spacing themselves and preparing for the inevitable.

Never had Kang seen such an absence of confidence in the great warriors.

He snatched every Raza staff and broke it, then turned to his new objective. As he moved closer, taking his time, gaining his breath from the exertion against the priests and their foul science, he thought absently that a more tactical maneuver would've been to fire on him while locked in the deadly grip of violet energy. Ranged around the compound were dozens of the Astake powered armor, carrying their vaunted plasma cannons. He could see their tall, Shogun-esque helmets outlined in the shadows, his former brothers in arms, standing there, waiting. Had they shot him then ... Perhaps weakened by the energy they could've brought him down.

Now they would never know. So confident had they been in the power of the priests.

Facing down the two Kazerai he began to feel his first doubts. Akido had been no easy match. His worry, however, was less that he could destroy two of them at once, as he soon learned that he could, but whether their destruction was required. As their fight raged across the compound, bringing collateral destruction of epic proportions, to structures, Astake, and others, even the wall itself, superhuman bodies whipping back and forth, leaps and blows, Kang wondered if he should let the Kazerai live. Was it truly necessary that he have no challengers? As he came to realize how superior he was to their efforts he thought, maybe, they could prove useful. Maybe they could be swayed, made powerful allies.

But it was too risky. If his coup was to work then he must be the indisputable force, the power that could not be reckoned with, and the presence of the Kazerai would always call that into question. As he stood over the last one to fall, watching his old comrade draw his final breath, he decided he'd made the right choice.

No challengers.

Confirming his power was no fluke. Nothing could stand against him.

He looked up from their final resting place, where the battle ended, far across the Compound at the other wall, a line of Astake standing in the distance, watching him.

Waiting.

They would not attack.

He'd won.

It was a new beginning.

And at that he laughed.

Invincible.

CHAPTER 24:

SEABORNE

"WANT THE REST OF MY BREAD?" Jess wasn't hungry, nor did Bianca seem to have much of an appetite. Still, she offered.

"No," Bianca spoke quietly. Then, with a little more feeling: "No thanks."

As expected, on the first night of their journey Bianca lost it. Went from terror to rage, directing that anger squarely at Jessica, saying things that could never be taken back, possessed of an intensity that, at first, Jess found shocking. Despite the pure hatred of her words, however, she understood Bianca's pain. Felt a powerful empathy for her friend. In many ways Bianca's fate *was* her fault.

Precarious moments passed after that, during which Bianca made a grab for the Icons, determined to have the one that would take her home, heedless of the consequences, ready to fall to her death in order to get out of there. But Jess kept them from her and at last Bianca's rage led to grief then, when the tears were gone, a brooding sort of resentment that lasted what seemed like forever. Thankfully that eventually gave way to a gathering—if reluctant—acknowledgment of the situation, followed by a slowly forming determination to make it through their hopeless predicament and, finally, a few apologies.

After that Bianca went quiet.

Jess set the bread off of the side and adjusted herself on the uncomfortable cot. There were two cots in the small "stateroom", one for each of them, a little head off to the side. Otherwise there were no amenities. Not even heat, it seemed, and she shivered and threw the ratty blanket over her feet, hugging her arms to her chest.

The bread was at least, for such accommodations, fresh. The food in general had been decent so far, actually, a mildly pleasant surprise and a bright spot on an otherwise dreary, frightening voyage. They'd been left mostly alone and neither had thought—or cared—to roam about the ship. They weren't prisoners, per se, but right outside their measly room was a dangerous-looking and very functional machine room, lots of piping both large and small, metal stairs going places they probably didn't want to explore, wisps of steam and plenty of grease. Crew came and went, checking this or that or—what appeared to be their true purpose for coming down to bilge level—ogling the two girls through the large porthole in their door. This, of course, only added to the creepfest of being fugitives on an old ship, on an alien world, completely at the mercy of the greed or fear of the captain and their escort. To say Jess was on edge would've been putting it mildly.

Once or twice, especially during the roughest seas and most aggressive slap-and-surge of the perpetually groaning vessel, she thought to find her way topside, to get some air and possibly puke over the railing. Instead she'd mostly just puked in the head.

Now the wave crests had become long; a slow up and down she'd gradually grown used to. Maybe she had her sea legs. They said you got them after a while, and being at sea for her was, mercifully, no longer a problem. She no longer felt affected by the constant motion. Bianca, on the other hand, was not so lucky. She still looked quite green.

They hadn't been given any new clothes, nor had there been showers—nor would they probably have taken one even if it had been offered—and so they still wore the plain black Dominion clothes given them by Darvon's daughter, Egg. Jess felt grimy, her hair was greasy, still loosely tied in the twin ponytail whips from MMA class—a time that seemed an eternity ago—and she knew there would be little chance to look better before she saw ...

Zac.

Troubled by all the unknowns, all the possible ways their reunion could fail, she nevertheless clung to that future moment with unflappable hope. Even as she argued against herself, played her own devil's advocate, the conviction that it would all end as she imagined prevailed. They would be together. He would welcome her. He would not be spoken for. Their future would be as bright and limitless as the sky above.

And as she shook her head at her own, sappy musings, as she thought of his embrace, she shivered again—only this time not from the chill. Sappy or no these thoughts of Zac lifted her, realistic or not they were her rock, and she found it hard to believe how far she'd put him out of her mind back on Earth. Now that she was here, so close, the anticipation was nearly killing her.

If he does *have another girl I'll take him from her,* she thought, realizing how insane that was but not caring. *Zac is mine.*

It was a maddening loop, and at the heart of it she had—every now and then during the mentally draining journey—snapped completely to reality and nearly had a breakdown herself, realizing she'd thrown her whole life away, essentially, on the silly notion of coming to this world where she didn't belong and reuniting with a boy she only hoped was still available or even accessible.

A few feet away Bianca curled up on the other cot, pulling her own blanket around her against the cold. Her eyes were vacant. She seemed, however, to be gaining strength. Building her resolve for the unknown ahead. She wasn't going back to her old life, that was certain, but Jess had real hope for getting her back and had told her so, and finally her friend was holding steady.

Jess was thankful for it.

She herself had continued to grow distant from that prior reality. This was the second time around for her and she had a strong feeling it was going to be the last. Bianca might find a way back in. Maybe. But Jess ... never could. Not now. It panicked her a bit, but mostly she allowed herself to become dead to it. The reality was that she felt like a girl out of time. An anachronism. Her mom, her dad, her sister; each of them would have their own feelings, their own loss, and maybe she would see them again, one day, their relationship entirely changed but connected nonetheless.

Or maybe not.

She only hoped the guys back on Earth hadn't done anything to them. The fear of that, the fear of harm coming to her family, worried her more than the fear of never seeing them again. She didn't want them to be affected by her troubles. That, however, was probably dreaming.

For a while she'd made attempts to crack the password on the laptop. She glanced at Bianca, then down at the backpack containing the Icons and stolen computer, close beside her cot, recalling the forceful convincing it took to make her friend give up on trying to use the Icon to get back. To make her stop grabbing for it. That first night Jess hardly slept, keeping a close eye on her friend.

The laptop, however ... she'd hoped the laptop might at least shed some light on the mysteries surrounding the two groups of guys and whatever the hell was going on back on Earth. Of course she'd been unable to log in. Frustrated she'd tried uselessly all day, knowing in her mind it would never work but determined all the same then, at last, gave up and put it away. She hadn't looked at it since.

"Hello?" A voice on the other side of the cabin door. Jess looked up and saw their assigned escort at the portal, peering in. She pulled the blanket tighter, wondering how long he'd been standing there.

Reluctantly she motioned him in.

He entered quickly, closing the door behind and filling the small space with his sleaze. There was very little to like about the guy but Jess tried to be friendly. He was, after all, the liaison between them and their eventual freedom.

"Get enough to eat?" he checked their plates, seeing the leftover bread. Bianca pulled her blanket up over her mouth.

Jess nodded, answering for them both. He smiled a broken smile. Every time he came he looked greedy, and she couldn't tell if it was merely anticipation of the payment waiting at the end of the journey or if he wanted to rape them or something. Maybe he hoped they'd start to like him? Or maybe he was just trying to drink them in, get an eyeful then go back to his cabin and play with himself.

If he *did* try to rape them it would be the biggest mistake of his life. She could guarantee him that. She would choke him out, break his neck and take over the whole damn ship, sail it east, run it aground, jump off and go find Zac. It was as simple as that. In a way, in her most vivid moments of rage, she wished he would. Wished he would push her over that edge; give her reason. Though she knew any such action was ridiculous, she wanted an excuse to stop cowering in that dingy room. Any catalyst to move, to inspire her to bust out and take charge.

He continued grinning, completely missing the flash of intensity that passed behind her eyes. "I tell the chef to make it special for you, every time." He licked his lips and, again, she didn't know if he was thinking of the delicious food or of them. "This heap is crummy enough. You should at least eat well."

Jess thanked him, painfully. He lingered.

"We're almost there," he said.

"Good," she wished he would just go away. What did he want?

"You know," he went on, pretending concern; "the captain, he's been making noises like he wants to sell you guys to someone else."

Jess sat up straight—wished she hadn't, realizing this was the sort of reaction he was hoping for. The guy was an idiot and she was sure there was some stupid, selfish, perverted, ulterior motive for telling them this. From his delivery alone it seemed, at least to his mind, the captain's threat was hollow, but he wanted to bring it up anyway and see what extra he might get out of them. Their pleas for him to save them? The two helpless little girls?

She sat back slowly.

"I've been talking him out of it, though," he assured them. "Don't you worry. I'll take care of you two."

Yep. That's what he wanted. Wanted them to be beholden to him, to owe him big for their safe passage. To have their indebted devotion.

Jess hurried him along.

"Thanks for letting us know," she said. "We know you'll

get us there safe."

The man nodded. Failing to come up with a good way to keep the conversation going, he reluctantly turned and left.

Jess slumped further; pulled the blanket up around her shoulders and found herself hoping they were almost there.

For the umpteenth time steeling her resolve.

* * *

KANG HELD THE DELICATE human form by the neck, feet dangling above the floor, hanging limp from beneath colorful cleric robes. He studied the devious face, still twisted in agony, eyes wide and empty. He'd barely had to squeeze. The combination of the man's stark terror and Kang's gentle grasp had been enough. But no matter. Kang had nothing further he wanted to say. Certainly nothing further he wanted to hear. The brief, shameful whimpering, pleading for his life ... that was already enough. Kang had learned the man's name, his position, and that was it.

Fezna. New leader of the High Council. *Ex* leader of the High Council. Kang looked at the bodies laying around him on the decorative floor of the expansive lobby. The rest of the Council. Gathered there at the base of Vivitak, the Emperor's tower, out of some strange belief that the divine power of the Emperor would save them.

It was the first place Kang went, of course. After dispatching the Kazerai, unchallenged by any further attack, watched by many, waiting to see what he would do. With the sun rising, strolling across the Imperial gardens, directly to the tower of Vivitak, long held inviolable by their religious doctrine, finding the robed clerics huddled inside.

He dropped Fezna in a heap among the rest.

There were others waiting. Uniformed soldiers. Officers. The Shogun. He looked at that frivolously robed man now, remembered Yamoto, former head of the Dominion military, the one for whom Kang had, indirectly, worked, standing with his former aide, Damas, who now wore the uniform of that station.

"You are now Shogun?" Kang said to him.

Yamoto, too, was afraid, but unlike the others stood proud, putting on a brave face, not making a sound. Waiting for what fate befell him. Kang could see Yamoto had done all he could, and if he died now he would die with honor. *Resolute acceptance of death.* Kang recalled the operating maxim taught by the Emperor himself. Any good Shogun—any good warrior—would have that as their final security. The rock upon which their courage would be built.

He admired Yamoto for it.

Good.

Now that he was here, now that he'd eliminated the greatest possible resistance, the Kazerai; now that he'd killed the major members of the conniving, fact-twisting Council, conveniently assembled for him in one place, removing the potential for their meddling mysticism and prophecies; now that so much had been accomplished in such short order Kang felt, at last, ready to begin.

He chuckled. Yamoto looked a little confused by the sound.

"It's funny," Kang explained, looking around the room, "that you were all gathered here, in one place. I needed to find you anyway. You've just made it easier."

Yamoto spoke. "They thought it safest," he looked at the dead clerics. "I warned them." His derision was clear. Yamoto felt no loss at their passing. Kang looked at him directly and smiled.

"I always liked you, Yamoto. You were a good commander. I'm sorry you've been reduced to ignoring your own advice in favor of the orders of a bunch of simpering idiots." He went to one of the ornate doors; the way up, to the Emperor's inner sanctum.

"I'm going up," he announced. "You should follow."

They all stared at him blankly.

"To the Emperor's chambers," he clarified. "Here, at the end of my journey and at the beginning of my reign, I would have the appropriate audience."

Damas exhibited some courage. "The Emperor?" he

asked. "Why?" By then they all knew who Kang was; their old Kazerai, transformed, the recognition of it perhaps as much a shock as what he had become; but there were doubts as to what was left of him.

He walked over to Damas. Others in the room tensed as he moved. Damas swallowed. Part of Kang wanted their undying allegiance, the more realistic part knew he would probably have to settle for fearful obedience.

But that would be enough.

"Do not question me," he said, no malice in his tone; simply an order he would not give again. "I require your presence."

"Of course," Damas said at once, and Kang could see the hesitation in his eyes as the words left his mouth. Was he ready to submit so quickly to this beast that just killed the last of their Kazerai and their High Council? This intruder who was now demanding access to the Emperor himself? That holiest of holies? More than that, had he just showed weakness in the eyes of the others?

But, Kang noticed, none of the others seemed to care. All realized what their own reaction would be. No one standing there had enough devotion to the dead Emperor to defy Kang. None would try and resist the inevitable.

"This way," Damas turned and headed across the lobby, Kang and the others following.

A few locked elevators and several long, absurdly useless, decorative halls later, they were standing in the outer chamber at the uppermost floor of the towering Vivitak. Yamoto, Damas, five senior officers and Kang.

A place where no one went.

Kang stepped forward and stood before the ornately carved door, savoring the moment. Beyond it lay the Emperor, in his repose, waiting for the day Anitra would be united and he would rise again to lead them.

Today is that day, thought Kang. *And I will be at its head. Not you. Sadly, Kagami, you will not be returning.*

With an easy nudge he pushed in the heavy door, bolts snapping away in a pop of splintered wood and metal. It groaned inward and hung on its hinges as he stepped across the threshold, into the Emperor's chambers.

Inside was about as lavish as he expected, the room filling the entire upper floor. High windows all around its circular circumference allowed only views of the heavens above, the morning sun rising outside, filling the room with warmth, glinting on gilded trim and precious stones. Kang walked further in, eyes fixed on the golden sarcophagus at the center, perched regally atop a white marble dais.

All quite breathtaking.

Behind him the others followed; appalled, scared for their lives yet unable to resist the temptation of seeing what had, until then, been impossible taboo. In that sense Kang had freed them, if only a little, and he sensed the curiosity behind their fear.

Of course they had no idea how far he intended to go.

At the sarcophagus he ran a hand along an edge, feeling the engravings, then ... punched through. The sharp sound of the blow made everyone jump, jerking their wandering attention from the sparkling beauty of the room and locking it directly on him.

Kang jerked the heavy lid free and tossed it aside, imagining it must be impressive in its heft, feeling as if nothing in his grasp. It cracked and broke apart as it flew through the air and hit solidly against the far wall, dust filling the rays of sunlight. As the noise of that action subsided he noticed all present were still flinching.

He stared down into the coffin. Inside lay the mummified Emperor, wrapped in extravagant gold robes, ancient flesh and white hair giving him a semblance of his original form.

Kang reached in and jerked the body free, ripping away the robes and pulverizing it, crumbling it to pieces. He could not resist laughing as he did, hurling aside chunks of decay and holding up the robes, mark of his new station.

"What now, your legacy?" he yelled, gloating. His audience stared back, speechless. He stepped up and stood atop the dais, holding out the robes.

Shouted: "I am your new Emperor!"

* * *

ZAC WATCHED THE FADING SKY, admiring the hues of deep, cobalt blue, reflected in the wide lake. The still waters were a perfect mirror of the clear, beautiful sky, no breeze tonight to disturb them; joined at the horizon, split by distant, rolling hills, backlit in silhouette against the fading light. The sun had slipped below the hills minutes ago and in the cloudless sky its final orange hues had been replaced by dark blues, layer upon layer; brighter at the horizon, curving overhead until behind him deep blue became the black of night. Stars poked through, their reflections appearing in the water amid the amazing colors.

It was a beautiful scene.

He breathed in the fresh forest air, turned and walked a little further along the lake—at length bringing the lighted buildings of the nearby Venatres outpost into view and dispelling a bit of the setting's magic.

Back to reality.

His current post was at the Venatres/Dominion border, working with various Venatres units to monitor and hold in check the growing Dominion presence. Following the battle at the Crucible the Dominion had stormed the Venatres shores with a fury and, unexpectedly, established a sizable foothold right there in Venatres lands, putting the Venatres on their heels ever since. Word was the Dominion were building their forces in preparation for the next surge. Zac had come back with the Venatres retreat and been working with them ever since.

In the midst of that he found plenty to keep him occupied. Siding with the Venatres had been a boon for them, but even the chaotic injection of his fighting prowess had done little to stem the tide. Like the Kazerai of the Dominion he was great at creating pandemonium, at performing specific missions, but in the overall scheme of war he managed only to create a minor impact. The Dominion still came. Poised, ready to attack. This time, he feared, they might sweep further, taking still more land.

As he made his way slowly along the edge of the lake, killing time before the next meeting, he noticed one of the outpost soldiers jogging toward him, an urgent expression on his face. Zac waited for his approach.

"Stal," he recognized the man. "What's up?"

"You've got a call."

Zac had one scheduled for the morning; wasn't expecting one now. Immediately he began thinking of possibilities. Was the Dominion moving troops?

"Command," said Stal. "Intel Branch. It's Satori. She asked me to come find you."

"Satori?" Now his mind went in an entirely different direction. What could Satori want? They hadn't spoken in a month. Now that she was with Intel their paths rarely crossed.

"She's holding."

Zac nodded. "Well," he started moving and Stal followed, "let's see what she's got."

CHAPTER 25:

TROUBLE

THEIR ESCORT CAME FOR THEM mid-day. The man was on edge, more so than usual, and for once it looked as if his mind was finally on other things. Other, more pressing things. Maybe they'd arrived? Jessica's spirits rose at the thought of this.

They followed him up rusty stairs, one flight then another, level to level, rising from the depths of the bilge, she wearing the backpack against her chest, hugging it close and not caring whether anyone suspected it to contain anything valuable or not. Bianca was wide-eyed and stayed near enough at every step to touch. Their escort climbed ahead, looking back constantly.

At the top of the last flight they emerged into the sunlight, topside, and Jess squinted against the glare. As they stepped onto the deck she raised a hand to shield her eyes, the sun overwhelmingly bright after the prolonged gloom of the below-decks cabin. She got her bearings and looked in the other direction ...

Land!

Sweet, sweet land, right there, stretching across the horizon, all the way left and right to the ends of her vision. *Yes!* That had to be Venatres. And there, directly in their path, clear enough to make out, was a dock.

"Come on," their escort nudged. "Captain's waiting."

A few crewmen were in view, ranged around the deck of the cargo ship as it prepared to make port. Their escort led them aft to the bridge island, a three-floor building at the rear of the ship—just like an old merchant marine vessel of Earth—and they began the ascent of yet another set of metal stairways along its outside. Windows wrapped the top and Jess could see a few people up there on the bridge, running controls or standing around watching. The crew, overall, seemed sparse. A typical compliment for a cargo ship.

Moments later they were at the top.

"You know," the captain addressed them as they walked onto the bridge; no introductions, no hellos, no preamble, "that's Dominion controlled land." He pointed to his right, to the southern horizon. "Just over the line."

They'd never met the captain before now. He stood apart from the rest, checking readings; a plain, unremarkable man, balding with a serious paunch. *Talk about a beer gut*, thought Jess, amazed at just how far it hung over his belt. Four other men shared the bridge, average guys of various ages, terribly unexcited about their jobs.

"Should take you there," the captain went on. "That's what I should do."

Jess glanced from the captain to their escort. The gap-toothed man was nervous. So was she, of course, but their escort's nerves came from the greedy notion that he might lose whatever payment he had coming. Jess knew nothing of his arrangement, but it seemed as if whatever he was counting on depended on them getting to *this* port safely— which probably also had something to do with why he'd restrained himself from trying anything "extracurricular" on the voyage.

Of course, that compulsion didn't help her. Just because he seemed to have a stake in their arriving didn't mean he could do anything about it. He just stood there, looking sick.

"Can't believe I'm putting ashore here," the captain continued speaking as if he had an interested audience, or as if he was just going to speak and didn't care if anyone listened or not. "They don't respect free trader agreements. Risking my livelihood, that's what I'm doing.

"At least the Dominion keep their word. Not like these goddamned Venatres." He took a moment to look Jess over, then Bianca. Studying them closely for the first time since they entered the bridge. Jess held the backpack tighter. "What I *should* do," he said, "is keep one of you as security."

Across the bridge one of the crew looked ashore through binoculars. The others steered the ship. No one paying them much attention at all.

"Maybe try and sell one of you to the Dominion." The captain toyed with the idea. "Wonder what they would pay?"

Jess glared at him. Mind at a heightened state of alert. She scanned each of the targets on the bridge. Each man complacent beyond belief, locked in a sort of automatic lethargy; the rote mechanics of bringing the ship to port. It would take precious instants for any of them to wake enough to handle a sudden threat. She calculated her moves. She could drop the two closest crewmen before the other two even knew what was going on. In the ensuing shock she could no doubt take those two as well—none of them looked athletic in the least—and the captain would go down with no more than a massively hard kick to the nuts. Bianca could be counted on to just stand there in shock, out of the way. The escort would have to be taken care of, of course, but he seemed like such a sleaze he'd probably just turn and run as soon as she broke bad. She'd then lock the door, grab the wheel and hold them steady, right into the dock. Smash. With grim determination she mapped it out, mind on that other plane; eager to execute. Itching to go berserk and make each of them bleed, heart racing in anticipation of imminent, brutal action.

But it wasn't to be.

"Captain," one of the crew got his attention. Binocular guy. "There's a group assembling on the dock. They just flashed the signal."

The captain looked toward the dock. Jess did too. At that distance it was difficult to see things as small as people, but she thought she could make out a small group standing at the edge. A glint of light flashed from among them, probably the signal.

The captain harrumphed.

"Flash them back," he said. "Looks like we'll go ahead as planned." Then, more to himself: "They'd better pay."

Lucky for you, thought Jess, still on the brink. *Lucky*

for you.

* * *

KANG TUGGED AT THE FABRIC of the Emperor's golden robes, situating them across his scaly shoulders. Bulky and flowing as they were, they were too tight and they shredded in places as he pulled them on. So far it was a ridiculous getup, but he was wearing them, at least for now. A mockery, truly, of that divine station, to be draped upon such a beast as he'd become, a yellow-skinned demon— complete with horns—masquerading in the Emperor's old attire, and the fact that he wore the clothes of a dead man, taken straight off that dead man, only added to this sense of the macabre. But it was his decision and he was sticking to it.

He relished the nervous expressions of those around him.

"Sir," Yamoto stood firm before him, backed by the other officers that had borne witness to his ascension. They gathered in the Shogun's chambers at the top of the Tower of Light, Yamoto long since out of his Shogun robes and back into his military regalia. Yamoto seemed fine with this, in truth. There would be no more Shogun. Kang would hold title of both Emperor and Shogun and would rule, in fact, as a god.

"We have word from the Imperial Guard," Yamoto completed his report. "The last of them have been rounded up. They're in detention."

Kang nodded. "Good."

He had not yet decided how to restructure the pervasive religious tenants that held together the framework of the Dominion, but he thought the few remaining clerics might somehow play a part. He could either kill them and rule the dominion as its absolute, unquestioned head, sweeping away all beliefs they'd lived their entire lives by, or he could fit himself into the existing dogma in some as yet unknown way.

"There is," Yamoto went on, "a considerable confusion

at the moment. If we are to transition—"

"Where is Horus?" Kang interrupted.

Yamoto paused. "Sir?"

" 'Lord' ," Kang corrected him. He liked Yamoto. He seemed less fearful than the rest. Ready to get on with things, if uncertain in the face of such dramatic change. Kang knew how hard it must be. He also knew he needed loyal officers to command. But it was probably time to set precedent.

"I am your Emperor," he noted.

Yamoto nodded. "Lord," he rephrased. "Do you mean Horus, the once Kazerai?"

"Once?" Did that mean he was dead after all? Horus hadn't been among the Kazerai to challenge Kang and he would be, if still alive, the only Kazerai left. Kang had so far assumed he was killed in the blast, Kang himself somehow shielded enough in the ground to survive, but there was also the idea that Horus lived. If so, what had become of his arch-nemesis?

Yamoto looked to the others in the room, standing nervously in wait; each of them wanting to have answers but, in this case, having none.

"We don't know, Lord," he said. "Following the Crucible he disappeared. We thought him dead, but learned he had begun working with the Venatres. He works with them now, though his location is rarely known."

Rage seized Kang, quite unexpectedly, and as his visage clouded over the officers in the room took an involuntary step back. Yamoto, even, moved. Just a little. Kang grinned, excited that his mere expression could have such an effect.

Then the rage returned, rolling over him, bringing with it hatred and the memory of how Horus had handled him. How Horus, if Kang was to be honest, defeated him.

No more. If Horus lived he would find him. Destroy him, now that he could. *Yes!* Avenge this horrible disfigurement, wrought as a result of Horuses' victory. And in the bargain remove that—potential—challenge to his ultimate rule of this world.

All else could wait. It gripped him like a shot.
Horus must die.

* * *

IT TOOK FOREVER TO MAKE PORT. Jess stood with Bianca on
the bridge, watching the crew go about their methodical
docking routine. Those crewmen with them on the bridge
coordinated those below, ambling to and fro across the
deck, pulling lines and hauling them in.

Time seemed to stand still. Jess burned with impatience
to just flee the bridge and leap over the edge to the dock, but
she used the time to scan the waiting group of Venatres,
trying to spot familiar faces; a dozen men in uniforms,
themselves waiting impatiently as the ship tied off. And
though she knew there was no logical reason for him to
be there she could not stop looking for Zac. He had to be
with them. He had to have come. It was almost like she
could sense him, or so it felt, but after a thorough scan of
the area, again and again, searching buildings, shadows,
places that might hide him—*why would he be hiding?*—
everywhere; looking even in the surrounding water (like he
would actually be swimming to her!)— she was forced to
conclude he wasn't there.

Hope could be a powerful thing.

One face she did recognize, on the third or fourth
sweep of the small group: Lindin. She remembered him,
commander of the Venatres forces. Standing among the
Venatres he and a few other officer-types looked to be
heading things, and at the sight of him her nerves eased.
Lindin was a decent enough man last time she saw him.
She'd left unexpectedly then, of course, after he'd told
her he wanted to question her and would see her in the
morning, but there should be no bad blood between them.
She was returning and she expected him to be helpful this
time as well.

Many agonizing minutes later the all clear was given
and the captain and their escort went ashore. Jessica
and Bianca were brought down to the deck, just short of

the gangplank, held there surrounded loosely by several of the crew.   She felt dirty in the days-old Dominion clothing, vulnerable, hugging the lumpy backpack. Bianca continued to crowd nervously against her, fear inflamed once more now that they'd reached this new juncture. Each new change seemed to affect her—though Jess noticed her reaction now wasn't as bad as before.

Bianca was starting to build a little courage.

The ship swayed gently in the waves lapping ashore, bumping against the dock, ropes creaking against its bulk as they went taught then slack again. In the distance rolled green, forested hills. The air smelled of the sea, the sky overhead blue, and for an alarming instant Jess snapped out of her head.

This was not Earth.

She steadied herself.

"I recognize one of them," she said softly, so only Bianca could hear—needing to speak, to bring her mind back to the moment. "We'll be fine."

Bianca looked to the men at the end of the gangplank. Lindin had moved to the front and was addressing the captain. The captain, in turn, seemed to be making a show of it, but Jess was confident all would go as planned. There would be no turning back now.

Sure enough, within moments the fat man accepted what appeared to be payment and was waving them down the gangplank. Without a word the crew stepped aside and let them pass.

Safely at the bottom Jess breathed a sigh of relief.

"Easiest profit I've made," the captain commented as they were handed over to Lindin and his group. Their escort eyed the captain doubtfully, looking back and forth between him and the small, heavy bag he held in one hand. *Interesting*, thought Jess. Like paying the village blacksmith with coins or something. Maybe it was even a bag of gems. Who knew.

All that mattered was that the captain seemed satisfied and, with no further comment, made his way back up the gangplank. Their escort followed, glancing back now and again at the two girls he would never see again.

"You can give that to Jacob," said Lindin. Jess started at the proximity of his voice. She turned to look up into his gaze. He was now standing quite close.

"Hi," she said and extended a hand. "Lindin, right?" Handsome, gray-templed, George-Clooney-esque Lindin, official with the Venatres.

"Yes," he took her hand.

"Jessica."

He smiled patiently. "You've become a legend, Jessica. I think we all know your name."

"This is my friend, Bianca," she introduced her.

Lindin took a moment to shake Bianca's hand, clearly caring little for introductions, then turned immediately back to Jess.

"You can give that to Jacob," he repeated. For a moment she wasn't sure what he meant, then realized he was talking about the backpack. Unconsciously she clutched it a little tighter.

"Why?" she asked.

"It has the devices, correct?"

She hesitated, not liking the sudden impatience in Lindin's eyes.

"Yes," she confirmed.

"Give it to Jacob." Lindin pointed to one of the men in the group. A younger, athletic-looking guy, who seemed just as eager to take possession of the backpack and its contents.

Jess wrapped her arms still closer about it. "I can hold it for now." Of course she'd known she would be giving the Icons over to them, at some point, but now that she was here, now that she saw how anxious they were to get their hands on them, she began to fear for their loss. She needed one of them, at least, to get home. If she ever went home.

What were the Venatres going to do with them?

"It would be safer with Jacob," Lindin insisted.

Jess scanned their faces, finding them all unfriendly in that moment.

She didn't want to give the pack to anyone.

Then ...

What?

Overwhelming, all at once, that same sense she'd had earlier when searching the docks as they made port, only now it couldn't be denied. That feeling, that silly, tingling sensation she'd been so quick to dismiss but that had never really left and it was now screaming at her, like her own personal Spidey-sense or something.

Instinctively she looked up, over everyone's heads, squinting into the sun ...

And saw something.

A figure, arcing toward the dock, airborne from a tremendous leap. Curving through the sky directly for them.

Nearly flying.

Everyone turned to follow her excited gaze.

Bianca screamed. Lindin and the Venatres stepped back, stumbling into each other as Zac impacted a hundred feet away at a crouch and looked up.

Jess was already halfway to him.

CHAPTER 26:

STALEMATE

NEVER HAD SHE RUN SO FAST. Jess hit Zac even as he was rising from his landing; hit him at a full sprint as absolutely fast as she could, not slowing even one little bit because she knew she didn't have to and *whump!* was crashing into him with every bit of emotion she'd been sitting on for months; enough to bowl a linebacker over and he laughed and swept her back and around, soaking up her momentum in a twirl and holding her to him. The lumpy backpack came between them, against his chest, sliding as he rose to his full height. She cursed its intrusion, wanting to feel him against her, wanting to hurl it aside and squeeze him to her with everything she had. In that first instant everything was a blur. She felt him set her to her feet, strong arms wrapped around her, enclosing her like in the safest space that ever was; heard him say her name—even as she said his breathlessly, overwhelmed, more than once. He held her and she buried her face against him, over the top of the confounded backpack; all other thoughts, all noises, all troubles for that briefest of instants fleeing to the far corners of the universe, leaving her locked in the timelessness of his embrace. Wrapped in serenity, ecstasy ...

It was heaven, and she relished it.

Too soon the reactions of the others came crashing in.

"What are you doing here?" An alarmed Lindin rushed up on them and held short, respectful of the Kazerai's strength.

"I came for her." The rich sound of Zac's voice thrummed in her ears and she thrilled with it. She looked up, into his handsome face—worrying all at once that she herself must look terrible. *Hideous!* But if she did his reaction did not betray it, smiling down on her with pure admiration. *You came for me!* she grinned. And for an instant fell into his piercing, blue eyes.

"Hi," he said, directly to her, ignoring the others entirely. Her heart fluttered.

"Hi," she returned. It was stupid, it was dumb, it was amazing, it was the most incredible verbal exchange in the history of ever and she loved it. Right then she was one-hundred-percent sappy, romantic teenage girl, bubbling over with emotion. Zac had come for her and to hell with everyone else. She felt giddy.

"You're supposed to be on the Northern flank." Lindin was quite obviously flustered.

"I was," said Zac, turning his attention briefly to him. "But this was more important." He turned his gaze back to her as he said it and her heart swooned. He looked exactly as she remembered. Over the intervening months, as she thought of Zac, again and again, she wondered if, in her mind, she might have—just a little—embellished his hunkiness. But as she held him now, not letting go even though everyone was right there waiting, feeling the depth of his chest, the power in his arms, looking up into his wonderful eyes as he looked down into hers in all his handsomeness, all his tallness …

Her memory was spot on.

He was as hunky as ever.

"Goddammit," Lindin looked around, trying to make sense of this new development. Trying to gather his thoughts, it seemed, to get things back on track.

Slowly Jess let go of Zac, reluctantly, but staying right up against him. He in turn looked to Lindin and the other Venatres. Zac wore black pants and boots, with a short-sleeved shirt that showed off his arms. With muscles like that, Jess thought, and at his height, he would've been strong for a normal man. As it was he was Kazerai, and she knew the strength in those limbs was a thousand times even what they appeared. He could toss everyone there in the water with ease, then waltz off with she and Bianca into the sunset, one girl on each shoulder.

She shuddered.

"Look," he kind of apologized. "I didn't mean to throw anyone off. I just came to make sure she's taken care of. That's all."

Jess reached and held his hand, so smitten she couldn't stand it. He squeezed it back and she looked over at Bianca and grinned sheepishly. Her friend just stared, freaked out by everything that was happening—not least of all by Zac's incredible entrance—but realizing, if nothing else, that Zac was an ally. And in that moment it occurred to Jess that Bianca had no idea what Zac was capable of. Other than the little demonstration back in the playhouse those many months ago, Bianca had never witnessed Zac's full potential. Knew nothing of it. Seeing him leap in through the air like that must have her mind in overdrive.

Lindin continued to look beside himself, a string of curses building. "She's got something crucial to our future," he said, no doubt hating that he had to explain himself. Diplomacy, not force, was the only solution and it was killing him. He, too, knew Zac could toss them all in the drink and there was nothing they could do.

The only way was to reason with him.

"I know," said Zac. "Remember? I know exactly what she's got. I know how she got here."

"But you don't know how important it is!" Lindin fairly exploded. Jess stopped staring furtively at Zac and put her attention on the other man in this standoff. Lindin wasn't a bad guy. She could see that. He had the best interests of the Venatres in mind and the Venatres were the good guys. She had no idea *why* he wanted the Icons so badly, but could accept that there was probably good reason.

"Maybe I don't," Zac admitted. "But I know how important it is to *her*." The implication in his statement was that *she* was more important than any of their desires and that, of course, made her swoon all over again.

Lindin looked as if he truly would explode. To his credit, however, he found his way to a calm center and, when he spoke, it was with remarkable, if forced, reserve.

"I know it's important to her," he agreed. "But these devices contain information we alone can take advantage of." Lindin looked as if he'd already said too much. "I can't make any promises," he was quick to add, looking directly at Jess. "All I can say is that, at a minimum, you will get them back."

Zac looked to her. "Them?"

"There's two now."

He raised an eyebrow.

Jess turned to Lindin. "You can have them for whatever you need," she said. "Obviously. I brought them here to let you. But I want to be kept in the loop. My life," and she glanced at Bianca, "our lives, whatever comes next depends on these."

Zac added a demand: "Take them with you."

Lindin balked. "We'll take them somewhere safe. As planned. They'll be taken care of."

"Take them wherever you take the Icon," Zac insisted. "I mean, Icons. Jess and her friend," he looked at Bianca, "Bianca, right?"

Bianca's eyes widened, surprised Zac remembered her name after all that time—she'd only said it once, back in the woods on Earth—and the fact that he *did* remember seemed to elevate her mood all at once. She smiled and nodded.

Zac went on. "And me, as their guardian."

Zac was so wonderful.

But this was clearly too much for Lindin.

"You— I can't ... Not—" He couldn't finish a thought; realizing, of course, that whatever he said didn't matter. Zac was staring him down, tall and determined, and Lindin had to resign himself to the fact that there was no choice. Jess could almost see the switch as it flicked over. Nothing he tried would be worth the effort. Sullenly he caved.

"I wasn't going to hurt her."

Zac seemed to grow a little taller, if that was possible. "I'm not saying you were. But you owe her and you know it." He looked down on Jessica and she felt the passion of his defense. Zac was her strength.

Her everything.

Lindin shook his head; prepared to accept the hand

fate dealt him. "This is the most classified project in the Venatres arsenal. *No one* knows about this."

Zac shrugged. "You can trust us."

Lindin nearly screamed.

But he didn't.

"If I do this," he said, "you need to understand that. No word of this gets out.

"Understood?"

Zac and Jess looked at each other. She squeezed his hand. They in turn looked to Bianca, who had the blank expression of one who was going along with whatever was decided.

Everyone nodded.

"Understood."

Lindin, still grumbling, began rounding up his men.

* * *

YAMOTO WATCHED AS KANG observed a group of workmen with mild disdain, positioning a new throne on the dais where the Emperor's coffin once stood. They were in the process of converting the uppermost chambers of Vivitak, the Emperor's previous place of waiting, into the monster's new chambers.

Yamoto stood to the side. He and Damas spent the earlier part of the day briefing Kang on the current positions of Dominion forces, strategic plans and so forth. Kang, who used to be a Kazerai in Yamoto's employ, who was now something so far beyond anything they'd ever seen. Kang, whom he at first expected to exhibit more interest, based on that past, who instead seemed reluctant to put his full focus on the current state of affairs, more concerned with the spoils of this new grip on power.

Yamoto watched him. Kang, in turn, watched the workers. Here was ... a man, with nothing to fear, who could destroy anything and himself could not be destroyed. Why should Kang care what anyone expected of him? What anyone thought? They were his to command, unquestionably, yet ...

There *was* a flaw to that reasoning.

Yamoto weighed his words.

"When should I schedule your address?" he asked. Kang seemed not to hear, consumed as he was with the placement of the throne.

But he did hear. "Address?" he queried.

Yamoto calmed himself. Standing next to this yellow-skinned, horned abomination, wrapped in the Emperor's golden robes, recognizing his mental instability ...

Whatever had happened to his vaunted Kazerai the horns now made him taller, his grotesquely inflated physique even more intimidating than the mere horror of disfigurement. That, of course, and the fact that Kang's new strength, quite factually, seemed to have no limits. It taxed Yamoto. There was nothing that could be done—in a sense Kang *was* as a god—and so Yamoto's only hope was to steer him, somehow, using only his will.

"To the people of the Dominion."

Kang squinted. Yamoto struggled to read the monster's expression. Suspicion? Confusion?

Hate?

"I do not intend to address these people," Kang went back to watching the workmen, and Yamoto realized it was disdain. Kang was filled with it.

"You must." Yamoto's words were bold, he knew. Perhaps too bold, but he had to push. This was his first battle, the first test of that very will, and he would either die or gain ground.

Kang's reaction, however, was mild. "I am their god," he said. "They do not need me to tell them that."

"Not true." Yamoto swallowed, regretting not thinking his words through. Kang looked back at him, slowly, and Yamoto steadied his gaze. Trying not to look defiant, desperate not to look weak. "They know little of you or your plans," he said. "Only that the Council is no more, and that a monster now occupies the halls of their god. To them you are a usurper. A demon."

Kang bristled. "I am their Emperor!"

"You're not," said Yamoto. Then, carefully: "Not yet."

Kang didn't kill him. He did, however, step close.

"I *am*." He studied Yamoto. Yamoto did not quiver, knowing Kang weighed something rash. Perceiving that, somehow, through the mania, Kang thought him useful. Yamoto was saying what had to be said, it was all he could do, and as Kang reined in the rage that nearly slapped his general across the room, Yamoto saw that the beast realized his words, clearly, were not insolence but advice. Difficult advice. Necessary advice.

Kang laughed a little. And for a moment Yamoto wondered if Kang himself would be so brave if the tables were turned. Would he stand up to a monster that could end his life in an instant? On a whim?

Probably he would not.

"What do you suggest?" Kang asked coolly.

"As powerful as you are," Yamoto began, "you have nothing if the people set themselves against you. I have no doubt you could, given time, destroy all of us. Every one. It's clear there would be nothing that could stop you.

"But where would that leave you? One man, in charge of all this?" He waved an arm around the room. Then he exhaled and lowered his voice. "There will be a revolt if you begin your rule behind closed doors. A monster that has defiled the form of the divine Emperor? There may yet be a revolt, even so, but your chances are better if you make yourself known. Recall the significance of this dogma. Of this belief. I've hated it my whole life. You hated it. You know you did." This spoke truth to Kang. "But it is what the people *believe*. Once you served within it, as did I. But you hated it even then." Kang did. He knew he did, and Yamoto could see the truth biting. "You know the strength of it. There must be a transition, if only a token one. Something to define the New and explain away the Old.

"Chaos is not the way to rule a people, or a world." Yamoto steadied himself. "Address the Dominion." It seemed as if he was getting through. "Promise them greatness. They may fear you at first, but they can be rallied. Only, however, with visibility. Only by starting your rule right."

Kang studied him.

"I am a god," he said quietly, testing Yamoto just a little further. "I need no acceptance."

"Even a god needs acceptance. A hated god will be left in nothingness. Forgotten."

Kang kept a stern visage. As if wanting Yamoto to waver.

He did not.

Kang relented.

"Very well," he said, and turned back to his scrutiny of the workmen. "Arrange it."

CHAPTER 27:

MOUNTAIN RETREAT

JESS SAT BESIDE ZAC in the back of the van, comparing the size of his knee to her own; gauging the power in his legs, listening as he answered meaningless questions put to him by the Venatres handlers. She, Bianca and Zac sat in the back of the large windowless van with four uniformed intelligence agents, enroute to their "top secret" destination. She held the backpack, still wearing it on her chest. Two other vans had started out in the same convoy, and she imagined they must still be near, rolling along the smooth Venatres roads; a procession that all seemed rather in the open, making her wonder if the Dominion had satellite tracking or some other sort of surveillance. Their little caravan of white trucks must be pretty obvious.

She leaned into Zac, deliberately, letting herself go with the sway of the vehicle, feeling his solid mass against her, feeling the weight of his proximity with every one of her senses. Sitting next to him was nearly unbearable, after everything, sharing that small space with the others, dying as she was to be alone with him, to ask so many things, to tell him so many more. Now that she'd actually *found* him it was killing her that their first moments alone might yet be far away.

"Really?" one of the group asked, not believing what Zac had just said.

"It's true," he confirmed.

And as he continued his dialog with the Venatres, who themselves had never met one of the legendary Kazerai, interrupted occasionally by Bianca, who was coming out of her shell and asked Zac a few questions about his power and what he could do—as all the others talked Jess studied his every move. Discreetly, of course, acutely aware each time he looked at her, even a glance; the way he held himself, whether protectively or otherwise—everything—trying desperately to glean the substance of his feelings.

Realizing now, without a shadow of a doubt, she was head-over-heels in love. As if there was ever any question. Back on Earth, over the intervening months, she'd just been suppressing. Zac was the one, and it was killing her not to be able to talk.

Did he feel the same about her? Had he ever, really? No matter anything else that had happened up to that moment she couldn't stop worrying he'd moved on. Not knowing *that* little bit of information, whether or not he'd found new love—that more than anything was killing her. There he was, right there—*he's right there!*— and she had no idea. Angry she couldn't just blurt out the question and find out once and for all.

Then—surprise, surprise—Bianca did.

"Do you have a girlfriend?" she asked from directly across the van. Zac looked to her and Jessica's mouth fell open. Her friend just popped, without thought or care, the very thing burning in Jessica's mind. Jess, fighting with ideas of how to subtly find out, how to carefully discover what she so anxiously needed to know, maybe ask a few oblique questions or something, and now Bianca throws it out there like asking Zac if he had a cat. Easy. Nothing to it.

For a moment it hung in the air. Zac shifted.

"Why do you ask?"

"I don't know." B was so casual, so relaxed. *How does she do it?* Jess wondered why her own courage escaped her. But she knew why. It was because this was Zac, and Zac mattered.

More than anything.

"You just seem so ... beyond normal," Bianca elaborated. "I just wondered if there are girls like you. Like if you've got a super-powered girlfriend or something."

Zac considered this. "I don't know how much Jess told you," he explained, "but my wife was killed." Briefly he seemed to relive the tragedy and, as Jess saw his expression change, she nearly reached for him. But the notion was too absurd. It passed quickly and Zac resumed talking.

"I haven't remarried," he said. Then: "I'm unattached."

And there it was. Everything she was dying to know, divulged. Bianca, in her innocent, direct way had learned the answer.

Which allowed other worries to take hold.

Was Zac interested? On her last visit they'd kissed. In fact their last kiss *he* initiated. They'd said things. Gazed into each other's eyes, in ways beyond that of mere friends. His farewell months ago was filled with passion, the kiss she would remember forever, his greeting back at the dock was way effusive yet ...

As subtly as she could she adjusted her hair, greasy after days at sea, knotted in strands. The Dominion clothes were frumpy and, by then she was sure, giving off a powerful funk. She must have bags under her eyes. Grime on her skin.

Of course Zac chose that very moment to turn to her, face to face, and ask: "How about you? Are you married now?"

She actually choked, coughed a little, even as Bianca laughed at the question.

"Married?" her friend sniggered. "We're too young to get married." Then she sobered and looked around the interior of the van—as if imagining all the strange things outside. "At least on our world." Jessica's eyes were locked to Zac's, watching for his reaction. Before he could respond, however, Bianca threw out a bombshell: "She's got a boyfriend though."

Why her friend chose now, of all times, to be her usual TMI self left Jess speechless. All she could do was stare gap-mouthed at Zac, unable to think of anything to say in response.

Mortified.

"Well," he seemed to resign himself to the idea, too fast, and her heart sank. "I'm happy for you," he said. "I'm glad you were able to get your life back on track."

No! She couldn't let him believe she was taken.

"It's nothing," she found her tongue, tried to be mild—

all the while wanting to yell everything in one breath, to tell him how she'd just tried to live her life as he wanted, how much he meant to her, how much he dominated her thoughts, her dreams, how much she was his, completely, how she wanted to be with him forever and ever and how nothing—*no one*—else mattered.

She made herself adopt an easy smile. "I think I need to come to grips with the fact that my life is never going to be normal." She swallowed, harder than she wanted, hoping it didn't betray her desperation. "Having a normal boyfriend isn't really an option," she gave an awkward shrug.

Relax!

"To tell the truth, I've already let him go."

Bianca looked at her in surprise. "You're gonna break up with Mike?" Jess wished she would just shut up. *Stop talking!* But Bianca powered on, clearly disappointed. "You two are so perfect for each other. It took you long enough to get together. Sheesh."

Jess stared pointedly across the van, making her eyes wide, hoping Bianca would get it. *Can't you see?!* Bianca, of all people, should recognize she was in love with Zac. Yet her friend seemed oblivious to what was right in front of her. Had all the trauma of the last few days messed her up that badly? Did she hit her head somewhere along the way?

Jess tried to beam it into her, to make her get it. "We left all that behind," she almost winked, knowing how ridiculous that would be but that determined to make her point. "Mike wouldn't understand any of this. Girls have boyfriends. Girls leave boyfriends. Mike was a boyfriend. But I'm hardly a girl anymore." She looked to Zac, trying to make *him* get it. "There's no way Mike can be part of my life now."

"That's too bad," said Zac, though it seemed he said it because he thought that's what he should say. Because it was the polite thing to do, to feel for someone's loss. Jess searched his expression, looking for more.

"Mike will get over it," Bianca said, and Jess snapped her attention back to her—seeing she was finally having the

Ah ha! moment. "Happens all the time," Bianca dismissed the idea of a break-up with a casual wave of her hand. "Especially for us teens." Then, laying it on thick: "We're all about the drama."

Zac nodded, not really understanding.

But Bianca didn't know when to quit. "Too bad, cause every guy would *love* to have Jess as their girlfriend. They've all got their eyes on her. Only she's too self-conscious to know it."

What are you doing?

"I mean, look at her," Bianca pointed. "She's beautiful. She could date any boy she wants, if she ever paid attention."

This isn't helping! Now that Bianca had done the one-eighty she was overcompensating. Jess concentrated, willing herself not to be embarrassed. *Look at me? Please!* Don't *look at me!* She looked worse than she ever had. Desperately she commanded herself: *Don't turn red; don't sweat; be cool; be calm.* It wasn't working. She needed to swallow, her forehead was beading and her cheeks felt flush.

Dammit B!

"Look how cute she is," her friend might as well have been shining an interrogation lamp on her. Jess was becoming really, really annoyed with chatty B. "She would make any guy happy. I've always known she was looking for true love. To be honest I never thought Mike was it."

Then, with a theatrical sigh: "Jess is a true romantic."

Suddenly Zac's proximity was too much. Jess needed space to catch her breath. There he was, face barely a foot from hers as Bianca turned the screws on her embarrassment. Ice blue eyes—*so blue!*—looking at her with a mixture of admiration she didn't deserve and a certain curiosity she could not fathom. But there was nowhere to go and, frustratingly, she had no idea what to say.

And, again, Bianca stepped in.

"I still can't believe that leap," she moved on. Whether she intended to take the heat off or not, it worked. Jess relaxed. But only a bit. "Holy cow," Bianca continued to marvel. "Are you some kind of mutant or something? Tell the truth."

Zac looked between she and Jess. "Mutant?" For him this had become a back and forth between Bianca sitting across from him and Jess sitting beside him. One girl he wanted to talk to, the other just kept talking.

Bianca shrugged. "Yeah."

Jess wiped her sweaty brow when Zac wasn't looking. "He's not a mutant, B. He's like a super soldier, would be the best way to describe it. The army did stuff to him. He was given a kind of boost that made him ultra powerful." In truth she had no idea what was done, and she wasn't sure Zac knew the exact mechanics of it either. The results, however, were quite clear.

"He's Kazerai," one of the Venatres offered. "An enhanced Dominion warrior."

"Like, *really* strong?" Bianca wanted to know.

Now Jess gushed a little. "Beyond strong," she laid a sweaty hand on Zac's thigh and took it away.

"How strong?"

"Superman strong," said Jess.

Bianca looked at her with a raised eyebrow. "Go Jess," she said, as if her friend had just scored big. "A super hero."

By then Zac's confusion was obvious. Jess became desperate to take control of this wildly meandering conversation.

She looked up at him. "How have you been?" It was a dumb question—and it made her blush even more—but it was all her overtaxed mind could come up with.

"Good," he said, himself ready to be done with the current discussion. "And you?"

"Good." What a ridiculous exchange. How could "good" begin to sum up what either of them had been through? Yet the brief and inane banter served to smooth the turmoil. Since being in the van they really hadn't spoken directly to each other without the others being involved in the conversation. And as he looked into her eyes, ready to say ... God knew what but something tender, maybe even funny, a joke or something to chase away the absurdity of this long ride, she anticipating his every word ...

The van slowed.

One of the drivers up front called back and everyone shifted at his announcement. The van was curving, pulling into a sweeping drive. Shortly after that it stopped, the rear doors were opened and a brisk gust of cold air swirled into the warmth of the compartment. Jess shivered, a chill crawling over her mildly sweaty skin as she squinted into the bright sunlight. It was late afternoon by the looks of it, the sky a brilliant, cloudless blue, and as she looked further outside the van at the surrounding scene she realized they were on a mountain, a range of snow-capped peaks all around. Snow was on the ground, piled at the sides of the wide road.

"Let's go," one of the Venatres was saying, jumping out the back. The rest followed. Jess noticed the two other vans were nowhere in sight. Zac rose, helping her though she didn't need it. She relished his gentle touch. Bianca got up and Zac helped her too, and together they stepped to the ground.

Outside the vista was breathtaking. They were indeed on the side of a mountain, a wide, sloping one, in a range of similar heights, snow on the ground as far as the eye could see, a sharp chill in the air. Jess hugged her arms across the backpack, holding it to her and shivering in the thin Dominion clothing.

They'd pulled up in front of a sprawling "house", like a château or a mountain retreat, built into the side of the mountain, probably halfway to the top, judging from their altitude and the mass of the peak looming directly above them. The slope was rocky, peppered with snow and green fir-like trees, towering to a misty height. Jess took in the breathtaking beauty as Lindin walked back to them from the front of the van. The rear doors were closed and the van pulled away, down the drive, curving around the side of the house and into the mountain. Though she couldn't see where it went Jess imagined it must pass through some sort of secret entrance.

"This way," Lindin wasted no time. The others gathered behind and followed him up wide, wooden steps onto the beautiful, wide, wraparound deck, across to a pair of decorative front doors. It was just like a ski lodge, a giant fireplace burning inside the expansive interior, flickering light inviting through tall windows. If this was a secret base it sure was a nice one.

Inside was as warm and cozy as it looked. Lindin kept up the pace, not stopping to say anything or make comments. The great room was probably a hundred feet in all directions, floor-to-ceiling windows on two sides, the other sides built into the mountain, heavy wooden chairs, couches and other lodge-like things everywhere. No people save a few uniformed agents. Jess was reminded of old film clips of Nazi Germany, of Hitler and his generals working out of castles and other vacation-like locations. This all looked kind of the same; people in brown and black suits, all business in a leisure setting.

Before they made it far a man was striding with purpose toward them, followed by several others of seemingly lesser rank. Lindin reached for the backpack. Jess hesitated, then, with a glance to Zac, took it off and handed it to him. He in turn handed it immediately to one of the junior officers.

"Get that to the team at once."

"Yes, sir."

And the man and the others were off in a flash. The senior officer arrived and engaged Lindin.

"Josef," Lindin greeted him.

"We have news," the man reported. "From Osaka. We need to brief you."

Lindin turned to the four agents with him.

"Wait for my call," he said, then nodded toward Jessica, Zac and Bianca. "Then bring them down."

CHAPTER 28:

THE NEW EMPEROR

KANG TOOK HIS CUE, a nod from Yamoto, and strode to the far doors of the Imperial chamber. Beyond the doors a grand archway led to an expansive balcony overlooking the city and the courtyard far below. As he passed through and out onto the balcony he made sure to wipe the sour expression from his face, replacing it with a forced benevolence. Or what he hoped might, at least, be taken for an engaging demeanor. It probably didn't make a difference. There were no demons on Anitra. No yellow-scaled monsters. He could smile his fang-toothed smile all he wanted. The people of Osaka would still fear him. Perhaps even loathe him.

But that didn't matter either. He did not today hold this address of the populace to assure them. To win them. He held it at Yamoto's insistence, at his own acknowledgement of Yamoto's correctness, in principle; his sole purpose to let the people know the way things were going to be from here on out. To apprise them of the New Order.

To introduce them to their new God Emperor.

He walked to the balcony edge, amping his last few steps into a purposeful stride, posture straight, bold, horned head held high. He caught his image in several reflective surfaces, the golden imperial robes hanging all wrong across his jaundiced form; a mockery of humanity.

It nearly made him laugh.

At the railing he stopped. Waited. Damas stood to one side, Yamoto following to stand nearby. Several other important aides gathered near Damas in a pre-arranged formation. Below, far below, in the Imperial courtyard, thronged thousands of Osaka's citizens. The rest watched on video, all citizens of the empire, this grand moment broadcast across the breadth of their lands. The address had been arranged hastily, nearly same-day. As soon as Kang relented to Yamoto's suggestion he insisted the address be done at once. Remarkable how many had shown up on such short notice. Of course, events of the last days had them all keenly on edge, wondering what would come next.

The tower was so high it almost made the whole affair seem ridiculous. Kang himself had insisted on making the address from the pinnacle of the great spire, from the balcony outside the Emperor's chambers; Vivitak, his new home. Individuals in the sea of bodies below were barely discernable. Probably not at all to the human eye. If he chose, however, with his sharp vision he could pick out details. Faces. Each of them fearful. Watching his image on the video monitors placed among them, many more looking up, gazing at something they could not see distinctly but which looked back on them with gloating in its heart.

"People of the Dominion," he began, voice deep, scarred; broadcast on speakers everywhere. "Welcome to the New Age." He surveyed them. Looked beyond them, into the distance, across the land he now ruled. "I am your new, immortal leader," he said. A bit of an egotistical statement, but if anyone deserved to be an egomaniac it was him. He could, right then, leap down among them and kill half before they could flee the courtyard. It annoyed him to be standing there at all.

But Yamoto was right. Kang kept reminding himself of that.

"You have known me," he said, "once. I was a citizen of the Dominion. One of your greatest warriors. You knew me then as Kang, greatest of your Kazerai.

"In the battle for the Crucible I was ... changed. Caught in the explosion of its destruction. I survived. Too powerful to be killed, I was instead transformed into the force you see before you."

And of a sudden he thought of something, completely unplanned. An idea, right then, in the moment, a million eyes upon him. An idea that had not been spoken of in any of his conversations with Yamoto or the others.

An idea that aligned perfectly with his arrival.

"In the time of my absence," he voiced it, "buried as I was in the sands of that wasteland in my crystal shell, I was yet aware. And in that awareness I was visited by Kagami, our great Emperor in Waiting." He watched for reactions; saw the expressions of confusion below, saw doubt pass across the faces of the uniformed men sharing the balcony with him. But among the people confusion changed quickly to something else. Intrigue? As the moment stretched he imagined some even expressed ...

Hope?

This was, after all, the core of their belief. Each looked to a future where the Emperor returned. It was as Yamoto said. They *believed*.

Kang smiled at his own brilliance.

"In that vision he told me I would be reborn, more powerful than before, a vessel for our domination. Kagami said I was to usher in our final and complete control of this world." This, too, aligned with their most fervent ambitions. In this, he thought, he must remember to assign divine power where they would accept it most.

It would make for the easiest transition.

"I doubted at first," he said. "Though I could not explain this disembodied awareness, I nevertheless did not believe I would be reborn. Certainly not like this." He raised his arms to the sides and turned slowly, left to right, letting them see the full measure of his deformity.

Now that he had the spotlight he could do whatever he wanted, say whatever he wanted. And in that same moment he realized it was probably best not to go too far. Best to stick to the script, as it were.

"So I am here. To continue that legacy, to ensure our destiny is realized.

"My first order of business will be to remove the last resistance to our rule, and claim fully the world of Anitra in the name of the Dominion."

Silence, at first, then, as the pause stretched, a collective murmur of agreement, followed by uncertain shouts, then cheers and, soon, the entire courtyard was cheering. A glorious sound, welling from the ground below.

Welcoming the promise of their new Lord.

* * *

JESSICA'S HEAD WAS ON A SWIVEL. They followed their escorts deeper into the underground mountain complex, the whole place unfolding before them as if some super-secret operation. Earlier Zac was called away, shortly after Lindin left. Not long after that others came for she and Bianca and took them down an elevator to a sophisticated set of corridors, plain gray halls that looked more like a movie set for a James Bond villain or a NORAD command bunker. Important-looking people bustled among the high-tech setting, obviously up to things of great significance.

"I still can't believe we're on another planet," Bianca whispered. Just as amazed as Jess she kept looking left and right, up and down. The halls were lit by long lights, not unlike the fluorescent bulbs they were used to in institutions on Earth, yet another Earth-like thing that was either the result of some natural evolution of discovery and invention or the product of an impossible parallel universe.

It was indeed hard, at every turn, to believe they were anywhere other than home.

"I assume it's another planet," Jess also kept her voice low, "but I don't know for sure. That device could connect anywhere. All I'm sure of is that we're not on Earth." She patted her chest involuntarily, still feeling the absence of the pack. Though this time around she could not simply go back home, it still panicked her slightly not to have the means to do so readily to hand. She recalled everything she'd been through on her last "visit", what it took to get the Icon and go back the first time.

She looked over. Bianca had been overwrought for so long it was like her adrenaline had finally run out. Jess couldn't tell if she was actually calm or just wiped. Either way her friend was, for the moment, taking everything in stride.

Suddenly Zac walked into view, ahead at the next cross-hall, saw her and turned for their small group. Impulsively she nearly ran to him again, but this time held her enthusiasm in check. As he approached it looked as if he too suppressed the urge to run. Just as he reached them and their escorts Lindin appeared from the other direction, a few other officers in tow.

The groups met at the center. Jess took Zac's hand, only half listening as Lindin began speaking. She thrilled with the feel of his warm grip, wondering if they should be holding hands at that moment but not caring enough to let go.

"Things in Osaka are not good," Lindin spoke directly to him, consumed with bigger things. "We have word that the Kazerai killer may in fact be Kang."

Jess felt her eyes go wide. That short statement held two impossibilities.

Kazerai killer?

Then: *Kang?!*

"Kang?" Zac echoed the word reverberating through her head.

Lindin nodded. "He made an address to the Dominion."

Questions fought suddenly to be voiced. From the look on his face Zac was just as shocked as Jess was—though he clearly knew a few more particulars leading up to this revelation.

"Wha ..." she stammered, "how is he alive?" Then to Zac: "I thought you killed him."

Zac's blank stare confirmed he thought so too, and that he was just as stunned as her.

"What do you mean, Kazerai killer?" she stared up at Lindin. Confused, scared—trying to make sense of how this could be.

"More can be explained later," he said, "but so far we believe it *is* Kang, transformed somehow in the blast. Detailed images, now that we have them, show this is likely true. It looks like, when the blast at the Crucible went off it didn't kill him but, rather, altered him somehow.

"The fact that he was able to kill not one Kazerai but all

three—two of them at once—leads us to believe he's grown more powerful as a result."

Three!? Jess was overwhelmed with the thought of this new danger. Until that moment she'd drawn comfort from the fact that Zac was impervious. No matter what happened he could never die. He would always be her strength, an unshakable foundation. Even if they were just friends, she never had to worry of losing him. Zac was a constant. Now that was in doubt. Now, apparently, the Kazerai could be killed. Whatever Kang had become …

How did he survive?!

It wasn't fair.

But Lindin was already moving on. "In the meantime we have to move quickly. We—"

"Jessica!" A voice from down the hall. A girl's voice, one that was familiar yet … Jess looked, found the source and, as she spotted the bright red hair coming toward her, recognition came crashing in.

"Satori!" She released Zac's hand and ran for her, troubling thoughts fading for the moment, replaced by an overwhelming kinship in that instant that blocked out all other concerns. Satori must've felt it too for she ran at her with just as much enthusiasm. They met and embraced.

"You came back!" Satori spoke into her ear, cheek to cheek. Then she held Jess by the shoulders at arm's length. "You look like hell," she laughed. "Every time I see you it's like you've been to war!"

Jess grinned. It was true. The last time she was with Satori was on the field of battle. Standing there now Satori was clean and pressed, same bright red hair but this time wearing what looked to be an officer's uniform. Black, unlike the brown worn by Lindin. Jess was surprised to find her there at all.

"You're part of this?" she asked.

Satori nodded. Then Satori glanced past her, at Zac.

"I knew you'd reach her."

Jess looked between them, realizing Satori must've been the one that tipped him off.

Lindin perked up at this little revelation.

"Wait. You told him?" He narrowed his eyes and glowered at her. "I should've guessed."

Satori just scowled back. "I had no idea what you might do." She refused to be apologetic. "I know you hate what we did but she saved our asses, in case you've forgotten."

"I keep telling you people I wasn't going to hurt her!" Lindin seemed miffed that Satori might think so. That anyone might think so. He stared hard at the red-headed commander.

Then shook his head, disgusted. "Thanks to you he got involved." He looked at Zac. "Now that you got involved you got everyone involved." He glanced pointedly at Jess and Bianca, then back at Satori. "There was no need to bring them here."

"Well it's done now. Besides," Satori's eyes flicked knowingly between Zac and Jess, "I knew they'd want to see each other."

At this Jess blushed, tried unsuccessfully to cool the heat from her face—then noticed Zac was blushing as well. The sight of his lightly pinked cheeks made her heart skip.

Did that mean ... ?

She still didn't have an answer, and suddenly wanted desperately to divert everyone's attention. Lindin took care of that for her, reminding them, quite pointedly, they were all standing in the middle of far more important things.

"We don't have time for this." He looked to one of his aides. "Has Nani arrived?"

"She's down with the ship."

Jessica looked at Satori, then Zac. *Ship?*

Lindin seemed torn. "This is why I didn't want to bring any of you here." Though it was clear he'd already come to a decision.

"Things have obviously evolved," he said. "And are continuing to evolve. What I'm about to show you is the single greatest secret on this world. It was certainly never my plan to show it to you, but then neither was any of this." He looked pointedly at Zac—and a little at Satori. Then at Jessica.

Satori maintained her defiance. "You wouldn't have

your little toys if it wasn't for her."

Lindin pressed on, ignoring the interruption: "We're so close to figuring this whole thing out it's possible—just possible—you can shed some light.

"At any rate we're going down and I'm going to show you. Below us, in the heart of the mountain, is the reason we were so determined to get the Icon." He gathered himself a little straighter. "Believe me, it wasn't just to make the Dominion angry."

Then he turned and was off, the officers with him motioning everyone else along.

Satori fell into step beside Jess and Zac.

"What is it?" Jess asked.

Satori couldn't resist a knowing grin.

"You have to see it to believe it."

CHAPTER 29:

CHARIOT OF THE GODS

JESS REALIZED SHE WASN'T MOVING. Was barely breathing, in fact. Moments ago she, Bianca and Zac had been led by Lindin and his group through a final, heavy door, like a giant vault, into a massive cavern that looked to have been carved from the dark rock of the mountain itself. Inside was fully as big as the interior of a domed NFL stadium—huge, all at once—towering ceiling formed of arches and wrought with design work that gave it an alien, almost gothic feel. The space was so large all sound had that unmistakable, dull, blanketed quality, the way things sounded when in an enclosed volume of that size. Mist hugged the ceiling three-hundred feet up. Human technicians moved about on the floor, equipment buzzed and a bustle of small-scale activity echoed throughout the cavernous space. Activity that was totally incongruous with the alien architecture and scale. All that, however, escaped her immediate notice. Only at the fringes of her awareness did she even perceive these things; barely, as one might perceive the beautiful lawn surrounding a magnificent castle. For her entire focus was glued to what sat at the center of that colossal cave. Nearly spanning its length and breadth, filling it, squatting in an aggressive stance on heavy struts, an affront to reason that could be nothing other than ...

A starship.

If the prior halls of the facility weren't interesting enough, this ... this right here ...

This was downright mind boggling.

But there it was. Lethal in form, sweeping out at the rear; wide, black body spread out and swooping forward; a silhouette that gave it a predatory shape, poised like a falcon in the final moment of attack, casting a shadow of doom across its prey.

"Whoa." Bianca's mouth hung open. She was the first to speak, way less stunned than Jess would've expected. In fact, compared to the way Jess was feeling right then Bianca seemed fairly composed.

"A UFO," her friend marveled.

Jess struggled to take it all in, to absorb what she was seeing, but the craft was just too dominant. It had to be three-hundred feet long, maybe more; over a hundred wide. Shiny black, no windows she could see; no markings save a handful of purple lines that traced odd patterns over its smooth, glossy black surface.

Though no one had said anything about it—nor even mentioned exactly what was in store as they made their way down—she knew at once the Venatres did not make this. The Venatres *found* this, somehow, and the cavern with it. No one had to tell her that. The teams of technicians, the equipment ... the Venatres were trying to make sense of it just as much as she was. How long they'd been at it she couldn't know. Months? Years? Certainly since before they tried to steal the Icon.

Somehow the two, the Icon and this starship, were related. Jess shook for an instant; made herself stop.

"You recognize it?" Lindin mistook Bianca's UFO comment for some deeper understanding.

Bianca just stared at him.

Lindin prompted, "You called it a UFO?" Though as he asked it was clear he recognized the truth of what he was dealing with. A teenage girl who was as awestruck as any of them. Bianca didn't know anything.

"An Unidentified Flying Object," she spelled it out.

Lindin seemed let down.

Jess drifted back to the starship, mind buzzing so hard she thought she might actually lift off the ground. The spectacle before her—though she shouldn't have been entirely surprised by much at that point—the sight of it was making her dizzy. Like having an out-of-body experience. Driven by a sense that this craft being there was entirely wrong.

And entirely right.

And it was that, that dichotomy of perception that suddenly drove the separation of self and, as these feelings tightened about her, she was gripped by sudden panic. A fleeting, intense moment where she fought the absurd impulse to run. To get out of there, flee the scene, get to safety. Anywhere but there. Only, of course, there was nowhere to go. She wasn't even on her own world.

And at the thought of that the panic seized her in force.

"How long has it been here?" she asked, in a hurry to quell the irrational fears hedging in. Threatening to send her into what could only be madness. She could see it, right there, the feeling of what it would be to go mad.

She could not allow herself to cross that line.

"We stumbled on it five years ago," Lindin answered, voice distant. Jess shuddered, continuing the fight within. The cave, the ship, the people around her, her future, her past—all held nothing but panicked doom. There was nothing to which to cling. No point of stability on which to set her sights in this sudden sea of insanity. She thought to clutch Zac but was afraid if she did he would recoil from her sudden, inexplicable terror.

Lindin went on: "But it's been here much longer than that. A long, long time. Hidden away. It was built by the ancient Anitrans. Specifically by a race called the Kel."

Jessica's gaze was drawn involuntarily back and forth across the shiny black colossus. It was immaculate. The Venatres had no doubt cleaned it, perhaps even repaired it—such as they had the technology to do. It had probably sat in that underground cavern for all that time but, still. How could it look so new?

Grasping at such mundane considerations was helping. She worked harder to evaluate the facts before her. Its size, how it sat, details of its smooth surface.

"The fallout of the Great Wars left little behind," Lindin went on, and she related that period to what she knew from talk of the Prophecy. "We've found few artifacts." He fell into a moment of marvel. "So little even to piece together the history of what happened, and now this. A whole, entire, starship.

"Somehow this cave was abandoned and never found. We believe it belonged to a Kel warlord. Some sort of private warcraft, not a part of the official Kel fleet.

"We've been studying it, piecing together its function. In the process we've learned a bit about the Kel and managed to decipher their language."

Slowly Jess was getting a grip. Lindin seemed proud of the whole thing, which was understandable. The Venatres were sitting on something beyond amazing and, unless the Dominion were also guarding some similar secret, this was a game changer. With this the Venatres could no doubt obliterate any Dominion resistance, enforce any ideal they chose. With this starship the Venatres could rule the world.

Lindin started walking, heading under the left "wing" and across the expansive floor, toward a concentration of technicians working near the front of the craft. As the group followed Satori stayed close, speaking for Jessica's benefit.

"This is what they wanted the Icon for," she confirmed. "After I let you take it and go home I got raked over the coals." For a brief moment she seemed to relive the pain of that episode. Then: "In the process, of course, I learned the truth of what was going on. Once I did they had to bring me in. Took away my field command and made me part of the intelligence arm."

It seemed Satori wasn't entirely pleased with that outcome. Jess tried to listen, but couldn't stop staring at the ship as they walked beneath and alongside its looming form.

With effort she dragged herself back to the present.

"Thanks for helping me," she looked directly at Satori. "As it turns out I'm stuck in this ... whatever you want to call it. This life. But at least I got to go home for a few months.

"I owe you."

"Are you kidding? We owe *you*. Never forget that. And don't let these guys bully you. You're way more important than you think. And you brought *two* Icons?" Satori shook her head. "Lindin's got a permanent hard-on right now."

Jess sniggered—more of a nervous reaction than anything, though humor didn't appear to be Satori's intent. The comment was merely part of her normal conversation and she kept talking as they walked.

"That's why I notified Zac. Just to make sure we kept some perspective on things."

Nearby Bianca and Zac only half listened, consumed with their own thoughts, gazes roving around the staggering interior of the cavern.

"He's a good guy," Satori glanced at Lindin walking up ahead, "but with this much at stake I didn't want to risk him getting too overzealous and you getting shorted somehow."

Jess nodded; couldn't seem to unglue her eyes from the ship. It was too real. Too *un*real was more like it.

The group came to a halt.

"This is Nani," Lindin was making the introduction as they walked up to join him where he'd stopped. Standing before him was one of the technicians, a girl, probably in her late 20s—looking like a grad student or something and enough out of place among the others that she drew Jessica's full attention. She had natural, white-blonde hair, cut in an odd way that almost looked like she did it herself; that kind of skin that would probably brown easily to a golden tan, but which in her case hadn't seen the sun in a long time. Bright blue eyes completed the Swede genetics. The way she carried herself was nerdy, no doubt—a cliché scientist or a bad stereotype—but it was more like she just didn't do anything to help that image. Like with a little work she could pull it together and look nice. She was frumpy, even her lab coat managed to look frumpy, and she was probably of the sort that was annoyed each morning she even had to pick out what to wear underneath it.

Jess found herself fascinated she was making these Bianca-like observations, and wondered what her friend must be thinking.

"Nani heads the discovery team," Lindin continued the introduction. "She's overseen everything on the project."

Nani raised a hand in greeting. Nerdy all the way to

her mannerisms, but Jess only half noticed as she was immediately shocked to learn Nani was in charge of figuring out the massive, technologically god-like machine dominating the space. How could she, younger than most everyone in sight, outstrip the knowledge of the dozens of other technicians busily at work all around them? How did this Nani earn the top spot over all those other candidates? Jessica's gaze swept those nearby, spotting many older, gray-haired, intelligent-looking men and women, each of whom looked more qualified ...

"I believe the devices will work as expected," Nani looked between Jess and Lindin, getting right to the matter at hand. She seemed impressed, maybe even a little nervous, to be meeting Jess in the flesh. "There do indeed appear to be shared functions. We've already been able to apply what we know from the craft to access the Icon's core mechanics."

Wow, thought Jess. Nani had only had the Icons for such a short while.

"I'm Bianca." Her voice interrupted the moment. Everyone looked at her. "Don't ask me how I got here. Long story." She laughed awkwardly, whatever impulse that had prompted her to speak now gone.

Nani smiled, almost like she found the random introduction refreshing. Bianca grinned. Like two dorks at a party, thought Jess, both realizing they were out of their element. Nani had no idea how to dress, and Bianca had no clue just what the hell was going on.

They were perfect for each other.

Jess looked to Nani. "What about the laptop?" she asked, curious how the Venatres would handle the Earth technology.

"The computer?"

She nodded.

"Standard binary storage. I believe we'll be able to use it."

Lindin looked to Jessica and Bianca, eager to unravel all they represented. "We'll want to debrief you both."

And as he said this, as Jess realized how much more was

still ahead of them, how much they'd been through already, she felt the sudden weight of their Dominion clothes, dirty from days at sea; her greasy strands of hair, the grimy feel of her skin.

"First I want a shower," she said.

"Yes," Bianca agreed wholeheartedly. "Me too."

* * *

DARVON'S OLDEST DAUGHTER, EGG, returned to the living room with a fresh bottle of rice wine. Seated on couches and chairs around the low table at the center were several senior members of the Conclave, including her father and, adding to the sense of gravity, the Daimyo himself. Taking care not to interrupt their conversation she filled the empty glasses and topped off the rest, watching the light catch the red gemstones of her shiny silver bracelet. It was the bracelet given her by Jessica, the angel, as she set out days ago on the next phase of her great adventure. Egg could hardly stop staring at it. Such a beautiful thing, so unusual for the Dominion. Too unusual in fact; something she could never wear outside the home. But there, around the house ...

There she wore it always.

She listened to the men speak as she finished filling their glasses.

"The report is that the Icons are now safely in the hands of the Venatres," Chom was saying. Word was Jessica made the trip across the sea and was now safely with a team of specialists in "enemy" lands.

"The lockdown here continues," said Grisha. "We were lucky to get her out when we did."

Grisha always seemed worried. Afraid, even. Egg placed the wine bottle to the side. *Interesting traits for a revolutionary.* But then, maybe he added balance.

"All of our movements are on hold as of now," the Daimyo spoke. The rest of them nodded, somber, attentive to his every word. "With the arrival of Kang we suddenly have much greater things to consider. This is a radical shift that could send the entire Dominion in a different direction."

The Daimyo, as a member of the ruling elite and as the Conclave's highest placed man, was given grave consideration in all things. They relied on him for the means to execute, and fund, many of their covert activities. The whole matter of Kang and his declared ascension to the Emperor's throne was stunning in and of itself. It was as if the world had been turned on its head overnight; every citizen of Osaka was reeling.

"Is he making plans for an invasion?" asked Chom.

"Those plans were already in action," said the Daimyo. "What he plans now is anyone's guess. But my sources are telling me he's impatient to the point of fury. It's all Yamoto can do to keep him in check. In fact, it was Yamoto that convinced him to officially assume the role of Emperor, hoping thereby to contain him—if only in some token way. Otherwise he was sure to run amok across the entire Dominion.

"There is no doubt of the damage he could—would—do."

Each of them seemed lost. What Kang had done already was ... inconceivable. Even to a people who fielded the mighty Kazerai. Here was a monster, a beast that could not be stopped; that could, in theory at least, destroy them all. The contemplation of it was enough to make Egg shudder.

"For that we may owe Yamoto a debt of gratitude," the Daimyo said. "In this act he may have saved us from a more terrible fate.

"Yet it does not change the fact that we are in for drastic change. We will have to rethink our strategy. The Conclave may need to resort to even greater levels of subterfuge."

Again they all nodded, though in this case Egg suspected they were just out of ideas.

Her father, however, had no shortage of passion, and filled the resulting silence with an excitement that seemed misplaced under the circumstances.

"None of that matters," he enthused. "Jessica has come. Once again, at just the right time. *She* will save us."

Everyone in the room stared.

"Kang is nothing before the force of the Prophecy," her

father went on. "*He* is the demon. We mistook Kagami and the others before. *Kang* is the one. It could not be more perfectly described. Who can deny it? The Golden Age is upon us." Egg cringed as he leaned forward in his seat, trying to get them all to see what, to him, must surely be obvious. "The angel is with us," he was so full of confidence, "we've done our part. We got her where she needed to be. The Prophecy will be fulfilled.

"This should be a time for celebration. Not moping about how bad things are." At this he raised his glass, an impromptu toast, waited a moment then, when no one else raised theirs, took a swig. Egg could see his cheeks were red with the alcohol and he was probably buzzed. Her own cheeks had grown red as well, though her blush had nothing to do with drinking.

For a brief moment she thought simply to leave the room.

But Chom spoke. "Darvon's right," he said, slowly raising his own. "This is a time of great things. Our purpose has been to throw down this regime and bring back hope, prosperity. We've based that on fantastic things, crazy things, but that belief has kept us strong. Kept our purpose alive.

"And now look. Months ago an angel *did* fall from the sky. And she changed our world. *She changed our world.* In ways we never imagined. Would never have thought possible. Now she returns and, at the same time, a monster arrives. One that can ruin us all. Straight out of the Prophecy, as Darvon says. Can we deny it? If the fantastic becomes reality, does that make it unreal? If the impossible happens, then is it still impossible?" He was on a roll, almost poetically so; one of those unplanned moments where inspiration and opportunity crossed and something perfect came to be. "We *are* in the midst of the Prophecy," he declared. "Among us Darvon has always held the highest belief. Now, in this hour of darkness, he alone sees the light.

"This *is* a time to celebrate. To rejoice, if we're worth one ounce of our professed faith. So I say," at this he raised his glass higher, "to our victory."

The others, inspired by this take on the situation, raised theirs as well—with a round of "to our victory!"s, at which they all drank deeply, lowered their glasses and smiled. Everyone in the room, grinning with fresh hope, happy in that moment, the mood completely shifted. Darvon beamed, his usual unabashed happiness, thrilled they'd managed to realize the joy before them, his smile outshining them all.

Everyone, that is, except Egg. Only her smile was wider, so proud of her goofy, stupidly optimistic, overly simplistic father. Every time. Every time he did it. Just when she thought she couldn't be more embarrassed, just in that moment something would happen and she would see right through it. Straight to his heart, straight to the purity that was her dad, and she would love him more than anything in the world.

CHAPTER 30:

A CERTAIN KIND OF MAGIC

BIANCA HAD GONE WITH SATORI to find their rooms. Both she and Jess had a chance to shower and get fresh clothes, after which they sat through rounds of questioning by Lindin and a few others and were, at last—well after dark—shown back upstairs to the main lodge. There Satori offered to take them to their quarters, an offer Bianca accepted but which Jess, for the moment, had declined. Exhausted as she was, as wonderful as a bed would feel right then, there in that warm chalet; a wood-beamed illusion that, temporarily at least, with its flickering firelight, might chase away the stark reality of her predicament—as much as she wanted to lose herself in its comfort, she was not yet ready for sleep.

She could not stop thinking of Zac.

It looked like they would finally—*finally!*—get time alone, and the anticipation of that had her floating. They'd been together off and on a whole day, surrounded by others at all times, unable to reconnect and it was driving her crazy. She yearned for him.

It felt funny to even think that.

I yearn for you.

She smiled to herself.

So, after Satori and Bianca left, she grabbed a big, fluffy blanket from one of the couches, wrapped it all about her, thick and bunchy and high around her ears, dragging the ground at her feet, went outside into the night and stood at the deck railing in the darkness, just at the edges of the warm glow shining out from inside.

The cold night air was biting.

Zac had been called to more meetings in the labyrinth below but asked her to wait for him. She shivered as she recalled that brief conversation. When he sent her up to

288 DAVID G MCDANIEL

the chalet above the complex the look in his eyes had been as eager as her own, and the witness of that—that he might crave this moment as much as she did—sent her fantasies soaring. She was downright giddy.

This whole being a fugitive on two worlds had its emotional highs and lows. Exhilaration, stark terror, raving panic, serene calm. There seemed to be no middle ground where adventure was concerned. Boredom or complacency? Never. Those feelings were long gone. If emotion was life then she'd lived more in these two trips to Anitra than most people lived in their entire existence. As a result she'd been learning to let go. Which, right then, was exactly what she was doing.

Completely.

Letting.

Go.

Yes there was trouble at every turn. There always was. But in that moment she was happy and she let herself experience that emotion fully. Reveling in it, gushing with the power of her desire for Zac, thoroughly soaking up the absolute bliss of standing there waiting for him to arrive.

She shrugged the bulky blanket higher and it pushed her freshly washed hair up against the back of her neck, bringing a fresh rush of goose bumps. With one hand she reached up inside its fluffy mass and pulled it across her mouth, then tighter. Only her eyes and the top of her head were now exposed.

She had to admit she was nervous as she stood there in the cold, shivering from more than just the temperature. As much as she longed to be with Zac she was, after so many months of anticipation, shaking. This was it. Their first moment alone in all that time. What should she say? Should she open with, "Hey"?

Or how about just, "Hi"? Or maybe, "What's up?"

Ugh.

What would *he* say?

More importantly, what should she *do*?

Should she be coy? At least at first? Saunter to him kind of casual? Let him come to her?

Should she kiss him? Would he kiss her? Any moment he would come walking out onto the deck, find her and ...

The shaking escalated and she consciously held herself still.

Brrrr!

Overwrought though she was, there was no denying the intensity of the cold. Behind her the fires inside the chalet flickered their warmth, before her spread a deep night salted with stars. Horizon to horizon, dark masses of the surrounding mountains outlined against the celestial display. The chalet was inviting, yes, but she *wanted* to be outside. For one thing it was the one place they could definitely be alone. Plus it was beautiful. Here and there in the distance shone other lights, not many, structures with electric bulbs nestled against the slopes; hidden in the trees or peeking out. Mostly the entire area, as far as she could see, lay blanketed in a peaceful night.

It was spectacular.

Beneath it all, of course, far below in the heart of this very mountain—in stark contrast to the natural beauty all around—was the starship. Its image was burned into her mind's eye; indelibly, like the after-echo of a bright flash. A dominant force, and for a moment that same panic she'd felt when first seeing it flirted dangerously with her composure. Quickly she pushed it aside. How strongly it affected her! A thing so amazing, so alien ... it, of all things, was what suddenly made Anitra out of this world.   To that point Anitra had been so much *like* her world it hardly seemed a different place at all. Now with the starship it suddenly became true space opera. If the circumstances she found herself in the middle of to that point weren't already epic, now this. A real, actual starship. And it looked as if the Icons she brought might hold the key to unlock it. What that would mean for the balance of power on this world, to say nothing of what it meant for the future, probably of *both* worlds ...

The door to the chalet opened. Out walked Zac and she ran to him. Flew. Just like on the docks, the instant she saw him, thoughts scattered to the wind. As fast as she could without regard for how silly it might seem, blanket snapping out behind like some ridiculous cape—admonishing herself for ever having been nervous about what she was going to do.

Of course this was what she was going to do.

He laughed as she charged into his embrace, a jumble of limbs and big, poofy cover. On impulse she wrapped it around him, pulling him in as much as he would fit, eagerly bundling him into her cozy cocoon. He stuck out head and shoulders at the top, arms outside and wrapped around her, but it was heaven; the mass of his body against her; his strength, both the obvious she could feel—a big boy with sturdy limbs—and his real strength, the Kazerai strength that could not be perceived but which she knew was there, waiting, coiled beneath the surface. Incredible, impossible power.

She shivered.

He wore no special, warm clothing yet gave off a subtle, smoldering heat that tingled her whole being as she pressed into him.

She craned her head, chin against his chest, looking up into his face, lips too far away to make the first move. That was *definitely* the first thing she wanted. Would he kiss her? He didn't, but the sparkle in his eyes, the absolute admiration in his gaze in that moment was undeniable, making it as passionate as if he had. It sent an unexpected thrill through her. The moment stretched and she found herself in awe of how absolutely incredible he was. Handsome, important, powerful. He could have any girl he wanted. Why he chose to be there with her, plain, nobody Jessica …

"I've been waiting all day for this," he further inflamed her desire.

"Me too!" she gushed and caught her next outburst. *Just be natural! Stop obsessing!* Her serenity of an instant before was in jeopardy.

But if he thought her silly it didn't show. He just grinned and she grinned with him, wide, smiling so wide it hurt and she tried to be amused by her own foolishness.

"I can't tell you how I've missed that smile," his eyes twinkled in delight. She recalled the way he said that before. *I remember everything he's ever said to me.* "It's like your whole face smiles. The way your eyes squint. The more you smile, the more you squint." Of course that only made her smile wider—if that was possible—so happy and at the same time so conscious of just how wide she *was* smiling, realizing that, indeed, she was squinting rather terribly. But she couldn't stop. Gently he reached and touched her face—*his hand is so warm!*—making her shiver. Then, to cover the reaction she shivered again, on purpose, pretending as if the cold affected her.

He took his hand away; seemed to concentrate.

"Did you notice they're changing color?"

She steadied herself beneath his gaze. Unsure what he meant.

"Your eyes."

My eyes?

"Little gold flecks," he said and, again, raised a hand, this time to point, the tip of his wonderful finger filling her vision. "There," he pointed, "there. All around. Like gold glitter." He lowered his hand. "It wasn't there before."

She didn't know what to say. *Cool?* That's what she almost said, mortified as she realized how close that word was to coming out of her mouth. She blocked several more stupid comments, *Neat! Awesome!* fighting mightily with the impulse to stammer something—anything—to fill the void. Reason prevailed. It was *okay* to just be there with him, to accept his quiet admiration.

And so she was silent. And as she held her tongue all she could seem to do was keep grinning, like an idiot, growing ever more frustrated with how difficult it was in that moment to just relax and be herself. Surely Zac must've noticed.

"They're quite stunning, actually," he said, then faltered and she saw, as if an epiphany, he was feeling his way through this just like she was. He too felt awkward. It was a revelation, in fact, and it calmed her, finally, restoring a bit of the thrill; leading, of course, to the additional realization that her conversation thus far had been completely vapid. So far all she'd said was, *Me too!*

Terrible.

"Thanks," she worked herself back up to Jessica Prime, throwing a little attention back his way: "I've always loved the color of yours. They're like pale ice."

And it was his turn to be uncomfortable. Making him look more kissable than ever, the big, strong Kazerai fidgeting ever so slightly in the shadowy firelight.

She continued smiling up at him. How he could be the warrior she knew him to be, an ultimate bad-ass—beyond the comprehension of any human warrior—and yet be so ... not a warrior at all.

In so many ways Zac defied description.

She craned her neck harder, not so subtly, reaching her face toward his. Their lips were an easy foot apart, leaving the actual kiss up to him. All the signs were there, the signals—there was no way she could be wrong in her judgment of his intentions.

Was there?

No, she decided and, in one chilling moment, made the further decision to be outrageously forward. A step off the cliff that, once taken, could never be undone.

"Look," she said, "you're too tall for me to kiss you. Will you just bend down here?"

The moment of terrifying uncertainty passed and ... it didn't bomb. With a curl of amusement at the corners of his mouth, perhaps even grateful to be rescued from his own struggle, Zac leaned in.

Emotions flooded through her as their lips touched, a rush of anticipation that was more than mere passion—driven by the amazing feel of the kiss itself ...

Love.

"I've missed you so much," she breathed into him as her eyes closed. He kissed her harder and she felt his longing; pressed into him with her own, releasing every bit of tension, every bit of pent-up uncertainty—all of it breaking free in a shuddering wave that just kept coming. Every fiber, every piece of her; the heat of his body, the complete and utter confirmation that he *did* feel the same way about her, no question and it was unspeakably liberating—so intense her shuddering ecstasy reached new heights and she began to worry she might actually collapse.

He separated but stayed close, warm forehead to hers. He smelled so wonderful. She caught her breath, eyes still closed; held fast to him even as he, in turn, held her in his arms. She would not fall; would never fall—could never, as long as he held her. The chill of the night impinged.

"I knew you'd come back," he mirrored her desire, voice thick, driving her yearning ever harder. *I yearn for you.* He shook his head gently against hers. "I had no way to make it happen. It felt strange to be powerless to do anything. That ever seeing you again was completely in the hands of fate. The Icon was with you. There was nothing I could do.

"I always listened for news, ready to rush to Osaka if I heard word."

Jess swallowed.

Zac was steady. Warm breath inches from her own. She could *feel* him talk; the gentle sound of his rich voice.

She opened her eyes. Images, fears swirling across the movie screen of her mind. So much was at stake, so much could change so quickly on that world; the raw instability of their union dominated her thoughts.

"What do they have planned for you?" she asked, worried she was already jumping too far ahead. "The whole Kang thing. You don't think they'll ..." She couldn't finish; closed her eyes again. She was there, now, she reminded herself, with Zac. Now was the time to enjoy. Thoroughly, no thoughts of the future.

But what if ...

"There would be no point," he answered. "Why send me to fight him? I'm no different than the other Kazerai. Kang would dispatch me as easily." She swallowed as he continued: "This could become a real problem for the Venatres. I don't think it's had time to sink in." She felt him raise his head and she opened her eyes; looked up at his strong profile as he, in turn, gazed out into the dark distance. "It's only just sinking in for me."

She pulled herself back into him. Wrapped him harder in their blanket burrito; tightly, face to the side against his chest, squeezing him full of her desire. Her hope. Her everything. Wanting, in some strange yet undeniable way, to absorb him. Like as if to merge their very beings; such that the squeeze did not seem nearly enough and, as she thought this realized that, despite her infatuation, she tempered her embrace. The way she would if hugging a normal man. Not that she could crush a normal man, of course, but neither would she squeeze one as absolutely hard as she could. Certainly not as hard as she now wanted to squeeze Zac. No one did that. It would hurt.

But here was Zac. A man she wanted so badly, more than she'd probably ever wanted anyone, and right then she wanted to squeeze him so hard—until she popped— and had the sudden, bizarre idea that, with Zac, unlike any other man, she actually could.

She could hug Zac as hard as she ever wanted.

Would he even notice?

Before she could consider further she went with it. Squeezed, as hard as she could—as absolutely hard as she could—waiting for a reaction and getting none—crushing her arms around him until it *felt* like they became one, like a complete fusion of their being, her eyes stinging like they might actually burst with the pressure. *Squeeze!* When at last an involuntary grunt escaped her she snapped to reality and relaxed her grip, dizzy for a moment from the strain; worried he'd noticed though totally, *totally* fulfilled. She'd hugged him *so* frickin *hard*. She could hug him no harder, could compress no more of her desire for him into a physical embrace. It felt incredible to have done it and, whether from the exertion or her own intense satisfaction, she swayed with lightheaded euphoria.

And, of course, Zac didn't notice.

"It seems you always arrive at the crux of something major," he commented, mind on other things; not so much as an *ugh* or a *Hey!* or even a *That was tight.*

Nothing.

What was his threshold? His skin gave like that of

a normal man.   She felt bones and muscles beneath. Squeezing him didn't feel like squeezing a robot or a tree or anything like that.   He felt entirely normal.   Yet, at some point, his body would not give. This she knew with certainty. Had witnessed it. At some point Zac became indestructible. At the level of human touch he felt quite normal. Beyond that ...

She could make indentations in his skin. He flushed, blood moved about beneath, just like any other human. At least it seemed to. So tender yet ... so hard.

He looked down and stroked her hair, and for a fleeting moment she wondered what the rest of him was like; how it all worked.

Was he even capable of sex?

Was he insatiable? A beast in the bed that needed twenty women to fulfill?   Did he kill women on accident in the heat of passion? Frail, dainty flowers beneath the might of his bulldozer power? Were the great Kazerai fed armies of maidens behind closed doors to tame their wild lust?

Whoa.   She dragged herself back from this absurd tangent. *Where did that come from?*

She was tired. *Exhausted.* She reminded herself Zac had a wife once, Kitana. One wife, no others, which meant he was probably perfectly normal in that department.

At about that moment Satori walked out onto the porch. The intense, red-headed commander showed momentary weakness as she stepped into the cold, grimacing and hugging her arms about her chest as soon as she hit the frigid night air.

She started over. "I see you two are staying cozy."

The massive blanket nearly hid Jessica, wrapped around she and Zac where they embraced. She pulled it from him and released him, hugging it back around only herself.

Not yet! Jess wanted Satori to go away. *Come back later!* Zac had only just got there.

"It's a beautiful night," he commented.

"Easy for a Kazerai to say." Satori made a nod to his minimal attire. He wore only the black short-sleeve shirt and slacks and stood comfortably, looking as if he were enjoying a balmy evening at the beach.

"I got your friend settled," she spoke to Jess as she came closer. "I think she'll be fine. She seems to be adjusting."

Jess pulled the blanket tighter. Satori had already begun to shiver.

"Let me show you to the room," she said. Then, on second thought: "Or I can just leave you two alone." She smirked, though her mouth took an unnatural slant as she fought to keep her teeth from chattering.

Jess turned to Zac. Embarrassed all of a sudden; indecisive; wanting nothing more than to spend the rest of the night with him, if that were even an option ...

"You go," he said. "I have to get back to Lindin. I made them let me come see you, but they're expecting me.

"To be honest I'm getting tired of all the discussions."

"Tell me about it," Satori agreed.

Jess slipped a hand from the warm blanket and placed it on Zac's chest. She gazed up into his eyes, acutely aware of Satori's presence.

Zac leaned and kissed her on the forehead.

"Come on," Satori was in a hurry to get back inside.

It was too soon, but it was time to go. Time, finally, to rest.

Zac was so sweet.

Jess reached and touched his cheek; smiled, then turned and followed Satori. And as the door opened and she stepped into the warmth of the fire-lit interior she looked back. Zac had already turned to the railing, standing tall, broad shoulders framed against the starry sky.

Warrior.

Romantic.

Gazing into the night.

CHAPTER 31:

REBEL LEADER

IT WAS LATE. Willet crouched in a tall stand of grass beneath a star filled sky. The clump was one of many in the wide, open field, overgrown and filling the untilled, unplanted tract of land directly outside Midbay; a field that had probably once been a booming farm. Signs of that probable past were all around; idle equipment, storage sheds—many still in good shape—orderly rows of soil that had not yet eroded as the wild encroached and reclaimed what man left behind. Ironically Willet had never been to Midbay when it was a bustling Venatres township, but now that it had been invaded and claimed by the Dominion ... now Midbay had become quite familiar to him. And this old farmland, hastily deserted when the Dominion began their occupation, sitting unpatrolled outside the perimeter of town, had become quite familiar indeed.

It was his way in.

He gazed across the gently rolling slopes to the lights of the one- and two-story buildings in the distance. Many of the Venatres inhabitants remained, as was the case with other cities and towns invaded by the Dominion on their wrathful push into Venatres lands. Prisoners, yet free in a sense, expected to carry on with the daily infrastructure, keeping the city alive while the Dominion occupation mustered forces for the next push.

The broader Dominion invasion had begun shortly after the destruction of the Crucible, a daring sweep across the sea to Venatres shores, furious resupply and a near-maniacal drive over several months, all the way there, to Midbay, just shy of the major city of Northhold. Expectations by the Venatres were that the Dominion were catching their breath. That they would stage more attacks. For the moment, however, they had, perhaps, stretched themselves thin. An invasion across the sea was not the most militarily sound tactic. Driven by their passion for revenge it had, so far, worked, yet it was precarious. The facts remained: They were securely entrenched on Venatres shores, holding land, resources and citizens, and it was all the Venatres could do to maintain their current position.

Willet rose, remained at a crouch and sprinted closer, stopping at another grassy stand.

Although he usually took this field by way of entry, he always tried to use a different approach. To cover his tracks when he could but, in truth, had never seen the Dominion put much attention on that side of town. The field was in the south, away from the larger Venatres forces staring them down in the north and, whether from overconfidence, bad tactics or simple, sloppy disregard, he'd been able to slip past the guards and infiltrate the town easily every time.

Ahead he could see his destination. The sign out front of the small building was barely discernable at that range, though he could make it out easily from memory: Café Ecco. One of Midbay's most popular watering holes before the Dominion occupation, or so Willet was told. A place for festivities, celebrations. It still attracted a large clientele, though of late the mood could hardly be called more than somber. After a day of doing what they were supposed to beneath the Dominion yoke the good citizens of Midbay gathered at the café to drink and forget for a while before shuffling off home. No festivities. No celebrations. Just a healthy dose of inebriation to make the suffering fade.

His contact would be there tonight.

He sprinted closer, ranging within sight of the few lazy sentries walking that edge of town, should they bother to look his way. He could hear the bustle from the tavern, the music, could see the faces of the people gathered outside. Midbay was an old town, stone buildings lined one against the other, streets narrow, alleys plentiful, and his way in tonight was just over the next small hill and down through a series of long shadows cast by a row of inadequate street lamps.

He watched as the Dominion soldiers walked their predictable pattern, waiting for the best opening. The distant thrum of music and conversation drifted on the air. The bar was in full swing. Overhead a meteor flashed across the starry sky, tail extending then evaporating as it burned up in the atmosphere. Gone as quickly as it came.

It reminded him of Jessica.

Satori called earlier to tell him she'd returned. When Jessica left those many months ago Willet had hoped they might see her again but, rationally, never expected it to happen. From what little he knew of her and her world there was no way she would return to Anitra by choice. Unlike what Jessica was used to, Anitra was a world at war. Fighting had been the order of the day for as long as Willet could remember; border standoffs, invasion attempts and all else, and Jessica had landed right in the middle of the worst of it. Not something she would willingly rush back to, he was sure. Despite the fact that, when here, she'd risen to the challenge—despite the fact that she overcame all odds to dominate, to become a hero—despite all that, Willet did not think she really wanted to jump back in. Sad as it had been to say goodbye he was sure that, once safely home, her name would simply fade to the status of legend.

He was curious what brought her.

Satori had been brief. Their call was regarding other things; the tactics of the moment, the chaos of Kang's return. There was now little doubt the monster was, in fact, Kang. But none of that impinged as much as the news of Jessica. Willet was thrilled. Jessica had saved his life those many months ago, and though his life had only been on the line because he went with her to help, the way she came back for him, the way she brought Satori and came to his rescue in the middle of an attack, fighting their way into the compound and out ... That was a debt he hoped someday to be able to repay. The entire Venatres owed her a debt, no doubt, but he himself intended to make good on it.

Up near the alley one of the soldiers moved.

For the mission tonight he wore dark civilian clothes.

That combined with his own, dark skin concealed him in the night.

The sentry paused, seemed to consider something, scratched at his shoulder then turned and went back the other way, evidently deciding he was bored with that direction. Willet watched until the man was far enough away then rose and sprinted the final distance, in and out of shadows, over the hill and dipping down into the alley where he pulled quickly to a slow, meandering walk. People within the city were rarely checked for documentation and, even if Willet were stopped, his story was tight enough to handle most scrutiny. So far, after numerous trips, no one had ever asked him a thing.

At the end of the alley he turned right, onto the main street, found his way down to the next block and went right again, continuing his leisurely stroll to Café Ecco. Within minutes he was blending into the crowd outside, just another of the locals, waving to a few who knew him, finding his way to the bar and ordering a drink. As he waited he turned to face the interior of the café, elbows leaning back on the countertop, pretending to be relaxed. He spotted his contact, a man named Dox, seated at a table in the far corner with another man, Dox's lieutenant, Gervin. Inconspicuous, both of them; trained soldiers, residents of Midbay, recruited after the invasion to supply what intelligence they could on the Dominion forces. So far Dox had been invaluable. A real professional, as far as Willet was concerned.

His drink came. He tipped the bartender and made his way over to the corner table.

"Dox," he said as he walked up. "Gervin."

The two nodded, casual, as if Willet were just another friend come to chew over the desperations of the day. Willet sat.

Dox took a pull from his drink. Set his glass down and looked across at the new arrival. "Interesting news."

Willet took a drink from his own glass and savored the taste. Midbay might be a city under siege, but their supplies were still better than those in his own small forward base.

These little trips often ended up quite pleasurable.

"Lots of interesting things happening right now."

Dox flashed a wan smile. "Who knew the Dominion would be taken over by the devil himself?"

Kang had become the topic of discussion in most circles, and not just militarily. Every man, woman and child on both sides knew of the Beast by now, though most information was quite new and quite sensational. Kang had, literally, burst upon the scene. Now their entire planning hinged on what he would do next.

Anything was possible.

"Is he a madman?" Willet was only half asking. Most reports pegged Kang as a wild variable. He wondered if Dox had any new news from within the Dominion ranks.

"Everyone thinks so. I can only imagine what the crew closest to him are going through. We're clear across the ocean, getting information through the filter of command. Dominion leadership here doesn't know what to make of it, to be perfectly honest. There's confusion across the board."

"But no talk of mutiny?"

Dox shook his head. "Not yet. They're prepared to follow Kang's orders. He's such a disruptive force, no one's wrapped their heads around this one. And Kang isn't giving them much time. You thought the Dominion was bad beneath the rule of the Council? So far Kang promises to be a hundred times worse." He took another, longer drink, that one not for show but, honestly, because he needed a stiff drink, then said grimly: "We think the whole army may surge any day. A foolish move, no doubt, but Kang doesn't seem to be factoring reason into his plans."

"I expect the worse."

"You think they'll move on Northhold?" That *would be* foolish, but if true would leave the Venatres reeling. They expected such a move of course, eventually, but the Dominion showed no signs of readiness. Nor were the Venatres fully prepared.

"They're gathering their strength. Massing forces outside the city. You've recorded that."

Willet had.

Dox shook his head. "Kang doesn't seem to care whether they're ready or not."

"How much of that do you think is speculation?" In a chaotic situation like this it wasn't unreasonable to expect all sorts of outrageous hearsay to be flying every which way. The army was buzzing with concern over what their new god-Emperor would have them do. Vocalized fears were in no short supply.

Dox took another drink; glanced at Gervin. "We've tried to keep a neutral eye on it. Not get caught up in the hype. Near as we can tell what's real is this: soon, maybe even within days, Kang will order some sort of attack. Probably against Northhold. Militarily that *is* the next logical objective.

"However, in light of the fact that we're dealing with an unstable mind—and perhaps 'unstable' is even too generous a way to put it—in light of that we should be prepared for any possibility."

Now it was Willet's turn to take a long drink. He put the glass down; held it on the table; looked around the bustling, if subdued, café. People trying to relax. Trying to forget, at least for a little while.

Facing a future that held little hope.

* * *

"I TIRE OF PLANNING!" Kang whirled in place. He stood across the throne room, near the balcony, glaring at the small group gathered in his presence. At the head of them Yamoto held himself tall, thinking just how tired they all were. *We tire of you*, he thought. Kang was not physically tired, of course. Yamoto doubted the monster would ever tire. They were well into the early hours of a new day, after a full day of non-stop planning, and their new Emperor showed no signs of wear. Quite the contrary. He was riled up and Yamoto was certain if he relaxed his steerage of the insane beast, even for an instant, bad things would happen. Kang was a madman, one who could, if the urge took him, wreak unimaginable havoc. There was absolutely nothing keeping him in check. No balance to his power. Not threat of assassination, coup—not even a mishap or disease. Nothing. The *only* thing holding things together, at the end of it all, was the concept of order. Protocols, insisted upon by Yamoto himself, none of which had more than weak consequences for their effect. Which meant Yamoto could not relax. Which meant he had to keep himself—and the others—focused. He glanced at each of them in turn.

To a man they were exhausted.

"He *is* there!" Kang pointed across the room to the large map on the far wall, the one he'd been referring to throughout this arduous "planning" session. Time and again, as he did now, he kept coming back to his obsession with finding the last remaining Kazerai, Horus.

This time Yamoto had had enough. As Kang went there, yet again, Yamoto very nearly snapped. But the threat of death was extreme. Kang could, and likely would, kill him with little provocation. Yamoto would never have lashed out at his old Shogun, or any of his superiors, even had he been angered with their decisions. Calm resistance, that was his way. But never had he been so angry as he was right then. Not only was Kang insane, he was a pompous ass. Yamoto was through with this line of insistence.

But he took a deep breath. Repeated what he'd been saying all night:

"We have no idea where Horus is, Lord." The Lord part was becoming increasingly difficult. Kang reminded him of an obstinate child. *A child with the strength of an army.* It was like a cosmic joke. A prank the universe played on them. "He's as likely there as anywhere. We cannot, no matter how much you desire it, go off on a random chase into enemy lands, striking for something we're only guessing is there." Now he knew he tread in dangerous territory but no longer cared: "To do so would be tactically foolish."

"Then we draw him out!" Kang was spinning up and Yamoto feared, this time, he might not be able to rein him in. The beastly, golden-robed, horned mockery of an Emperor surged across the room to the map, some crazy idea gaining steam. Wild-eyed he tapped it with insistence—poking holes in the stone behind the paper in his enthusiasm. Yamoto shuddered with the sheer power Kang possessed.

"Here!" the monster said, stabbing the area around the Venatres city of Northhold—the area where he was convinced Horus would be found. Yamoto regretted ever mentioning Horus had been reported there. Wished he'd foreseen the potential for Kang's fixation. "We attack Northhold," Kang announced. "*I* attack Northhold."

So caught up in Kang's fury was Yamoto that he failed at first to notice Damas, who had broken slowly from the group and was now moving toward the beast. Kang, too, failed to give him any attention. Yamoto wondered what Damas was up to. Kang still had not acknowledged his proximity though Damas came closer, unnaturally close, desperately concealing nerves. Yamoto could see that now. Kang made everyone nervous, of course, but Yamoto couldn't shake the feeling Damas was fighting some greater terror. Uncertainty.

What was his general planning?

"That could certainly work," Damas pointed to the area around Northhold on the map, drawing Kang's attention. "No matter where he is he'll have to respond."

"Yes!" said Kang, happy to have something more than the dumbfounded stares he'd been getting all night. Damases' feigned agreement worked. "He'll have to respond!" Kang enthused, latching onto that idea.

Yamoto had no idea what Damas was doing, but he was not about to allow him to encourage Kang's insanity. Still, for now he watched.

One of his other generals, however, seemed to misread the situation. "Lord, we have the means to stop a Kazerai," he said, adding a logical observation to the clearly illogical conversation. "Horus has not yet been a threat to us. Disruptive, perhaps, but never in open combat.

"He knows we alone possess the technology to contain him."

"I do not care!" Kang bellowed and Damas, so close to

him, cringed; took a step back. "I will not have one of *them* alive while I rule!"

Kang simply could not abide another who might even remotely be a threat. Yamoto expected a bit of a grudge was at work. Horus was, after all, the one who stopped him. Add that together with the psychology of a man who'd been mutated into a monster and it was no wonder Kang was so determined to see an end to the man he considered his arch-nemesis.

"That is wise," Damas tried to get his agenda back on track, confirming for Yamoto that he was, in fact, up to something. Never one to be like this Damas was so obviously at odds with himself right then there was no doubt he had an ulterior motive. Kang, on the other hand, was too caught up to notice.

"However," Damas stepped ever closer, "I would suggest Midbay." He pointed to that city on the map, to the south of Northhold. "We already hold that area. Our troops mass for the next phase of the invasion. If you take your attack to them, ahead of our assault, perhaps threaten existing Venatres interests, civilian interests, Horus must surely respond."

Now Damas had Kang's full attention. Kang looked eagerly to the map and the Dominion's top general went closer and … Yamoto noticed his hand moving upward. An awkward action Damas tried with great difficulty to make seem completely natural.

What are you up to, my friend?

Somehow Kang completely missed it. Either clouded by his own passion or so full of unwavering confidence in his own might, he completely failed to respond as Damas brought a silver syringe from his pocket and jabbed it hard into the scaly hide. Right in the shoulder, spiked skin exposed through the shredded silk of the Emperor's golden robes. Yamoto doubted Kang's skin could be pierced, but as he watched in amazement he recognized the specialized syringe; a cocktail of chemicals designed to stop the beating heart of a Kazerai. A prick should be all it would take. They had two controls, really, for the Kazerai: the Raza energy to hold them, the chemical agent to kill them. Both highly guarded to the point of being arcane. Rarely used, there yet existed a means to end the lives of their greatest warriors. The syringe was it. A fail-safe, if you would, and Yamoto expected this was what he now witnessed. Somehow Damas had gotten hold of one, prepared it and steeled himself for this moment.

He felt a surge of pride at his general's action.

At first Kang didn't notice, so caught up was he in Damas' enthusiastic support. Damas stabbed him even as he finished speaking his last words of encouragement. Almost as if Damas were, quite out of place yet plausible enough, giving Kang a congratulatory slap on the shoulder. *Great idea, Emperor! Good job!*

But that wasn't it. Not at all. And as Kang realized what had happened he staggered. Reached and snatched the syringe from Damas in shock. Damas hissed and pulled back what was likely a broken hand, smacked aside as Kang took the silver syringe from him. Surely by now the rest of the officers in attendance recognized what Damas had done.

Keenly they waited, expecting ...

But Kang did not fall. Damas was terrified. He watched in horror as the Emperor staggered, reeled to the side, affected by the cocktail but not yet succumbing to it, steadied himself and ... backhanded him, even as Damas turned to run. The blow folded him in half, sending his body flailing against the far wall with a wet thud and the abbreviated echo of a choked cry—cut short by the murderous impact. He fell in a twisted heap, head turned back across one shoulder to stare vacantly at all of them, gore oozing from a cracked skull.

Yamoto tore his eyes from the mess. Kang stared back at him, clearly thrown off by the serum but not dying. With a great effort he gathered himself, shaking off the effects. All at once he turned to stare at the syringe in his fist, eyeing it in disbelief. Recognizing what he held.

But ... he was overcoming it.

Then a deep, shuddering breath, followed by a powerful

snort as the horned, yellow beast shook his head. He straightened.

Steadied.

Seemed to come to his senses all at once. Expanded his chest, shoulders and head back, leaned forward and ...

Roared.   Deafening   in   the   small   space,   absolutely crushing; an expulsion of sound that rattled the walls. And as each of them gripped hands fiercely to the sides of their heads, eyes squinted shut, Yamoto wondered if his ears would bleed.

The sound diminished, changed, and he realized Kang was laughing. Fury had morphed to mania and Yamoto looked up, lowering his hands. Kang's laugh was not as loud as the roar but it was obscene, and Yamoto struggled to remain calm in the face of a situation that was completely beyond his control. They were, as they had been all along, at the mercy of a mad god. And while he admired Damas' effort, not having known anything about it in advance— not having, he noted with some small regret, thought of it himself—now that it had failed he realized, with devastating hopelessness, they had nothing left to try.

There was, indeed, nothing that could stop Kang.

Suddenly the beast was standing in his face, sneering at him with that hideous grin.

"Nothing can kill me!" he hissed, echoing Yamoto's very thoughts. "Did you really think that would work?"

For an instant Yamoto worried he would be blamed then, in a moment of defiance, *wanted* to take credit. Wanted to be allied with Damas, who he considered a hero for his action, no matter if it cost him his life. Better to be remembered a hero than live in fear beneath the rule of an abomination.

But integrity, above all, motivated him.

"I had nothing to do with this," he said honestly, and was satisfied with the sound of contempt in his voice. It was not a plea for understanding, rather a statement of disappointment. *I had nothing to do with this,* his tone implied, *but I could not have been more satisfied if it succeeded.*

Kang, however, did not care either way.

He whirled on the others. Yamoto was certain, from the smell in the room, that at least one of them had soiled his pants. "I cannot be killed!" Kang yelled at them, loud but not so loud as to do more than make them cower. "Not the Raza, not the serum, not the great Kazerai themselves— nothing can stop me!"

Yamoto wanted so badly to be able to hurt him right then. To break him, somehow. Make him suffer.

Kang leered. Turned and ambled over to the dead Damas. "He had one good idea," he said and turned back. "We go to Midbay," he informed them. "At once."

They stood an instant too long.

"Go!" he ordered and the rest of them fumbled against each other in their haste to be off, to make preparations for whatever random thing the demon had in mind.

To get out of that room as quickly as they could.

Except for Yamoto. He turned more slowly, watching Kang seethe, feeling a remarkable calm in the face of instant annihilation. There was nowhere to run, quite literally. Nowhere to hide. If he was to die there was no way to stop it.

And so why not push back?

Resolute acceptance of death.

Kang saw this defiance but seemed instead to make the decision to work with it.

"See that they prepare an adequate force," he instructed Yamoto directly. "I want four airships to depart with mine."

Yamoto stared a moment longer.

And left the room.

CHAPTER 32:

LATE NIGHT RENDEZVOUS

BOOM! AN EXPLOSION ROCKED the metal floor. Jess kept her balance better this time and continued across the room to the archaic wooden door—out of place against the riveted green-iron surfaces of the small space. Beside the door was a sleek, high-tech access panel.

It was the same dream as before. *The same memory,* she reeled a little as the absolute reality of the scene overwhelmed her, artificial as she knew it to be. Sensations were too strong, too detailed. It was like *being* there, though she knew she wasn't.

Carefully she played it through, wondering all the while whether she might take control and run things differently.

There were no windows. Diffuse light came from the same unknown source, the door before her covered in complicated runes.

Another explosion and she lurched to the side.

Too real.

She steadied herself with a hand on the wall. The same battle as before took place outside, rocking the floor with pulsing blasts. More hits and she stumbled.

All was as it had been.

Looking down she saw she wore the same armor, in her free hand the long, curved sword of blued steel. She studied her hands more closely. Were they even human? Nearly too perfect to be human, too exquisitely formed; pure, unblemished skin, not a freckle or other mark to be seen. She took a big pull of the acrid air. As before tactile feedback was amazing; the wall beneath her palm, the armor against her skin. The shiny panel beside the door.

She turned to that as the battle outside continued to intensify. This time the vibrant edge to the dream did not begin to fade as before and, in a moment of panic, she struggled to awaken. For a terrifying instant she remained locked in that other reality.

I'm trapped!

Then ...

Sat with a gasp.

It was dark.

She looked around, frantic.

Forcibly reminding herself where she was.

In the room at the chalet.

Then: *Anitra.*

Not Earth, not home and, again, the panic washed over her.

She fought it. Centered herself. It was the room she and Bianca fell asleep in that night.

Quietly she slid out of bed, shaking; went to the other bed and checked the mounds of blankets and pillows. Empty. Bianca wasn't there.

Where'd she go?

Instead of growing more alarmed, however, she felt herself calming. She looked out the curtained window. Definitely still night. She'd slept most of the previous day, Bianca too, rising only to eat together then both went straight back to bed. Jess hadn't even looked for Zac, so tired was she from their ordeal. She had no idea what time it was, but it was odd Bianca had risen without her and gone off alone in the middle of the night. At the same time it wasn't as alarming as Jess might've imagined. They were in a mountainside chalet, in the middle of the frozen nowhere, perched atop an underground complex filled with the good guys.

Wherever Bianca went she would be in no danger.

Jess stood still for a moment in the dark room. Thoughts sucked back into the dream, or into her head, or wherever they went at times like this; the swirl of troubled contemplations that consumed her. Earlier, during their time up and about, she'd at last seen the videos of Kang. Images that iced her veins. And not just because Kang had somehow morphed into a freak of nature. Not because she knew how powerful he'd become. It iced her veins because

Kang looked …

Kang looked like the beast from the Prophecy. She remembered Darvon's words, from the last time she was there, when they were making their escape, chit-chatting in the car as she drove through Osaka, on the hunt for the Icon. Incredibly, though Darvon only mentioned it those many months ago, in idle conversation, she remembered his words clearly:

A great demon will come, it went, *yellowed like the sickness of death, and the angel will vanquish the beast and bring to heel the vast armies it commands.*

Was that Kang? The Conclave never took those words that literally, as far as she knew, but this was about the most literal representation of them she could imagine. *A great demon. Yellowed like the sickness of death.* Could the Prophecy really be happening? If so …

If so what did that mean for her?

Awake now she went to the bathroom and turned on the light. Shook off those considerations and went to the sink. And, despite time already spent there in the chalet, despite everything she'd been through, found herself shocked at the fact that everything was *so* normal. *Completely* normal. Indistinguishable from a hotel room on Earth. Beds, lamps, bathrooms, toilets, lights—everything. Maybe each was a little different; so call it Europe instead of the Midwest. Still it was difficult to believe—especially at times like this—that she was anywhere but home.

She stood before the mirror and looked at her sleep-styled hair. The dream must've been restless. She ran water and rinsed her face, found a towel and dried off, holding it tight over her whole face before exhaling into it and dragging it slowly down to her chin. As she patted dry she leaned close, looking carefully into her eyes. Zac said they were changing color. Were they? She hadn't noticed. They'd always been brown as far as she was concerned (Bianca always tried to call them hazel) but upon inspection they did, indeed—looking at them closely—seem lighter.

Huh.

Had they always been that way? Was it her imagination?

Zac said they were different. She peered closer, studying them more carefully than ever, scrutinizing every angle and there, peppered across each pupil if she looked close enough ...

A constellation of gold.

Whoa.

You had to really look, but once you saw it ... it was *there*. To Zac's uncanny vision it must've been quite obvious. How long had they been like that? According to Zac it was new. Last time she was on Anitra the gold in her eyes wasn't.

Her face was nearly on the glass as she turned this way and that, focusing on the tiny anomalies—tingling at the thought Zac had actually noticed such a subtle difference in the color of her eyes. Were the gold flecks anything to worry about? Everything else seemed totally fine. She felt fine. Maybe traveling through the Icon gateways caused it.

Weird.

She withdrew and looked herself over. The gold didn't stand out at a distance, even now that she now knew it was there—other than to make her eyes seem lighter somehow.

Idly she brushed at her hair; tried to make it lay flat, tried to give it some kind of style. Failing that she grabbed an elastic band, wet it and pulled it back into the usual ponytail. When she cinched it tight it stood high and away from the back of her head and swished when she moved, making it at least look peppy. Flirty. *I've got the right face for a ponytail*, she thought, turning her head left to right. Good thing, because she wasn't very skilled at making her hair do much else. *Just lazy* was probably the real reason, though it was easier to blame her lack of a style on talent. Which, of course, was also the result of being lazy.

All roads led to lazy.

Now fully awake she decided to go find Bianca. She went back into the bedroom and got dressed. Moments later she was out in the chalet and looking. After checking the main hall, finding it empty at that hour—tempted to sit a while by the large fire which burned as brightly as ever, obviously tended throughout the night—she continued on to the rear of the main building until she eventually found a uniformed Venatres.

"You're Jessica," he said as she approached. Of course for them she was somewhat of a legend. She swallowed the sudden rush of uncomfortable emotions.

"I'm looking for my friend," she said before he could say anything else.

"The other girl? I saw her earlier. She was asking about the underground complex. I sent her to talk with Josef."

Jess looked around, finding no clocks, wondering just what time it was exactly. She remembered the name Josef.

"Where's Josef?"

The man led her to him and Josef, in turn, escorted her back down the metal caverns beneath the mountain, all the way to the cave containing the Kel warship. Once again in the presence of the mighty machine Jess felt that same sense of foreboding, unable to shake it as Josef led further into the vast interior space. Some of the scientific teams were there, though in all it was much quieter than earlier. In fact it was amazing she and Bianca would be given access to such a heavily classified thing at all, but they'd already been in there once, already knew about the starship and, though the Venatres appeared similar to Earth agencies in many ways, they obviously had their differences. These efforts to comprehend the logic of the situation, however, did little to dispel her mounting discomfort.

Then she saw Bianca. Standing with, of all people, the project's lead scientist, Nani. As soon as her friend saw her she smiled, white teeth beaming against her brown face and Jess felt an immediate sense of relief. Not so much that she'd found her friend but, rather, that Bianca seemed happy.

Jess called to her. "What are you doing down here?"

Josef saw she'd achieved her aim, took his leave and headed back the way he came. Jess thanked him and kept walking. Toward the work area, where Nani and Bianca stood in what had apparently been some sort of animated conversation. Jess could not imagine what her bubbly, fashion-conscious friend from Earth would be talking about with an alien scientist.

"I woke up," Bianca explained when she was close. "My head was all screwed up. I was wide awake, freaked. I almost woke you but I wanted to be strong. When I couldn't go back to sleep I decided to walk around. Ended up down here." She glanced at Nani, then back at Jessica and proclaimed: "This place is like Area 51!"

Jess looked around the interior of the massive space, lingering on the dominant form of the Kel warship—unable to keep her eyes from it. "Are you kidding?" She shook her head. "This makes Area 51 look like Disney." Images from the dream flashed across her mind, the runes on the door and the markings on the Kel craft. The starship was like a magnet for her eyes, and not just because of its size. The more she tried to ignore it the more she couldn't.

Forcibly she made herself look away. "Do you guys ever take a break?" she asked Nani, wanting to strike up idle conversation. It had to be super late. Most of the science crews Jess remembered from earlier were gone but some were still there, working as feverishly on the project now as they had been then.

"Yes," Nani assured her. "In fact, I was just wrapping a few things up when Bianca came down. It's hard to break away, as you may imagine. Sometimes I go without sleep. The Icons you brought have given us a whole fresh set of information." She glanced at the Kel warship. "I think we finally have what we need to make this thing work."

Bianca looked to Jessica. "They can test it soon," she said, enthusiastic. "The Icon has info on Earth." She seemed happiest about this as she looked back and forth between Jess and Nani. "Nani says once they test it we can go. Can you believe it? They can actually take us home in a starship." She was thrilled.

But going home was a thought on which Jess was trying not to dwell. She suspected that, no matter anything Nani might've said to Bianca, others would make that decision. Taking them home would not be the first order of business.

Her eyes drifted back to the starship. She made herself scrutinize it, steadily; analyze it without emotion—not having much luck with the prickly tingles creeping up and down her spine. It looked so incredibly powerful. Huge; sturdy; lethal. Nothing like the wispy shapes of typical UFO descriptions. If form followed function, even a little, then this thing was deadly. She looked for sign of cannons, missiles or any other sort of weapon. It was a private craft, Lindin had said, having belonged to a Kel warlord. Overall the ship was quite smooth, with only a few irregularities; mainly several large, recessed grooves.

"Does it have guns?" she asked—surprised for a moment she spoke her internal thoughts aloud.

But Nani answered without hesitation; eager, it seemed, to field questions. "The Kel were warlike," she nodded. "It has energy casters," she pointed to the grooves, "and kinetic rail guns. Not unlike the ones we use, though much more advanced." Then she shook her head slowly, contemplative. "Unfortunately we haven't had a chance to test them. Not in here. Would probably make too much noise." The way she said it was not apparently funny at first, then Jess realized she was, in her own way, making a joke. Nani hazarded a tiny smile and Jess smiled with her, then Jess laughed and Nani did too. It was as if Nani wanted to make sure everyone got it first. Bianca joined in and together the three girls shared some emotional relief. It was a bad joke, but Jess relished the sound of their laughter as it echoed hollow in the large, mostly quiet space.

Nani went on. "It should fly," she said, then glanced around and spoke a little more quietly—though there was no one close enough to overhear: "As far as I'm concerned they could've taken it out by now. The transit drive is really what they're after.

"That's what getting the Icon was all about."

Bianca grinned, at both Jessica and Nani, excited to be part of this high-level discussion. They were talking about, dealing directly with, things that could affect an entire world. Things that could get them home. It was exhilarating. Jess had to admit she felt it too.

Nani kept her voice low. "The Icons are Kel artifacts

from around the same time period." As she spoke Jess was, again, amazed at the longevity of the technology before them. The Icon she and Bianca used, Zac before that and Emperor Kagami before that, had been buried on Earth a thousand years. This ship had apparently been sealed up there in the mountain just as long. "They use the same quantum entangled mechanics," Nani explained. "The Icons contain a location pair which restricts them to transit between two points. Kind of like a small, personal starship engine.

"The transit drive aboard the *Cearcrux*, however—"

"*Cearcrux*?" Jess asked, twigging on the name. "Is that the name of the ship?"

"Yeah." Then: "It means *Reaver*, in the language of the Kel, or something like it." Hearing the Kel word had been vaguely disturbing, but Jess dismissed it as Nani went on: "Its transit drive can be set with multiple coordinates and has advanced navigation as part of its operation. I've set the coordinates from the two Icons and," she paused, "I believe it will work.

"There are tests needed," she cautioned, "but everything plugged in perfectly. All our preliminary work has paid off. Everyone thought this would take much longer. I did too."

"Wow." Jess tried to let the concept settle. Bianca cut short her reverie.

"I know, right?"

Nani began putting things away. Jess studied the ship. Looked at Nani. Talking to Nani felt more like talking to an older college friend, not the chief research scientist over a monumental, ultra-top-secret project.

Monumental is hardly the word. World-changing is more like it.

History changing.

But Nani was pure scientist. Political machinations meant little to her. She was all about the discovery. Uncovering the new frontier.

Why can't we all be like that?

"So you were able to get into the laptop?"

Nani kept putting things away. "You mean through its

intended interface?"

"Um, yes."

"No, but we were able to plug in directly."

"Directly?"

"To the hardware. In doing that we enabled the user interface. Kind of a reverse entry. But it's working."

For some reason that, perhaps more than anything right then, excited Jess the most.

"Did you get anything off of it?" she asked.

Nani nodded that they had.

"What did you get?" What kinds of things was the mystery agency hiding? Anything?

Nani shrugged, continuing to put away items at the workspace. "We got it all. Transferred everything. Haven't had a chance to evaluate it yet, not fully, but we grabbed the entire contents of its storage."

Jess hesitated. Then, without thinking further:

"Can I borrow it?" Technically it was hers, in a way, but ...

Nani, of anyone, should be able to appreciate her interest. She hoped. Nani of anyone should understand her curiosity.

She did.

"Sure," she said without hesitation. Jess had expected a short battle, or at least a pause. She was taken with how quickly Nani agreed. And, again, recognized the difference between Earth and Anitra. On Earth, at an installation like this, there would've been a mile of bureaucratic process before any such release would've been granted—even if Nani was willing.

But she didn't wait for Nani to change her mind, or to see if such a process existed. In no time she had the laptop in hand and was hurriedly saying thank-you and good-bye—worried Nani would realize something, or someone else would intervene, all the while dying to get back to the room and take a look. Nani gave her the passwords, even showed her the things of most interest. According to her the science team went in directly on the items most relevant to their research and others were reading and evaluating the rest. At that point, since all data had been transferred, the laptop itself was, for the Venatres, little more than a relatively useless piece of foreign technology.

Which meant Jess was free to do some research of her own.

Curiously Bianca chose to stay behind, resuming whatever conversation she'd been having with Nani—which was fine with Jess; at least that way she'd be alone—but as she left the hangar she found her interest in the contents of the laptop temporarily crowded out by a greater interest in the odd friendship clearly developing between her friend and the girl scientist.

Once the duo were out of sight, however, and she was a few steps into the hall, that curiosity fell quickly away. Replaced again by thoughts of what amazing secrets must lay within the Earth computer hugged tightly to her chest.

CHAPTER 33:

TRUE LOVE

IT WAS LATE. Lindin couldn't seem to find a good point at which to call it a night. More reports had just come in from Midbay, indicating the Dominion forces were preparing for mobilization. Now he'd just finished reviewing sketchy details from agents in Osaka, telling of yet more drama within the upper ranks of their enemies; specifically that an attempt had been made on Kang's life and that preparation was being made for a direct attack—by the new Emperor himself—on Venatres soil.

Where the Dominion was concerned things could not, it seemed, get any worse.

Yet there was good news. Excellent news, in fact. Nani had been able to divine settings from the Icons faster than expected and it looked as if, far in advance of any expected timeframe, they were ready for a trial run of the great Kel starship. Which, if it worked, would, in one scientifically astounding swoop, catapult the Venatres to a whole new level of capability.

On the one hand an enemy that had been attacking since they wounded it mortally at the battle of the Crucible, led suddenly by a seemingly unstoppable monster. On the other salvation. Or at least the hope of it. The starship was theoretically untouchable, based on what they knew so far. If it worked they might use it to bring the enemy to heel.

But he dared not reveal it at the wrong time. That the Dominion had absolutely no idea of its existence ... that alone was remarkable. If the starship failed in its first tests, which would be highly visible—no putting it back into hiding after that ... if it was lost somehow and recovered by the Dominion ...

There were so many ways this could become a catastrophe

of epic proportions.

And so the Venatres sat at a crux. And so Lindin could not call it a night. Sleep wasn't an option anyway. Not until he collapsed. Exhaustion would take him when the time was right.

Until then he worked.

* * *

GOD SOMETIMES YOU JUST DON'T COME THROUGH, the music managed to fill the bedroom, despite coming from the small, built-in laptop speakers, *Do you need a woman to look after you?* Tori Amos sang as Jess sat cross-legged on the bed, mind expanded in contemplation of the screen before her; thoughts swirling, filled with incredible details of the info she'd read so far.

I gotta find why you always go when the wind blows, Tori lilted along, *tell me you're crazy, maybe then I'll understand.*

The laptop screen glowed brightly in the semi-dark, one small lamp in the corner its only competition. The white radiance cast the rest of the room in stark light. Jess drifted to the present, settling on the scene before her.

After Nani gave her the laptop she'd hurried off, asking after Zac along the way and discovering he was, even that late, tied up in planning. She had no idea what was going on that called for so many meetings, but Zac had been in high demand since they arrived. And so, dying to pour through the contents of the Earth computer she rushed to her room, climbed eagerly into bed and flipped it on. A bit of nerves as she waited to make sure it worked, then tried the passwords, but everything took and she was in and breathing a sigh of relief, scrolling and clicking at will. That was what felt like hours ago. Sitting by herself in the middle of the night, hunting through pages of digital information, pictures and all else. It felt very much like being a teenage girl again, surfing the web, only this was not the web. The information she "surfed" was right there on the laptop, and was so significant, so far beyond the typical juvenile urges that might keep a girl up late at night

...

It was absolutely mind-blowing.

Tori finally got old. Jess clicked and brought up the laptop's media player, scrolling through the selections to see what else she could find. Though this was, she'd now confirmed, a US government laptop, it was nonetheless a normal laptop with the usual bits of personalized BS. Whoever it belonged to had a folder of songs and it didn't take her long to start playing music. She found it curious the owner even had Tori Amos, imagining a stiff, suit-wearing G-Man, but if there was one thing the last months of world hopping had taught her it was to expect the unexpected. An album labeled Metal caught her eye. She flipped through it; found a song to begin. Pretty much the exact opposite of Tori Amos, she thought—*who was this government guy?*—and clicked to play.

As the opening riffs ground from the tinny speakers she found herself taking a deep breath, drifting with the intensity of the heavy drums, receding once more into that realm of speculation where she'd just been so deeply immersed.

One didn't live on Earth, in any modern society, without exposure to wild speculations, conspiracy theories and "what ifs", to say nothing of pop culture and its endless stream of doomsday scenarios, ancient alien TV shows and all else that fueled the imagination. The idea of secret societies was as old as mankind. Vampire cults, Illuminati, reptile men. The list went on. According to theorists these societies were everywhere, working their evil machinations among the unseeing; craftily manipulating the sleeping masses for their questionable, if unfathomable, purposes. Jess herself had always found it hard to believe there might not be *something* unknown on Earth, secret things, accessible only to the initiated, though she was sure nothing extreme—and she certainly hadn't devoted much time to the contemplation of such possibilities. Where that was concerned she'd never formed an opinion, and if forced would probably have placed herself somewhere on the sane side of the discussion, much closer to the non-believers than the so-called whackos.

Now things were different. Now she'd gone to another planet, one with humans on it, visited alien cities, seen advanced technologies, witnessed the reality of super men and—right there in front of her—was a US government accounting of a group on Earth, a secret society the likes of which she'd never heard.

It hadn't taken long to clear up the confusion as to who was who in that little battle back in Boise. The guys in suits were in fact an agency within the US government, the owners of the laptop, a Black Ops group that had, as expected, extreme latitude in their operations. They'd certainly behaved with impunity once they decided to close on her. Nameless, faceless—a group with a clear License to Kill. In all the info on the laptop they referred to themselves only as "Project Ophiuchi", a reference to the discovery that led to their inception. Their tentacles, however, reached into every branch of government. Even, it seemed, into many global organizations.

How long they'd been on her trail she hadn't yet discovered, but pictures on the laptop of her going about daily activities—along with a full bio—gave her an icy chill—actually made her skin crawl—and were difficult to look through. The stuff on her was current, the oldest pics taken not that long ago—including, to her horror, Vegas—confirming those paranoid suspicions—but their investigation leading to her apparently went back further, to data gathered around the time of the "twin disturbances". The disturbances, of course, being the thunderclap in a clear sky that occurred last summer over her neighborhood when Zac came through, another a few days later when she returned in the Skull Boy armor. No one had apparently reported the one when she and Zac disappeared from the playhouse (perhaps it was muffled) but of course her absence was noted and a connection drawn, and there were evidently many people that noticed the others. Many more than she suspected. The fact that no one bothered her for so long afterward did not, apparently, mean it had gone undetected.

It took time for those reports to rise through the chatter. Project Ophiuchi was constantly monitoring. Like the NSA or something these guys checked everything, crunching data into discrete nuggets, patterns and so forth; running them through algorithms designed to identify leads. Those in turn were investigated, more so as they showed signs of value and, a few months after the disturbances, Ophiuchi had narrowed things down to a handful of correlations in the area. Most notably the girl who disappeared during the exact same time frame, reporting afterward a suspicious case of amnesia. At that point the noose began to tighten. Why they were so methodical she might never know, but when the hammer finally did fall she was already onto them and, as it turned out, the whole thing blew up in their faces. Now here she was, back on Anitra.

But those were just the surface events. The layers beneath were ripe with unbelievable, fantastic connections, most notably what led to the birth of the "Project" in the first place. *That* alone was an eye-popper. Back in the late 60s, in the Rockies, right there in America, a man hiking a remote area had stumbled across ...

An Icon.

It took her a few minutes to digest that bit of information. They didn't call it an Icon, of course, but the pictures and descriptions could make it nothing else. Obviously this was the second Icon, the one she snatched from the warehouse—right from out of their hands—and brought with her to Anitra. The one Nani and the scientific team now held deep in the mountain below, along with her own.

The man who discovered that Icon was found dead near the device, signs of a short fall but, more curiously, evidence of exposure to a vacuum. A *vacuum* had killed him, right there in the woods, in the middle of nowhere. Reports from the local coroner questioned the obvious signs of burst blood vessels and expanded organs but drew no logical conclusions.

Of course the government was quick to step in.

All was taken over by then Project Blue Book, shortly after which Project Blue Book was terminated and Project

Ophiuchi formed.   Unlike Blue Book Ophiuchi was completely Top Secret. As near as Jess could tell, from what she'd read, no one even knew of them. Even now. Before the inception of Ophiuchi, when Project Blue Book first tested the Icon, they learned—as had she with her Icon—that it phased the holder out of existence. They took the Icon to a lab and, after some evaluation, tested it.   Perhaps the test was an accidental activation, she couldn't be sure from reading the records, but one of the Project twisted it and was gone. When that man was then found back in the Rockies, where the device was originally discovered—also dead from exposure to space—they began to determine the Icon was a transit device between two very precise locations. A base was set up in the Rockies at that point and, after more trips with men in space suits, taking numerous readings, it was determined the connecting point, a point in deep space, was in fact in the star system 36 Ophiuchi, some 19 light years from Earth.

At that point the whole thing was buttoned up and Project Ophiuchi was formed.

Which, in turn, triggered a response they would never have expected. For, as the Project soon discovered, there was *another* device like theirs on Earth, maybe even more, that had been known about by a small group of people for nearly a thousand years.

Which was where the secret society came in. And which was where, for Jessica, her skin really began to crawl.

The Bok, they called themselves. Esehta Bok. A name taken from—and here was the part that, just when Jess thought she could be no more blown away, managed to blow her away—the language of the Kel. The same aliens that made the starship sitting right there in the mountain complex on Anitra. The same aliens that made the Icons. The Bok were humans but, according to their own history, had been at war with the Kel a thousand years ago when they founded their society on Earth. Jess deduced this was likely during the period everyone here kept referring to as the Great Wars, and in the fallout of that the Esehta Bok were left isolated on Earth.

Shortly after that they went into hiding.

For a thousand years they came forward in the shadows. Prior to the formation of the Project the Esehta Bok had, therefore, remained completely unknown. Project Ophiuchi learned of them for the first time when the Bok attacked. The channels employed by the Bok were apparently even more far-reaching, more hidden even than those of the US Government. The Bok knew of Project Ophiuchi and the Icon before the Project learned of them and, in a decidedly brazen move, staged an assault that very nearly succeeded. Commandos, much like those used in the Boise warehouse district—Jess had concluded, now, that that was likely what the second group of players in that fiasco were— infiltrated the new base in the Rockies and almost got the Icon held by the Project.

Almost.

They failed, and in the bargain alerted the Project to their presence. Now aware of the Bok the Project began their own effort to uncover their bold nemesis. An effort that to date had been, largely, a failure.

According to what the Project knew, what Jess could find on the laptop, Esehta Bok meant, in the language of the Kel, "Defenders of the Secret" or, literally, "Secret Defenders". Project records were sketchy at best; the Bok had remained invisible for a thousand years and weren't easy to expose. Even now that they had the full attention of the Project and its bottomless budget, they remained mostly a mystery. In fact, what little the Project *did* know about the Bok was from a few remotely connected commandoes captured during that initial raid (men hired by the Bok but not actual Bok), along with a few minor hacks into Bok records using vague leads from other disconnected sources. They had been otherwise difficult to crack.

But they knew a little.

For starters this group, the Bok, counted themselves superior to everyone on Earth, having once been part of a technologically advanced civilization when Earth was heading into the throes of its Dark Ages. They were arrogant. Their group back then had been small, Earth remote—and unheard of among their confederacy of worlds—and when they came to Earth their own worlds had been engaged in a civil war. One that, as near as the Project had been able to determine, was going badly. As a result the Bok were stranded. Exactly how that happened or whether it was absolutely the case the Project didn't know. What they did know was that, a thousand years ago, this small group of Bok tried to establish a beachhead on Earth, a place for their larger group to escape to and, when that failed, they were left behind. Having few options and being far more advanced than the people of Earth they tried, of course, to take over. That failed, for though they were more knowledgeable than the humans of that time, superior in their own ways, the Bok were never able to parlay that advanced understanding into absolute control. Indeed many were persecuted, burned as heretics, etc. The usual sort of thing that happened around that time in Earth's history, especially to anyone introducing a high level of knowledge (which could only be deemed sorcery) into a sea of ignorance. Seeing therefore the impossibility of Plan B, those Bok left alive receded to a sort of Plan C, choosing to go underground and come forward since that time as an elite—beyond elite—secret society.

Building a dossier on them had proven near impossible. If Project Ophiuchi was super Black Op, the Bok were a black hole. It was only when they made that first daring raid on Project headquarters, back in the 70s, that the Project even became aware of them. So began the conflict between the two groups, along with, for the Project, the process of discovery, decades of difficult investigation into their invisible foe leading, eventually, to the battle at the warehouse from which Jess only narrowly escaped.

How, or why, what very nearly amounted to an encyclopedia of information had come to be on this laptop, she could not imagine. But there it was and she'd been bending every ounce of IQ to the understanding of its contents.

The attackers in the battle in Boise were most probably mercenaries in the Bok's devout employ. Theirs was an almost religious society, steeped in ritual and special knowledge, or so it was described, and the Bok therefore employed zealots for such operations. There were recorded instances of similar attacks. Jess imagined this one, the attack in Boise, was done the same way. Making it yet another attempt by the Bok to acquire the Icon held by the American agency. They clearly saw value in it, great value, and along the way the Project came to learn the Bok most likely held one of their own, if not more than one. The sparse data maintained by the Project told them the device belonging to the Bok likely went to another world or worlds. And so, more than anything, more even than their desire to eliminate the Bok and fully understand their nemesis, the Project wanted to possess that other Icon (or Icons). Just as the Bok wanted theirs.

Of course the Project had never been able to capitalize on their own device. After a while they stopped using it to pop to and from the distant star system, having gathered what info they could. Attempts to send anything larger than a few men failed. Large equipment transfer was out. There were other problems. The closest thing to the point in space where the Icon connected was a massive gas giant. It had been photographed many times (pictures were on the laptop and it was beautiful; a giant, purple planet, wrapped in shimmering clouds) but, close though it was in a relative sense, the Jupiter-like planet was still tens of thousands of miles from the device's transit point. Other planets were in the star system but there was no feasible way to reach them. Equipment advanced enough to study them was too large to make the journey. As amazing, as absolutely stunning as it all was, the device slowly, over time, became little more than a novelty.

The Project examined it but had not yet been able to figure out its function. They didn't know how to take it apart. Scans—better and better scans as the years wore on and Earth technology advanced—revealed little. None could tell how it worked. Jess was impressed that Nani had so quickly been able to understand the devices, but she had the Kel starship, not to mention the more advanced Venatres equipment behind her. It wasn't fair to compare what they were doing there on Anitra with what was available on Earth.

And so, mostly, the mission of the Project had turned to "Get the Bok." The disbanding and acquisition of their immediate rivals. According to the latest information on the laptop the Bok, too, were switching tactics. Moving away from their passive infiltration of world institutions, gearing up for a more aggressive attack. Apparently, after a thousand years, they were once again about to make a bid for the world. A young, dynamic leader had assumed the head of the organization, a man named Lorenzo Fertiti, an Italian, and the Project had been watching him closely. Very closely. Lorenzo had emboldened the Bok, exposing more of their tendrils (it seemed the Bok had agents in nearly every global institution, more so even than the Project, which was chilling in itself—talk about conspiracies come to life) and, therefore, gave the Project more angles from which to attack. Lorenzo was cocky. Too cocky, perhaps, and this, his ego, had become the Bok's greatest weakness—and the Project's greatest opportunity. Even as Lorenzo made bold steps forward, the increased visibility required to do so gave the Project more and more exposed points on which to set their sights.

Jessica, to her great surprise, knew something neither group did. Namely that the Icon she used was also found on Earth, by a Japanese man about 150 years ago, which he then used to travel to another world. Anitra. Whether Anitra was the world the presumed Bok Icon went to she had no idea (the one she stole from the agents was the Rockies Icon, which transited between the Rockies on Earth and deep space around the purple gas giant, at 36 Ophiuchi), but the whole intricacy of the devices and their tangled history was starting to make her head hurt. If nothing else she was, by now, convinced Anitra was in fact another planet, another real point in space, just like the Ophiuchi star system.

As far as the Project knew (from what she could see on the laptop) the Bok did *not* know of her Icon. However, as was now obvious, the Bok *did* know where the members of the Project were going to be on that fateful day in Boise, which made her believe they might know more than the Project realized.

Did that mean the Bok also knew more about *her?*

Other possibilities. Did the Bok have more than one other Icon? Would commandos come dropping through somewhere right there on Anitra?

One thing was certain, these last few hours with the laptop had been an awakening. A mind-bending, all-caps: AWAKENING.

Already she knew so much. She'd thought, before, that her time on Anitra, the first go-round, had been an awakening. It was, of course; hugely so. Now though it was like that awakening had been supercharged. So many more pieces of the giant puzzle that was the Truth were in her hands. If she ever *did* get back to Earth this information would prove priceless. Now she knew the fundamentals of the Bok and the Project, who those groups were and how and why their little drama back in Boise played out the way it did—and what to expect from both. Now that she'd paired it in her mind with everything she knew on *this* end ... suddenly she knew more than both sides. She knew what Lindin and the Venatres knew. They had no idea the things the Bok and the Project knew, or how they related to Earth. The Project and the Bok knew nothing of the Anitrans and their discoveries. She did.

Suddenly, right there, at that juncture and at least for a little while, she knew more than anyone.

Oddly it made her feel, not burdened, as it had before, but prepared. No more mystery about who, or what, she was dealing with. On either side. Whether that ultimately changed her own path, whether it headed her life in a vastly new direction ...

Well, her life was *already* headed in a vastly new direction.

But there were too many variables between her and what came next to imagine exactly how things would play out. Probably the Venatres *would* go to Earth. After all, it was another world like theirs. It was impossible to imagine they *wouldn't* go. When that happened ... maybe she could involve herself in some higher capacity.

That was an idea.

As a liaison, or an ambassador even, between Earth and Anitra. Get herself a pardon for what she'd done. She was plugged in at a high enough level here, on Anitra. How hard would it be to get a role like that? Months ago the Shogun, though evil in his conniving, had even suggested such an idea. Maybe if—when—the Venatres went, she could achieve an amnesty of sorts. The Project held power on Earth, and now she knew all about them. Maybe she could bring Anitran technology; help root out the Bok and expose what they were hiding. Full disclosure of everything, pardon by the Project and a new world for all. There had to be a way to secure her future, and as she thought of it ... it gave her a comforting sense of hope. She tried to let it carry her. Only, that thinking led to other things.

The Golden Age.

And with that the promise of the Prophecy echoed uncomfortably in her mind.

Absently she wondered why the Venatres kept the starship hidden for so long. Five years since its discovery, no evidence she'd seen in their everyday things of any super-advanced technology that might've been derived from it. Maybe they'd incorporated some of the discoveries in ways she hadn't observed. Or maybe they were withholding *everything* until they had the Icon technology and could make the whole thing work. Whatever their choices, the Kel starship was currently the biggest secret ever.

She took a deep, cleansing breath and leaned forward; continued reading, scrolling through information that was, taken by itself, earth shattering yet, taken with the whole merely part of the bigger picture.

Then a word caught her eye.

Priestess.

She zeroed in on the screen, halting her slow scrolling. Something she'd missed. She backed up and read from the top.

... The Esehta Bok claim their order originated with the dogma of a Kel priestess from another world.

She read it again. Breathing shallow.
Continued:

Their existence was based on her teachings. Their claims are that there was a large-scale war in progress at the time, among several worlds, possibly a result of those teachings. It would appear that the earth was not part of that war, nor on any of the channels of those forces. Earth was, therefore, to be a refuge for the Bok. We can only imagine that the war was going badly. From that we can also assume that the earth, once discovered by the Bok, was kept secret from these other forces. There is no evidence to support the idea that any extraterrestrial war, at least not one of significance, ever made it to these shores.

There is no corroborating evidence for much of this.

We can conclude, then, that the founding Bok were a small group. From their own records, those few we have been able to obtain, they were ultimately unable to make an impact on Earth civilization at that time. Their small numbers gave them nothing beyond their advanced knowledge with which to attack their objective. Their priestess was apparently lost in battle. As a result they were soon forced underground, forming the secret society that exists today ...

Jess leaned back.
Skin crawling way more than it should've been at that point, or so she thought. But she could not shake the

sense that these Bok and the Prophecy and, to her alarm, she herself, were connected.

Could this document be referring to the same priestess? A *Kel* priestess.

Aesha.

The same priestess that started the Prophecy?

A knock at the door and she lurched. Her heart started racing. Quickly she killed the grinding Metal music and shut the laptop—unnecessary, perhaps—got a grip, looked at the door and called:

"Who is it?"

Bianca would've entered without knocking. It was her room too, after all. Which meant it was probably one of the Venatres.

"It's Zac."

Her heart shifted gears, thundering now.

She gathered her wits and found her voice. "Come in."

As the door opened and he did she swallowed, debating how to act. Put away the laptop? *No.* She raised the lid, opening it back up—trying to return smoothly to the way she just was, watching as the computer came out of the hasty hibernate. Get up? Give him a hug? Act casual? Act pleasantly surprised? Act absolutely thrilled, which was the way she felt beneath her sudden, sweaty nerves? *Say something!* Say what? And as she botched any attempt to come to a decision Zac made it to the bed and sat.

His sudden presence was overwhelming. Too much. Exacerbated by the very real, physical presence of him as he plopped at the foot of the bed, pushing the mattress down heavily and lifting her up. In an effort to seem relaxed she stuck her arms out behind her and leaned back, awkwardly—failing, utterly, to look composed.

"You're up late," he commented.

Desperately she tried to clear her head. It was impossible. Switching from the total immersion of moments ago to the social demands of now had her completely off her game.

If she even had a game.

Get it together!

"I've been reading," she glanced at the laptop, login

box up and waiting. She leaned forward and typed in the password.

"That the computer?" Zac studied it.

"Yeah," she said, then, managing to calm a bit, added: "I can't believe what's on this thing."

Zac reached and touched the edge of the lid, testing its feel. "What did you find?"

"Incredible stuff," she leaned back again, doing a better job this time of being natural. "You should see some of it."

"I'd love to," he enthused, and for a weird moment, the way he said it ... she imagined those same words in front of other things. *I'd love to kiss you. I'd love to marry you. I'd love to ...*

She focused. "What are *you* doing up?"

"I never sleep, remember?" Now that the initial shock was gone the reality of him being there weighed on her. It was late. Very late. They were alone.

"They finally let me go," he explained.

"They've had you in meetings since we got here."

He sighed. "The Dominion is in a very ... volatile state right now. A lot going on." Then: "Kang has really turned everything on its head. All new strategies and no way to predict what's next. In a sense we have to be ready for anything."

She was sorry she asked. She didn't even want to think about Kang right then. Ever.

She tried to be more engaging. "So what brings you by?"

He shrugged. "I heard you up."

"You were checking on me?" Immediately she hated the way it sounded. Like she thought it might be creepy or something, which couldn't be further from the truth. She *liked* the idea of him checking on her. In fact, if he stood watch outside her door all night she couldn't have been happier.

"A little," he admitted. Then: "I heard music. What were you listening to?"

She glanced at the laptop, taking the opportunity to shift to a more comfortable position.

"Music from Earth," she said. "Can you believe these

dorks had iTunes?" Even as she finished the sentence she realized she'd just given him two words he probably didn't know, dorks and iTunes. He only asked about the former.

"Dorks?"

"People who have no social skills," she shrugged. "You wouldn't expect them to have good music."

"Who were these dorks?" he asked quite seriously. Nervously she giggled at his address of the government agents as dorks. Then wondered if the giggle sounded lame, or if he'd take it the wrong way. Then wondered why she couldn't just get over the flustering nerves that had her mercilessly in their grip.

"Part of my government on Earth," she made it sound casual. "The ones that had the other Icon."

A quiet moment passed between them. Jessica's heart continued to thump in her chest as she willed it to ease, certain he could hear it.

Zac pointed to the laptop. "Can you play some more?"

It took her an instant to realize he was talking about the music.

"Yeah." She moused to the media player, almost asked what he wanted to hear but that was pointless. Of course he wouldn't have any preferences. He didn't know any Earth songs. He'd profess to like anything she picked, that much was certain, but what would he *really* like? What would be the coolest thing to share? Were the right options on here? Something special, maybe even something that could become "their" song? This would be the first time they'd listened to music together.

Oh, the pressure.

She scrolled through the list, impressed with how much this government guy had, growing more nervous as Zac watched, waiting, found something safe, clicked it and lowered the volume.

Zac smiled as the song began and closed his eyes. After a minute he said: "You guys have such great music. I loved those songs on your phone."

She recalled when he had her phone, the last time she was on Anitra, and wondered just how much he got to listen to. How much he got to see. Had he looked at the best pictures of her? The worst? That phone was long gone, everything with it, but she recalled it vividly. It had been a part of her. She remembered how she felt when he told her he had it. Remembered everything about every short instant they spent together. And she realized, if you added it up, including and right up to this moment and these minutes right now, she and Zac had probably been "together"—in each other's presence—a grand total of one day. If that. Probably less.

She felt like they'd known each other a lifetime.

He opened his eyes and looked at her, his own gaze soft. "Why'd you come back?" The question was phrased intimately. Curious.

"You mean here?"

Of course he meant here. *Duh!*

He nodded.

"I don't know. I was being chased."

He accepted that, asked no more, and only as he closed his eyes again and drifted in thought, mind on the music, did she realize she could've said more. Could've told him how she came back to be with him. How the thought of him was what impelled her, what really made her take the ridiculous step of running from the authorities, taking the Skull Boy armor and the Icon—taking *their* Icon—and making herself a fugitive on her own world. *I came for you! I ran here to be with you!* But it was too late for that answer. Too awkward. No way to fit it in as an afterthought without coming out all wrong.

And so she sat. Watching him, trying not to fidget, studying his expression as he continued to sit with his eyes closed. There were words forming, it seemed, thoughts; she could see. She wondered what he was about to say.

"The entire, short time I've known you," he opened his eyes, "we've always been on the run. Always in the middle of a fight. It's nice to have a few peaceful moments."

She found herself lost in his youthful face, her own mind buzzing. *Zac.* Sitting there in the low light, heavy on the bed in front of her, tall and handsome in his simple black uniform. Unlike earlier such moments it didn't become awkward. Felt perfectly normal, in fact; sublime, and only when the song ended and silence fell over them did she even realize they'd been sitting there staring at each other.

"Do you believe in fate?" he asked, and the question enflamed the thoughts swirling within her.

She very nearly blurted, *What?*, but caught that moment-ruining question as she cast about for the appropriate response. The pause stretched and she decided to say simply: "Yes."

Zac smiled, then his eyes sparkled. "The circumstances of our meeting were intense," he reminisced. "I can't help feeling we made a connection. As soon as we saw each other. Something I can't explain except that, maybe, we were fated to meet." He looked at her, needing to know: "Is that weird?"

"No!" she gushed. Went on before she could stop herself: "I felt that way too! When I first saw you I was like, 'There you are!', like you'd been missing or something. I couldn't say that then, things were too freaky right then—I mean, you just fell out of the sky—but that's how I felt." She swallowed. Why did she keep losing control of her own mouth?

But Zac, as always, didn't seem to care. "When I became a Kazerai," he began, had a thought and reached to push the laptop aside, removing that barrier between them. As he slid closer her breathing grew shallow, heart racing all over again—at his proximity, at everything in that moment. He was suddenly right there, within easy kissing distance …

She wanted so badly to kiss him.

God!

But he was talking. "When I became a Kazerai," he continued, no real change in his mannerisms. It was as if he just wanted to be closer, not that he had any ulterior motive in mind.

But oh how she did.

"I knew deep down I was doing it for some other purpose. Unknown even to myself. I still don't know, exactly." He drifted. Came back. "They choose only the best Astake to undergo the process. Unlike the others, though, I didn't want to be a Kazerai for the usual reasons. Others fought for the honor, out of pride. Desire. Lust for power. For me it was different ..." She waited, intent, heart skipping on unabated. When he continued it was as if he'd jumped ahead. "I always used to look up at the stars. Like I wanted to be out there in the worst way. Like, there was something I needed to do, somewhere I needed to go.

"Almost like, there was somewhere else I needed to *be*."

"Me too!" she blurted, thinking in the same instant that if she couldn't quit being an idiot she was going to go lock herself in the bathroom. The last thing she wanted was to scare him off.

But there was so much they had in common! So much they shared. Why was she worried? He obviously liked her the way she was. Already he'd had plenty of opportunities to react to her outbursts, to her dumbness, but he hadn't. She'd kissed him, boldly, she'd said things—she'd done enough already to send him running. He'd certainly seen her at her worst; crying, terrified, crushed, dirty, confused. Yet there he sat, alone with her in her room—*he came to me*—moving closer, not further away, and there were no signs of him running anywhere.

Quite the opposite.

And so she decided, with an overwhelming rush of relief, to stop adjusting what she said or how she said it. To stop trying to be something she wasn't. To just be herself. Obviously he was perfectly fine with that.

It felt liberating.

"I've always dreamed about something beyond Earth," she carried on, determined now. "Other worlds."

Zac nodded. "For me I thought becoming a Kazerai would get me closer to that. I didn't know how, but I struggled for it.

"Then, right before we met, I was given ... whatever it was, it was supposed to make me open to suggestion. A drug. It didn't, really, but it did clear my mind. I remember thinking I should use the Icon. My instructions were to get it to the Venatres. But I had this nagging idea it was meant to be used. That I should activate it. When the guards attacked ... I did.

"The combination of what Kitana gave me and the blasts of the guards as I twisted it ... I think all that knocked me out. Left me totally blanked. When you found me, after I fell ... for a while it was like I was a clean slate."

A bit of Jessica's rising euphoria faltered at the thought of Zac's former wife. It had been months since her death but Jess felt for him—all the while wondering what changed. How did *he* feel? Was he still in mourning?

"I'm so sorry," she offered.

He seemed to get what she meant. "Ours was an arranged marriage." He looked almost apologetic, which fascinated her. "We didn't choose each other. All Kazerai are assigned a wife. Families with eligible daughters vie for a chance. Being selected as the wife of a Kazerai means gaining favor with the ruling dynasty.

"Kitana was special, though. I knew at once, when we were introduced, she was beyond the greed of her parents. It was clear in her expression. In her eyes." He faded again, lost in the memory. "She came with a higher purpose. When she did what she did, when she used me ... I know she understood I was with her. That I forgave her." He paused. Then continued in a more reserved tone: "We got to see each other once more, before she died. I was trapped in the Raza field. The witch was taunting me. Using Kitana to get to me. Then, when Kitana took her own life ..." He stopped talking and, to Jessica's dismay, his eyes glistened. No tears fell but they were there, sign of his emotion—held in check by whatever strength he possessed. The sight of it pained her.

"I broke the field," he said, eyes drying as he moved to that part of the memory. He seemed in awe of his own action, of what he himself had done. "I broke the field. Too late, though, and I wasn't able to save her. And I wasn't able to do it again." At this he stopped and, this time, it appeared he was done.

Jess felt empty. Unsure what to say. Zac was drifting

and, as she watched him, sad for him, an entirely natural curiosity overtook her and she asked quietly:

"What's it like? Being a Kazerai?"

He brought his focus back to the present.

Back to her.

Shrugged. "Weird at first. I'd aspired to it for so long, to be chosen. Once I went through the process ... for a while it was amazing, to be so strong. So impervious. Then it was like I had nowhere else to go. Nothing left.

"There are certain sacrifices you make." He paused, still lost in his thoughts. Went on: "But I knew I wanted it for a reason. Like I said, I had this conviction it would get me out there." He glanced up, gaze beyond the confines of the room. "To the stars. Don't ask me how, but I truly believed it would.

"Turns out I was right."

Then he surprised her. "What about you? What's it like being you?"

The question took her off guard. "Me?" What was there to tell? "Nothing special." Even as she said it, though, even as she thought it, she hoped he would feel different.

He did.

"Hardly," he disagreed. "You're amazing."

The way he admired her made her blush.

"But I mean about being an angel," he looked on her now with a developing wonder. "What's *that* like?"

She was confused. How much did Zac know about the Prophecy? What details?

And—and this worried her—did he place as much stock in it as the fanatics of the Conclave? Did he place as much stock in *her*? Surely he couldn't believe she was an actual angel.

Suddenly: *Is that why he likes me?*

The possibility of that made her heart sink. What if *that* was the driving force behind his unexplained attraction? What if he was only drawn to her because he thought she was some sort of divine savior? *Just like all the others.* And as she thought of this she realized it made perfect sense. Boring, plain Jessica had no chance of attracting a handsome super guy.

Of course not.

A crushing feeling began to squeeze her chest and a frown, an uncontrollable frown, took over her face.

Even as a smile spread slowly across his.

"Lot of pressure, huh?"

And she saw he was teasing her. Poking fun, in his own way, having had his own experience being the center of such regard. And the sadness vanished, as if whisked away on a breeze. She kicked him lightly. "Ha ha."

He laughed.

Said: "After you left I got an earful. Especially from Darvon. Of how you were the one who'd come to save us all. I learned all about you and your legacy. Darvon admires you more than you can imagine."

"I can imagine." She forced herself to stabilize. "At least when they expect amazing things from you, though, you can deliver. I have no idea what they see in me."

Now Zac eased his teasing. His admiration again became genuine. "What you did is remarkable. How can you not see that?"

She snorted, a dumb sound but she refused to dwell on it. "How can *you* see it? I mean, you can jump a hundred feet in the air. I can't do that."

"Come on," he paused and looked up, searching for words. "How to explain it." He shook his head. "Results," he settled on that. "We accomplish things—*we* accomplish things. Not to get philosophical, but the fact is we accomplish what we accomplish by whatever tools are necessary. All that matters is the result. I'm big, you're small. I'm strong, you're not. It doesn't matter. Results." He looked into her eyes. "You can't deny the results of what you've done."

She couldn't, actually. When you put it that way. She was reminded of Darvon and the same point he tried to make, finding it odd that both men would draw the same conclusion. She'd definitely gotten results. And now that Zac mentioned it, in addition to all she'd done last time around she had to consider what she'd done to get where she was. Escaped two powerful groups on Earth, both bent on catching her. She had their laptop there on the bed beside her. Stole their Icon and got away, then got to safety in the enemy city, then got *out* of the enemy city and all the way here. Some of that was her, some of it the work of others, but all of it was a result of what drove her. All the result of *her* determination.

Maybe results *were* all that mattered.

Zac looked into her eyes and his admiration continued to expand. "I guess what I'm trying to say is you're the single most incredible person I've ever met." Then, with what might've been a slip added: "I feel like I've finally found the one I've been looking for."

And all at once her spirit soared.

Why did she keep doubting herself?

Now it was his turn to look uncomfortable. "This may sound strange," he fidgeted, trying to recover his composure—unbearably cute as he did so—and she wanted to grab him more than ever, "but I didn't seem to have any purpose until we met."

He looked away, then tried to hold her gaze. She was quiet. What could she say? Nothing, really, so she didn't. Satisfied that, at last, she was in command of her own tongue.

He went on. "I felt like I was working toward that moment, toward finding ... you," he made motions with his hands, trying to understand, "though I had no idea why. I didn't know who it was I was trying to find, or even that I was trying to find anyone, only that, when I saw you, you were it. How that worked, how things fell into place, across such impossible distance, against such incredible odds—when I had no plan for anything ... I can't explain. Results, I guess." He gave a little smile; that wonderful, boyish, slightly lopsided smile of his and she melted inside.

He shook his head. "The strangest thing is, somehow, I knew this day would come. I knew we *would* be together again. As the days turned into months, in my heart I still believed. I was impatient, every day you were gone I couldn't stand it, but part of me was calm." Finally he made himself shut his own mouth and Jess smiled to herself that he was having just as much trouble as she was. As if a small epiphany she realized: If you let someone talk long enough you often learned amazing things.

Life lesson: Be quiet and listen.

Now it was her turn.

She felt her cheeks flush. "From that moment in the woods," she began, "even then it was more than the crazy circumstances. Before that I never felt like I belonged. Mostly I just chalked those feelings up to teen angst. Every teenager feels like an outcast. But in my heart I knew that wasn't it. I'd felt that way my whole life." She recalled: "Mom and Dad were always trying to cheer me up." Then: "Like you it was like I was waiting for something. Kind of like you wanting to become a Kazerai.

"I was obsessive, always learning things, always reading, always training—fighting, motocross, gymnastics, chess, science, whatever—trying to know everything I could, trying to be perfect at everything, though I had no idea what for. I could've cared less about the medals, the praise, I had no one I wanted to impress. Not even a sense of accomplishment. I just ... did stuff. Then in the last few years I gave up. Like, since I couldn't figure out what the hell I was working toward, there was no point. I started trying to be normal. Which wasn't going well, by the way. Then, in the moment I saw you, it was like, 'Okay. Now my time has arrived. Now I've got to *do* something.' The way things developed after that ... there's no rational explanation for the way I reacted. I should've freaked and turned you in, like Bianca wanted to do. But I didn't. Then, when we dropped through and ended up here on Anitra ...

"I was so scared." She paused, startled to re-experience that emotion more strongly than expected. The replay of those events had become such a part of her psyche she very nearly paid them no more attention; like thinking of food or what to wear or any other daily, regular thought. The strength of it in that moment was entirely unforeseen and she felt the fear all over again. Fear of being lost; fear of all she'd left behind; the undercurrent of panic that had been with her since then, ever present, driven by so many things.

She searched Zac's eyes, looking for stability.

And became acutely aware of the tension between them. A different sort of fear. It had been there all along, of course, throughout the whole conversation, but in that moment it became painfully obvious. They were alone. In a room. For the first time, really, not under immediate duress, not surrounded by others. Not expecting anyone. She'd been digesting significant loads of information all night, reading from the laptop, now Zac was with her, discussing yet more significances, deep imponderables, and suddenly all she wanted was to hold him.

More than that.

She swallowed down a wave of frightened desire, hoping he didn't notice. *But surely he notices.* His senses were too attuned not to. *How do I smell?* If pheromones worked on normal people what did they do to him? Did he have super nostrils? Did she smell like a raging hormone bomb? Nervously she looked away, certain she'd already betrayed herself. Thinking—*praying?*—Bianca might whisk in, thinking someone might knock and break the spell but acutely aware of the reality that, for that instant in time, they were alone.

In a bedroom.

On a bed.

Is this it?

She slid her hands across her lap; looked down and started playing with one of her feet. Her heart was jumping in her chest. What to do? Every internal discussion she'd ever had flashed across her mind. Was right there before her. Every conclusion she'd ever drawn, every decision about Zac, about wanting him, about waiting for him … All her fantasies were staring her right in the face. There he was, right there—*he's right there!*—sitting on the bed in front of her. Just the two of them, all alone.

Dreams had, to her frightened realization, become reality.

She had no idea what to do.

As if from a fog she felt Zac's fingers beneath her chin.

Lifting, gently. He raised her eyes to look into his and only then did she become aware of the fact she'd been staring down, lost in this inner turmoil. His face was close, a passionate tenderness in his gaze, a deep and unexpected understanding of all she was going through ...

"I want this too," he whispered, confirming his own feelings in the matter. As if he could read her mind. He must've sensed it. But then, how hard was it to see? Even a normal boy could've read the signs.

His words resounded in her head.

I want this too.

Then: "I want *you*, Jessica." And emotion bit. Hot tears blurred her vision. "We could give in to our infatuation," he told her, beginning an explanation she wasn't sure she wanted to hear. "We might find it here. We might not. I'm a wanted man. A knock could come for me at any second. Bianca could come back. Too many things could happen.

"Our time right now is not our own."

He looked so deeply into her. It was if they became one, the mere act of his gaze filling her with his being.

All she could do was nod slowly, chin resting gently in his fingertips. Understanding yet ... not understanding at all. Confused. Hopeless yet so full of hope; sad, overflowing with joy; the unfettered high of simply being there with him, coupled with ...

"This moment," he said, "*this* moment, of all moments, should be ours. Completely. Right now it isn't.

"Now is not our time," he said, a certain fervor in his voice—even as he so clearly restrained his own desire.

His voice was nearly a whisper. "Now is not our moment."

She nodded, unable to muster words of her own. Knowing what he said was right, taken with his restraint, taken with his wish that their first moment together be safe, that it be theirs, completely—taken, more than anything, with the understanding that they would, in fact, have that moment, one day, and the sustaining thought of that, perhaps, more than any other, released the agony gripping her heart. The battle of what was right and what was good, and what was craved and what would, for now, be denied, and, like the discovery of something lost, it eased her mind. Boldly she put a hand to the side of his head and stroked his cheek. Ran her fingers around his ear. He leaned and kissed her and she fell into his embrace.

"I love you," she released every bit of pent-up emotion as the words escaped her lips, into his, breathing the words into him, aching with the strength of it. *I love you!* This was not some young lust. Not a product of the crazy circumstances in which they found themselves. She said those words not because he was an exotic example of a man and she wanted him. She said them because it was true. She had always loved him. Loved *him*, and the words came from deep within her soul.

Never had anything been so real.

"So much," she whispered.

"I love you," he told her in earnest, and the comfort of that, as he held her close, brought forth more tears; silent tears, tears of joy, warm as they trickled down her cheeks to the corners of a bitter-sweet smile.

He held her. The knock never came. No interruption ruined the wonder of their time in each other's arms.

Soon, minutes, or hours—lifetimes later; she didn't know, just that the timing was perfect, exquisite in its beauty—a ray of light peeked over the horizon out the window. The morning sun, climbing slowly into the sky.

They lay together and watched it rise.

CHAPTER 34:

THE CALM BEFORE THE STORM

KANG PACED THE FLIGHT BRIDGE of his airship. Since "awakening" from his transformation he had not slept, nor did he feel the need. Same as when he was Kazerai. It was difficult even to be still at times, and now was one of those times. The thought of ending Horuses' life had him too impatient to wait calmly until his convoy of airships arrived in Venatres lands.

He glanced at the pilot and navigator at their flight stations, looking intently out the forward screens.

Everything was on automatic at that point, nothing but open ocean as far as the eye could see. The small convoy flew low above the waves, beneath detection, heading into the morning sun as they made a stealth approach toward the distant Venatres lands. As such Kang suspected the crew's concentration was not genuine. More probably they merely pretended to be engaged, not wanting to turn or otherwise make eye contact with the beast pacing steadily behind them. He snorted. It made them jump. To that he smiled.

They were weak. Slaves to his whim. As a Kazerai, even then, he had evolved so far beyond them. Susceptible only to the technologies of control built to contain the powerful warriors. This next evolution, whatever he'd become—a form impervious to those same technologies, as had now been demonstrated—had left him completely untouchable. Bringing with it a certain exhilaration that, in fact, he could do whatever he wanted and no one, no thing, could stop him.

Part of him wondered—the reasonable part, perhaps—whether those emotions might last. He'd never been a philosopher, but in his most lucid moments it occurred to him that what made one happy was challenge. Overcoming obstacles to achieve some goal. Right then he was happy because he was on his way to meet a challenge, and achieve a goal. No more Horus. No more Kazerai. Beyond that he would take over the world. But, and this *did* trouble him: what then? Those objectives seemed close at hand. He was confident they would be gained. Leaving him ...

Where?

Like waking to a game you could never lose. A game where you made all the rules. The novelty of that, it occurred to him, would wear quickly.

It was not anything to worry over yet, nevertheless the prospect was undeniable and, while the notion of being all-powerful was, at the moment, a heady proposition, the actual realization of that end, he had to admit, could become more troubling.

Even a god needed something to fight.

* * *

JESS SLEPT MOST OF THE DAY. The sun was setting as she lay awake in bed, stretching; luxuriating in the warm sensation of a thorough rest. Zac left earlier that morning after being called away, shortly after they watched the sun rise, and when he was gone she fell straight asleep. Those additional hours of rest were exactly what she needed. No troubling dreams, no fitful tossing and turning. Physically she felt great.

Mentally too, she had to admit. After everything she'd learned, after seeing Zac and spending the night talking she felt less concern, more acceptance of what lay ahead. Her curiosity flared as she wondered where Bianca had been all night—she didn't recall her ever coming back to the room, though her bed was made—and Jess determined to find out.

First a shower. In no time she was in the soothing spray, thoughts flipping idly between Bianca's whereabouts and Zac—thoughts of Zac spurring different intrigues altogether. The warm water was invigorating, but ultimately the urge to keep moving drove her from its embrace.

Soon she was dressed in the comfortable, if plain, Venatres clothing, hair wet and tangled loosely about her head. She decided not to spend any time on it, not even a ponytail, went and put the laptop in a drawer, got her keys, left the room and locked the door behind.

Outside in the hall the chalet seemed more like a themed hotel than a topper for a high-tech military complex. It stretched on with an identical layout, room after room, elsewhere adopting more of a mansion feel, and after reaching the end of the long hall she entered the larger portion, making her way across the dining and kitchen area just outside the guarded entries to the labyrinth below, out to the Great Room.

There she heard Bianca.

Got you.

She picked up the pace at the sound of her friend's voice. It reached her from the expansive seating area along with a few other voices, and as she got closer she found a handful of people lounging on couches before the large fire. Satori, sitting with Bianca, along with a trio of young Venatres men, each dressed in uniform. Satori's bright red hair stood out among them.

"Hey," Jess called as she neared. They all turned, five heads in unison over the backs of the couches. Satori smiled. Bianca brightened.

"Jessica!" she enthused. "You're awake."

"And you never went to sleep," Jess retorted, reaching the sitting area and coming around the end of the couches. A large, overstuffed chair sat to the side facing them, near the fire. She chose that and plopped into its soft cushions. "You're going to burn yourself out. Where have you been?"

"Around." It wasn't a coy response. Bianca just didn't seem to have a better answer. "Mostly in the lab," she elaborated. "Before I knew it it was daylight." She paused, then said slyly: "Someone said Zac went back to the room so I, um, stayed away." She only partly tried to suppress the smirk stealing across her face. Satori didn't suppress hers at all. Jess blushed as everyone looked at her, including the three young Venatres men. The innuendo was not lost on them.

"By the time I did come back you were *out*," Bianca finished, emphasis on the "out", hand motion and all, "so I changed and kept looking around.

"Met the guys," she introduced them: "Harad, Ja'zing and Gert." They each lifted a hand or nodded in turn, smiling, and Jess nearly sniggered as Gert was introduced. Why the name struck her as funny she couldn't say, but she found herself actively turning her mind from it lest she start giggling. Adding to the humor of it Gert was easily the cutest, most handsome among them. In all none of the guys looked to be over twenty. Young soldiers, probably fresh into service.

"Nice to meet you," she addressed them as a group.

"We're attached to the guard," said Ja'zing.

Bianca smiled. "We're going for drinks later."

Drinks? Wow. Jess found herself amazed with Bianca's overnight transformation. She'd *really* settled in, and was clearly excited at the prospect of going out with a bunch of cute boys.

"There's a little bar upstairs that opens after dark."

Harad spoke directly to Jess, almost impatient to say something. "You're a legend," he marveled.

With his words she lost a bit of her marvel for her friend and felt herself slump. She still found these moments difficult; never knew what to say, never knew how to act when *bonk* the spotlight was suddenly flipped on and shining right in her face. There were obvious reasons she was the center of attention. Stranger from another world. Possible harbinger of an ancient prophecy. The logic of it, however, did little to dispel the discomfort.

She tried to play it off. "Anyone would've done what I did."

Harad was skeptical. "Bring down the Crucible? Kill the Shogun and the High Council ..."

"None of that was me alone. I had help." She glanced pointedly to Satori, as if to suggest *say something*.

"Hey," Satori held up her hands, "we all just played our part. Jess was the one that pushed."

Harad turned back to Jessica, insisting: "See? You're a hero."

She didn't know what to say. And so she tried to make herself appear humble. Mostly she was just embarrassed.

"They've been talking about you non-stop," Bianca pretended to be annoyed. As if maybe they should've been talking about something else. Like her.

"We were hoping you'd show up before we had to leave," Ja'zing added. "So we could at least meet you. And look. You did." He leaned forward. "But alas, we must depart."

"Don't!" Bianca played the pouty teen to perfection.

"We have to!" Ja'zing was just as dramatic, and for an instant Jess could only imagine the banter that had been going on before she got there. Apparently teen drama wasn't much different no matter what world you were on. She wondered how long Satori had been sitting there suffering.

"We'll see you later," said Gert.

Bianca relented. "Fine." Her feigned disappointment was thin. The idea of going to a bar, as the guest of three young men, had her terribly excited. With a few more exaggerated farewells they left, Bianca watching and making loud comments across the room until they were out of sight. When they were finally gone she, Jess and Satori sat quietly.

Jess made eye contact. "You're holding up well."

Bianca shrugged. "I'm trying to make the most of it. I know we'll get home." She brightened. "Hey. At least no homework, right?"

"True," Jess agreed. Then, with a resigned little smirk: "I didn't have my report ready anyway."

Bianca gave a knowing laugh. "Miss Farrington."

Jess chuckled with her, sharing the understanding of the thing that was Miss Farrington—and the absurdity of homework in contrast to their predicament. Absently Jess thought on what really *did* come next. Reminded of what waited on Earth. And now ... now the additional glut of information from the laptop, suggesting what *really* lay in wait ...

Though the moment right then was about as tranquil

as any you could ask for; crackling fire, comfy cushions, orange dusk outside the beautiful floor-to-ceiling windows ... it was hard to shake the clinging reality that their ordeal had so much yet to be resolved.

Bianca's contemplations weren't so deep. She was thinking of the bar. "We should all go," she suggested. "With the boys. Three of us, three of them."

Satori deferred at once. "Oh no," she shook her head, red hair flipping across her shoulders. "The club is for junior officers. I try not to get involved."

Bianca turned to Jess, mouth open to speak.

"I'm good," Jess said before she could ask. "I think I'll just hang here by the fire." Eagerly she turned to the side in the big chair and threw her legs over one arm, letting her feet dangle toward the flames. With a thought she reached and slipped off the short Venatres boots, scooched down further, stretched her legs and held her soles to the heat.

It felt wonderful.

Bianca shrugged. "More fun for me."

Jess sighed, turning her feet this way and that in the soothing waves of crackling bliss. Closed her eyes. The chair mushed around her, forming a rapturous embrace, managing to push aside some of the worry. Maybe she could capture a little peace after all. The whole sensation— the comfort, the warmth, the quiet and the serenity of everything in that moment—it was a little slice of heaven she did not want to end.

Of course it didn't last.

"So?" Bianca had her probing voice on. Jess wasn't getting off that easy. "What happened last night? Between you and mister super mutant?"

"Not a mutant, B." She kept her eyes closed, pretending to revel in the rapturous comfort.

"Whatever. What happened? We're all friends here."

"Nothing," she refused to be baited.

"Nothing nothing? Or really nothing?"

Jess leaned her head back, exasperated, but kept her lids shut. "Nothing."

"You lie! You guys were in there alone. *Past sunrise.* I

saw him leave. Don't think I wasn't keeping an eye out."

Now Jess turned her head and stared at her.

Then a new voice: "Hello?" It was Nani.

Thank God.

"Nani!" Bianca enthused, forgetting Jess for the moment and taking on the role of greeter. Jess only hoped Nani would not be roped into this discussion, included as a "friend" in their little group for girl talk and enlisted to help make Jessica dish. Maybe with Nani's arrival they could move on to something more relevant. Or maybe just be quiet altogether.

Ha. Good luck with that.

Nani walked up, blonde hair a mess, lab coat in hand. It looked as if she'd just woken up. Jess could only imagine her sleep schedule. Probably not many hours each day.

Bianca held out a hand: "Have a seat." Nani looked to be feeling out of place but chose a spot on the long couch near Bianca. Jess turned a little to the side in the chair so she could face them, though she kept her legs over the arm, reluctant to remove her feet from the gentle heat.

Nani had a dorky sort of innocence about her. Like a genius child trying to understand the world. Jess had a feeling she'd been holed up in labs most of her life. Her passion for understanding was tangible, and she was obviously beyond brilliant.

"Did you find anything?" she asked as soon as she sat, speaking to Jess; eager to know what she might've learned from the laptop.

Jess nodded. "It's amazing, actually, how deep this goes. How connected our worlds are." She knew Nani shared her passion for mystery. And here, she thought, was a chance to get the conversation onto things she *did* want to talk about. She seized the opportunity. Put aside her desire to just sit there and be quiet, knowing that would never happen anyway, pulled her legs from the arm of the chair and turned in the cushy seat to face them directly. She crossed her legs, pushed her drying hair behind her ears and leaned forward.

"For starters I discovered there's a group on Earth," she

began, "that has ties all the way back to the Kel at the end of the Great Wars. You guys haven't looked at any of this yet?"

Nani shook her head. "So far we're trying to put together information relevant to the starship. There's a group on Earth with ties to the Kel?"

Jess nodded. "From what I can tell they may hold the keys to much of our shared history. Anitra *and* Earth."

Nani's intrigue was on the rise.

Jess went on. Proceeding to relate the story of the Bok, the Earth agency after them, the Project—who very nearly captured she and Bianca—and what she'd learned. Nani had questions, Bianca and Satori too, and Jess was amazed she had answers for nearly every one. She really *had* absorbed a lot from the information she poured over. Amazingly everything stuck.

Nani had her repeat the Bok/Kel connection several times, as blown away as was Jess to learn there was a group on Earth with ties to the ancient Kel, in action around the same time the *Reaver* was left hidden on Anitra. She vowed to dig more into those bits of information as soon as she could. Jess went on, unspooling her discoveries, Nani adding relevant comments on this or that topic, information related to what her team was putting together, updates on their progress and so forth; Bianca had her own, uniquely Bianca concerns and questions, about how things Jess discovered related to their lives on Earth; Satori, too, put in her perspective, but all eyes were on Jess as she did most of the talking, surprised by how much she had to say. Relating what she'd learned, many points spinning off into discussions and even a few philosophical debates, but always with her in the lead. Satori, Bianca and Nani hung on her words as she pieced together the tale of their history.

At some point she noticed it was dark. The conversation had begun to slow, then meander, and as it did one observation stood out above the rest, unrelated to laptops, secret societies, government agencies and all else:

Bianca had found a friend in Nani.

Though the two were practically polar opposites, it was clear they were hitting it off. Bianca had spent the whole night with her in the lab, leaving only when Nani called it quits. Now, sitting there on the couch, they were like total besties. Jess was happy; it was giving Bianca some much needed stability. For her part Nani seemed fascinated by the fact that Bianca was from another world. Bianca seemed fascinated by, well, she just seemed fascinated by Nani. The thought of the two of them hanging out made Jess smile.

Somewhere along the way Jess turned to the side once more, making herself comfortable during the long discussion, feet stretched out to the warm fire, and she realized a certain quiet had descended on the group and each of them was caught up in their own thoughts. Night had fallen and it was as Jess felt herself doze—*man I'm tired!*—that the boys returned.

"Bianca!" someone shouted from across the room. It was Ja'zing.

Bianca turned on the couch.

"Hey!"

"You coming?" All three were there, cute in their uniforms, eager to begin an evening of fun.

"On my way," B called and hopped up.

Jess stopped her. "You haven't slept. You're really going to do this?"

"Yep!" she said cheerily.

Then turned to Nani.

"Let's go."

Nani looked startled.

"Who? Me?"

"Yes, you!" Bianca laughed. Nani could not believe she was being invited. Or, rather, expected to go.

"I'm on my way to the lab. I've already spent too much—"

"You practically live there," Bianca waved a dismissive hand. "Actually, you *do* live there. Take a break. And not just to sleep. Come. Have some fun."

Nani looked around. "I just did."

Bianca stared at her. "What? This? This was your

break?"

"There's too much to do. I need to—"

"Come on!" Bianca reached and took her hand, pulling her to her feet. Jess realized Nani had probably never been in a situation like this, confronted with a social butterfly insisting she throw responsibility to the wind and do something just because it was fun. For her it had to be a novel concept. Her resistance was weak. Bianca tugged her around the couch toward the boys.

And with a "see ya" to Satori and Jessica was off, leading Nani by the hand.

Jess called after them: "You better not snore tonight!"

Bianca ignored her, angling her chin up and skipping the last little bit as she joined the others, hand in hand with Nani tagging reluctantly along. Together they went off, all but Nani laughing—who still looked uncertain but definitely growing more fascinated with each step. The small group headed upstairs.

Leaving Jess and Satori alone. Together they listened to the diminishing sound of boisterous voices as the others went off to the club. Music had begun filtering down, not loud enough to be disturbing, and if Jess focused on the crackle of the fire the distant sounds of revelry faded into the background. Again she found herself wishing the elements of that moment were set within a different life. One that didn't have the trauma of a violent past behind it, the deadly uncertainty of an apocalyptic future ahead. It was so pleasant right then; she hated that it was squeezed between such brutal bookends in time.

But those things were not now. As before, she made a conscious effort to be in the moment.

"You've captured the heart of a Kazerai." Satori's comment shattered the gathering serenity; seemed to hang in the air. Jess wanted to ignore it, to continue sitting there quietly and pretend she hadn't heard. She thought to change the subject, to just say something else in exchange.

But there would be no getting around it.

"I don't know how," she said meekly.

"If you don't know then I certainly can't explain it to you.

He's fallen for you."

Jess turned to the intense, red-headed field commander. Coming from her this gave Jess pause. Satori did not speak from any ridiculously placed awe. To her Jessica was no mythical angel. Satori simply spoke what was.

"You even got him to change his name."

Now Jess shook her head. "That was only because we didn't know his real name." But it did little to diminish the point.

"Whatever," Satori said. Then, giving advice: "You need to figure it out. He's a real catch but he's in demand. A freelance Kazerai, here in Venatres lands? Available, on the free market? Do you know how many girls have had their eye on him? Do you know how many girls secretly dream of a Kazerai husband?"

Husband?! But Satori's statements only reinforced Jessica's fervent hopes.

Desperate dreams.

She looked at the ex-commander; beautiful, subtly Asian features. Lounging comfortably on the couch. Smirking. Felt the heat rising to her cheeks and knew she needed to change the subject.

"How did you end up here?" she asked. She looked around the chalet. "You didn't fight it? This seems a bit calm for your tastes."

Satori seemed willing to move on. "I *couldn't* fight it." She reflected on a more painful time. "I got myself in a lot of trouble giving you that Icon."

A short exhale of breath and a shake of her head. "I had no idea at the time. Not really. I thought losing it would actually be a good thing. I wanted to help you and it didn't seem like a bad way to do it. Boy was I wrong.

"Anyway," she said. "It's all worked out in the end."

Jess nodded. The moment stretched and she said no more. Tired after the hours of discourse already behind them she found herself fading. Quietly, before the crackle and pop of the flames. Lids flickering. Desire to say something waned behind this fresh tranquility until nothing would rise above the inertia and she let herself go. She glanced sleepily at Satori, who was alert but caught up in her own thoughts, more than happy to let the conversation die. At some point someone came and tended the fire. Added fresh wood and it burned brighter. As far as Jess knew it had been burning since she got there. Maybe it was always lit.

The whole place made her think of some upscale timber lodge. Like Vail or something. The flickering, fire-lit glow, warm and cozy, their reflections across the room in the night-blackened windows. Like she was on vacation, hanging out after a day on the slopes. All that was missing was hot cocoa.

That and maybe a life to go with it.

Upstairs the music thumped. She recalled the plain Dominion bar Darvon took her to back in Osaka, during their escape, wondering if this Venatres bar was just as boring. From the sound of the music it wasn't.

"Sounds like fun," she roused herself a little, mumbling, trying to muster enthusiasm. It ended up sounding feeble. "Maybe we should go up and check it out." Maybe Zac could meet them there.

Like a date.

"You don't look like you're doing anything else tonight," Satori's voice was distant. Jess realized she was probably right. Her eyelids were sagging, worse and worse, and she felt her body calling for more sleep. Not surprising, considering the length of time she'd been running on an adrenaline high. More rest would continue to restore her. Still, the impulse to rise and do something was strong.

How is Bianca still going?

Even as was thinking this she felt herself nod. Snapped to; tried to make sense of her surroundings.

And drifted off for good.

* * *

"Am I interrupting?" Zac called. He could see he startled Satori, who sat on the couch facing the bright flames, deep in thought. Jess was in a chair beside her fast asleep. Satori looked in his direction.

"Where've you been?"

"Where do you think," he made his way over to the cluster of chairs and couches, furtively glancing at Jessica as he came around. She looked so comfortable. So beautiful in the warm glow of the firelight. He chose a chair across from Satori and sat, stretched his legs out in front of him and leaned back.

"Meetings," he said.

"The Dominion making a move?"

"Probably. Command has me reviewing everything they've got on Kang, the new Kang, which isn't much, trying to assess the threat." The Venatres called more meetings than Zac ever thought possible. When he was with the Dominion, misguided as they were, they were at least brief in their briefings. Since he'd been here at the mountain complex the Venatres meetings had been non-stop. Especially now with the uncertainty of Kang.

"Is he coming?"

Zac nodded. "Airships. Staying low, evading detection. We're not sure of his destination, though we suspect he's headed for the front." The thought of the possibility of battling Kang, now that his nemesis had become a Kazerai-killing beast, troubled Zac. As yet they had no detailed information, but for the last several hours of assessment and planning he'd been facing up to the very real possibility that he would, in fact, be called upon to stand against this unstoppable menace. How they would expect him to do that, how they would expect him to fare any better than had the other Kazerai ...

But it didn't matter. If it came to that, he would go. And despite the reality of what had already happened, despite the sheer power Kang had already demonstrated, Zac could not make himself feel the fear he knew he should. He felt as indestructible as ever. As if he could, if it came to it— somehow—rise to the challenge and defeat Kang.

For the moment he let it pass.

Decided to have some fun.

"Your man's been sending quite a bit of intel," he winked, watching Satori's reaction. "We wouldn't know half of this without him. You should give him a kiss for us."

She cringed, as expected; he grinned as she scowled. Satori was one tough girl. It was hard to get a rise out of her and Zac imagined few people tried. He, however, enjoyed getting under her skin when he could. After all, what was she going to do? Punch him? Hurt his feelings?

A heavy breath from the sleeping Jessica drew his attention.

And it was Satori's turn. "Speaking of, 'your girl' filled us in on some interesting tidbits tonight. She found a lot on that computer from Earth." Satori didn't have to be a magician to see his own admiration. Still, he managed to look at her as if he were confused.

"My girl?"

Satori chuckled. "You truly are something. I've never seen a more fairytale bunch of crap."

Zac pretended to be hurt.

Satori shook her head. "God."

"We've kissed," Zac admitted, trying to defend himself. Then with more certainty, knowing there was no point being evasive: "You have to admit we've both been through a lot. We're getting to know each other. Mostly until now its been total chaos every time we're together." Satori wasn't buying it. He scooched around a little in the chair. "We have a complicated relationship." It came out weaker than he wanted.

"Please," she laughed at him. "What relationship *isn't* complicated? Sure, you're a specimen of superhuman strength, she's a girl from another world, but give me a break."

Jess snorted, smacked her lips and wriggled in the puffy chair. She curled into a tighter ball and fell into a deeper sleep, hair falling softly across her face. Glowing shades of brown in the gentle firelight.

She was so beautiful.

Satori waved a hand in her direction. "Put her to bed," she said.

Zac nodded, agreeing. "This conversation was going nowhere anyway." He stood and Satori stuck her tongue out. He grinned, went over and lifted Jessica, heart melting as he curled her gently into his arms. Though he felt the change in weight the act of holding her took no more exertion than simply standing there without her. Holding her was totally, completely, a zero effort. The tremendous strength that came with being a Kazerai ... it was fascinating. Truth was he'd still not gotten used to it. Maybe he never would. Fortunately the finer things, touch, smell—none of that was diminished, and he gave quiet thanks for that now. His threshold of pain, of tolerance, was off the scale. His strength, immeasurable. Sensations, however, were quite intact, and right then he relished them. The feel of her contact. The heat of her soft body close to his. Her wonderful, wonderful scent. The tender rise and fall of her chest.

Pure bliss.

"You're so smitten," Satori chuckled from the couch behind him.

It snapped him from his reverie.

"Be a gentleman," she admonished.

"I will be. You know I will be."

She nodded slowly. "I know. You're always a gentleman. That's one of the things she loves about you." Then, with a subtle shift to absolute sincerity added: "She's lucky to have you." She regarded him, standing there with Jess cradled in his arms. "You two were made for each other."

Zac thought to say something but decided against it. He found Jessica's boots, laying where she'd dropped them, and stepped over to get them—but as he leaned down Satori waved him on, reverting to her normal, brash self: "Leave them. Go. Get her to bed before you drop her."

He opened his mouth but remained silent. He straightened, turned and carried her off.

Loving every minute of it.

CHAPTER 35:

APPROACH

DAMN. Lindin hung his head. He'd just been on his way to grab a few minutes of sleep. He leaned tiredly against his desk.

"The convoy could be anywhere," his aide reported. The man had arrived before Lindin could even get out of his office; he was the chief military liaison there at the mountain complex, the one who had been giving regular updates from all points. A disturbing picture was being painted. Dominion forces at Midbay were mobilizing, whether prepared or not, in conjunction with what was expected to be the arrival of Kang. The new Emperor's convoy of airships had been flying mostly undetected across the ocean, various lookouts able to spot the group along their route and triangulate movements, giving them at least a vague idea where the madman was headed.

Until now.

"On his predicted path he should've passed within detection of at least two outposts," said the aide. "So far they've seen nothing. Either he's dropped off his pace, or is proceeding on an entirely different course. Best guess is that he still intends to hit Midbay, but our certainty on that has diminished." The aide scratched his head absently. "Let's put it this way. No matter where he makes landfall he's close."

"Maybe they all just fell in the ocean." Lindin knew he was on a short fuse. He studied the man, fresh faced, realizing how tired he himself must appear.

But the aide understood and mustered a smile. "If only we were that lucky."

So. It seemed Midbay would, indeed, be the final battleground. Lindin had hoped Kang would continue as he had been and they'd end up with a confrontation away from occupied areas. Of course that was a foolish hope. Nevertheless one he—and others—had entertained.

Perhaps if they could catch the convoy soon enough they might shoot the airships down before they made it.

Idly he wondered at the starship hidden beneath him in the bowels of the mountain. If ever there was a call for the alien starship's potential it was now. Do a test run? Try to use it and go hunt down the airships? Take them down over the ocean? But of course that was a foolish thing even to consider. Far too many unknowns remained. Far more stood to be lost if it failed than could ever be gained from stopping one small convoy.

The aide went on. "As if to confirm this possibility, the Dominion in Midbay are definitely gearing for assault. Possibly within the next day, possibly even sooner. Our confidence is high. They will attack soon."

Lindin sat. Venatres forces north of Midbay were already mobilized and the stage was set.

It looked as if sleep would have to wait a little longer.

* * *

IT WAS THE DREAM AGAIN. Jess stepped across the strange room, explosions rocking the floor; went to the archaic wooden door set against the riveted green-iron walls. Beside it was the same sleek, high-tech access panel.

As before she played things through, working in some subtle way to take control. The battle outside rocked the walls. Another hit and she steadied herself.

All was as it had been. She was dressed in the same armor, in one hand the long, curved sword of blued steel. Her hand not her own yet ... definitely her. *She* held the sword. *She* wore the armor. But *she* was not Jessica.

Then a voice, calling to her. "I'm not leaving you!" it said. She turned but caught only a glimpse of a figure through a sudden billow of smoke. All this she saw in an instant, heart racing as an explosion flashed and hammered her awake.

She sat bolt upright. Struggling for breath.

"You okay?" a familiar voice came from a bright light in the distant dark. She snapped to it. Saw a figure silhouetted in the doorway.

Bianca.

Light splayed around her friend, flooding into the darkened room.

I'm in bed.

Her breathing steadied. Another figure was with Bianca, visible in the light of the hall. Jess identified her as well.

Nani.

Bianca and Nani had evidently been standing there. Jessica's startled awakening must have shocked them.

She found her voice. "I'm fine."

Hurriedly Nani wished Bianca goodnight, bid her make sure her friend was okay, then the door closed and the room was fully dark. Bianca came over and stood beside Jessica's bed. In the near pitch of the darkened room Jess could tell she was looking at her cautiously. Her face was barely readable, but her posture said it all. "You sure?"

"Yes." Though Jess wasn't sure at all.

"Bad dream?"

If only you knew. "Yeah."

Bianca stood a moment more, then stepped across to her own bed and sat.

"You were totally quiet when we got here. I had to check to make sure you were even alive." In the darkness Jess could see her friend's face still showed concern. "I went back to say goodnight to Nani then all of a sudden, Bam! you were like, '*Kalistima!*' or something."

"Kalistima?"

"I don't know. Sounded like. Loud, too. You sat up like the Exorcist. Like some kind of demonic announcement. *Kalistima!* Nani and I both jumped. You were sitting straight up, eyes wide, this look of ... fury on your face."

"Like you'd just told someone to do something and they'd better do it or else. It was freaky."

"Weird," was all Jess could mutter. She tried to piece together any part of the memory that matched. Nothing did.

Bianca watched her silently a few seconds, then began getting undressed. Jess realized her own clothes were still on. She'd last been awake out by the fireplace, she recalled, remembering vaguely Zac bringing her to the room and putting her to bed. She'd roused from her deep sleep as he carried her, enough to catch glimpse of him, the hall and, finally, the darkened room as he laid her down, covered her and kissed her head. At which point she fell back into a rapturous slumber.

Now this.

She shuddered.

Bianca was down to her underwear, went to the bathroom, peed and flushed, turned out the light, returned and climbed into bed. She lay back and yawned, sounding tired.

She ought to.

Jess looked around, suddenly disoriented. "What time is it?"

"Middle of the night."

She could see Bianca's shape in the gray darkness, laying and looking up at the ceiling. Jess remained sitting. "Did Nani stay at the club the whole time? Didn't she have work?"

Bianca chuckled. "That girl can party. It was crazy. I bet she's never had that much fun in her life."

"You kept her out all this time?"

"She's a big girl. Besides, if she wanted to go she could've gone. It wasn't like she was hiding." Then, as if the thought of that was an inside joke snickered: "Hardly."

Jess tried to imagine the nerdy Nani getting down at the club.

Bianca recalled: "Probably danced with every guy there."

"You got her drunk?"

"Did I say that?"

"So she just started dancing with everyone? Completely sober?" That seemed unlikely.

"Not a drop." Then: "For a moment I even thought she might go home with Gert."

Jess cocked an eyebrow; realized Bianca would never

see it in the dark. "You're a bad influence. You're here a few days and already you've got their lead scientist—who happens to be working on their most important discovery ever, by the way—in a club partying when she should be working."

"Jealous?"

Jess ignored her. "Then you nearly get her to go home with one of the local soldiers? Who probably also has his own restrictions and could get in big trouble."

Bianca smiled, teeth barely visible in the gloom. "Pretty cool huh?"

"I should never have brought you."

"I tried to get you to take me home." Bianca said this in her best 'I told you so' voice. Rolled her head to face her and, even in the dark, Jess could see her eyes widen as if to say, 'Huh? Am I right? You know I'm right.'

Jess laughed, unexpectedly, and it felt good.

"Besides," Bianca added, satisfied. "She's mostly done with her part. Truth is, she's dying to take it for a spin. Man! Can you imagine? A frickin starship. Can you even imagine how epic that will be? She says it's totally ready to go, now it's all politics. Lindin's the one holding the cards."

Jess sat quietly. Pondering just how quickly Nani had been able to adapt the Icons, how much she'd hit it off with Bianca and how much Bianca, in turn, now knew about this ultra-top-secret project. Despite her often juvenile crudeness Bianca was a sharp girl. And a good friend.

A great friend, Jess had the sudden thought. *She really cares about me.*

"Listen," Jess spoke with sincerity, "I know I said I'm sorry, but I really am. I never, ever wanted you to end up in the middle of this. You don't deserve this mess."

Bianca dismissed it with a simple wave of her hand. "They would've found me in the house anyway. Who knows? Maybe this worked out better.

"At any rate, I have to blame myself for getting involved with such an obvious freak in the first place." She looked pointedly across the space between them. "Something told me weird stuff was going to happen around you. I *knew* you were trouble, from the moment we met, when you first moved to town. But I became your friend anyway." She sighed. "It's on me."

Jess re-crossed her legs; got more comfortable on the bed.

"So Nani's on her way to the lab?"

"Yes." Jess could see a wry smile on Bianca's lips—as if to reassure her constantly worrying friend. "All is well."

The next words out of Jessica's mouth were probably ill-advised, but came before she could consider the consequences: "How about you? You decided not to hook up with one of the boys?" She had no doubt Bianca could've if she wanted. Her friend's ability to snare boys had, though Jess would probably never admit it to anyone, always fascinated her.

"Nah."

Jess found that hard to believe. "No?"

"Harad wouldn't leave me alone. But I decided against it."

"Did you dance with him?"

"Yeah." The way Bianca said it made it sound like she'd danced with him a lot. And enjoyed it.

When she said no more Jess queried cautiously; knowing, again, she tread in dangerous waters but too curious to heed her own warnings: "Did you kiss him?"

"Nah."

"Not even a kiss?"

"Felt a little strange," her friend shook her head in the gloom, "I don't know how they do things here."

Jess clicked her tongue. "Kissing's kissing. Everywhere." She couldn't stop thinking of Zac.

Bianca shrugged. "I have to admit, I was a little nervous."

"You?" Jess was incredulous. *Bianca? Nervous?* "No way."

"I was."

"Why?"

"I don't know." Her friend thought about it a moment. Then: "I wasn't sure I was ready to see his ding-dong."

"Wha—" Jess spluttered, despite an effort not to. "*Ding-*

dong?"

Bianca just shrugged. "He *is* an alien. You never know."

"Who says he was going to show you his ding-dong?"

"What else would he show me?"

Jess scrutinized her. Bianca seemed unusually punchy. "Are *you* drunk?"

"Only the boys drank. Nani and I stayed sober."

Jess shook her head. "You know they're human like us."

At that Bianca rolled sharply to face her. "Not Zac," she said, startling Jess with her sudden shift—even as her friend mused: "I wonder what *his* is like."

Jess swallowed, thankful the darkness hid her reaction. "He's human too," she defended. "Just stronger somehow. Everything else about him is normal."

"Really?" Bianca propped herself up, eager to know more. "Have you seen it?"

"Bianca! Can we please talk about something else?"

Her friend pouted. "What am I supposed to think? I don't know what you guys did when you were here last time. You've already kept so many secrets." Then: "You still haven't told me what you did last night."

"I *did* tell you. Nothing. We kissed."

"Kissed?!" Bianca leaned forward, mouth falling open. "See? That's not 'nothing', Jess. You're keeping secrets." She held out a hand, curling her fingers into her palm a few times as if to say "come on", beckoning: "What else?"

Jess squirmed. "That's it."

"Sure, sure."

There would be no winning that back-and-forth. Best to move on. "Anyway, I'm sure he's quite normal." Only ... was he? She *did* see things last time she was here— though she would never tell Bianca lest she be forced into an embarrassingly detailed description. After Zac's fight against the Astake when they first arrived, after being burned clean by their plasma cannons, she saw. In the midst of the insanity of that moment, her life in incredible danger, a million things freaking her out—that being just one of them—all she knew, all she recalled from that snapshot of chaos was that he seemed utterly ...

Perfect.

Hardly normal. At least not ... by looking. All of Zac, physically, was like some kind of perfectly sculpted, perfectly chiseled dream guy from a magazine or something. She found her thoughts rushing, wondering—as she had on the cold porch with him—how the Kazerai worked. *Was* he normal? Could she count on it? Should she?

Did it matter?

She swallowed.

"So you say." Bianca, luckily, failed to notice her hesitation. Jess hoped that meant they would be able to move entirely away from the subject, but realized in the next moment that wasn't going to happen. Just because Bianca failed to home in on the awkward pause did not mean her friend was done.

Hardly.

"What if it's mutated?!" she latched onto a new idea; seemed to imagine wild possibilities.

Jess cringed. "He's not a mutant, B."

"Super human. Whatever." Bianca was undeterred. "Maybe it's strong like him. Maybe you can do pull-ups on it." Then: "*Ooh!*" she had an even better idea. "What if it grows *huge*? I mean, like, really big, like the size of a leg or something?" She laughed at the idea of this. "A third leg! Maybe he can haul ass on it, running like a tripod! Gives him extra speed!" She arched her back up and down where she lay, mimicking a ridiculous three-legged lope. Jess sniggered—to her dismay—tried to cover it quickly by chiding her friend.

"What is *wrong* with you?"

But Jess knew there was no stopping her.

"He's beyond human, right?" Bianca made a case for her theory. "He's a warrior, right? Like, a super soldier, like you said? They made him with a purpose. I mean, I'm assuming. And it probably wasn't for breeding. What if he can control it, like an arm or something?" Her imagination gained strength. "Whip it out and it turns into, like, another arm and he starts pounding people!" At that she rolled and jumped to her feet, on the bed, bent and hooked an arm, elbow at the waist, forearm sticking out in a fist, and began flailing it around like a club, jumping back and forth as she pounded imaginary opponents. "Boom! You want some of this?! Boom! You too?! Boom! Oh yeah! Get some! Boom! Boom!"

Jess started laughing. She didn't want to. Did not want to support her friend, especially in this, but couldn't help it. It was too much. Seeing Bianca jumping on the bed, in the shadows, forearm sticking out from her waist like a club, fist and all, clobbering people with gusto ... too much. It was appalling, it was hilarious, and as Bianca went on, jumping higher, putting more into it, feeding on Jessica's inability to stop laughing—laughing harder, in fact, as her friend amped the hilarity, making more and more ridiculous comments, each worse—and funnier—than the last—Jess was at last blinded by her own tears. It was the stupidest joke ever but she was gone. Her stomach hurt and she could not stop laughing. She turned away and told Bianca to knock it off. Begged her. It took a few tries but eventually her friend relented and flopped back to the bed, tired from the exertion. She stared up at the ceiling as she caught her breath.

For a long time they both just lay there, giggling. Every few minutes B would throw out another zinger, on a roll—full of demented inspiration—bringing on another round of laughter until, at last, some time later, they settled out and each new joke only made them smile.

At length Bianca spoke. "I needed that," she said, breathing easier now.

Jess had to admit she did too. "Me too," she said. Hoping it didn't encourage her friend further.

It didn't.

"You're impossible. You know that." Jess raised her head to look across at her.

"I know."

"I'm glad you're able to find humor in the middle of all this."

"I'm probably just delirious."

Jess nodded. She herself was delirious, that was for

sure. Bianca seemed to grow more contemplative.

"I feel like we're all of a sudden adults," she said, taking a moment to consider their predicament. "We were getting so close on Earth, but even after you're eighteen it's not like you get your independence overnight. You may go off to college, or even get your own place, but all the ties are still there.

"It's like no one really *treats* you like an adult for so long after that. You've almost got to wait until you're thirty or something.

"But now, since we got here, now that I've been coming to grips with it it's like ... bam. We're adults. Grown up, that fast."

Jess studied her in the dark. Feeling a huge sense of relief after the gasp-inducing laughter. Her body actually felt lighter. That they could be where they were, in the middle of what they were, and yet have an outburst of naughty hilarity worthy of the best slumber party ...

It felt good.

"Yeah," she agreed. "I had that same thought last time. Like I'd grown up. I didn't want to. What I would've given for Mom to come take me home. But I rose to it. Then, when I did get home, it was like ... I knew I could do anything a grownup could do. More than most grownups, actually. Yet I was still considered a kid."

A long silence followed. Jess lay quietly on her bed, looking across at Bianca. Trying to read her friend's expression in the gloom. She could see the white's of her eyes, looking up at the ceiling, but could get no bead on what she was thinking.

Then Bianca spoke. "How will we go home?" she asked. Jess thought about an answer, but Bianca's question ran deeper: "I mean, how will we really go home? There's the starship. And if that doesn't work there's always the Icon. Maybe another suit of that armor. I know *how* we'll get home. But, how do we *go* home? We can never go back to our old lives, Jess." She turned her head to the side, looking at her. "Our lives on Earth are over."

Jess took a deep breath, unsure how to respond. At

length she said simply: "I know." The teen mind was a tough animal. This she knew from experience. Mentally they would pull through. Though their lives were irreversibly changed, though they could never be "teenagers" again, Bianca would be fine in the end. Different, but fine. They both would.

"I mean," Bianca faced back to the ceiling, trying to make sense of what had been little more than mindless fear until then. Emotionally in the last day she'd swung from terror to frivolous fun, and was now settling somewhere in between. Working to put a rational take on the reality of their insane situation. "Those guys back on Earth ... No one is going to protect us. And even if they did, we'd have some serious explaining to do. After all that we're not going to have a few interviews, go home, get checked back into school and be back in Physics Monday morning. Not like you did last time."

Jess nodded.

"This is it for us," Bianca concluded. It sounded like her voice hitched, like she was about to slip back into terror, but as she went on it was clear she'd found strength. Jess was impressed by how far her friend had come. "We're now onto a completely different track," she said. "We're young, our lives are ahead of us. None of that has changed. But I'm probably not going to be a vet with a practice back in Boise."

Jess smiled.

Said: "Probably not." Her friend had always dreamed of becoming a vet. "Though, and not to sound stupid, it isn't entirely out of the realm of possibility. The way I see it our world is going to change. In a big way. It has to.

"No, we won't ever be in high school again. We'll never be anonymous teenagers. That's for sure. To be honest I have no imagination, even, of what all this is going to do to both Earth and this world. All I know is that vets will still be vets, and cities and towns and houses and ... all of that will still be. Things are going to be crazy, no doubt, but they won't—they can't—be that drastically different. Not because I don't want them to. Because it just isn't possible. *Everything* about our way of life won't be swept away. Most of it will be the same.

"I guess what I'm trying to say is, maybe when all is said and done you *can* still be a vet. If that makes any sense."

Now it was Bianca's turn to smile. Jess could see her white teeth in the gloom.

"It does," she said. "But I may have changed my mind by then. Maybe I'll be a starship captain instead."

Jess laughed with her. It felt good to let go, to see the vast possibilities that were always there, even in the midst of a crisis.

Then a knock at the door and they both jumped.

"Jess? Are you in there?"

It was Zac.

CHAPTER 36:

THE BATTLE BEGINS

THE DOMINION WAS ATTACKING. Willet heard the distant pulse of cannons and the thunder of explosions rolling across the land long before any intel reached him. Somehow the Dominion had decided to move, ahead of the Venatres forces' best predictions, and since then Willet had been operating solo behind the lines, in the heart of Midbay and now, in the gray light of the pre-dawn hours, found himself making his way carefully along an alley at the outskirts, through the shadows, drawing up on the familiar Café Ecco.

The intensity of the battle had grown. To his experienced ears it had also moved closer, telling him the Venatres were, for the moment at least, pushing back. Which meant the Dominion, miraculously, was already losing ground. Early into the conflict and the Venatres were making a statement.

He hoped they had the energy to see it through.

There were three enemy brigades to the north of the city, stationed there after Midbay was taken and gradually bolstered over the last weeks. Astake, powered armor, light infantry, artillery and mounted troops, making for a formidable force arrayed against the Venatres. Over the last weeks Willet and his teams had pieced together detailed info of what the Dominion were bringing. He knew well what his Venatres comrades were up against. Even still, it had been his assessment they were prepared and could hold, if not repel, the Dominion—perhaps even retake Midbay at the end of this inevitable conflict.

He moved further up the alley, to within sight of the café. Most of the Dominion's focus was now at the front, but it was still dangerous to be where he was. There were sentries about, as well as the Dominion's own reconnaissance teams, snipers and all manner of other units, each tasked with keeping eyes on their claimed prize. Willet dared not walk too boldly there in the city as he had before—there was no way to "blend" when every other civilian was now cowering indoors, under curfew—but at the same time he did not want to be caught looking suspicious.

He stopped at the back door of the café. This one led into the kitchen and, if his info was correct, should be open. He paused for a moment, continuing his careful ruse—just in case he was being watched—turned to the north to watch the sky, as if truly the curious spectator he pretended to be, and paused. Explosions flashed against the night in rapid staccato; small, large—the air popped with flashes of heat and energy, too furious, too frequent to get a good gauge of the darkness in that direction. Though seeming to make a casual sweep, he scrutinized every detail in nonchalant fashion, piercing the shadows far and near, looking for sign of any observer.

He found none.

Like lightning and subsequent thunder each flash came before the rumble, but the battle had risen to such intensity it was difficult to match one with the other. Now and again a flash more tremendous than the rest would set the sky ablaze, followed seconds later by the obvious explosion that went with it, giving him a chance to estimate the distance of the conflict.

It wasn't far.

Satisfied the Venatres were reacting to the Dominion with more effectiveness than predicted—and satisfied he'd found no one watching him—he went for the door, opened it and slipped inside.

"About time," came a voice from the darkness. It was Dox. Within the walls of the building the sounds of the battle diminished, though the air shook with a steady pulse. Dishes and fittings in the kitchen rattled with each. Willet gave his eyes a moment to adjust.

"Sounds like we've got them on their heels," Dox added. "At this rate it won't be long before they're pushed right back here, into the city."

Willet nodded. "From what I understand the First

Cavalry and Eighth Infantry are pushing south along their outer brigades. They'll close ranks from behind in a pincer. Not much info being passed right now, even on encrypted channels." Willet found his way to one of the cupboards. His eyes grew more accustomed to the dark and he soon found what he was after: one of the small radios he used from within the city to relay info. Rather than risk getting caught with one on him, he'd some time ago hidden a few at strategic points around Midbay.

He took this one out of its hiding place and stuck it in his ear. Turned it on. Voice recognition acknowledged him and activated the encryption. He passed it his code and a channel was opened. An operator on the other end answered.

"Confirm."

"Willet. One Nine Seven."

Pause. "Confirmed. Go ahead, sir."

"I'm at checkpoint Three with a report."

"Ready."

"Observations on the East flank confirm units moving in support of the Malek Brigade. I count nine squads of Astake powered armor. Last location fourteen by five closing on the front at fifteen. That was ten minutes ago."

"Copy, nine squads."

"What's the overall report?" Willet asked. The operator was just a relay point, passing information like Willet's to commanders and those running the battle, but due to his position might have heard things. This was a strictly formal communication sequence but Willet was curious. He chose to engage the man as a comrade. "From out here it sounds like we're pushing them back."

Another pause. Then the man said: "Seems that way from here too. Hard to tell, but most of what I'm hearing is that we've got the upper hand."

Willet could almost swear there was a hint of excitement in the man's voice. A cautious edge, but nevertheless hope. Perhaps the Venatres could win the day. Turn this defensive response into a full-blown route and give the Dominion a little of what, until then, the enemy had only been handing out.

"That's great news." Willet appreciated the friendly exchange.

The man's voice dropped on the other end, an air of concern in it. "We seem to have lost Kang, though."

"Lost him?"

"They're trying to pinpoint him. So far no luck but we think he'll be in sight of the shore soon, we're just not sure exactly where."

Willet nodded. "Copy. I'll check in again shortly."

Formality returned. "Copy. Out."

Willet left the earpiece in. His days of subterfuge, at least here in Midbay, were at an end. The battle they'd been planning for was at hand. From this point on he was a combatant.

He turned to Dox. "Where are the others?"

"Gervin has them spaced around the northwestern perimeter, two near the port."

"Everyone in contact?"

Dox tapped his earpiece.

Good. So that left Kang, still the wild variable and now gone missing. No one knew where he was. Not even his own troops; if they knew Dox would've known and Dox knew nothing. Dox was about as plugged in as an outsider could be. Apparently Kang's arrival was to be a surprise for everyone.

Much importance was being placed on the beast and how to deal with him, and rightly so. The Kazerai had been bad enough. But from the latest intel it appeared Kang was susceptible to none of the things the Dominion used to control the super warriors. Kang was stronger. And, to make matters worse, by all indications insane.

What a lovely day this is going to be, thought Willet.

He looked at Dox.

"You ready?"

Dox nodded.

Willet managed a smile. "Let's see what we can do to make things interesting."

* * *

THE NERVE CENTER OF THE MOUNTAIN COMPLEX was buzzing. Jess hurried to keep up with Zac as he led she and Bianca into the command area, brushing past guards that were, at that point, little concerned with who came or went. All focus was on the developing battle.

"Zac!" Lindin called as he caught sight of them.

He curved for Lindin and Jess followed, Bianca close behind. Zac had come for them in their room with little explanation other than that the complex was about to go to war, hurried Bianca into her clothes—not bothering to wait outside as she dressed and not seeming to care, just pacing restlessly and appearing to Jessica distant—then hustled them down to the command room. The Dominion was attacking at Midbay and Zac felt the girls should be there, with him, to hear firsthand the progress. Jess was happy he came for her, but that small happiness did little to dispel the fear clenching at her throat.

"We've found him," said Lindin, looking even more ragged and tense than Jess would've expected, even under the circumstances. It looked as if he hadn't slept in days. He directed Zac to a set of screens being monitored by several technicians. "Just now." The mountain complex was not a military hub but there were a lot of very important people there, and Jess could see everything to do with the battle at Midbay was being transmitted through that room. The whole place was filled with tension.

"Kang?" Zac asked and Jessica's heart went to ice.

Of course Lindin meant Kang.

Lindin nodded, grim. Orders continued to be barked around the room, calls for this or that feed, aerial images showing the field of battle, scrolling columns and other info ticking off troop dispositions and status, operators hustling back and forth or sitting glued to monitor screens. On the displays Jess looked at a plotted line moving slowly on an arc across the water. Directly for Midbay.

"We've had 'thopters swarming up and down the coast," said Lindin. "We finally found him." He pointed. "We don't have the range or the speed to catch him, but we've been able to pinpoint his approach."

Suddenly the radio speaker at the console blurped. "Flight Twelve confirming visual."

"Go ahead Twelve."

"I have Dominion airships moving south by southeast on this trajectory." Coordinate info was passed, locked at the upper right of the operator's screen. "I make it one thousand by six hundred.

"They're coming in low and hot."

"Five?" One of the officers in the room counted the dots on the screen, incredulous. "He brought *five* airships all the way across the ocean? For this? That's most of the fleet."

Lindin's expression confirmed the insanity of it. Kang had become a wild variable in every regard. "We don't know the airships' absolute capabilities," he said, "but this is the fastest and the furthest any have ever been pushed. After flying that low and that hard we don't know what to expect out of them. We suspect many tolerances have been exceeded. My guess is that they're nothing more than a show of force, a ride for Kang so he can get here and wreak havoc."

Jess remembered vaguely that the airships were a uniquely Dominion thing, closely-guarded technology like the Kazerai, rarely used in combat. Rarely risked was probably a better way to put it. They were also, to her understanding, few in number. The Dominion's most costly hardware, and Kang had just run a marathon all the way across the ocean with, apparently, nearly all of them.

"Transmitting visual feed," the 'thopter pilot reported over the radio speaker.

"Got it.

"Here we go."

And the screen switched to show the view from the pursuing Venatres aircraft, flying into the sunrise. A few other 'thopters in the same formation could be seen off the wing, but everyone's attention was drawn to the five shapes ahead and below: wide, swooping; insect-like outlines of the airships, black hulls and gold markings casting intimidating silhouettes against the ocean, stark against the sea-green waters over which they flew. At least three of them gave off dark smoke—one quite heavily—reminding Jess of old video footage of American military aircraft burning fuel too richly. Like B-52 bombers trailing dark vapors in their wake. The smoke curling out behind the airships, however, seemed more a sign of abuse. Lindin's suspicions could be right: they might've pushed the mighty craft beyond tolerance.

"Will they make it?" someone asked. A small crowd had gathered, Kang rapidly becoming the centerpiece of the show. Jess was sure he always had been; the battle at Midbay something they'd merely been preparing for, Kang a threat with a potential for which they had no real answer. It was with a certain fascinated horror they stood watching the feed of the deadly airships, imagining their more deadly cargo, pulling further and further away from the pursuing Venatres aircraft as the enemy convoy headed relentlessly for the distant shore.

"They'll make it." The tone in Lindin's voice said he wished it wasn't so.

Everyone stared at the dark shapes as they got smaller, outpacing the ornithopters. Around them the room bustled with the energy of the unfolding battle at Midbay but a sort of isolated quiet had fallen over the small group gathered around that console. Jess looked to Zac. He watched the leading airship with a different sort of regard. While the others tracked the progress of the airships with fascinated disconnect, a human curiosity imagining what tragedy it might foretell, Zac knew the implications for him were much more personal. Jess realized this too and, while nothing had yet been decided, nothing had even been discussed, she found herself resisting the urge to clutch him as he turned to Lindin.

"Why is he doing this?" he asked. But Jess suspected Zac knew. Suspected she did too. "Why come all the way here, to this battle? Is he trying to make a statement? Is he really that crazy?" Jess saw it in his eyes.

Zac knows.

When Lindin spoke she did clutch him. Reached for his arm and pulled herself to him.

"We've been getting more info over the last few hours," Lindin began, clearly having prepared for this but hoping the moment might never come. "It seems our fears have been confirmed. Kang is after Horus." For an instant, as he said this, Jess breathed a sigh of relief. *Yes! He's not coming for Zac!* But it was a foolish instant and her hopes crashed just as quickly. Realizing what she'd known all along:

Kang came for revenge.

"You're the last Kazerai," Lindin said. "And it would seem Kang is determined to remove all challengers. That is his one and only focus at the moment. Not to mention the fact that, well, you and he have a little history."

He tried to smile at the weak joke, an effort at levity in the midst of this very serious situation, but couldn't. His attempt to lighten the mood failed.

Instead things became even more somber.

"We think he wants to draw you out," said one of the senior officers, looking grim.

Jess swallowed. "Zac," she got him to look at her, heedless of the others in that moment. Heedless of everything. It was she and Zac; only them, no one else.

"Zac. You don't have to do this. Don't let yourself be baited," she implored. And as he stared into her eyes ...

She pulled back.

Never having seen him look the way he looked now.

Zac had always, in every moment, been so full of life, so full of confidence, determination. A certain disregard for the seriousness of things. In everything they'd been through, every ordeal, in the heat of each trial, no matter what difficulty they faced, she'd never seen him look so ...

Lost.

CHAPTER 37:

HERE BE DEMONS

"There he is," Willet pointed over the horizon, spotting the trails of black smoke in the early morning sky as the airship convoy made its way toward shore. He and Dox had been listening for sounds of their approach since confirmation from HQ, but the terrific volume of the clash between the Venatres and Dominion forces—which continued to draw closer as the Venatres perpetrated their miraculous route of the enemy—nearly overwhelmed all other sound. Not so anymore. The airships, belching the sustained explosions that kept them aloft, could now be heard.

And, in that instant, could at last be seen.

Dox followed Willet's outstretched arm.

"He" had become their focus. "He" was Kang and, by then, all they cared about. The airships themselves were unlikely to be fit for combat. They might cause trouble, or, having delivered their cargo, might simply turn and head to safety. No one knew. No one cared. All the Venatres worried about at that point was what was aboard.

Kang.

Willet watched the five mighty craft draw closer, thunder expanding, black smoke wafting behind them in poisonous trails that scarred the blue morning sky. Missiles found and sought them out, intercepted by rapid-fire plasma beams from the airships themselves, defenses that could not be penetrated.

He and Dox had managed to sabotage one command and control position there in the city and had been in the middle of coordinating their next strike when this development brought them to their current position.

"What's the plan?" asked Dox.

Willet shook his head. "Observe his touchdown and track him. Feed reports to Command so they can coordinate whatever response they can. I'm open for ideas."

Dox had none.

* * *

"HE'S LANDED," came the report. By then info and images on Kang's movement had been transferred to a large screen on the far wall, everyone in the control room watching. Jess stood beside Zac, clutching his arm harder than ever, both of them transfixed by the giant video feed. Satori had joined them. Somewhere nearby Bianca stood. Jess had tuned everything else out. She tried to steady herself, caught up in what had become for her a very small world: Her and Zac. And the very real fear, growing each second, that he would leave. That duty—ridiculous, pointless duty—would dictate he run off to meet Kang in battle. Only to die stupidly and for no reason. Who would make that decision? Lindin? Someone else?

Would Zac listen?

Waves of bitterness chased waves of fear, leaving her alternating between trying not to shake and trying not to scream.

"We've got a reconnaissance unit in the area," came a report. "I'm getting a request for communication. They're near the landing site." On screen the images of the airships loomed ominous; five giants maintaining a tight formation as they flew right over the heart of the city, descending. Pursuing aircraft circled overhead, taking the images looking down, the console operator switching between feeds. All those watching cringed as the giant airships slowed, circled and blasted in for a landing, obliterating small buildings beneath them as they did; debris billowed high on all sides in a hurricane of force as the engines of the massive craft hammered everything to dust.

Kang was truly a monster.

"That area of the city is reported evacuated," one of the operators checked, answering the unspoken question hanging in the room. "Should be clear."

Then: "Reconnaissance unit on scene. Connecting."

"... yes," came a familiar voice. "Requesting an open channel."

"Go ahead, recon unit."

"Willet here." Jess brightened slightly and a surge of hope passed through her—*Willet!*—though there was little he could do to help any of them. Still, hearing his voice brought her a brief instant of joy. She looked and noticed Satori had also brightened—though her expression clouded rapidly with concern.

"We've positioned ourselves near the airships," Willet's voice continued. "I'm going to feed what info I can on Kang's movements."

"Copy."

On screen the view from above showed clouds of debris dissipating slowly, clearing enough to vaguely make out what transpired on the ground. The 'thopters continued to circle the landed airships and it wasn't long before a figure emerged from the lead craft. At that resolution it was hard to make out details, but the figure, while human-like, was definitely not human. It had horns and looked more like a yellow demon.

Jess squeezed Zac tighter. She wasn't the only one to react. More than a few in the observation room put hands to their mouths or gasped in witness of the live image of what they'd only seen limited images of.

"I see him," Willet continued to narrate. "Here. Transmitting." And as he said this a new feed came in, from Willet on the ground, and the operator shifted that view to the large screen. Now they had a clear, ground-level panorama. The demon figure, alone, no one else emerging, moved among the wreckage on the other side of the closest craft. His legs could be seen atop a pile of rubble, then he came down, moved forward and stepped into view in front of the massive, black airship.

"Hold on," Willet zoomed, bringing the image up close and personal.

Kang was terrifying.

"Whoa," over the audio Willet concurred. "That is one scary looking bastard." Kang stood as if posing, looking away from the camera, horned head turning this way and that, muscular arms at his sides, spines on his back. Yellow, scaly hide ... Surveying the destruction that had already been wrought. Contemplating, it seemed, where to begin.

Jess glanced across at Satori. The red-headed commander's concern had grown. A lot. She now looked like Jessica felt, as if wanting to scream at Willet to get the hell out of there. You're too close! she seemed to be thinking. He'll see you! What are you doing?!

Jess looked up at Zac, who in turn gazed levelly at his destiny.

She swallowed, hard. Determined this would *not* be his destiny.

Kang was *not* going to draw him out.

"Come," she said sternly—her normally soft voice strong in that moment—tugging at his arm to follow. Zac didn't move. She wanted to yank him, to hurl him across the room and throw him in a chair, stand in front of him with her hands on her hips and tell him exactly how it was going to be and demand he knock any—*any*—idea out of his head about even *thinking*, about even *considering* going out there to fight that thing.

But there would be no yanking. With all her might—with power tools—she could not so much as bend Zac's pinky. Not if he didn't want it. So, patiently, she got his attention, nodded her head stiffly to the far side of the room and started that way.

Reluctantly he followed.

"Tell me what you're thinking," she said as she walked him quickly away from the crowd. Many eyes followed. Obviously Zac was the center of attention—which made them both the center of attention—but she didn't care. She was *not* going to sit by and let him commit suicide. Especially just because a bunch of selfish other people wanted him to.

She stopped at the other side of the room, stood in front of him and held his biceps, like one would if talking to a child. But this was no child. She felt the size of those biceps; knew the strength they contained.

Terrified she was about to lose him.

"What are you thinking?" She wanted to give him the benefit of the doubt, but she knew exactly what he was thinking. What everyone was thinking.

"I can't deny this," he admitted. "They need me."

"You can't go out there," she told him.

"I'm not sure I have a choice."

"You do have a choice. Zac. You do." Then, more desperate than she wanted to sound: "You *do*."

"Who else is going to stop him?"

"Who else—?! He killed three Kazerai!" Now she knew all eyes were on them.

"I can't stand by and do nothing." He shrugged. "I can't hide from this."

She wanted to slap him, and very nearly did. Maybe that would snap him out of it.

"There has to be another way," she tried to speak as calmly as she could. It didn't come out calm at all. It sounded a lot more frantic than anything.

He held his hands out to either side, failing to treat this with the seriousness he should.

"I'm the only one who even has a chance," he said.

She exploded.

"Chance?! *Chance*, Zac?! You've got *no* chance!" Then, horribly: "He'll kill you! You'll die out there!"

She recoiled at her own words.

No! It was way too loud, way too forceful and … the most awful thing she could've said. Everyone in the room was staring.

For an instant she fought the urge to run away.

But Zac didn't react. He just stood there, boyishly naïve and ready to do what he must, not even flinching. As if she hadn't just utterly betrayed him. She was shaking, horrified. She put trembling hands to her cheeks, then to his; held his face and looked into his deep, blue, trusting eyes.

"I'm so sorry," she practically whispered. She shook her head, trying not to cry. Feeling so absolutely low. Feeling more terrible than she ever had in her whole entire life. *What have I done?!* Wanting so badly to take everything back, growing sick to her stomach as she realized she never could.

Her words could never be un-said.

"I'm so sorry."

* * *

KANG STOOD WATCHING as another building collapsed in on itself. This one was about five floors, similar to the last, but the time it took to crush enough load points to bring it down was proving far more boring than expected. He'd not yet tested his strength in this way, on such large targets, and while his power was proving to be as near limitless as he suspected, he was yet a small form compared to the things he was trying to destroy and, in the end, the results were far less dramatic than he'd expected.

"*Horus!*" he bellowed, wondering what kept the mighty Kazerai. Surely Horus knew what he was up to. Not long ago Kang spotted a recon team shadowing him, far away amid the ruins, no doubt capturing his every move on video, which was exactly what he needed and so he'd been pretending not to notice, hoping their broadcast would lead to what he really wanted: the arrival of his nemesis.

So far it hadn't.

"*Horus!*"

He waited a moment as the echo of his roar bounced across the city, then strode off in another direction—careful not to move too swiftly and lose his unwitting camera crew.

So far this area of town had proven to be evacuated and he was starting to take notice. At first he wanted to test his strength, compel Horus to come stop him. Now that Horus was failing to show—*surely he must be near!*—it was time to make things more interesting. The military was ignoring him, wisely, which meant he was being left to his own devices. For now. Which meant, perhaps, Horus would eventually come. But Kang would not wait for eventualities. And so if destruction of property would not draw him out, then perhaps loss of life would.

Where are you all hiding? he wondered, gazing across the breadth of the city. He knew there were civilians there. Perhaps they'd gone to the other side of town? He thought to make contact with one of his commanders and find out, but this was his little adventure and he was having more fun going it alone.

Leaping slightly he bounded toward an area south of him, in his line of sight; landed, sniffed the air and trained his acute senses for the sights and sounds of humanity.

He made another leap, checking back discreetly to make sure he'd not lost the recon group. Then spotted ...

A school.

Yes.

What's more, peering from one of the upper windows he saw a handful of faces. Young faces. *Naughty little children,* he grinned, watching as they saw him and recoiled in horror. Surely their teacher or whomever must've given them explicit instructions to remain out of sight.

With a bigger leap, pushing off with such force he felt the pavement crack beneath him, he was arcing through the air and landing atop the three-story schoolhouse, impacting with a thud that sent mortar and tiles shooting into the air. He rose to his full height. Turned slowly atop the roof, pausing briefly to watch the battle from that vantage, taking place a few miles north of town. Smoke and fire, explosions, the thunderous flash of cannons, fiery trails of rockets, vehicles maneuvering for position across the battlefield. Making note of the fact that, to his dismay, his forces appeared to be losing.

Have to fix that, he determined.

But first Horus.

He watched until he caught sight of the recon team far below and far away, just now arriving near the point from which he last leapt. He waited until they saw him, made sure they could see, then decided to drop through the roof.

Bang! he stomped a hole in it and fell through to the next floor with a crash. Screams greeted him. He looked around, keen eyes piercing the temporary cloud of dust.

Four older children, probably teenagers, hiding crouched against the wall. They leapt immediately to their feet and scrabbled out of the room, fleeing down the hall.

Slowly he walked after them, watching as they reached the far end and disappeared around the corner, banging into each other in their desperation to get away.

Oh, yes, he grinned. *This will do nicely.*

CHAPTER 38:

THAT WHICH CANNOT BE IGNORED

"IT'S AN ULTIMATUM." Lindin turned to Zac. Everyone watched the transmitted images from Willet's team. Kang was inside a boarding school and, reports now confirmed, the building was occupied. His efforts to draw Zac out had taken a turn for the worse. Now he appeared bent on doing whatever it took to provoke a reaction.

He was forcing their hand.

A hush descended over those watching.

Then Willet's voice came over the radio. "Hold on. I think I see him." Willet had been moving carefully around the school perimeter, trying to observe what he could. "Switching to IR." And his transmitted image flipped to show heat signatures within the building. Kang was there; disfigured, horned shape striding methodically through the halls after running children. As if in no particular hurry.

"My god," someone said quietly. All watched in horrified anticipation, certain something terrible was about to happen. Jess kept looking at Zac, watching for his reaction. Since her earlier outburst she'd been quiet, just holding his hand as they watched. When she'd reached for it she was afraid he might reject her, hating her for what she said, but he didn't, and she clasped it tighter now as he gazed on the images of Kang.

Dozens of heat blobs, both large and small, scurried around the floors of the school building, a deadly game of hide-and-seek, those there in the control room gasping as a child would occasionally come close to Kang, encounter him, then turn and bolt the other way, Kang making no effort to give chase. Jess could only imagine the terror inside that building. Could only imagine the screams. Was Kang laughing at them? It was clear he was toying with them. He'd moved quickly to the lower floor and smashed the doors closed and was mostly just corralling them as they tried to find a way out.

"Hold on," Willet moved closer and made an adjustment. A group of three larger children managed to make it to a door that Kang hadn't smashed and escape. A small cheer erupted in the control room as they sprinted clear, cut short as everyone held their breath, wondering if they'd get away.

But Kang either didn't notice or chose not to bother, and soon the kids were sprinting into the distance, far from Willet and his small recon team. Willet tracked them a moment more then turned back to the school building.

"One small victory," he said quietly, and everyone watching seemed to nod in agreement.

Their relief was short-lived.

"Oh no," Willet brought in his focus, drawing their attention to a section of the building. Kang had a smaller form in his grasp. Hanging from one hand, kicking and thrashing. Jessica's heart rose into her throat. Kang moved with purpose now, up stairs to the upper floor then further, to the roof. As he exited onto the roof Willet switched to visible light and zoomed in on the demon, striding to the edge of the roof, child in hand. A boy, looking to be eight or so, thrashing wildly to get free.

At the edge Kang turned his demonic head this way and that, looking far and wide. Fangs glinted in the sunlight. He found Willet far away on the ground and looked right at the camera, gloating for whoever might be watching, then held his arm straight, dangling the boy out in space. Zac tensed, squeezed Jessica's hand so much it hurt, leaning forward at what Kang was about to do. Only Willet's voice cut the silence, his transmitted audio as he bore witness firsthand to the evil atop the building. As if forgetting he had an audience.

"No," he said. Then, imploring: "No. Please."

And Kang released the boy.

The child fell screaming and Willet looked away, horrified, camera going with him and, mercifully, the only thing those gathered in the control room saw in that instant was the ground beside him.

The screams of the falling child came to an abrupt end and ... a terrible quiet. The wind, the distant battle—all other noises were as nothing.

Then a tremendous roar spiked the audio.

"*HORUS!!*"

Willet jerked his gaze up, camera on Kang where he stood, horned head thrown back, arms stretched wide at his sides like a crucifix, echo of the bellow on his lips.

Summoning the one he sought.

It took Jess an instant to realize Zac was gone.

Just then, released her hand and rushing away, toward the door and out of the room.

"*Zac!*"

She whirled and raced after him.

He continued, slowing not one bit. His long strides were so fast she had to run to catch him.

"Zac! Please!" but her pleas were weak. She knew it. Felt it. The abomination had to be faced or it would not stop. It was terrible, it was horrible, but Zac had to go die. None of them could stand and watch any more of this. Least of all Zac. He, like he said, was the only one who even had a chance.

She began crying as she ran. He kept striding, on his way, not stopping, not even looking back.

"Zac!"

Then another voice shouted from behind: "Do you want me to fly you?" It was Satori, chasing after them. She was the only one; the rest remained in the room. Not even Bianca. No one else came; only Jess and Satori, chasing after Zac. The three of them alone in that empty corridor.

Zac glanced back at Satori but kept on. "I'll get there on my own." Then: "This is between me and him."

Satori stopped. Jess kept rushing after him, alternating between a jog and a walk as Zac maintained a relentless pace. Satori fell out of sight and Zac was soon heading upstairs, Jess chasing him weakly like a child.

"Zac!" she implored.

"I'm going to kill him," he continued walking, heading

up. The certainty in his voice was chilling and for an instant she believed him. But it was foolishness. She stumbled but kept up. He didn't seem to care.

"We're in love!" She didn't know why she said it, it was a stupid thing to say right then but, somehow, it worked. He stopped. Turned at the landing in the stairwell and stopped. She rushed up on him and grabbed his arms tightly now that she had him and stared up into his face, trying not to be a baby.

He looked down into her eyes, so tall, "We *are* in love," and she hated the way he said it. No tenderness. He was so angry right then. "But this isn't about us."

And he was off again. The short conversation over.

She ran after him.

Up the stairs, round and round, past a few sentries on duty, into the fire-crackling warmth of the unreal chalet, across the Great Room and out onto the porch, into the daylight. There he finally stopped. She rushed and grabbed him once more.

"I'm so scared!" she wept. They were alone on the wide timber deck, basking in wonderful sunshine beneath a brilliant blue sky, surrounded by snow covered fields. A scene that was far too beautiful for the tragedy they faced.

At last Zac reached his arms around her and held her, restoring a bit of tenderness. She sniffed away tears.

"I know why this has to be," she said, face turned to the side against his chest, "but please, just slow down. It's happening too fast!"

He turned her head up to face him.

"There will be no good time for this." He looked into her blurring eyes, his own, ice-blue pupils hard like steel. "This is killing me the same way it's killing you. But each second I wait is one more second he tries to make me come. One more person, one more child that might die. If I don't go …"

She waited, wondering what would be his next words but then Zac, strong, powerful Zac, did something she at first could not believe.

He shed a tear.

Just a little. She saw it, through her own. Welling in his eyes, red-rimmed, the rest of his visage steady. He cried not because he was afraid. Not because he feared dying. Not because he feared fighting Kang. He *wanted* to fight Kang—she could feel it, could feel the rage, the impatience within him and, though he knew the hopeless odds stacked against him, she could see he wanted this fight. Was determined to bash in the demon's head.

What he cried for was her. For them. Silent tears, and only a few, but their little tracks rolled freely down his cheeks, glinting in the cold sun, and this was the saddest she'd seen him.

"I don't want this to be it," he said, voice steady. "But it is. I don't want this to be the end of us.

"But, maybe, it is."

No!! she screamed in her mind.

"And if it is," he went on, "I don't want to stand around talking about it." Then his voice was filled with frustration: "We haven't even started! Our time together—" He looked away, too pained to continue. Her own agony flared, such that she thought she might seize up, right then, right there. Fall to the deck in a puddle and expire. Was this truly the end?

He calmed.

"I could never say the things I need to say," he shook his head, looking desperately into her eyes. "Not at a moment like this. How could I? How could I have that conversation? Now, with so much at stake? With every second another child dying. Another life ended."

She reached a shaking hand and wiped away his tears.

"He wants me, Jessica." He began to reclaim his determination. "But I don't think he's ready. He thinks he is. But he's not. I'm going to make him wish he'd never come.

"This ends now."

Jess shuddered at the sudden intensity in his gaze. And, for a fleeting instant, feared for Kang.

Maybe Zac *could* defeat him.

She took a deep, shuddering breath.

Zac reached and stroked her cheek, holding her close with the other arm. And his next words made her question herself for ever doubting.

"In our short time together," he said, pushing back her hair, "we've made it through one impossible thing after another, out of nothing more than our own hope, our own determination. This is just another of those times. Does this thing I'm about to do seem impossible? Yes. Does that mean it's doomed to fail?" And he looked deeply into her, hand twining her hair.

"No."

And she believed him. With all her heart, she believed him.

"I didn't mean what I said," she shook her head slowly. "I was just scared."

"I know," he reassured her. He bent and kissed her and she tasted the salt of their tears; a passionate kiss, emotions all out of whack amid the angry frustration and she gave into it, feeling his resolve, melting into what became, for her, a bitter sadness backed by desperate hope. When he withdrew they both had, at least, made peace with what was about to take place.

Zac was going to fight.

"You're so beautiful," he whispered, earnest, and she reached and dragged him to her for another embrace. When they separated she managed a reassuring smile, and he touched her lips gently with his fingertips, gaze filled with love.

"I'll do everything," he said, "*everything* in my power to see that smile again."

She tried not to cry. Tried to prop up the bravery of the moment, to be strong for him.

Then: "Stand back," he said and moved away. He took another step, crouched and ...

Leapt into the air. Hard off the porch, heavy timbers creaking with the launch, thrumming beneath her feet— flying impossibly far into the distance where he landed in a plume of fresh snow a hundred feet away. His sudden absence wracked her. Gone, just like that. Far out there in the field he leapt again, harder that time, no porch to be concerned with, no frail human girl to worry over, and that time he was *really* soaring, in an arc high into the sky; far, far into the distance.

It was a staggering display of power.

And in that instant she felt her knees wobble and hope gathered force and soared.

He's so strong! She watched him head rapidly into the distance. *How can he lose?*

Two more giant leaps and he was out of sight, over the foothills and on his way to battle Kang.

Gone.

But his absence was too sudden. No matter any fledgling hope, no matter any shade of inspiration it was too soon. Too soon to be gone and off to that end.

She turned back to the chalet and leaned against the railing.

Putting her face in her hands to hide the tears.

* * *

WILLET WATCHED IN HORROR as Kang dropped another child. He seethed with impotent rage, absolutely nothing he could do to stop the heinous carnage being perpetrated by the beast.

Duty compelled him to stay on station, to report what must be reported, to relay this tragedy frame by frame, all the while wishing he could simply turn it off and run away. Put it all behind him, as if it never happened. Wipe the nightmare clean. But he knew he never could. What he witnessed would be with him forever.

As the beast stood there atop the roof, gloating, the thought of shooting him in the head with a high-yield missile, of punching one down his throat, fought mightily with Willet's reason. It was a foolish notion, one that would have no effect and only cause more harm in the end yet ...

It was a difficult urge to contain.

A voice on the radio penetrated the fog of his fury. Someone was trying to get through. He looked to the side. Dox was there. The others of his small team.

As aghast as he was, horrified.

He struggled to clear his head. "Go ahead."

"The Kazerai is on his way," came the voice of the operator on the other end. Willet looked again to Dox. Spoke a reply into the radio.

"Zac? He's coming?"

The operator's voice was filled with emotion. "Yes."

Willet stood at once, without thought, and ran toward the school waving his arms.

"Hey!" he yelled. Again, louder: "HEY!" This was exactly what Kang was after. "I know you can hear me! You!" Kang was far away but Willet had no doubt he could hear as well as the vaunted Kazerai. Probably better. "*HEY!*" Kang had been headed to grab another victim but paused and turned. Looked straight at Willet. Willet stopped and shouted, as loud as he could:

"Horus is coming!" It occurred to him, only as he stood there, vulnerable, in the open, that Kang had probably just been using Willet's team to get what he was after. Which meant if Zac was truly on his way Kang would have no more use for them. Would he jump down and kill them right there?

In a strange way Willet hoped he would. He'd love nothing more than the chance to punch the demon right in the face. After everything that had happened there that day that would be the best way he could think of to end his life. All his hate channeled into an unrestrained strike. His last action in this world.

"Horus is on his way!" Willet held his arms out to the sides, defiant. Willfully tempting fate. Wanting a reaction out of the thing. Wanting to anger it if he could. Wanting to infuriate it, in truth, to make it seethe with the same rage he felt.

Kang just stared at him.

Then, slowly, a fanged grin spread across that evil expression. Willet thought he heard him cackling.

He glanced at Dox. At his small team.

Had an idea.

He turned back to Kang, who still stood atop the school,

looking almost as if he were in glee.

"Not here!" he shouted. "He won't fight you here!" He pointed to a distant area, a park of sorts, free of buildings and free of people.

Kang stood laughing quietly, staring at Willet as if he'd not even spoken.

And Willet wondered if the beast was totally insane.

CHAPTER 39:

FACEOFF

JESS WAS CRYING SOFTLY when Satori found her. At the sight of her Jess sniffled and stopped, not wanting to look weak before the tough, red-headed commander. The chill in the air had begun to impinge, and though the morning sun was warm on her back she hugged her chest, shivering. As Satori came close, stopped and stood beside her at the railing, she was struck by the quiet of the moment. As if not noticing before. Pandemonium reigned in the control center at the heart of the mountain below; had been going strong when she left. Beyond the great peaks a war was being fought; people were dying. Zac was leaping off to meet his own end. Yet, there on the porch, in that impossible moment, all was calm.

Fresh sobs ached in her throat, fighting to be released, but she swallowed them down.

Beside her Satori put her hands on the railing. Jess watched her from the corner of her eye, bright red hair blowing gently as she gazed in the other direction. For a long moment she simply stood there, making Jess wonder why she came. She felt compelled to say something, anything to break the awkward silence, but didn't want to talk. Not to Satori, not to anyone.

Finally Satori did.

"Don't know why he refused a lift." An idle comment.

Jess turned her head to look directly at her, even as Satori continued staring out toward the distant mountains. The way Zac had gone. Jess turned back to face the chalet. Felt the tears drying on her cheeks in the cool air; icy streaks, the unmistakable evidence of her emotion. She wiped at them.

"Probably just as fast," Satori noted, more to herself. "It's not that far."

At that Jess looked down at the deck; wiped away more of the frozen tears and hugged her arms tighter across her chest.

"I hate this." She didn't want to get into a conversation but Satori wasn't going anywhere. Maybe that was her plan. Stand there until she said something. Well, it worked. Now she was talking. "I wish I'd never come here in the first place. This has been," she waved a hand at all the intangible things in her life, "the best and the absolute worst that's ever happened to me. One minute it doesn't seem like I could be more happy, then it's like I could never be more crushed. I'm terrified, I'm thrilled, and just when I thought I was getting used to the ups and downs ... This. Now it's over, and the whole thing is going to end in sadness. My whole story will be a tragedy."

When Satori spoke it was quietly. "That doesn't sound like you." Her gaze remained fixed in the distance. "I never would've expected you to feel sorry for yourself."

"I'm not feeling sorry for myself."

"What do you call it?"

Jess had no answer.

"Sounds to me like you're giving up."

"I'm not giving up. It's over."

"Is it?"

"It *is!*" Jess knew her anger was excessive but didn't care. Any hope she had was at an end. "Zac is gone! He's dead!"

Satori seemed surprised. "What? When?" Now she was looking directly at her.

"Don't be a smartass."

Satori let the silence hang, then said pointedly: "He's not dead yet. Not as far as I know."

"Oh stop." Jess turned away, trying not to cry again. "Don't give me that crap. It's over and you know it."

She felt so hollow inside.

But Satori just shook her head. "I've been in too many lopsided situations to ever believe that. So have you, in case you're forgetting. Look what we pulled off at the Crucible. Look what *you* pulled off to even be standing here right now."

Jess stood with her arms crossed, defiant.

Satori stared at her. "I want back the Jessica I know."

Jess didn't want to be bitter. Didn't want to sound like a whiny bitch. Satori didn't deserve that. She just wished she'd go away and leave her to her grief.

But that wasn't happening.

With as much calm as she could muster she asked: "So what do *you* think we should do?"

Satori shrugged. "Do? I'm not sure there's anything to do." Now she became firm. Voice taking on an edge, chastising Jessica for her attitude: "But moping and crying aren't the solution either. We owe him, Jess. *You* owe him. Zac is on his way into the belly of the beast, off to face Kang—for all of us—because he knows it's the only way. He could've run from it. He didn't. He's out there because it's the right thing to do. The least *we* can do—the very least—is have faith.

"You can't give up on him."

Jess continued to stand solidly.

Heart aching.

Satori was adamant. "He's not dead. I'm *not* being a smartass. He's not dead yet and you know it. I know it. And until he is, as long as he has a single breath left, we—you—*you* of all people, Jessica—can't give up on him."

Jess felt her lips pinching in anger.

How could he run off on me like that?!

And … was that it?

Was *she* the one being selfish?

It hit her like a wave.

Of course she was.

All her emotions, all her reactions, against Zac, against Satori, against the whole world in that moment, were being driven by selfish desire.

How could you leave me?! She wanted to scream. Already had, in a sense, and as the regret of that settled she began to feel even lower. Her heart sank. Until then she'd managed to shift the feeling of losing Zac to anger; now she was sad all over again. Yet, even as that crashed over her the absolute epiphany of it, of what drove her emotions, cleared everything away like a stream of water over sandy glass, leaving her with perspective. And she found her core. Deep beneath, always there, and at the center of that strength she knew—completely knew and understood—regret fixed nothing. Regret was useless, and right then it was threatening to hang her with inaction. Solutions were what she needed.

And so she made herself look. At the situation. At everything.

Satori kept talking, of course, still trying to make her point, not realizing she already had. "He stopped Kang once." She shrugged. "Maybe he can do it again."

But Jess got it. The wheels were turning.

What *was* the solution?

Then ...

An idea

She looked up sharply. The idea gained substance in a mad rush—insanely fast—coalescing to a picture of exactly what she had to do.

What they both had to do.

For this idea to work she needed Satori, and the crystal clarity of what she suddenly had in mind chilled her.

She made eye contact with the battle-hardened commander, wondering if Satori could see the nervous worry in her stare. What she'd just envisioned ... Her plan was only seconds old, final bits of it still forming, yet there were already a hundred ways for it to fail.

Crazy.

It was suicide.

However if it succeeded, if it *did* work, somehow, then maybe, just maybe ...

Kang would be gone. And Zac ...

Zac would survive.

Jess hesitated. Then, carefully:

"I have an idea."

There must've been a mad fusion of excitement and terror on her face; Satori's own expression shifted in response, a growing mixture of curiosity and ... definite

worry. *What's she up to now?* she seemed to be thinking.
Jess had already been a huge pain in her ass. Already
almost cost her everything. Satori frowned. What was
running through her little teenage mind?

Jess swallowed.

"How fast can you get us to the scene of the fight?"

"Midbay?"

Jess nodded.

"Why?"

"I'll tell you in a second." And she was off across the
porch, through the doors to the chalet and headed below.

Hoping Satori would follow.

* * *

KANG HAD FINALLY MOVED TO THE PARK. For many long, nerve-
wracking minutes Willet watched as the yellowed demon
stood atop the school, cackling like a madman, unmoving,
wondering what rash thing he would do next. Wondering
whether he would murder more innocents—wondering,
in truth, whether he would just come kill them all—until
at last the beast leapt. Of a sudden, sending up a cloud
of dust and debris from the roof as he launched, arcing
through the air, above and over Willet and his team, across
the sky as if shot from a giant catapult, landing in a plume
of dirt on the wide swath of green Willet indicated.

Willet and team followed and the monster stood now
on the wide open field, in the distance, surrounded by
precisely pruned and landscaped trees. Willet and his
team had begun creeping closer, cautiously, each step
increasing the fear of being exposed in the open with the
beast yet determined to reach a better position. To assist
Zac however they could.

For Willet had a plan.

As they drew up through the trees he waved his team
closer, gathering them within a tight group. Dox plus
three others. Two of them carried equipment, munitions
and other items for demolition. Everyone carried rifles
and plenty of bullets. Useless in this situation, of course,

but Gervin packed something bigger. A missile launcher. Equally useless, more or less, not enough to take out Kang, but now that the monster was in the clear perhaps Willet could help Zac get the fight off on more even footing.

He looked across at Gervin who crouched nearby and the two exchanged a nod of understanding.

Gervin was ready.

Behind them the battle raged. As the Dominion forces had been compressed tighter and tighter against the outskirts of the city they at last held and now, it seemed, the brief Venatres advance had been brought to a halt. Reports were that a standoff was developing. At any rate Willet did not expect that clash to encroach on the showdown about to take place there in the park. A stark contrast, he noted, looking out over the beautiful, tranquil setting, to the chaos behind them in the distance. An island of calm at the heart of a city under siege.

He looked at a few of the buildings at the far edges, toppled earlier by Kang in his seemingly random rampage. Willet and his team had observed it all, watching in stunned disbelief as Kang demonstrated what appeared to be untouchable power. There was no way even a Kazerai could've done that much damage. Not that swiftly, at any rate. Certainly not that easily.

Which made Willet worry all the more that Zac was in over his head. He could not last long in this fight.

But at least by coming the demon had been temporarily stopped. Drawn away from his monstrous crimes. For the moment he was contained. Willet watched the thing standing there in the middle of the park, waiting, deformed chest and shoulders heaving as it took deep, billowing breaths—fearing what Kang would do once he was finished with Zac.

Consciously he steered his mind from those fatalistic thoughts. Zac was coming, knowing full well what he was up against. Willet owed it to him to do everything he could to help. More than that, he owed it to Zac to believe.

Across the park Kang eyed the small team. Willet kept expecting him to leap to them any second and simply kill

them. Based on what he'd seen it would take Kang no
time at all. A few bloody moments and Willet and his men
would be ripped to shreds. But Kang didn't. He just kept
checking to see that they were there, and Willet began to
assume he still wanted an audience. Maybe he expected
them to broadcast the fight. Whatever his motivation, it
was clear he found them no threat. Surely he must realize
they were armed and might not continue to sit idly by, yet
even the possibility of their attack did not compel him to
pre-empt it.

It was almost as if he didn't care.

A shadow passed across the sun and Willet looked up.
A human form, arcing in from a giant leap—bigger and
farther than any Kang had yet displayed—arms and legs
out for balance. It was Zac. Down he came and *whoomp!*
landed before them, a few dozen yards downrange from
where Willet and his recon team crouched; a perfectly
placed landing that threw up a wall of dirt as he hit and
dug in to a stop. It was such a spectacular entrance that,
for a moment, Willet wondered how anything could stand
against Zac. *How could anything defeat that?* Zac had
always been the mightiest of the Kazerai. Nothing could
stop him.

Except Kang. Willet's surge of hope came crashing back
to reality as Kang snorted at the other end of the park, a
noise like a steam valve going off, the mere act of which blew
up a cloud of grass and dirt from the ground at his feet. He
did not charge. Simply continued to stand there, crooked
horns framing his visage, staring across the hundred or so
yards separating he and Zac. Looking on the new arrival
with what Willet could only describe as grim satisfaction.

Yet ...

For an instant Willet thought he saw something else.
Another emotion passed across Kang's demonic expression,
even at that range. Concern? That seemed unlikely.
Nevertheless Kang did not greet Zac's arrival with the same
sort of sneering confidence with which he'd so far treated
everything else.

Perhaps the beast had doubts.

For his part Zac *did* seem unconcerned, and this managed to further inspire Willet's hope. The Kazerai rose from his landing methodically, almost dramatically— glanced briefly at Willet and his team, gave a small nod of acknowledgement then faced his adversary. Zac stood in an easy stance, arms at his sides, hands balled into fists. He wore the black Kazerai pants and boots. Somewhere in his journey to the battlefield he must've removed his shirt and was now bare-chested.

Even without his Kazerai strength Zac was intimidating. Tall; broad; muscled. *With* the strength of a Kazerai ... Again Willet found himself believing that maybe, just maybe, Zac could win this.

For the moment neither combatant moved.

Then Zac addressed his opponent.

"How does it feel?" he bellowed across the distance. There was no strain in his voice yet it was loud beyond measure.

Kang stared at him and frowned.

"Must suck, looking like that," Zac went on. Willet wondered if "suck" was something Zac had learned from Jessica. Some slang from Earth. Wherever it came from it made perfect sense. It would indeed "suck" to look like Kang. Willet could see a bit of anger flash across the eyes of the beast.

"I'm guessing your throne's not too comfortable," Zac went on, making note of the spikes along Kang's spine. "Emperor. Maybe they can cut some holes." Kang's vanity, when he was human, was legendary, and Zac was twisting a knife right into the heart of it. Willet could see Zac was getting to him.

The dark-haired Kazerai twisted harder. "You forgot what it was like, didn't you? Being human. You've been so caught up in this new power. But when you saw me ... I could tell it all came rushing back. You called me here to get rid of me, but all I've done is remind you of what you've lost. Now that you see me you realize it's all gone. You'll never be human again. Never know any of the things you once knew. You stand there, power incarnate, more alive than you've ever been, and yet you could not be more dead."

Kang becoming enraged. He bellowed back: "You're the one that will be dead!"

Zac smiled. More of a baiting smirk. "We'll see."

Willet was starting to enjoy this. But the banter was dangerous; merely putting off the inevitable. There might be a point to angering Kang but Willet didn't see how it could continue.

It was time for his gambit. He signaled Gervin—even as Zac set himself and said to Kang: "Shall we?"

Kang growled, leaned forward to charge and ...

Gervin shouldered the launcher and the missile streaked across the green field with a hissing roar, a blur of rocket fire that impacted the demon square in the chest before he could move.

BOOOOM!!! the explosion lit the park; a fireball of heat, the target way too close for that yield of an explosion. Instantly the wave of overpressure and booming repercussion rocked them. Willet knew it was coming, braced himself, shielded eyes and ears in that instant between instants as the missile found its target—Kang so focused on Zac he completely missed his opportunity to dodge—but the blast was too overwhelming. Willet felt himself lose his footing and go tumbling, banged backward and disoriented.

But he couldn't let that happen. Desperate not to let this chance slip he caught his tumble and staggered as the rush of hot air passed over him, to his feet and forward, back out into the park, coughing, in the direction of Zac.

"Zac!" He yelled. Found him, ears ringing, vision spotted but clearing enough to see Zac's dark head of hair, then the bare skin of his upper torso. He stood more or less the way he had been right before the missile was fired, unaffected by the blast but nevertheless confused for the moment.

As if unsure how to react to this new development.

"Go!" Willet yelled at him. "Pound him!"

Zac got it. Leapt forward, one leap, clear across the park, hitting the felled Kang somewhere deep in the burning trees. Willet could not yet see well enough to spot Kang's fallen form but Zac landed straight and true, laying in a flurry of punches and Willet assumed Kang had, for the moment, been knocked back and maybe even knocked out. He didn't dare hope any real damage had been done, but his objective had been achieved. He'd made it so Zac at least got in the first blows. Vision returned. Focus. He watched Zac unleash destruction on his stunned target.

Worried it would not be near enough.

CHAPTER 40:

SMALL HOPE

THE MORE JESS THOUGHT IT THROUGH ... what she had in mind, if she was even able to pull it off, would not completely solve the problem. It would, instead, trigger a new series of problems, each more difficult than the last and, in that sense, was the worst idea ever. In view of everything, however, it was the only idea that had any chance. And so she was doing it. It was the one thing that could, ultimately, save Zac, and if she didn't hurry it might be too late. Each second out there fighting Kang was one more second his life was in jeopardy. One more second he could die.

"Where are we going?" Satori stepped quickly to keep up as Jess maintained an impatient jog. Time collapsed; there was no more of it left; she had to get there now and that desperate impulse prodded her all at once, as if physically, and instead of answering she picked up the pace to an outright run, ignoring Satori completely and rushing below, leaping the final set of stairs to the long hallway leading to the lab.

She stretched her pace down the wide corridor, making for the far, vault-like door, bootfalls striking hollow in rapid staccato. A pair of guards waited. They drew rigid as the two girls sprinted toward them, raising their guns in sudden alarm.

"Emergency business," Jess called out, not knowing what else to say but in too much of a hurry. She hadn't given the execution of this plan much thought, focused instead on the bigger picture. All she knew was she had to get into the giant room beyond.

The guards looked to each other as she raced up to a fidgeting halt, anxious, Satori right behind. *Move!* she wanted to yell.

"They need the artifice specs," Satori interjected, forcing

her rank and knowledge into the situation. "Upstairs."

The way she said it made sense, a voice of reason balanced against Jessica's frantic urgency. Without further delay the guards nodded and let them in. No reason to question a senior intelligence officer, and so it was with a friendly nod and a "Thanks" from Satori that they passed inside.

Jess reeled as they stepped across the threshold, as she had each other time in the sudden and overwhelming presence of the giant black starship. She kept walking, fast, heading for the far side.

Hoping Nani was here.

"You wanna tell me what we're doing?" Satori asked as the heavy vault door closed behind, echoing across the massive space.

Jess looked across at her as they hurried.

"We have to get one of the Icons."

At the announcement of that Satori slowed and nearly stopped, then rushed to keep up.

Jess kept striding with a purpose.

Before Satori could protest Nani walked into view.

Yes!

There she was, stepping around one of the work areas, drawn to the sound of their approach. As if curious to see who'd come in the large door. She brightened when she saw Jess and Satori.

"Jessica," she called as they came toward her—growing slightly anxious when she caught the quick intensity in Jessica's eyes. "Satori. What are you guys doing here? Isn't everyone up in the control center? Bianca called down and said—"

"We need your help," Jess said as they reached her.

"Anything." Nani was so friendly. Jess really hoped they might one day get to know each other.

She sprang her demand.

"I need one of the Icons."

Nani's expression fell. Satori, too, was still in the middle of processing the revelation of Jessica's intent. She spoke directly to Jess: "What are you thinking?"

But Jess kept talking to Nani. "Zac has gone to fight

Kang."

Nani could do nothing but stare. The lump in her throat went up and down as she swallowed, desperately wishing, it seemed, that this wasn't actually happening. That Jess hadn't said what she just said; that she wasn't there making this demand.

"He can't win," Jess tried to explain. It still felt terrible to say it. "If Kang can't be stopped he's a threat to the whole world. He could ruin everything.

"The only way to defeat him is to get rid of him." She looked at both women. "There *is* a way to do that."

Understanding dawned on Satori. Slowly it began to settle over Nani as well.

"But ... how?" Nani wanted to know. Her voice had grown quiet. Fearful. She could see Jess was determined beyond measure. Could probably feel it, Jess suspected, as she was beaming it into her so hard it felt she might actually shove Nani backward without even touching her. "You want ... to use an Icon?" Nani shook her head. "To get rid of Kang? How will you reach him?" She glanced to Satori but got no immediate support. "And what if Kang uses it to come back? There's no—"

"Kang isn't going to use it," Jess assured her. "Zac will."

* * *

YES! KANG ENTHUSED, relishing the impact of his fist with Horuses' face, watching as his nemesis went soaring away. Kang had just tried to apply the same rear choke he'd used to break Akido's neck, but somehow Horus managed to squirm away. No matter. Now that they were fully engaged Kang realized he would kill Horus the same as he had the others. So far Horus was, indeed, proving to be superior, a more worthy match—living up to his vaunted status as the greatest of the Kazerai—but in witness of his meager strength Kang's confidence had returned. Now that they'd been going at it he realized, with certainty, Horus could not defeat him.

Which meant the world would soon be his. There would

be no one else to stand in his way.

The sneak missile attack hurt. He vowed to dispatch the small team of soldiers still watching from the woods once this was over. In fact he'd tried a few times already to send Horus flying in that direction, in the hopes of taking the battle close enough to kill them, but Horus managed each time to divert the clash. Horus was losing, but he somehow succeeded in confining their battle to that relatively small area. It was his only success in this fight, a small victory, but Kang hated him for it. More of Horuses' noble efforts to protect others. He was getting destroyed, yet even in that fought to shield the world from harm.

Kang sneered as his enemy hit the ground in the distance. *That will not last long*, he mused. *When this is over I will wreak such death and destruction upon this city as to make future historians quake with horror. This city, and you, will become my shining example. The thing by which I instill fear and absolute obedience into the hearts and minds of the world.*

After this day all will fear Kang. All will obey.

Horus rose. Again. He kept getting up, which frustrated Kang terribly, but it was to be expected. Mere blows were not going to dispatch him.

Kang leapt even as Horus did, meeting him in mid-air with a titanic crack of impact, bodies locking in combat as they shot off on a new trajectory.

Laughing in triumph, Kang gripped him and squeezed.

* * *

"So that's the other one?" Satori asked over the roar of engine and wind, looking across to the Icon in Jessica's hands. Jess nodded. "And it goes to deep space?" Jess could tell Satori still hadn't come to grips with the details of what they were doing.

Neither had she.

"Yeah," she shifted the shiny device, holding it carefully. Wondering: Could Zac survive in space?

But he had to.

At least long enough to get away.

They flew one of the smaller ornithopters, Satori at the helm. Jess sat in the co-pilot seat, watching the ground scroll rapidly below; feeling the power of the steam turbine through the superstructure, the mechanics of the beating wings, driving them furiously at speed.

Wishing the machine could go faster.

But Satori was on it for all it was worth. Reluctantly Nani had given them the specified Icon and they concealed it, made their way to the hangar and, with another easy explanation, were dusting off and on their way south. Heading for the battle at Midbay. Just now they were clearing the foothills, Jess leaning with the machine as Satori banked hard between the spectacular, tree-covered ridges; a breathtaking flight which, under other circumstances, she might even have enjoyed. Right then she held on for dear life.

Slowly she turned the Icon in her lap, double-checking for the tenth time the scratch made—by her—with the Skull Boy's armored finger. Making absolutely sure she had the right one.

This was indeed it. The one from the agents. If the information on the laptop was correct its two connecting points were Earth and deep space, somewhere in the star system of 36 Ophiuchi. This particular Icon had last been on Earth, which meant the next twist should send it to deep space. The twist after that would send it back to Earth. Specifically high above the Rockies.

She was basing everything on this.

Though there was little doubt the device would work as expected. No reason not to believe the info on the computer. What terrified her was the rest of it. First she would have to get the Icon to Zac, in the middle of a superhuman melee. Then he would have to activate it—while holding onto Kang—then, if it worked, he would have to fight free of Kang—in deep space—and activate it again, this time *without* Kang, leaving Kang floating hopelessly in the void.

Sending Zac plummeting over the Rockies.

That was the only way to be absolutely rid of the monster

and at the same time save Zac.

It could work. It *had* to work. But since the second activation would send Zac to Earth, not back here to Anitra ... That meant if it *did* work the plot only thickened. *She* would then have to get to Earth using the other Icon, no doubt with another suit of Skull Boy armor, land in the middle of whatever the agents had waiting at her house in Boise, then fight her way all the way to the coordinates in the Rockies. Hoping Zac remained, hoping he wasn't so injured after the fight that he was able to be captured by those same agents, rescue him, and only *then* snap them both back to Anitra.

Directly over Osaka, of course. Capital of the Dominion.

Her head hurt.

But there was nothing else. No other way. She'd already come to that conclusion. First Zac had to live, and this was the only chance to save him. Second, Kang had to die, and since there was no way to kill him this would accomplish the next best thing. They would be rid of him.

Rescue Zac.

Get rid of Kang.

Using the Icon would accomplish both, and from there she would just have to figure it out.

Not doing this would lead to only one outcome:

Zac dead.

Kang loose in the world.

She took a deep breath.

"So Zac pops there and leaves him?" Satori.

Jess nodded.

Step one had been accomplished. They actually had the Icon and were on their way to Zac. *One step at a time*, she steadied herself, eyes glued to the shiny device in her lap.

If the difficulties ahead weren't bad enough, she tried desperately not to think of the *other* alternatives. What if Kang got the Icon away from Zac? What if *he* used it and he, Kang, not Zac, appeared over Earth? How would she even know if that happened? Once Zac was gone she had no way to be sure. What if she did all this, then ran to Earth to rescue Zac ... only to find Kang there instead. She would've then sealed the fate of her own world.

Satori flew them hard through a long bank and roll.

This is going to work.

* * *

WILLET CRINGED. Zac had just squeezed out of yet another attempt by Kang to crush him and Willet wondered how many more escapes the great Kazerai had in him. Kang bellowed across the field in impotent rage, focused entirely on the kill; thwarted at every attempt. Early in the fight he'd seemed to derive some perverse sport from the back and forth, the pursuit of the inevitable end, but when it became clear that end would not be achieved easily Kang shifted efforts. Became more focused. Desperate.

Somehow Zac kept slipping free.

"Why prolong this?" the horned monster boomed. Zac stood a dozen or so yards from him and, for the moment, the two faced each other, sizing up their next move. Zac was bruised, even bleeding—something Willet had never seen one of the Kazerai do—while Kang looked as fresh as he had at the beginning. As fresh as he ever had, though a certain angry weariness had crept into his bearing. Unmistakable on his expression. Whether he was actually tired Willet doubted, but the beast's expression was definitely that of one who was done playing the game.

Kang was clearly anxious to end this.

Zac managed a smile. Even in the midst of certain doom. "You want me to just give up and die?" he shouted back.

Willet wanted so badly to be able to do something. Anything to help. But there was nothing. Another missile only risked driving Kang's anger. Somehow, some way Zac kept propping up the will to go on, but it had to end. Kang would eventually win this. And as Willet sought desperately for a way to prevent that inevitable outcome his radio beeped.

It was Satori.

"You have eyes on them?" her voice was suddenly in his earpiece. Not so much as a "Hello", no other announcement of her presence, and for an instant Willet was mute with shocked surprise. *What's she doing on this channel?*

"Satori?" Wasn't she back at the mountain complex?

"Zac and Kang," she said. "Do you see them?"

"Wha ... Yes. I see them. Where are you?"

"Circling to the west. We have a solution."

Willet made out mechanical sounds in the background of her audio. Satori was in a 'thopter.

What the hell?

"Give me your coordinates."

Hurriedly he gave them to her, knowing better than to try and question further. The tone of her voice told him all he needed to know. She was coming and he should do what she asked.

"Can you send someone to meet us?" she queried.

"I'll meet you myself," he signaled his team, who listened with interest to the radio exchange.

"She'll need an escort."

She? But for some reason Willet knew at once exactly who Satori meant.

Jessica.

And as he realized this he felt a tiny smile pass across his face, wondering just what the two women were up to.

"It's a park," he said. "Stay to the northeast side. That seems to be the safest. I'll meet you there."

"Copy that. We're coming in hot." Then, in an entirely conversational tone: "How's it going?"

He laughed.

"Terrible."

"How long has it been?"

It took Willet a second to switch gears.

"Since we've seen each other?"

"Yeah." The concentration in her voice made it obvious she was executing some sort of tight maneuver, probably avoiding the attention of the Dominion units as she flew. Her skill with machinery, however, was such that she could easily chat at the same time.

Willet sighed. "Months."

"Sorry it has to be like this," she grunted under the strain of the turn and added: "Bad timing or not you'd better have a kiss for me." Willet noticed the other members of his team grinning. There was a moment of silence as the channel remained open, other noises filling the background.

"Don't doubt me for a second," he said.

"Never." Then, with another strain: "We're here."

Willet rose. "On my way."

* * *

ZAC WAS TIRED. He hurt. It had been so long since he was either, he realized, that he'd forgotten how nice it was to live free of both. Pain and exhaustion had become foreign to him.

Not so anymore.

Kang lunged and he ducked and pivoted at the last possible instant, gripped one of the spines at the monster's back, pulled, twisted hard and released, flinging the deformed demon over and into the nearby trees. Many of the trunks in the park were broken or toppled from these impacts, but Kang's flailing body splintered a few fresh ones as he crashed through the woods to a stop.

Zac had managed to turn the last two attempts to grab him and thought he may have figured a way to redirect the beast, but it was temporary. There was nothing more he could do, that was now painfully obvious, nothing more anyone could do, and it would be he and Kang until the end. Until eventually, inevitably, Kang sank that one hold from which Zac could not escape. Then it would be over.

He was going to die in that park.

What bothered him was not that he himself would die. That was an end he'd come to grips with. What bothered him was that so many would die in his wake. So much would be lost. Once Kang won this battle it was over. This world and everything Zac cherished would be gone.

He'd resigned himself to his own death. Coming out there to face Kang he'd already accepted that likelihood. There was no resistance in that. What kept him fighting, what kept him holding on was that, though he knew he could not win, he *had* to win or else everything he'd known, everything he loved would be lost. And the conflict of those two realities ...

That was making his heart ache. With an emptiness the likes of which he'd never known, he stared that harsh inevitability right in the eyes. He was the only thing standing between Kang and the destruction of those he loved, and he was fading.

He strode closer to the trees, fists clinched. Seeking out his executioner. Waiting.

It was a great and bitter sadness. When he went he went with that last impression, that he had not died a warrior's death, in a battle that would be won, or even a battle that others might finish in his wake, but that he, in losing, left behind a hopeless tragedy that might never be undone.

And so he fought. The only hope for this world. Wanting to let go. Wanting to be done. *Needing* to die. Exhausted, in agony, yet ...

Unable to quit.

Kang came at him, bellowing louder than ever. Zac leapt over him this time, miraculously avoiding him once more. Kang dug in and caught his charge, throwing up a towering wall of earth with his momentum. Zac landed and looked past him, over his head, a dangerous moment of distraction, catching glimpse of the fires of battle in the north. Black smoke blotted out most of the sky. It was a tortured scene and its tragic beauty held him.

And there, framed against the roiling black: a lone craft. One of the Venatres ornithopters, cutting across the bleak horizon. For an instant he became consumed with it, admiring its stark elegance. All alone, small in the distance, insignificant against that massive backdrop of war. It flew fast, as if on a singular mission—though for what purpose he could not imagine. He had the fleeting idea it was there for him, an odd sense of familiarity, but was brought quickly back to reality by Kang's attack.

This time the beast caught him.

CHAPTER 41:

INTO THE FRAY

"THERE HE IS," Jess spotted Willet on the ground as Satori flew them in a tight spiral, heading down. As they continued their curve, bringing Jessica's view to the other side, she looked out across the city toward the battle beyond. It reminded her of the fields of Osaka, when she first arrived over Anitra months ago, image of that conflict burned in her mind's eye during those instants as she fell. It had been night then, the fires burning hellishly with no competition from the sun, but enough black smoke had gathered in the air above this one to give it a similar feel. Dark forms of both Dominion and Venatres units engaged across miles-wide swaths of terrain.

Then she was facing the other way as Satori continued their spiraling arc, descending rapidly. Jess kept searching anxiously for Zac, heart in her throat. She'd found the park Willet mentioned, sign of the conflict all around, but so far no sign of either Zac or Kang.

Then she saw them. Emerging from a row of swaying trees, a few felled entirely as the two small bodies threw each other with tremendous force. She gasped as she saw Kang's yellow, horned form. Put her hand to her mouth as she watched him hammer Zac into the turf.

Then the 'thopter was dropping below a smaller group of trees and touching down with a lurch. Willet was there, running to them.

"You ready?" Satori asked and Jess jerked her head to look at her. She knew her eyes were wide, knew she looked as freaked as she felt, but she was, indeed, ready.

She nodded.

Strands of Satori's bright red hair blew in the turbulent air coming through the windows. Outside the cockpit the giant wings cycled to a stop, mechanics whining in the heart of the craft, the steam turbine winding down to a throaty idle. Satori kept it spinning. The whole scene screamed action, danger, but for that moment Jess worked to find inner calm.

Behind them in the hold the door crashed open with a bang. She jerked and looked over her shoulder as Willet jumped in.

"I knew it was you!" he beamed, hurrying straight for her. She stood and put the Icon in her seat, taking him in an embrace. Willet was a soldier, tall and strong, wearing full gear and filled with the confidence bred of experience and competence. Though no superman he was still a powerful presence and Jess squeezed him tightly, relishing his strength. Absorbing the comfort of his friendship.

He would help her.

He hugged her just as tight. "I knew you'd come back," he said happily. "When Satori told me ..."

They stood there what seemed an eternity, under the circumstances, but Jess did not want to let go. Neither did Willet. It was Satori that accelerated the moment.

"Yeah, yeah. There'll be time for a reunion later. What about me?"

Willet released Jess and looked at Satori. A sly smile turned the corners of his mouth.

"Ah, yes," he said, and went tenderly to her, bent and kissed her where she sat in the pilot's seat. It was a wonderful kiss and Jess watched them intently. Like watching a movie, and only as they separated did she even think she probably should've been polite and looked away.

Not that such things really mattered right then.

Willet straightened. "So what are you girls up to?" He put his hands on his hips and looked between them; as if finding them at a party, not in the middle of a life-or-death battle. *Hey! What's up!* His stance was casual, engaging, a slight smile on his face. *Where's the keg?*

Jess was glad he was there.

Satori answered. "Jess has an idea."

Willet settled his gaze on her. "Surprise surprise," he said as if, of course, it was no surprise at all. Jess felt she must be getting a bad reputation. And this latest plan wasn't likely to change that. Quite the contrary.

"I need to get this to Zac," she said and reached for the Icon in the seat. Holding it carefully in both hands she lifted it and faced Willet. "It's the only way to get rid of Kang."

Willet eyed the shiny device. It was clear the Icon was still a huge point of mystery for him, such a guarded piece of their collective past. Whether he knew the details of the two she brought or not, whether Satori had filled him in on any of that, he would at least know exactly how one of these worked. And he would have, therefore, more than an inkling of what she had in mind.

"You want to ..." He kind of nodded toward the Icon. She could tell from the look in his eyes he did, in fact, understand.

"How?"

Jess inhaled.

"I've got to get close. I've got to give it to him."

Willet had started shaking his head and probably didn't even realize it.

"Close?"

She nodded. "I know that's going to be dangerous."

At that Willet glanced at Satori, who remained seated. "We all speak English here, right? Dangerous? Dangerous is playing with a loaded gun. Dangerous is ... walking down the middle of the street." He looked back at Jess. "What you're suggesting is a guaranteed death wish."

She appreciated his effort to lighten the mood. Willet had always been one of those people that found ways to keep a positive balance, even in the midst of bad things.

She shrugged. "So how do we do it?"

Again Willet looked to Satori.

But Satori had nothing. "She's counting on you."

At that he turned back to Jessica. Studied her a moment and ... held out a hand.

"I can't say I haven't done stupider things." Then: "So I just give it to him?"

Jess looked at his hand. Taken with his willingness to

help, to do this crazy thing just because she was asking. More than that she was compelled by the urgency of the sounds outside, the distant explosions—the knowledge of the other, more important fight taking place nearby. The one she could not see, or even hear, but which dominated her thoughts. She looked into his eyes.

"*I* have to give it to him," she said. Slowly Willet lowered his hand.

"You? I've already been out there," he said. "Why you?" Then: "Kang knows I'm here. He may not be as suspicious if I go with it. If you show up it will definitely tip him off."

Jess swallowed. She had no explanation to give. None she wanted to share.

Willet was shaking his head again. "It's too dangerous."

Meaningfully Jess turned up one corner of her mouth. "You mean a guaranteed death wish."

A small grin found its way to his face.

"I'm so glad we're friends," he said, and though it sounded like a joke he really meant it. "Knowing you has just been nonstop joy. Welcome back, Jessica. Life without you would be so boring."

Jess smiled with him. Worked to steady herself. "If I can get this to him," she said, "he'll be able to use it. He'll know exactly what to do. With it he can get rid of Kang."

Willet sighed, preparing himself for what was to come. Jess found herself taking deeper breaths.

"I'll keep the engine hot." Satori would do her part.

Willet stood to his full height. "Well all right," he clasped his hands together and held them tight. "Let's do this."

* * *

"*DIE!*" KANG ROARED, straddling Zac and punching him furiously, a flurry of fists raining down impacts that could shatter steel. Zac threw up blocks, deflected what he could, but Kang was too overwhelmingly strong, the blows too powerful ...

Zac realized he was finally done.

Whatever had kept him going until then, whatever

sense of duty, whatever impulse to shield others from this monster ... gone. He was running on automatic and it was over. He could not—would not—keep it up.

The fight had at last degenerated from the flamboyant to the primal. Conflict in its most basic form. No more exaggerated tosses, no more leaps, no inspired moves. Kang on top, pinning him to the ground, pounding away. Nothing more.

Zac lowered his arms.

The punches landed now, bringing with them more pain, and he hoped Kang would just finish him. Hoped, in those final moments, he would be wrong and the people he loved, those he sought to protect, would find a way to kill the beast after all.

Jessica.

She would be fine, he told himself. Made himself believe it. *She's strong.*

Regretting he was about to break his promise.

And Kang rolled him over and gripped him. Saw at last, through his rage, that Zac had succumbed and, once more, went for a choke. This time Zac would not struggle. This time it was over.

It didn't hurt at first, a respite from the agony of the strikes. Then, as Kang's forearms clenched either side of his throat, it did. A little, still less than the other, and he closed his eyes, trying to find peace in those final instants— even as Kang roared with the fury of exertion. Zac's mind faded. The only way to kill him was to break his neck, and he willed it to happen as the pain intensified.

What would death hold? Was it truly the beginning of the next adventure? Was there a heaven, as preached by their once Emperor? Heaven certainly did not lie at the other end of the Holy Relic. Earth was not heaven. Just another world like this one. Filled with as many problems.

Jessica.

Perhaps there was another place. A real heaven.

Any moment he would know the answer.

He only hoped he would not forgot.

And at the thought of that a heavy sadness washed over

him. Unexpected, of such an intensity that the pain faded and he nearly surged with a fresh effort to fight free.

What if he forgot?

A new start, another place ... whatever death might bring, these things did not frighten him. What frightened him in those final instants, as he lay there dying, what brought, of a sudden, such deep and terrible sadness, was the thought that he would forget. That in passing he would take no memory of who he'd been. What he'd done.

Who he'd loved.

Losing that ...

But it was too late. His decision was made. He had no fight left, and as Kang squeezed him with an intensity that could never be undone Zac ached for those memories.

What if he lost them forever?

No!

Then, above the roar of his executioner, above the pounding in his own ears ...

A sound.

A ...

Voice?

Calling his name.

Zac!

It came again, louder.

Then ...

Was it real?

Yes. He *did* hear it.

It *was* real.

Zac!

He opened bleary eyes.

Could it be?

CHAPTER 42:

A HERO IS TESTED

"*ZAC!!*" JESS SCREAMED at the top of her lungs, tears streaming down her face. But he couldn't hear. There was no response. No more movement. As if he were already ...

"*ZAC!!*" She stood atop a small hill, not fifty yards away, horrified as Kang squeezed the life out of him. Bellowing so loud ... She could never be heard above the monster's roar.

"*ZAC!!*" her voice cracked. Willet stood several steps behind, both of them vulnerable in a way that could never be described. She'd come slowly up the hill, terrified, looking for Zac, feeling like she walked into a cage with a pair of fighting tigers, nothing to shield her. Now she stood staring at him, Kang at his back, on the ground, squeezing him, killing Zac before her eyes.

"No!" she croaked and sank to her knees. In her hands she gripped the Icon.

Useless now.

The mark of superhuman conflict was all around; broken trunks, fallen trees, gouges of rich, black dirt, long ruts across the green lawn. All of that clouded over as hot tears filled her eyes. She sat on her heels, sensing Willet behind her, knowing there was nothing either of them could do. Nothing anyone could do.

She was too late.

She didn't bother to wipe the tears away. Everything became a blur of color, as if looking through a storm of raindrops on a windshield. The ruined grass of the field beyond, probably once a beautiful park on a sunny afternoon, people walking, children playing.

She knelt there crying.

Building new resolve.

What would be her last act. She was too late to save Zac, too late to stop what, she now realized, had been inevitable from the beginning. Fate. And there she was, at the end of the line, and there was still one possibility.

She would use the Icon.

Her life was over but she might at least make one grand, final impact. *She* could save them. Everyone. *She* could do it, be the angel they wanted her to be. At least she could do that. So many lives would be spared, at the expense of just one.

Mine.

Kang would want her. He was going to kill her; there was no question of that. Any second he would come to her, to gloat, to snap her neck ... whatever. He would not walk away and leave her there. And when he did ...

She would take him. Both of them, to the void. Deep space and the vacuum of a quick, certain death. Fling the Icon away and there they both would die. Kang gone from this world, she the hero they all expected her to be.

It was a perfect solution.

I am *the angel.*

She would save everyone and, in the process, go with Zac into the great beyond.

Kang's roar ended and she blinked watery eyes, seeing him toss Zac into the air. Blurry, just shapes at that distance, through her tear-filled vision, but she was appalled with the way he so roughly discarded the body. It was a horrible last act, and she hated the monster more than ever.

But it gave her clarity. Determination to make this sacrifice. Determination to watch him die. *I'll smile at him,* she vowed. *I'll look him right in the eyes and smile.*

And suddenly he was running for her. Faster even than she could process. She'd expected him to saunter over, to make a spectacle of it, not move so quickly ...

I'm not ready!

Hurriedly she fumbled with the Icon, heart lurching into her throat as all at once he was right there—

"Jessica!"

The voice penetrated her fog.

Wha—?

"Jessica," the voice repeated, soft but urgent. Familiar. A hand touched her shoulder and her mouth fell open.

It was Zac.

Watery eyes dried; as if brushed clear by a spring wind.

Zac!

There he was, right in front of her. She blinked, again and again, vision brightening, not believing it.

You're alive!

She couldn't speak.

In her silence he looked himself over. "You were right," he said with a lopsided grin. "I had no chance."

Zac! She remained speechless. On her knees, he squatting before her, face bruised and cut, smudged with dirt, body beaten but whole, looking worse than she ever thought a Kazerai could possibly look but ...

"Oh Zac!" Bright and alert, filled with energy, so happy to see her—*so happy!*—and her spirit soared, in that place and in that moment, even as her heart went out to him. For his pain, for his sacrifice.

For his love. Which he was practically beaming into her. Even in his beaten state he was the most incredible, the most wonderful man she'd ever known.

And he loved her.

So much!

But suddenly Kang was coming. Over Zac's shoulder she saw him gather himself for the charge.

The reality of their situation slammed home.

"Use it!" she jammed the Icon into his hands. No time for anything else. Hoping he would just do as she said. "Take him! When you pop out get free and use it again! Fast!" Then, to be absolutely clear: "Use it *twice!*"

Zac had also forgotten the urgency of the moment, so taken was he with her unexpected arrival. Without question he took the Icon.

Mustering the will for this final act.

And as he stood and looked down, only split-seconds left together, about to be gone into the unknown, his ice-blue eyes glinted and ...

There was trust in them beyond measure.

Jess shuddered.

"I *will* come for you!" she told him; her last words as he turned and leapt away. Hard, fast; so sudden she gasped and fell forward in the wake of it, watching as he impacted the charging Kang with a titanic smack that knocked the beast in an entirely new direction. She raised herself back to her knees as the two superhuman forms tumbled away, across the ground, locked in a concussion of limbs and turf, echoing roars of Kang's fury, Zac's yells and a blur of action ...

POW!

They were gone.

Jess sank to the side.

Gone ...

Slumping to the ground, staring at the spot they just were, out there in the torn-up field, faint wisps of grass swirling in the air around the vacuum of their absence.

She flopped and rolled all the way to her back, face to the sky.

She'd been expecting it. Knew what would happen— *planned* for it to happen only ...

The fact of it hit her with a strength that nearly took her breath away.

Zac is gone.

At length the noises of battle rose to fill her awareness. There all along, ignored until that moment. Hardly worth her attention before then, so much more at stake. Now the explosions, the shrieks of missiles, the staccato pop of bullets, thundering bomb bursts—these things began to impinge.

Their imminent threat did little to fill the void.

He's in deep space.

Her whole body buzzed.

"He did it."

It was Willet.

He'd walked up to stand beside her. He crouched at her side. Carefully, as if approaching a lost child.

"Zac saved us."

Jess turned her head to him. No new tears came. Maybe she was finally done crying. Maybe it was too much. All she knew was, right then, she felt completely, utterly empty.

She looked into the sky above, far into the blue depths, beyond the drifting clouds of black smoke, focus on nothing at all. Willet's word's echoed in her head.

Zac saved us.

Mind caught in the grip of one certainty.

Now they had to save him.

EPILOGUE

THE MASSIVE, purple gas giant loomed in the near distance, wrapped in a myriad of shimmering clouds. Floating impossibly still in the stark beauty of the void, a curtain of stars its brilliant backdrop. Colorful nebula drew a long, feathery thread across that same field of vision, adding variety to the image, depth; defining the scope of the stars and the vastness of space. In reality the planet was nothing against that majesty, of course, but there, at that range, it dominated the view.

Kel warlord Eldron had grown tired of looking at it.

He and his crew were in a wide, stationary orbit, taking their turn at the waiting game, sitting in their battle cruiser, watching that small area of space that had grown so terribly interesting to their leaders. Numerous anomalies had been recorded there, in that one spot, but had since— since the war council began putting ships out to watch closely—failed to return. No more signals. Nothing found.

A failure.

The purple planet was called Raag, named long ago for their ancient god of war, and since the anomalies it had become the focus of the Kel tremarch and her entire senate and, by extension, the entire Kel civilization. Under their direction a military presence had been established in that spot. At first, when the sensation was most fresh, an entire small fleet—whittled down over time until, now, a single cruiser was all that was maintained.

More than was needed, as far as Eldron was concerned. A simple satellite would've done.

He and his ship were on rotation. In a week they would be replaced and he and his crew would return to Kel. At which point he could finally stop staring at the boring gas giant.

A squawk at one of the consoles and he looked across to the crewman at that station.

"Identify." He sat a little straighter in his command chair. The bridge of the battle cruiser was long, filled with control stations, lit by the green glow of panels and screens but otherwise dark. A viewscreen at the fore end spanned the entire breadth; wide, tall, showing the colorful planet and field of stars without and, now, according to fresh readings ... something else.

"Energy pulse," came the report. "Quantum in nature." The crewman turned to him. Said: "It matches."

Now Eldron gripped the arms of his chair.

After all this time.

The anomalies, so meticulously recorded when first appearing in that spot, had never recurred. It was almost as if a joke were being played. Odd little flashes of quantum wavelengths, small yet containing, potentially, vast amounts of energy. Precise, unusual, always the same, randomly timed over the course of several years until, at last, forces were sent to investigate.

At which point the signal never returned.

Eldron had begun to believe it never would. Most of his fellow warlords felt this way. Felt the senate was wasting time, resources.

And now, here it was.

"Move on it," he commanded. Hurrying to recall orders. Working to put himself in the right frame of mind. So long and so many times had he sat, expecting nothing, it was almost as if he needed to remember what to do.

Pilots engaged the battle cruiser's engines and the mighty warship turned with a powerful thrum. Methodically they began advancing on the pinpoint in space.

Another crewman reported: "Cross-reference complete." Then: "It was the signal, my Lord."

The purple gas giant slid to the left, off-screen as they banked, then grew smaller behind them as they accelerated toward the coordinates of the anomaly.

Their waiting point had been determined based on earlier measurements, calculated to ensure adequate response time to deal with whatever might conceivably come with the bursts. And, hopefully, adequate reaction time should it prove dangerous.

The consensus among the Kel scientists was that the burst of energy was in fact a sort of portal and might, possibly, herald the arrival and subsequent departure of … something. What that something might be was anyone's guess. An advanced race? Something else? And so, to be as prepared as possible, their waiting standoff had been placed closer to the giant planet.

"What's there?" Eldron peered into the starry void on the massive viewscreen. From his command chair he selectively defined and enhanced areas, scanning wavelengths. Nothing he could yet make out. Maybe it was merely a localized burst of energy? If so, and if, after all this, their mystery signal turned out to be merely a scientific curiosity, then he *truly* hated to think of the time and resources wasted.

"What came through? Anything?"

History told of a time, long ago, when similar methods of travel were used to move between worlds. Records of that had been lost in the darkness following the Great War but, despite the ravages of that ending, the Kel Empire had risen again, rebuilding, mastering space with new, powerful warships. Quantum drives had been attained once more, but so much was yet missing …

It was speculated that this quantum signal was another race, using a similar drive, and if they could be captured the Kel might gain from their technology.

But Eldron saw nothing.

"Nothing as yet, Lord," came the confirmation.

It seemed as if the burst was, in fact, no more than an anomaly. Some undiscovered cosmic event. If there were ships or travelers involved they would surely have detected them by now.

"Wait."

Eldron looked in the direction of the crewman who spoke. Across the large, battle-ready bridge.

"I've got readings," the man went on, quickly swiping his hands across a display at his console. "Life-forms."

Eldron stood on impulse, surprised. Once on his feet he

decided to remain standing.

"Life-forms?"

The man checked further, not believing it himself. "Yes, Lord."

"No craft?"

"None, Lord."

All on the bridge were now reacting in surprise. Many glanced up from what they were doing, looking between Eldron and the screen ahead.

There are life-forms out there? seemed the unspoken question on everyone's lips.

The helmsman went on: "Closing. Locking in velocity. We will reach that point in three minutes at present rate." Then: "Recommended standoff?"

Eldron wasn't sure how to answer. "Are they still alive?"

"Yes, Lord."

"How many?"

"Two."

He stepped down from his command dais and strode across the bridge, toward the massive viewscreen at the fore.

"Two distinct forms, Lord. Unshielded. Getting strong biometric readings. Floating apart from each other, on trajectories as if an impact occurred following the signal. Just ... floating."

At the base of the tall, wide screen Eldron stopped. There he stood, looking up into the void, directly before it. The giant display stretched to either side, filling his vision.

Still he saw nothing.

"Close standoff on the nearest," he said. "Five hundred."

"Closing."

"Magnify."

The screen resolution was adjusted. And there, at last, he saw it. A small body, floating free in space.

"Hold." The massive battle cruiser came to a halt, steady, holding position in the void. Facing off against ...

What?

"Magnify further."

The helmsman did.

And Eldron took an involuntary step back.

"You have readings?" he asked, partly to cover his reaction. "You're certain it's alive?" It was. He could see clearly that it was.

Impossible.

"Yes, Lord."

"And the other?"

"Also alive."

The other life-form was not in this view, but Eldron could only imagine it was just as hideous. He stared at the one on the screen. The thing should've been a vacuum-expanded corpse. But it wasn't. There it floated, a beast straight out of demonic lore. Yellow, disfigured horns protruding from the sides of its head; helpless yet ... full of power. *Tangibly* full of power. Seething with a fury that could nearly be felt.

It floated on the screen before him, as big as him now in its rendering; as if he stood directly before it.

What is this?

The monster seemed to stare straight at him, unblinking though it "looked" at him from far, far away, through bulkheads and an armored warship's thick hull. It was as if the beast knew it was being watched and, in the knowing, stared back. Piercing their scrutiny.

Pure rage in its eyes.